Diary of A Sane Man

Bill Dughaille

Contents

Part One: Formation

Chapter 1: The Calm

April

Bill Dughaille

Friday 4th April

Mrs Phillips was late today. She normally turns up promptly, ten thirty-four a.m. every Tuesday, library book trolley in tow. When she finally walked into reception this morning she seemed more flustered than ever, not an easy task for someone who could fluster for England.

Now there's a thought – an Olympic flustering event. Or perhaps we should just start with a European competition. After all, the Yanks would never be good at it, and most of the rest of the world wouldn't understand it. Bit like cricket really – trouble is we keep losing at that as well.

Anyway, I digress.

Mrs Phillips has been having problems with her husband, George, who has never been the same since his funeral – she couldn't find him anywhere, and ended up leaving a message with one of the others, should he turn up. Behind that fluster lies a heart of gold and a mind of – well, I'm not too sure about that bit. I'm not saying that talking to the dead is necessarily a sign of someone who has lost touch with reality, but you have to admit that it is unusual.

'Do you know,' she said to me in almost a whisper, in case anyone should be within earshot, 'sometimes I wonder if he isn't avoiding me.' Since that is exactly what George had spent his last years doing it seemed not unlikely. I was torn between the urge to suggest that all she had to do was nip down to the cemetery, go about a hundred yards to the left, and she'd find him "resting" under a tombstone saying "Georgi Phippillis" – a slight misreading of Mrs Phillips' handwriting by a somewhat inebriated mason – and wondering why she thought whispering was safe when she regularly communicated with people she couldn't see.

How would you know they weren't eavesdropping right at that very moment? Archduke Ferdinand might be taking notes.

'Everything's been in such a state over there ever since she came over,' she confided solemnly.

"She" is some member of the aristocracy, recently passed into immortality. There have been, according to Mrs Phillips, some snappish exchanges "on the other side" between those who consider the whole thing pretty irrelevant and those who see it as a tragedy to be met with tearing of beards and rending of garments.

Presuming they do wear garments over there. It's not the sort of thing you like to ask about. Well, not of Mrs Philips, anyway. She can come up with some amazing explanations which make your brain hurt, and somehow almost seem to make sense. Almost.

I watched her as she happily dragged her library trolley off to the lounge to supply tomes of knowledge and steamy sex to various residents. I'm led to believe that, under current legislation, Mrs Phillips qualifies for the list of sane people.

Here at the Sunshine Garden Centre Institute For Those With Minor Cases Of Not-Quite Off Their Rockers, where I find myself temporarily in residence, we no longer have the sort of resident who isn't allowed to watch television or read newspapers or play with sharp objects, and just as well – we could get a bad reputation, people might think we were mad or something. Actually this place is, in fact, part of a highly secret government research project. Or that's what I wrote on the census forms last year, anyway. After all, if a pile of bricks can be seen as a work of art, I don't see why we can't be a highly secret research project. Reality is only perception viewed through dogma.

I like that saying. I don't know if it means anything, but it sounds good. I must try it next time I'm down the pub, maybe after a few pints.

The truth about this place – and whisper it softly if you will – is that it's a result of the great privatisations by a Labour government. It's the sort of confusing thing that happens just too often these days; a 'socialist' government whose entire history was one of nationalisation deciding to flog everything they could to the capitalists, because they realised that they – the government – were just plain useless at social institutions, whereas business folk knew how to run things. Of course, the business folk aren't really interested in running things, just in making money. It's the sort of thing that gives politics a bad name.

The idea that the capitalists were somehow more competent turned out to be a little wide of the mark. When this place was handed over to a private company to run, the company started off by trying to reduce all human content – employees and patients. It seems to be a reflex action in a certain managerial world to rid their company of as many employees as possible. Witness the rail company that got rid of the bulk of their staff, including drivers. A month later they were desperately offering ludicrous wages to hire drivers, as they had discovered that drivers were necessary to drive the trains. You would have thought that they might have spotted such a minor point, what with them being highly paid directors and all.

This lot here gleefully went down the road of leaning on the shrinks to release people into "care of the community" as it was (wrongly) called (though to be fair that was started by the Conservatives). It took someone at their head office a couple of months to work out that they were actually losing money, and a few more to work out why. The contract with the government stipulated that they would be paid according to the number of patients treated. Take away the patients, and you take away your revenue. Initially they attempted to renegotiate the contract so that payment was according to available rooms – they would have had the builders in double-quick to put up partitions – but apparently agreeing a government contract takes years, re-negotiating it takes centuries or a world war, sometimes both. They could probably have organised the world war, but the bean-counters pointed out that financially it wouldn't have been cost-effective.

Unless they could import cheap Indian soldiers.

So they had a rethink, and realised that what they wanted were a certain number of patients who could be classified as loopy, but not loopy enough to require 24 hour attention, or to need security guards to stop them indulging in anti-social behaviour such as blowing the place up or attacking visiting directors. Since they had already got rid of that sort of undesirable by declaring them well enough to go back into the community they were in an ideal position to take on a new raft of quiet, trouble-free fruitcakes, which they are in the process of doing. And so I find myself in a rather comfortable residence, three square meals a day, and all I have to do is pretend to be mad once a fortnight – or less if the doc's on holiday. All the latest newspapers, books, several television lounges, lovely gardens, a couple of decent pubs in walking distance. Far from the madding crowd. An ideal position in which to pursue the highest goal; the study of Life.

The trick, of course, is not to rock the boat. Let sleeping dogs lie. After all, when you're having such a good time, why upset people? If anyone's going to upset the apple cart I can guarantee it won't be me.

Saturday 6th April

Saturday is the day the gardening company comes to mow the lawn – or every second Saturday, since the cutbacks, and sometimes only on the third Saturday, if it's been raining too hard. For some strange reason most of the people go out to sit in the garden on Saturdays and Sundays, almost like a religious rite, despite the lawnmowers and the weather. Thursday and Friday were gorgeous, sunny days. Today, though sunny, is quite cold due to a freezing wind coming off Siberia or Alaska or somewhere. No-one was out during the week when it was warm, yet there they sit on a freezing cold day, wrapped up warmly and ignoring the mowers, because it's Saturday.

I'm probably making everyone here sound exactly the same, but they are very much individuals. You'd never make an army out of this lot – even the staff are a disparate rag-bag unlikely to agree the time of day. They had made lowly positions, such as security guards and porters, redundant, apart from Harry who did his back in one Sunday; because he couldn't do his job anymore they were afraid of trouble with the unions if they tried to get rid of him. Most of the nurses went, apart from Matron, who I think they were just too scared to try it on with, and she stayed on because she is so close to retirement. Fortunately she's extremely efficient.

Dr Hamilton, my doctor, spends most of his time writing textbooks on existing theories. I get the impression that he regards most of them as nonsense, which allows him to be marvellously neutral when writing about the subject, and apparently colleges and universities appreciate having such objective descriptions available – it makes it harder for the students to come up with straight answers. Personally I think he sees the whole thing as being somewhat amusing in an ironic way, and something to do which allows him to follow his real passion – golf, or keeping ferrets, or whatever it is. Not football, for some reason. Strange.

Arsenal and Spurs are to face each other on Saturday, now that's something to look forward to – Arsenal winning again, of course. If only they were showing it on the telly. I wish they'd get their priorities right.

Ms Dervish, the administrator and frightenly efficient – that's two efficient women, enough to make you fear for your comfort – says she supports Spurs, but only because her dad did. And she's got nice legs, so we can forgive her. If only she weren't one of the staff or I wasn't a resident I think we could get along quite well together. Although sometimes I think she doesn't quite trust me. There used to be a calendar on the wall behind reception desk until someone who shall remain nameless replaced it with the previous year's one. There was great confusion between people who believed it was Sunday and those adamant that it was Monday and wondering why the television schedules had suddenly changed. Ms Dervish didn't actually accuse me of being the one responsible. Well, not in so many words. Honestly, some people have no sense of trust. It was a scientific experiment. If you're going to be part of a secret research projects you have to have scientific experiments, don't you?

This morning I found Colin in our usual place, sitting on the wide brick wall next to the pine trees. Colin's one of the few people you can hold a decent conversation with. He's perfectly rational – insofar as anyone can be perfectly rational – but every time some doctor decides he's well enough to go back outside, he ends up in a sort of trance, staring at nothing until the horrible sentence of being sent into this strange place they call the "real world" has been lifted. Even then it takes him a few weeks to recover.

He looked up from the Guardian he was reading.

'Morning,' he called, gesturing to the wall next to him. 'Have a pew. Have you read this bit about Bethlehem?' I pulled myself up onto the wall. 'That depends,' I said, 'I had a look at the Independent earlier, and their version is that the Israelis are a bunch of fascist anti-Semites who are going totally against the will of the civilised world, and the Palestinians are a misunderstood, semi-enslaved people whose only fault is their generosity.'

'Not much different in the Guardian,' he said. 'I should have brought out the Telegraph as well – their story will probably be that the Israelis are a gallant people who are fighting desperately to defend themselves against a mad bunch of terrorists who use suicide bombers to slaughter innocent civilians in coffee shops.'

'You'd better be careful about bringing out those papers, you know Snaffle Sausage gets paranoid about some of the others reading them and getting over-excited.' Snaffle Sausage is my name for Doctor Adolf Snaflwurtz, a nervous psychiatrist who worries about almost everything. Personally I think he should be one of the residents, preferably in a different place, somewhere far away.

'Oh, well, at least it'll give him something to worry over. He gets quite worried when he hasn't anything to worry over.' He chuckled at this witticism. 'I do envy these people who can decide on one side or the other,' he sighed. This was not surprising coming from someone who has panic attacks while trying to choose between two brands of margarine in a supermarket. Not that he's done that for a long time – bought margarine in a supermarket, that is. 'How do you suppose they do it?'

'My suspicion,' I replied, after making a show of giving this the careful thought it deserved, 'is that people, on average, decide on their point of view, and then find evidence to support it, rather than the other way around.'

He nodded mournfully. 'You could be right, I rather suspect. But how do they manage it? Why don't they have doubts like us?'

'I think it's called mental self defence – or something like that.' Possibly ego. I must read up on Freud sometime. Bound to be a good quote or two there. Personally I think we're rather fortunate to be able to take a balanced, objective view of the world. I patted him on the shoulder. 'read the cartoons, Colin, the other stuff's just too depressing for you.' I left him slowly cheering up as he browsed the cartoons.

He used to be a highly paid computer programmer who could spot an error in thousands of lines of code at a glance, so I'm told.

He really does worry about things too much.

Tuesday 9th April

'Disgusting!' roared the major as I managed to slip into the dining hall just in time for a late breakfast. I wondered what the old fool was blathering on about this time. He's not a real major – used to be a plumber, according to his file, which naturally I haven't taken a sneak look at – but he tells everyone that he's a major (unit undefined), and carries himself around with a straight back in the sort of way he thinks a major would. This morning for some reason he had dressed up in what I can only presume was an undertaker's discarded suit, rescued from a skip somewhere or other, with some sort of extra sheen applied.

'Not even shaved, by God!' he continued, and I realised that it was me he was going on about. It was true that I hadn't shaved – I never do before breakfast, it would involve getting up even earlier. Shower, yes, shave, later. And it gives me that fashionable look.

'Insolent young puppies like you should learn some respect!' he shouted across the dining hall.

'Boggles, if you don't put a sock in it I shall come across and pour your porridge all over your shiny bald bonce,' I replied loudly, making sure the entire hall could hear. Baggle – the major – went red and furious, and suddenly concentrated on his porridge. He wasn't about to chance the odds that I would pour his porridge over his head. I probably would. It's the sort of thing lunatics do do.

After all, you do have to keep up appearances.

As I negotiated my way with newspaper and plate of egg, toast and bacon to my normal seat in the corner, I wondered what had got into the silly old fool to try his nonsense with me. I smoothed out the newspaper prior to tucking into breakfast. The front page explained Boggles' ancient black suit and mood of righteous indignation – royal funeral today. Apparently we're supposed to be in Mourning.

I can't stand people like Boggles. They climb on to any little bandwagon which might give them a little power by association. You would have found them in the Taliban, the Nazis, McCarthy's lot –

anywhere, anytime. No doubt gardening clubs and train- spotting societies are full of them. Why can't people be as easy going as I am? Live and let live. It should be obligatory.

I shall have to think of some suitable punishment for major boggles.

Friday 9th April PM

Otherwise known as 'later that day' ...

Mrs Gladstone stopped me on the way in to afternoon tea.

'I thought your threat to douse Mr Baggle in porridge was very unfair," she said, with a twinkle in her eye, 'you raised our hopes and then did nothing about it.'

'Er, not your favourite person, then is he?' I asked.

'Dreadful person, absolutely dreadful. We made the mistake of inviting him in as a fourth for our bridge game when Avril passed on. Dreadful. He always bid way beyond anything he could win, and then blamed his partner, or claimed that someone must have reneged – never his fault, always someone else's. Absolutely dreadful. It became so bad we had to give up playing. If we had another player we could have politely told him to get lost, but as it was there was no other option. Dreadful.'

'Dreadful,' I agreed dutifully. She shook her head sadly.

'Poor Janice, one of the other players, just went downhill from there. Bridge was the only thing that kept her going, really. Now you can get hardly a few words out of her. Dreadful. Absolutely dreadful.' While I sympathised with poor Janice, I couldn't help getting that feeling that I was about to be set up for something.

'Have you ever played bridge?' She asked, looking at me with eyes so innocent I could see the trap a mile away.

'Only on a very social basis, Mrs Gladstone, and that was many years ago. I'm afraid I'd never be able to play to your standard.' She laughed at the thought.

'Not at all, an intelligent man like you, I'm sure you'll pick up things very quickly.' If she thought I was going to fall for that old soft-soap, she was greatly misjudging me. Of course, I do like to believe that I have a certain native intelligence, and I can pick up some things quite quickly. But I don't succumb to flattery very easily.

'That's very kind of you to say so, Mrs G, I wouldn't object to the occasional social game when possible, but obviously I couldn't commit to a regular occasion.'

'Good, that's settled. I shall let you know when Janice emerges sufficiently to be able to follow a hand.' She moved to go, thinking, presumably that she had got me to agree to something. Some chance!

'But I must tell you that I am in favour of the monarchy myself. Possibly not royalty, but definitely the monarchy,' she said as a parting shot. 'And it was a wonderful funeral. Wonderful.' She moved off in quiet triumph.

I'm not sure of what she meant by the difference between monarchy and royalty – I know what I think the difference is, of course – but in this place knowing what someone else thinks they know can be quite an art form. If not impossible.

Okay, I admit I haven't a clue about the difference between monarchy and royalty.

They're spelt differently?

Right, so that's two things to concentrate on. Sort Boggles out subtly and avoid bridge with Mrs G. Oh, and keep out of trouble while doing it. Should be easy enough.

Wednesday 10th April

US Secretary of State to arrive in Israel for talks. More civilians killed by a Palestinian suicide bomber. Israelis invade another Palestinian town. England football striker has broken metacarpal. In doubt for the world cup.

Had my fortnightly session with Dr Hamilton. We were playing our game of "let's see who first gets bored with answering questions with questions". He had started with:

'So, is there anything you've been doing recently you shouldn't have been doing?'

One of those lovely questions not even Mother Theresa could have answered in the negative, and she's dead.

'Now that depends on what you see as something that shouldn't be done, doesn't it Doctor?' I replied.

'So you think that there are some things that shouldn't be done?'

'Based on your question I can only conclude that this is a position which you believe. I would be interested to know what those things are, and why you feel they shouldn't happen.'

'So you're suggesting that there aren't things that shouldn't be done?'

'I wasn't aware of saying that – could you tell me what it is that I said which gave you that impression?'

'You feel you've given me the wrong impression?'

'Your use of the word "wrong" is interesting – why do you feel that something is wrong?'

This sort of thing can go on for hours – a similar thing happens in parliament. But neither Dr Hamilton nor myself are made of stern enough stuff to handle it for more than a few minutes. He eventually broke with a direct, and very badly timed question.

'So, the greevils have been quiet of late, then?'

'Ssshh!' I commanded, looking around nervously, lowering my voice and putting a finger in front of my lips. 'Those bastards will hear you. They're just waiting for a chance to latch on.'

'Aaaah,' he said thoughtfully, and then lowered his voice to match mine. 'Aaaah, I see,' he whispered.' He seemed to think for a while, and then leaned forward and whispered, 'What if we give them a code word?'

I thought about this. 'So they won't realise we're talking about them?' I whispered back.

'Yes, something like – what about 'rats'?'.

'No, no,' I replied in a shouted whisper, 'that's too obvious.'

'Bats? Cats? Dogs? Frogs?'

Frogs I liked.

'Frogs,' I agreed. I resumed speaking in a normal voice. 'No, not many problems with the frogs lately. But you can never be too careful.'

He leaned back. 'Good,' he said, 'so long as the, er, frogs, are under control, we are definitely ... making progress. And I shall see you in another fortnight.'

I took my cue, and stood up to open the door. Behind the door Harry was waiting to be asked to call the next patient.

'So long, Doc, see you in two weeks.'

'Two weeks then,' he said as he made a note in his diary. 'Oh, and Harry – Harry, please don't forget to check the rooms for ... ' – he looked at me – 'frogs.'

Harry looked a little confused at first. Then he roared with laughter.

'Oh, you mean the GREEVILS, Doc!' he almost shouted in amusement. The bastard.

I screamed something like 'No, no', and raced out down the corridor, through the French windows, and dived into the spot in the middle of the rhododendrons.

The thing about frogs, you see, is they don't like rhododendrons. They can't spell the word. That's their big fear. Spelling. Grammar. That's why I have a dictionary in each corner of my room, and riffle the pages every so often. Carrying a decent newspaper helps as well.

And people like Harry do not help.

I stayed in the rhododendrons until Matron came out with the Oxford Concise and my tablets. Got a good sleep in the lounge behind the big couch.

The frogs lose interest when I'm not in the room.

Honestly, the things I have to do to keep a place here.

Thursday 11th April

Israelis and Palestinians still at war. England striker still has fractured metacarpal. Royal personage still dead.

A new recruit turned up this morning. I was just tucking into breakfast at my usual table when Matron ushered him in, like a duck nudging a chick in the right direction. Tonique was doing duty behind the breakfast bar this morning.

Poor girl, when her parents named her Tonique they must have hoped she'd turn out to be a model or actress or something, but she looks like the worst nightmare of any teenager – washed-out blonde hair, watery blue eyes, extremely pale face emphasizing livid spots of acne. And a perpetually nervous expression, as if she had something to fear, working amongst these nutters.

Still, it could be worse. She could have got a job in Woolworths or somewhere like that, having to deal with the fruitcakes who constitute the great shopping public.

The new recruit, a shortish, slim, wiry man, possibly mid-thirties, with a head twitch, walked – if that's the right word; "was shepherded" might be more accurate – up to the breakfast counter. Tonique picked up a plate as if it was likely to bite her, and Matron asked, 'Now what would you like for breakfast, then?' (Never use "we", as in "what would we like for breakfast". It's very patronising, and likely to drive some people crazy.)

The new recruit shook his head and pointed at something on the counter, and said 'Feck!' with a Scottish accent. Tonique looked at him in horror.

'Come along, Tonique,' Matron said patiently but firmly, 'bacon'. Tonique nervously put some bacon on the plate, just managing not to miss it. The new recruit, whom I instantly christened "Jimmie" in honour of his accent, looked around again, pointed at something, and said 'Feck!' again. 'And eggs, Tonique,' matron said. The eggs were duly added to a trembling plate. After another point and another 'Feck!', some toast joined them. Jimmie seemed satisfied with this,

19

and Matron told him to find somewhere to sit.

This is always an interesting occasion for a newcomer. He's about to enter the minefield of existing seating arrangements, risking the danger of taking someone's long-established chair, resulting in shockwaves which reverberate for weeks, and determine long lasting hateships. They can send a nervous newcomer to bed for days.

On the other hand Jimmie didn't look like the sort of person who would let such things upset him. More likely it would be the other person off to bed for a few weeks. You really don't want to get into an argument with someone whose vocabulary consists of the word "Feck".

Of course I had not obviously been looking at what was going on. The polite pretence of not watching people, which you find common in British society, was magnified a hundredfold in this place, so I also obviously didn't notice Jimmie look around, and then twitch his way slowly to my table. Only when he was right in front of me did I raise my head in curious surprise to find someone standing there.

'Feck?' he asked, waving his plate at the table.

'Feck', I agreed, gesturing for him to sit if he wanted. He put the plate down, sitting down carefully while his head twitched around as if checking to see that there weren't any arbitrary dangers that might be lurking in the near area, or possibly the Big Breakfast Burglar in disguise at the next table. Having sat down he looked at his eggs and bacon as if it were the first decent meal he'd had for ages, something to be admired before engulfing. He looked up, pointed at the salt near my elbow, and said 'Feck?'

'Feck', I replied, and passed the salt over.

'Feck', he said, thanking me.

I think Jimmie is going to be a welcome addition to the squirrel factory.

I wonder if he plays bridge.

Friday 12th April

Apparently it's the striker's metatarsal that's fractured, not his metacarpal. Which goes to prove that some people don't know their metacarpal from their metatarsal.

I wonder which is what.

Israeli prime minister ignores calls to pull Israeli army out of "occupied territories". Suicide bomber – young girl – blows herself up in Jerusalem a few hours before US State Secretary is due to meet Palestinian PM – meeting postponed until Palestinian PM condemns terrorism. Some people claim that the suicide bombers are the result of the desperation of the Palestinians. Others might point out that a religion which promises them martyrdom and 71 virgins in paradise might have something to do with it.

And do the women also get 71 virgins (or is it 72? – the figure seems to change from time to time). This is something I feel we should be told. The feminists could be quite upset otherwise.

If you get 71 virgins do you also get 71 mothers-in-law? That's something they've kept pretty quiet about.

Colin is in media-hating mode, as he does from time to time. Spends the day re-reading 'Rise and Fall of the Third Reich'. Ignores all newspapers, and walks out of the day room if the news comes on television. When I mentioned that the siege of the Church of Nativity in Bethlehem has been described as "barbaric" (by a Franciscan), he muttered something about Monte Cassino. Mentioning the rumoured "war crimes" in Jenin was met with 'Hamburg? Dresden?'.

He'll get over it sooner or later. Even if he has to take up reading the tabloids.

Saturday 13th April

FA Cup semi finals. Middlesbrough 1, Arsenal 0. Arsenal won, because Middlesbrough's goal was in their own net. Funnily enough Fulham managed exactly the same trick against Chelsea. So it's Arsenal vs Chelsea for the final.

Julie came to visit. You'd think by now she'd have got a boyfriend with a stable job and a penchant for washing the car every Saturday. Insisted on describing how she spent yesterday redecorating her spare room. Painted it in my favourite colour. I didn't even know that I had a favourite colour. Apparently it's apricot. It's supposed to be soothing.

Jimmie said his first new word this morning. Looked out the window and commented, 'Fecksunny'. I agreed. But outside it was also a bit fecknippy in the shade.

And Mrs Gladstone has apologised for the lack of bridge due to Janice's ongoing mental absence, but she has assured me that Janice will return to earth soon. In return I assured her that I fully understood and sympathised, and mentioned that I was so busy myself at the moment that we probably wouldn't have time anyway.

Then I went out and hid in the garden with a good book.

Tuesday 23rd April

Been laid low with a bad back for a few days. I wouldn't mind so much if it was a result of some energetic activity such as saving the world from a killer asteroid, but it happened when I reached across the breakfast table for a teaspoon.

I'm told Tonique was nearly scared out of her wits at the scream I uttered when whatever it was snapped or slipped. The few other people left in the breakfast room just carried on as if nothing had happened. They've probably learnt to ignore such minor things as blood curdling screams.

Tonique has been very good about things such as bringing me food though. Even though she's obviously scared witless by most of us she manages to overcome it and even do things she hasn't been asked to, which belies her appearance of being initiatively challenged. Maybe it's something to do with adolescence.

Colin has also started reading newspapers again, but only for my benefit – up until yesterday it was too painful to manage the distance between bedroom and the lounge where the papers are always laid out – so he brought them to my bedroom and read out snippets while I lay on my back and developed a hate complex about ceilings.

At least the back's almost fixed. Shall be wary of teaspoons for a while though.

Mrs Gladstone popped in to see how I was doing. While I've being laid up watching a ceiling Janice came out of her stupor to say something like 'Bridge? I'd love a game.' And of course the essential fourth player was flat out on his back. 'dreadful', she said, though I'm not sure whether she was talking about my back or the lack of a fourth player or Janice's state.

Mrs Gladstone did leave a book on "Basic Bridge", though. I've being desperately trying to crib words and phrases to remember basic bidding so that I can at least blag some of it. As far as I recall a lot of bridge is about bluffing, or at least that's the way I used to play it. But it is incredible how tired your arms get when lying on your back and holding a little book up in front of your face. I knew I was unfit, but this is ridiculous.

The major's apparently being muttering about "lead swingers", referring to me. He's one to talk. He does though, to great lengths. Mostly about how the country needs a firm Conservative government, they should bring back National Service, restrict the vote according to income, close down all left wing newspapers, lock up anyone unemployed and send them to work in chain gangs. I don't think he sees the irony.

Saturday 27th April

I see the papers seem to have given up on this business about the England football coach's love life, thank god. Swedish he might be, but also declared messiah while England are winning. Once they start losing he'll find out what happens to messiahs who don't deliver.

What possible public interest could there be in whether he's going out with one woman or another, or even both. He's the coach of the England football team, not some religious maniac trying to tell us all how to live our lives. If he thought that sex would help the team he'd probably arrange for a travelling brothel to accompany them to the world cup, and there's not a single England supporter who would criticise him if it worked.

Colin, Jimmie and myself were trying to catch some intermittent sun next to the pines this morning when I broached the subject. Now that's optimism. One of them is stuck in the past, and the other's contribution to any conversation extends to the occasional "feck". Colin merely shrugged his shoulders, and Jimmie carried on looking around checking for any possible attack by a passing free-range terrorist who might want to take over the asylum.

'Now I know a free press is essential to democracy, but you have to draw the line somewhere,' I said. One way to get Colin to make a contribution is to mention the word "democracy". He roused himself, and opened his mouth to say something.

'Quis Custodiet Ipsos Custodes?' said Jimmie.

We both looked at him in amazement. He looked embarrassed.

'Feck,' he said. It sounded like there was a question mark at the end of it.

'A good point,' Colin said quickly, as if nothing strange had happened. In this place you learn not to comment on other people's behaviour.

'But I don't know if you can regard the media as the guardian of democracy. It would be nice to think so, but they're hardly neutral.'

'And there are some things that aren't in the public interest,' I replied, 'such as the England coach's private life.'

'That depends on whether you regard him as a role model,' Colin pointed out. 'You could argue that he's corrupting the youth if his private life is dubious.'

'You could argue that the media is corrupting the youth. I reckon none of the youth knew anything about his private life until it was splashed across newspapers and the telly.'

'Feck,' said Jimmie. I presume it was agreement. Either that or he was giving the all clear in case we thought he might have spotted balaclava-clad gunmen crawling across the lawns.

'Not a valid argument,' Colin countered, 'you could say that about politicians. But the media has a duty to alert us to any potentially harmful dealings in parliament.'

'Ah, but the England coach isn't a politician. He doesn't pretend to know how we should live our lives. His job is to choose and train a winning England team for the world cup.'

'But what if his private life is bringing the game into disrepute? Footballers are punished if they do anything off the pitch which is considered bad for the game. Look at that Leeds player.'

'He was done for beating someone up after having a skinful in a pub,' I pointed out. 'That happens to be illegal, as well as being bad for playing football.'

'As far as I recall he was only found guilty of affray, not actually beating someone up.' He grimaced in an effort to remember something. 'What was his name?'

'I can't remember,' I replied. 'But tell me something honestly, Colin, you don't really believe that the press have the right to splash someone's love life across their pages, now do you?' He shrugged.

'No, I don't. But we have to explore the arguments for and against before taking an informed and objective decision.'

'Good, now that we've done that I reckon we can ignore the thinking bit and say that the press are a bunch of sods for trying to upset England's chances.' When you're as objective as we are you don't need to be caught up in all this agonised weighing up of arguments.

'Absolutely,' Colin agreed.

'Feck,' said Jimmie.

Monday 29th April

The Prime Minister (ours, not the Frenchies') has had another bright idea. This time we're going to take away child benefit from people who have kids which constantly play truant or cause a nuisance.

The last bright idea was to march troublemakers up to a cash point and make them take out money to pay an on-the-spot fine. Only they realised that (a) the type of troublemaker they would be arresting probably wouldn't have a cash card unless they'd nicked it off someone else; (b) if you did catch some drunken yobbo with a cash card (a stockbroker for example) all they'd need to do was to pretend to have forgotten their pin number; (c) even if you managed to get the money out of them, you'd have a bucketful of lawyers dropping on your head the next morning wanting to talk about the legality of taking money off someone too drunk to be capable, and (d) you'd be giving a copper on the beat the rights and duty of judge and jury.

To be fair, I can't remember if that was one of the PM's, could have been one of his cronies – but he's held his hands up to this one.

I pointed the article out to Matron while she was in the area, and she shook her head sadly. 'These politicians should think before opening their mouths,' she said, irritated. 'Any fool can see that it won't work without creating more work than it's worth.'

She went off briskly to do something urgent somewhere else. Or maybe she went off to do something briskly. It's a good bet that if Matron thinks something is a bad idea it's a bad idea – not morally or ethically, just practically. And to her mind impractical is unethical. She has a point.

There are the knee-jerk reactions from the usual interest groups. Save the Children (or whatever they're called) have immediately said that it will affect the poorest people the most. They might be right, but I don't see what difference that makes. Poverty doesn't give you the right to make other people's lives hell. Especially when most of those other people are just as poor as you.

'I'm always amazed.' Colin commented later, 'at the way people think that things like the dole and child benefit are somehow a god-given right. All they need to do is look at other countries to see how wrong they are.'

'Feck,' said Jimmie. You always know when he's around.

'The dole, benefits, minimum wage, they're all things which we as a society have agreed to do – well, more or less – either for moral or practical reasons. And like any agreement there's an onus on the other side to do certain things, primarily not to abuse the agreement.' He paused for thought. 'It's like hitting women,' he said.

There was a certain silence while we tried to work this one out.

'The dole is like hitting women?' I asked finally.

'No, no, what I meant is that it's the agreement. Men could use their superior strength against women, but there's a tacit agreement that they won't, and women shouldn't abuse that agreement and hit a man because they know he won't respond in kind.'

'Feck!' said Jimmie, with an enthusiasm which suggested he had experience of what Colin was talking about.

Personally I'm in agreement with Matron; I can't see it working as a practical proposition. You can see the bureaucracy forming a mile away – a new department to handle all cases. A panel to decide on who should be penalised. Guidelines. People to hear appeals. People to hear the appeals of the appeals. The government taken to court by people (who would need legal aid – the people, not the government). Cases would take months to decide, cost a fortune, and achieve nothing. And all that is before we start mentioning "European Court of Human Rights".

Still, at least it's an idea. It might well be a gimmick, as the Tories claim, but it does focus attention on the problem, and maybe if people think about it someone will come up with a proper idea.

I remain hopeful.

I must be mad.

May

Wednesday 1st May

First of May, May Day, loads of rioting, sorry, demonstrations, planned in London and Paris and places like that and we couldn't go! Not fair! If they were afraid of us causing damage they could at least have allowed us to go to Paris. We might have caused damage, but only to the French. Would serve them right for calling us a bunch of yobs.

Still, it appears that there was hardly any rioting worth mentioning, and nothing like the year when they gave the statue of Churchill a luminous green mohican. Personally I thought he looked quite good with it. I think he would have found it amusing. Especially if you put a glass of good brandy in his hand.

I'm not quite sure what they were demonstrating against, nor whether they knew in the first place. As far as I can see it was part Reclaim The Streets, part anti-globalisation, part anti-capitalism, and several parts various other. Still those in opposition weren't quite clear either. Some person e-mailed the BBC commenting that the demonstrators had got to London using capitalist railways and transport.

In which case it's amazing they arrived on time.

I'm sure I could organise better demonstrations. Just make sure they're all in the same place at the same time, shout 'MacDonalds!' very loudly and watch that lot start frothing at the mouth and breaking things.

But May Day is not only about demonstrations and riots. Miss Melly wished us a "Happy Belthane", which is apparently the first day of the spring-summer cycle for pagans. She was certainly wearing one of those long flowing dresses which could be associated with Celtic runes or whatever they are. I can't quite work out whether she was serious about the whole business. I've always thought of her more as a Women's Institute type person. Invoking bardic chants while going sky clad just doesn't suit her.

To add to the general atmosphere of the strange and unusual, Colin claimed this morning to have heard Kerry sing last night. Kerry, so the story goes, is a white-gowned pale beauty who is never seen during the day, and very, very rarely at night, and then only a glimpse as she disappears around a corner. When you hear her sing it's a portent of something important about to happen, like you're going to win the lottery, or an alien spaceship from the planet Vog will land in your cabbage patch. If you have one.

On the other hand, possibly, just possibly, and I mention this only as a small alternative, maybe someone else just left their radio on when they fell asleep, and the glimpses of Kerry are a trick of the light. I suggested that to Colin, but he accused me of "scoffing at other peoples' beliefs" and walked away in a huff.

Me? Scoff?

When I turned up for breakfast the major was sitting with a lovely black eye and bruised face, with the Omley sisters flapping around him, tending to his every need. They seem to think that he's the genuine article, and treat him like a minor god. They're also twins, and the sight of two identical blue-rinsed old ladies flapping around the major makes one wonder if there isn't some dark religious ritual going on.

Turns out that he'd nipped out for a couple of quiet pints last night. We're allowed to do that so long as we aren't on medication, or likely to be a danger to the public – like falling asleep in someone's shopping trolley (it's happened, and didn't half give the poor shopper a turn. The girl at the till was also a bit put out, what with him not having a barcode).

The major was enjoying a quiet pint – or whiskey, in his case – when some noisy squaddies from the army camp a few miles down the road turned up. In civvies, of course. He must have done something or said something that upset them, because they waited outside for him and gave him a going over.

That's what he says, anyway. Apparently his attackers were wearing face masks or scarves so he couldn't definitely identify them.

He does have a habit of getting up most peoples' backs by telling them what to do, not just army privates out for a drink. He's barred from four pubs in the area for just that reason.

On the one hand you can't let squaddies go around beating up some loony because he shouted at them. On the other you can't let people go around shouting at other people for no good reason. And on the third hand, if the squaddies believed that he was some anonymous officer pulling rank on them in a civilian pub, then you can't blame them for wanting revenge. It is, after all, abuse of power.

It's somewhat of a moot point. The army won't want any civilian investigations into their boys, and this lot don't want residents involved in court cases. It's amazing what effect a simple query can have on a jury, say like putting the major in the witness stand and asking him "So how long have you been a fruitcake then?" It tends to destroy the jury's confidence in the witness.

Local people start to ask awkward questions about safety and security with nutters roaming the streets. The people running this place don't want to have to have any more meetings with the local residents to explain that there is absolutely no danger whatsoever, and that the patients don't tend to float around with meat cleavers in their hands and murder on their minds. Besides which, people might start Asking Questions. Questions involving words such as 'taxes' and 'our'.

The major is fully aware of this, so he isn't likely to start demanding his rights either. It wouldn't take much to have all outdoor excursions monitored, and all visits to local hostelries banned. So if you fancy the occasional relaxing pint you'd have to convince them you were sane again – which would put you permanently on the outside, and it's a dark, cold world out there.

At least I presume the major is aware of this. I hope he is. Only takes one idiot to upset the fruit cart.

Friday 3rd May

They've voted a monkey in as mayor in Hartlepool. Not a real monkey – which would have been something – but someone who dresses up as a monkey for football matches.

A government source has condemned it as "devaluing the political process". Which is to say that he wasn't impressed by the electorate telling them that a monkey could do their job better. Or, having seen what they've done in London, where the mayor was hobbled when the wrong bloke (according to them) was elected, maybe the people of Hartlepool wanted to show their opinion of what the mayoralty was worth. Pity we aren't near Hartlepool, I might have stood myself. Just for a bit of light fun.

Spent a busy and interesting morning helping out in the admin/reception area this morning. They encourage this sort of thing, wrapping it up in some psychological mumbo-jumbo about how it helps residents take responsibility, and gives them something positive to do. They may well be right, but my suspicion is that it's also because they're trying to reduce admin costs. Or cope with the fact that the owning company won't give them enough money to spend on staff.

That's the strange thing about Ms Dervish. She's capable, intelligent, efficient – and extremely good looking if you go for women who wear expensive makeup, power dress, have long auburn hair (normally in a bun), and wear those little rectangular glasses that emphasize their stunning green eyes. Not that I would, of course. Just because she's stunningly attractive doesn't mean anything.

Apparently she worked with Dr Hamilton before, and took up the job here when he came to us. I have this suspicion that he pays her good money to type and proofread his books while appearing to do the admin here, which is why she's here rather than in a more lucrative job in the city.

These thoughts were rambling around my head this morning as I worked behind the counter in reception, pointing visitors to the meeting rooms, doing the odd bit of paperwork, trying to read various files I wasn't supposed to. I wonder what new visitors would think if they knew the nice man in reception was one of the residents. I often have the urge to make sudden noises to see the reaction.

Maybe tell them to go outside and wait by the swimming pool which we don't have – and then look at them as if they were mad when they finally made it back to confess a failure to find the pool.

Everyone has to have a hobby.

On the other hand you sometimes end up having to deal with some residents who have left their rooms and got lost, wanting to know things such as when the number 23 bus is due. You'd think they'd realise that there aren't many buses likely to appear in the middle of a small reception area, but some people fail to spot these elementary facts of life.

Such a one turned up this morning. Came in from outside – which surprised me – with a look on her face which would put thunder to shame. Not someone I recognised, which was strange, presumably a relatively new patient. Very smartly dressed, expensive looking handbag, quite attractive, late thirties or early forties, not the normal sort of appearance, but it takes all sorts.

'Where is she?' this woman demanded as she reached the counter. She certainly wasn't happy about something or other.

'Who would that be?' I enquired politely. You have to be careful not to upset them.

'You know who I mean. Where is she?'

I hate it when women do that sort of thing. "You know what you've done". Etc, etc. You go through the several and various actions or lack thereof which you might have committed in the recent past to try to work out precisely which one has caused offence this time, and even if you're as pure as the driven snow you're on a hiding to nothing. Julie did that all the time. Used to drive me mad. I think the Inquisition adopted much the same approach.

'I'm sorry,' I lied fluently, 'I'm new here, who are you looking for?'

'Her. The trollop. Do you have more than one trollop here? That wouldn't surprise me.'

'Ah,' I said, as much just to say something as to give myself time to think. Much as I would have enjoyed a nuthouse full of trollops – my most memorable girlfriends would never have qualified as Sisters of Chastity – I could not think of any currently residing chez nuts.

We have some people in because they think the Martians are out to get them, so someone who sees trollops everywhere is quite normal. Except when they're very, very not happy and look like they're ready to throw something – in this case probably everything. We keep the counter clear of any hurlable objects, but she was carrying a mean looking handbag, and even though I was taller and bigger than her, madness carries its own strength.

At that moment madness was busy looking around the reception area for any hiding trollops, and I took the chance to turn to the door to the admin office, hoping Ms Dervish could lend a hand, or possibly get Matron to lend a syringe filled with sleepy-bye juice. Ms Dervish appeared for a second, alerted by the noise, made some waving gesture with her hand and disappeared smartish. Which left me to cope with Trollop-finder.

They do this sometimes. Leave you to work out a problem on your own. It builds initiative apparently. I'd prefer to do without it, thanks all the same. Initiative can get you into all sorts of trouble. I turned back to crazy Jane and said, in my best bedside doctor voice, 'Why don't I take you to a meeting room while I find her?'

'I don't want to go to a meeting room,' she growled, 'I want to go to her office.'

'Of course, of course,' I replied soothingly, 'that's what I meant, her office is what we call the meeting room.'

'I'll bet it is,' she countered. I could only guess at what that meant.

'If you'll follow me,' I requested politely, coming round the counter and leading her towards the padded room we have for people who are a little too excited. It hasn't been used for ages, and I hoped the padding was still up to it.

I was about to say something about not being sure that "she" – the trollop – was in at the moment, but realised that could have crazy Jane racing all over the buildings in a room by room search, and confined myself to some comment about how she was sure to be in. When we got down the corridor to the padded cell I opened the door and ushered her in, calling to some non-existent person within, 'A visitor to see you, miss.' Crazy Jane swept in with the vengeance of the furies, giving me time to quickly shut and lock the door.

It's a good thing the cell was padded, and the door strong. The outburst from inside, once she realised that she had been tricked, was suggestive of a small explosion going off. And her language was quite appalling. Haven't heard that sort of language since I last found myself next to a hen party.

I pocketed the key and walked back to reception whistling. As I got there Dr Hamilton strode through the door.

'Am I glad to see you, Doc,' I said, 'I've just locked up a wandering resident who needs a really, really large dose of nighty-time tablets.'

'Have you really,' he asked in a rhetorical fashion. There was a strange look in his eyes. 'Perhaps you should give me the key,' he suggested.

'Of course,' I said, handing it over. 'I didn't touch her at all. No bruises, no damage, apart from what she's busy doing to the padded cell.'

'Yeeesss,' he said slowly, very drawn out, as if he were trying to decide on something. 'A very good job, but I think perhaps now would be a good time for you to be somewhere else. Out of sight.'

'Natch, doctor,' I replied. I know the drill. Keep everyone away while the trick cyclist goes in to calm the patient down. And best of luck to him, he would need a few tricks with that one. I quickly disappeared to the garden, and our sunny patch.

It was about an hour later that Dr Hamilton came out with crazy Jane. He put his hand on her arm as if to guide her to his car, but this was swiftly brushed aside, and to my surprise she marched to another car, and drove off raining gravel all over the poor doctor.

Well, how was I supposed to know it was his wife?

Sunday 5th May

Spent most of today trying to recover from celebrating Arsenal's victory over Chelsea in the FA cup Final – two nil to the Gooners, result!

It probably wasn't long enough since the last medication to slip out for a couple of pints, but Ms Dervish gave me the nod, so at least it was sort of legitimate. I think she was feeling a bit embarrassed at not helping me with Mrs H, and gave me more leeway than Matron might have.

As far as Mrs H goes, apparently she suspects Dr H of having, shall we say, liaisons, with a resident here. Which to my mind is sufficient evidence to reserve a place here of her very own. Dr H is far too fly to make that sort of mistake. Maybe if he were newly qualified and inexperienced, but he must have at least fifteen years in the job, and he's not likely to risk his career and mortgage over a bit on the side with a patient. He'd be slung out of whatever organisation it is that shrinks belong to. His textbooks would disappear from shelves faster than you could say "peacan pie".

On the other hand, never underestimate what foolish things humans will do.

Still, I can't see it – who here could prove so alluring as to entice Dr H from whatever vows he made when becoming a psychoanalyst? I presume they take some oath or other – like doctors with the Hippocratic oath. Must look that one up sometime. Maybe I can slip it into our next session.

It does mean that I've got to be careful on the reception desk in future – I don't think Mrs H is going to forget or forgive in a hurry. Which was a good reason (well that's what I said) for disappearing down the local on Saturday afternoon.

The trouble with these games that kick off at three in the afternoon is that you have to be there by two to book a barside stool with a view. Being on your own means making sure you don't have to move to replenish rations – i.e. order the next pint – or your seat will disappear pronto, so a stool at the bar is essential. On the other hand it does mean drinking pretty solidly for an hour before the game, and about two hours during and after, and then it's still early, so you have a few more.

Now I've never been a great pint drinker. Three at the most, and I begin to feel like a waterbed that's been overfilled. Which is a pity, because there's nothing like sitting in a local – a real local, where most people know each other – watching the footie or just reading the newspaper. But the alternative to carrying on with the pints is switching to the shorts, which can often be a very bad move. Matron does not like her residents turning up singing "There'll always be a welcome in the hillside", or whatever ditty you're suddenly convinced you can sing.

"Show me the way to go home" is a definite no-no. They might well do just that.

When I turned up at the pub I noticed Ginger Ferris sitting in one corner. Funny bloke. I call him Ginger because of his ginger hair. He's always dressed in some form of brown – brown shoes, light brown slacks, check brown jacket, cream cravat, little ginger moustache, brown walking stick. You'd swear he was some local lord enjoying his retirement, slumming it in the pub or going for long walks on his estate, but he's actually a resident, about twenty five. It's funny watching some people trying to work out why this apparent pensioner has the face of a twenty year old.

We exchanged waves, but didn't sit together. He likes his corner and his solitude. A lot of us are like that.

The game was as exciting as could be expected, both teams capable of taking it, but Arsenal's superior play ensured that they took the cup. I think I must have had more than I realised, because I noticed a distinct lack of coordination in the leg department when I stood up at the end. Normally I use this as a test – stand up and stretch every fifteen minutes or so to ensure that I'm as sober as I feel – but I guess I got carried away in the excitement, and forgot. It was fortunate that Ginger was leaving when I did, because he provided a handy direction device – or to put it more accurately, could remember the way home.

I must have been banging on for quite a while about how good it was that Arsenal had won before Ginger had time to point out politely that he was a Chelsea supporter. After which I think I waffled on about how good Chelsea were, and no better game was played. Ever. Absolutely ever, ever in the history of, well, whatever history there was. And god, wasn't there an awful lot of that. History. All over the place. Knee deep in the stuff.

As you do.

At least we made it back without breaking into "It's a long way back to Tipperary" – I think Ginger was actually sober, thank god. Though I vaguely recall seeing Ms Dervish in the admin room – working late, and on a Saturday, must be those text books – and have this horrible feeling that I might have said something about her allure. Quite loudly in fact. I might even have broken into "Her eyes sparkle like diamonds" before Ginger deposited me in my bed.

I think I shall pretend not to remember anything.

It's better than the alternative.

Monday 6th May

Putative prime minister assassinated in Holland.

Colin has reverted to form – more than form – and spends most of his mornings scouring every newspaper he can find. Ironically it's partly because Mrs Phillips delivered a library book he'd been waiting months for. He sees it as confirmation of Kerry's prophecies.

'You see, when Kerry sings things are going to happen,' he claimed smugly. Personally my feeling is that a seer who announces the impending arrival of a library book which is already overdue is somewhat underutilised in the prophecy world. But he's quite happy. And now, having received said book, he's reading the newspapers again.

'Lovely, lovely,' he muttered as he pored over the Guardian. He looked up guiltily. 'I don't mean it's lovely that he was assassinated,' he said quickly, 'of course that's tragic. I mean what he was. What he stood for.'

The would-be prime minister was branded by the ruling Dutch politicians – and others – as a fascist because he was anti-immigration. Unfortunately for them he was also a professor of sociology and gay. Liberals don't like gay Fascists. They find them confusing.

'Best thing that's happened since the war,' Colin said later, sitting on the wall in the sun, after he had exhausted every possible article in every possible newspaper, including the Express. I'm sure I even saw him dally over the Sun. 'Ever since the war Liberals and the Left have got away with simplifying everything into an Orwellian two-legs bad, four legs good scenario.' Colin's the only person I know who can say "Liberal" and "Left" with capital letters when he wants to. And "Conservative."

"Tory" he can make a swearword of.

'Feck,' said Jimmie.

Jimmie's the only person I know who can say "Feck" that way.

'Anything they didn't like was either "Nazi" or "fascist". Saved the work of having to think about anything. Or having to debate real problems. Just call the person behind an idea a fascist and the problem was solved. Funny thing is they were using Goebbels' methods even better than Goebbels did.'

'I do enjoy a good bit of irony,' I commented, for something to say. Colin made a noise which sounded like "Hmmph" to demonstrate his appreciation of my interruption, which was about nil.

'And along comes this chap who according to their dogma has to be a good guy, because he's gay. And a sociologist. But he's a bad guy, because he's anti-immigration. And he's anti-Islam, which makes him doubly bad, because the Palestinians are good guys because the Israelis are bad guys and the Palestinians are Muslim, so Islam must be good.'

I could see a mental "feck?" on Jimmie's face.

'I've never understood that,' I said, 'everything I hear about the Islam is pretty bad – to call them reactionary would be an understatement. Yet we keep being told how nice and loving most of them really are, despite their comrades in religion going around stoning people and generally acting like a bunch of barbarians.'

'Ooh, careful,' said Colin, 'you could get into trouble for using that sort of language.' He chuckled. 'That Dutch chap called Islam backward, and an imam returned the favour by describing homosexuals as worse than pigs. The Liberals didn't know where to put their faces.' He sighed. 'It's not just Islam, really. It's religion.'

'That's the thing about Christians,' I commented, 'they gave up religion long ago. At least in this country they did.' I thought that was quite witty, but there was no response. 'You have to wonder whether there really is a move for change afoot, as some papers are suggesting,' I added.

'I bloody hope so,' Colin replied. 'In any decent society someone convicted of something, like mugging say, would be taken out and given the good kicking he so richly deserves. With the Liberals and the Left the mugger became the poor victim – oppressed childhood, society was to blame, that sort of nonsense – and the real victim was left out in the cold. Things were turned on their head. And anyone who objected was a fascist and not worth listening to. Now hopefully, with wubbleyouwubbleyou two and Hitler and that lot so long gone we can start looking at things objectively again.'

Not often you hear Colin swear.

He knows all about mugging. It was after the third time that he'd been mugged that he found he couldn't leave his house. Locked the doors and bolted the windows. Couldn't walk down a street, not even in a group of friends. They had to drug him just to get him out of the house and in here. Turned out to be the same teenage mugger each time. The courts put him on probation.

The mugger, not Colin.

'Good thing he was gay,' Colin said. 'Otherwise he would have been just another dangerous fascist .'

'Feck! Poofter!' said Jimmie.

His word count is increasing. Now we just have to work on the diplomacy.

Wednesday 8th May

Good news. Arsenal beat Man United one-nil, at Old Trafford, Man U's home ground. Life does not come much better.

Bad news. Had a session with Snaffle Sausage today. Life doesn't come any worse.

Dr H is on holiday – most of them seem to be on holiday these days – and the eminent Herr Doctor Adolf Snaflwurtz has taken over his sessions. The man is so nervous he makes me nervous. Even sitting with his desk between us.

'You have a problem with authority,' he claimed.

'Do I?' I asked, wondering where this had come from. It might be true, but I hate to show it.

'What was your relationship with your mother like?'

I have to give him that. Unlike Dr H he doesn't bother listening to any questions a patient might have. Or any answers.

'Well, er, she was my mother, and I was her son. About the normal mother-son relationship, I suppose.'

'You think mother-son relationships are normal, then?'

'Why, don't you?'

'Have you ever seen your mother naked?'

'No. Have you?'

'What? Why should I have seen your mother naked? I have never met your mother. What are you trying to accuse me of?'

Hah, gotcha, I thought. He's so continually on the attack he has to trip sooner or later. 'I didn't mean my mother, I said soothingly, 'I meant yours. Was it a problem?' The trick is to subtly reverse the doctor-patient relationship.

'I do not have any problems with my mother. I have overcome all those. That is why I am now a qualified psychiatrist.'

'And an eminent one, so I'm told.' He blushed. Careful, I thought, not too much of the trowel.

'Some people seem to think so. My book has had many positive reviews.'

'Not surprising, doctor. I'm told "Illustrations of an Infant" was welcomed by the psychological community.'

'Illusions of Infancy!' he snapped. Whoops. 'I think you are trying to be funny.' Whoops again. 'You are a very supercilious person, are you not.'

When he gets excited his Austrian accent begins to appear. I call it German. That really upsets him. Calling Freud a German is even better. I think he has a problem with the Germans. I must try to introduce Hitler at some stage, and describe him as Austrian.

'Of course not, doctor, I just don't have a very good memory. Keep getting words mixed up.'

'Ah, yes? Interesting.' He made a note in a little book on his desk. 'I notice you are friends with Cecil McGowan,' he commented, picking up and opening a folder from the neat pile on his desk. In fact the whole desk was so neat it was irritating.

'Cecil who? Never heard of him.'

'Do not try to play games with me. I have seen you and he and Colin Smith together in the garden many times.'

For a moment I was stymied. Then the penny dropped. 'You mean Jimmie the Feck?' I asked in astonishment.

'I don't think it is helpful to describe people as "thick", and I doubt whether you are qualified to make that decision in the first place,' he responded angrily. I decided not to point out that I hadn't said "thick". I might have to explain what "feck" meant. 'And his name is Cecil, not Jimmie. Names are important to the individual. It is not very nice to tamper with someone's name.'

Now he might be right about that, but somehow I couldn't see Jimmie as a Cecil. I'm sure there's nothing wrong with the name Cecil, but it just doesn't fit Jimmie.

'Though I must admit Corporal McGowan's intellectual abilities might not be considered to be of the highest, it is not up to you to make comment on them.'

"Corporal?" I thought. I decided to slyly indulge in my skill at reading things upside down – the words were upside down, that is, I wasn't standing on my head – now there's an idea – as Snaffle had laid Jimmie's file down neatly and flatly on his desk in plain view. 'Sorry, doc', I murmured, looking down at my finger nails in contrition, making sure to get a good look as my glance dropped. And then again when I looked up.

If I were to be honest I'm not very good at reading words when they're upside down. God knows, I practise every time I'm in that office, but I'd never make a professional spy. But I did catch the words "Desert Storm", "Belfast", "Bosnia", "medals", and "court-martial", mainly because Snaffle had highlighted them.

'Just so long as you remember in future,' he said somewhat triumphantly.

Dickhead.

Personally I'm not convinced about the Herr Doctor's estimate of Jimmie's intelligence. I think Snaffle might be guilty of the mistake of associating someone's rank with their brain capacity. There are any number of reasons why people don't get promoted, and I could guess at some of Jimmie's.

Shortly after that the hour was up, and I had to leave without getting another look at Jimmie's file. But there will be another chance, when I help out in Admin. I don't think of it as snooping. It's information gathering. For self defence.

You don't want to find out the hard way that the person you're speaking to has a bad habit of suddenly throwing sharpened knives at imaginary devils.

After the session I gave admin and reception a hand – not to have a sly read of Jimmie's file, old Snaffle Sausage still had that – but partly because I'd promised, and partly to normalise relations with Ms Dervish so that we could pretend I hadn't sung any silly songs on Sunday. Turned out she was in a bad mood about something. You don't ask questions at a time like that. Especially you don't use the phrase "that time of the month". It's impolite. And dangerous.

'Why are men such shits?' she asked at one point. It's another thing women have. They ask questions like that of men who they know won't be able to answer. Unless you take one of two lines; put an arm around them and assure them that they are beautiful and that you would never treat them with anything but respect, while caressing them suggestively in such a way that lacks any respect – an option I felt not open to myself under the circumstances – or to reply something like 'because they have women as mothers', an option not to be taken without a clear line of retreat, and a sudden turn left or right to avoid unidentified but very solid flying objects. And my line of retreat was blocked by the reception counter. Last time I tried leaping over anything higher than a tortoise my head left a dent in a wall which had to be replastered. My head didn't feel too good either.

Still, could be worse. I remember an incident a few years ago, when I was still free and easy. A bloke at my local who was gay and as camp as the day was long, with whom I occasionally used to exchange social banter – I'm not his way inclined, of course, but each to their own – came out with exactly the same phrase – "why are men such shits?".

Not much I could say to that either.

Friday 10th May

They say that travelling by train is statistically far safer than travelling by car. That won't mean very much to quite a few families today; seven dead and many seriously wounded in an horrific crash. Back coach of a train came flying off the rails and ploughed into the railway station. The pictures shown on telly were incredible.

The minister for transport, local government and the regions – whatever that means, even if I've got it right – said he would demand an immediate inquiry. Just like the last one, no doubt.

The minister probably sees this as an opportunity; he's been in hot water recently, for a number of reasons, none of which he seems to acknowledge. First he told a television programme that a senior member of his department had resigned. Parliament weren't too chuffed because they have this idea that such things ought to be announced in Parliament first, not on some touchy-feely low grade television show, but the PM's (aka Princess Tony) New Tory Party have such a large majority they don't appear to give a monkey's about parliament. The minister finally went to parliament and announced the resignation there. Only one slight problem – the senior departmental member hadn't resigned after all.

It's the sort of thing you might remember. Turn up at the office, and someone asks, 'Have you resigned?' To which you answer, 'No'. 'You sure you haven't resigned?' 'Nope, I think I might have noticed.' 'You're absolutely, definitely, one-hundred percent sure you haven't resigned, then?' 'No, I have definitely not resigned.' 'I'll take that as a maybe then, shall I?'

Now his department have acknowledged that he hadn't actually resigned, not in the technical sense of resigning as such, and are due to pay him a couple of hundred thousand quid because he obviously can't carry on in the job anymore. The money coming from our taxes of course. And the minister blaming the head civil servant in the department instead of accepting responsibility as the head of department as he should. And he tried to refuse to come to parliament to make the announcement. Claims that he did not mislead parliament. Told them something that was undeniably false, but doesn't think that qualifies as "misleading".

And while this farce was being enacted by the head of the transport ministry, which covers rail travel, something was happening on the railway which would cost at least seven people their lives. Talk about people fiddling while Rome burns.

The trouble is that they're too busy playing politics to concentrate on what they should be doing. Which is why people never went for William Hague as leader of the Tory party. No doubt he was a brilliant politician, as seems the case, coruscating in repartee during question time, but people don't elect politicians to play games. If we wanted Sophists we could privatise the whole thing.

What can you do?

I think the major's losing it. He learned about Jimmie being an ex-corporal – from what source, I don't know, but he did have a session with Snaffle Sausage yesterday – and now he has requested that the dining hall be divided into "Officers and Ladies" and "Other Ranks" areas. He must be mad. What fool would accede to such a request?

Well, there's always Snaffle Sausage, I suppose. But I'm sure Matron will put him right on that one.

I have no doubt which section I would be expected to join.

But I think Herr Majoor – or is it "Hauptmann"? – will have trouble trying to sort out the "Ladies" from the "Non Ladies". It could be fun.

Tuesday 14th May

Sounds like the rail crash was the result of two missing nuts. Or detached nuts. Very strange, since the track was comprehensively checked ten days before, and visually checked the day before. Besides being crucial, the nuts are apparently too large for their absence to be overlooked. Time will tell.

Rumours floating around that British Marines in Afghanistan were let down by US troops who refused to block off the end of a valley, thus allowing a group of al-Qaeda to escape. I think most people have more or less mentally ticked off Afghanistan as being "over", thus ensuring that it will duly blow up again sooner or later.

I see a woman has been jailed for allowing her kids to play truant. Now that might seem harsh, but apparently this took place over the course of two years, and the relevant authorities had tried everything they could think of to get her to do something, but she just laughed them off. Now she's doing time, and not laughing anymore, so perhaps there was a point to it. The problem is that it's another half baked scheme from people who don't live in the real world. As a letter in one of the papers pointed out, teachers are much happier when that sort of pupil does play truant – it means there's less disruption in the class. The well-off kids don't go to schools like that, and the clever kids will manage anyway, but how would you feel if your kid was only average, but pulled down by others who will never appreciate education until it's too late?

You have to ask whether it's morally right to spend more time and money on anti-social elements than on those who aren't brilliant, but try their best.

But middle of the road plodders don't make the news.

I shall have to think about that one.

Mrs Gladstone caught me for a game of bridge today. I'd been lulled into a sense of security, presuming that the dreaded bridge game wouldn't appear, but it appears that Janice has taken a turn for the better, and was close enough to this planet to have a few hands his morning. Not expecting it, I didn't have time to think up a good excuse, which probably wouldn't have made any difference, because Mrs Gladstone had me sitting down at the table somewhere inbetween "Good" and "morning".

I'd rather expected that I would partner Mrs Gladstone as she's the best player, and I haven't played for years, and even then it was no more than social messing around. But I found myself sitting opposite Miss Melly – ex-music teacher, a quiet old spinster who refuses to be called anything but Miss Melly – who is probably a competent enough bridge player but nowhere near good enough to make up for my abysmal knowledge.

And sufficient of Janice may well have come back to us to allow her to play a hand, but I think quite a lot is still on holiday somewhere out there. She kept patting my arm and saying "I do enjoy a good rubber, don't you", which was bad enough the first time, but after the tenth time I was worried I might lose my mind, especially as she always chose the exact moments when I was doing my best to concentrate on the bidding. People have been killed for less.

And to add havoc to the chaos every time Miss Melly made a bid, Mrs Gladstone would ask me "What do you understand from your partner's bid?", which is technically legal, but I've never seen it used with such frequency. And then Janice would pat me on the arm and say "I do enjoy a good rubber, don't you", and I would end up having to ask Miss Melly to repeat her bid, whereupon Mrs Gladstone would repeat her question, and Janice would repeat her arm patting. At one stage I was losing hope that I'd be able to get out of there as anything less than a gibbering wreck, but finally three rubbers were over, and we had a total of about two points and Janice and Mrs Gladstone had about forty zillion.

Though I'm told it isn't difficult, I've never bothered to remember how points are made up in bridge. And somehow I doubt whether I'll bother now.

The truth of it, as I realised later, was that I'd been hustled by a pair of experts. Caught me coming and going, the sods. Good thing we hadn't been playing for money.

Idly chatting with the other two – or chatting with Colin, and Jimmie throwing in the occasional "feck" – I mentioned the subject, and Jimmie's eyes lit up for a second.

'Feck. Bridge?' he asked.

'Bridge,' I confirmed, 'that and the subtle art of distracting the opposition and trying to drive them round the bend. Why, do you play, Jimmie?'

He nodded. 'Feck,' he said, which I took as to mean "Yes, but it's been a while."

Suddenly things seemed much brighter. 'Jimmie, I think I may be able to find you a game,' I said.

It shouldn't be too difficult.

Thursday 16th May

Looks like the gay sociologist's party in Holland are going to win a serious number of seats in their election. Before he was assassinated the media had enough trouble trying to work out what he was, now they're really confused – people voting for a dead fascist gay maverick?

British PM doing his usual two-step dance routine over the euro – claims that it would be a "betrayal" of Britain's interest not to join. Funnily enough the anti-euro lot use the same word, only in terms of joining. But the PM keeps on doing this; one minute he says something to indicate that he's concentrating on the euro, the next he says that his position hasn't changed, quotes the five "economic" tests and complains that people aren't concentrating on the important local issues. Political sleight of hand.

And the transport (etc) minister, who will go down in history for something, possibly for being the most accident prone minister of the century, managed to add to the confusion by claiming that there would be a referendum on the euro early next year. Which the PM immediately denied. You can't help but feel that someone's telling porkies. As some satirist commented, the transport (etc) minister might finally lose his job, not for lying but because he told the truth.

I see a budget airline was proposing to operate cheap Sunday flights between Stornoway and Prestwick, but decided against it because locals are strictly Presbyterian, and no business or public transport is allowed on Sundays. I wonder if they still burn witches.

Do they allow striking of matches on a Sunday?

The German Chancellor has won his court case against a newspaper that claimed that his hair was dyed. I can't make up my mind whether it's ridiculous or not.

Bismarck would never have tolerated it.

Colin came rushing up this morning as I sat down to enjoy breakfast. I wish he wouldn't do that. It's not good for the digestion. Mine.

'Have you seen this?' he asked in his own unique mixture of breathless anger. He waved what looked like a folded card towards me.

'Colin,' I asked patiently, 'you don't suppose it could wait until after breakfast? Morning, Jimmie.'

'Feck,' said Jimmie, in an absent minded greeting. He was absorbed in finished his eggs and bacon, using a piece of bread to wipe up the last escapees of yolk on his plate.

'This is serious,' Colin insisted. 'read that.'

I gave a deep sigh, and took the proffered card. It read "OFFICERS AND LADYS ONLY", and looked like it was written by someone who had a serious problem with writing. I put it down and picked up knife and fork prior to commencing on the more important business of grub.

'I agree, Colin. Terrible. That in these modern days someone should make such a terrible spelling mistake.'

'It's not the spelling mistake,' he said, hopping from foot to foot. 'do you know who wrote this?'

'Your four year old nephew?' I asked through a mouthful of egg. Personally I think speaking with your mouth full is a disgusting habit, but under current circumstances it was either that or let the stuff go cold.

'Of course not. And he's my grand-nephew. I wish you wouldn't be so flippant. This is serious.'

'So you said. So who did write it?'

'The major. Put cards like this on all the tables that lot use.'

I thought about that for a moment. "That lot" would include the major and the Omley sisters, along with one or two others who thought they still lived in the days of the Raj.

'Mmm, I see. He's really losing it, isn't he? So what's the problem?'

'It's an insult! It's a calculated insult.' For some reason Colin was really wound up.

'Colin, it's a calculated insult by someone who isn't very good at arithmetic.'

'Eh?'

I sighed. Which isn't easy when you're about to take a bite of toast. The crumbs fly in unannounced. When I finished coughing, I explained.

'That was a pun, Colin. Calculation? Arithmetic? Yes? Okay, no, then. I don't see why you're so upset about it. I mean he is somewhat of a prize idiot. After all, it's not as if he put "Other Ranks Only" on our tables, is it? And you wouldn't want an "ossifiers only" card on your table, would you?'

We were interrupted by a quiet "feck" from Jimmie. Having exhausted all possibilities of any food remnants on his plate he had picked up the major's childish attempt at a place holder. I must admit it didn't sound like a polite or disinterested "feck".

'That's not the point,' Colin continued, 'it's the principle. He's gone out of his way to insult us, and to show how superior he is, and I don't intend to stand for it.'

'Righty ho. What do you plan to do? Give him a blanket party?' A blanket party is where someone has a blanket tossed over them to prevent them seeing their assailants, and is given a beating. Don't ask me where I found that one.

'Feck,' said Jimmie, who undoubtedly considered this an option, and a good one.

'Of course not,' Colin replied. 'But I shall think of something. You'll see.' He stomped off in suppressed fury.

I pushed my plate to one side, another breakfast half ruined. I lifted my coffee instead, looking at Jimmie. 'No blanket parties, Jimmie,' I said. He looked at me in innocent surprise, as if the thought had never entered his mind. 'Feck?' he asked, pointing towards the plate I had pushed away. 'Yeah, all yours, Jimmie,' I said.

He set about retrieving the undisturbed bacon to make a bacon butty. I watched enviously. I like a bacon butty as much as the next man, but Colin's outburst had put me off food for the moment. I suppose the army had taught Jimmie to eat where and when and what he could. And that nervousness burnt it all off, so he'd never have a weight problem.

Funny, that. So many people worried about putting on weight, yet for people like Jimmie it would be a good sign. Reminds me of something Julie once said, when we were out shopping once, many years ago. She commented enviously on how thin some woman was, and I pointed out that the poor woman probably had anorexia. 'Lucky thing', was Julie's reply.

There's nowt so daft as folks.

Later on I met Tonique walking back to the main building on my way to the sun trap. Unusual to see her outside. She nodded nervously at my greeting, and hurried passed. She's like that. Nervous of her own shadow. Jimmie was enjoying the sun when I got there.

'See Toni?' I asked. 'That poor girl should get treatment. If someone said boo to her we'd have the first woman on Mars.'

'Feck,' he replied, eyes closed, absorbing sunshine. I doubt if he even noticed Tonique beyond being someone – or something – providing food at meal times. He only notices people who are a potential threat.

'You know, Jimmie, you really should take more notice of the people around you,' I pointed out to him, unfolding The Times. There was no reply. I decided not to pursue it, and concentrated on the results of the Dutch election.

Monday 20th May

Prisoner JH6047 has achieved his fifteen minutes of fame – imprisoned for stealing golf balls. Not quite Raffles, still less the heist of the century, and even worse, it wasn't a hold up in a golf shop. He was merely taking them from the bottom of a lake on the golf course, where unamused golfers had given up any hope of seeing them again. Which begs the question of how he could be said to have been stealing them – surely it would have fallen under some maritime law of salvage whereby people can claim abandoned ships? But the judge considered it such a heinous crime that the felon should be locked up.

Fortunately others have seen the essential stupidity of this, and our man is going to be allowed to appeal. Most people think that he – the felon, not justice ass – was providing a valuable service by reclaiming the balls and selling them on at reduced, second hand prices to people who would promptly hit them back into the lake. At least the golf course owners wouldn't have to dredge the lake so frequently.

Foreigners coming to this country must wonder what we're like. We lock up mothers because their children truant, and enterprising recyclers for retrieving abandoned golf balls. The Japanese would be proud of us. What's next, decapitation for not bowing as the queen flies overhead?

And meanwhile people die on the railways due to incompetence and greed, and no-one gets even a slap on the wrist.

Maybe I'm in a bad mood, but it does sound incredibly silly. Maybe it's that the newspapers concentrate on the bad things, but there's enough of it to go round. Wembley is another example. They've been going round the houses with that one for ages now, and eighteen months after the last match there, even longer than after they decided to pull it down and rebuild it, they still haven't a clue what to do. Now they're talking about reopening it with a minor facelift to get the money to pay back the lottery loan which they got on promising that the new stadium would host athletics as well as football, except that now they don't think they can do that.

And it gets worse. Birmingham has spent a lot of money in laying out a plan for themselves to host the national stadium. The "Secretary of State for Culture, Media and Sport" – the longer the title the less it means – imposed a deadline of 30th April for the Wembley lot to sort out their mess, and no doubt Birmingham were rubbing their hands in glee, knowing that Wembley couldn't organise the proverbial in a brewery, but 30th April came and went, and the deadline was ignored by the politicos, leaving Birmingham not very happy at all, and who can blame them? Since Birmingham is arguably more central to the UK than London, and has, apparently, good transport links, give it to them, I say. Cardiff proved that they can build an international stadium for about £165 million (estimates seem to vary) – but Wembley's latest prediction is £715 million, and that's before they start coming out with excuses about overruns. And London has more than enough attractions. Madame Tussauds, for example, where the Wembley management could stand, and no-one would notice the difference between them and the other waxworks.

For some reason everyone is falling over themselves to state that, while there has been "mismanagement", "lack of adequate monitoring" and "we're 'an international laughing stock" , no-one is to blame. Like the fairies came along and did it while no-one was looking. You can smell a committee a mile away.

It's almost enough to make you angry enough to stand for election yourself.

The quote I really like is from Sport England, the body which decides on allocation of lottery finances to sporting bodies: "We have this amazing ability in this country to stab ourselves in the foot and to go on reviewing things until we completely kill them."

I have this kind of mental image of people in suits sitting around a conference table with knives sticking out of their shoes.

Popped out for a quiet Sunday evening pint last night, to a different pub, much closer than the usual. I'd heard that The Rose and Crown – it's the pub's real name, believe it or not – had a new landlord, and apart from having had enough of listening to Colin planning his revenge on the major, and Jimmie whose mind seems further away than ever these days – I was interested to see what this new landlord was like. The old one had a definite prejudice against anyone from here. He'd serve them, but the drink would be slammed down on the bar, suds frothing everywhere, just to make sure that the would be drinker knew that he wasn't welcome. My theory is that he was afraid of the inmates, and adopted an aggressive stance as a sort of pre-emptive strike against any suggestion of abnormality.

Which is ironic if you look at his regulars.

The other theory is that he was just a nasty piece of work who liked frightening people.

Anyway, the new landlord's name is Pete, and a very friendly type he is. The place was pretty empty, so I sat at the bar and he and I had a long discussion about the issues of the day, such as whether England should be relying on a single striker so much, and how you can't trust the Argies.

Ginger Ferris had beaten me to the pub, and he was sitting in a corner seat with a pint in front of him, staring into somewhere only he could see – personally I reckon he's making sure he can still remember every Chelsea player since 1945; it's the only thing left of importance to him.

The landlord kept glancing at Ginger in what I can only describe as confused apprehension. Finally he came out with it.

'Here, you know those loonies from up the hill? I reckon that's one of them. When I took this place over from Mike he warned me about them.'

'What, him?' I asked, nodding in the general direction of Ginger, 'Slasher Edwards? The Razorman? Oh you don't want to worry about him, he's harmless.'

'Slasher? Razor?' he asked with a face full of fear and a voice filled with panic. 'Why they call him Slasher then? Razor?'

Fortunately I was only half way down the first pint of the two I had promised myself, otherwise I could have got carried away – in more ways than one. I've learnt that the law of unintended consequences doesn't only apply to those who mean well, it can have nasty effects on those who are trying to stir. I patted him on the arm.

'I'm joking, Pete. Ginger over there – well, I call him Ginger, don't know his real name, to tell the truth – he's a very quiet Chelsea supporter. The most harm he'll ever do you is to bore you silly with statistics about the Blues.'

He seemed to relax a little. 'What's he in for, then?'

'Now, Pete, that's a personal question, very impolite to ask. And he's not "in" for anything. He's a voluntary patient. Could discharge himself if he wanted to.' That seemed to calm the landlord down a bit. He was a bit over-energetic about wiping the bar in front of him though. You get to recognise when people are a little nervous.

'So how come you know all about him then?' he asked. The question I had hoped wouldn't come up. I drained my pint glass and held it for a refill.

'Because I am one of them,' I said. It was one of those make or break moments.

He looked at me nervously for a moment. He seemed to come to a conclusion. He took my glass, placed it in the wire tray holding dirty glasses, picked up a clean one and began to pull a pint for me.

'You don't sound ... um ... '

'Like a fruitcake?'

'Well, no, I didn't mean that at all, you, er ...' He put the pint down in front of me, and I held out a five pound note. He shook his head.

'On the house,' he said. 'My first night and all.' He leaned forward, elbows on the bar. 'You know, I've spent all my life in the pub trade, but I've never had loonies as regulars before.' There was a moment of companionable silence. 'Don't know how the missus will take it. She should be okay. But I do have two teenage daughters, and from what Mike told me I've been dreading you lot coming in here.'

'Pete, your daughters, they help you here in the bar?'

'Yup. eighteen and seventeen they are, and ever since they were old enough I made sure they did their bit. Pay them for the work, of course, but just so long as they get an idea of working for a living.'

'So they're not unused to the sight of people acting, how shall we say, strangely? Otherwise known as four parts pissed.'

He laughed. 'No, they know how to handle themselves.'

'In that case, I'm afraid they'll find us really, really boring. Not a single homocidal maniac amongst us. Most they'll have to do is remind us where home is. Pete,' I said, raising my glass, 'I'd like to buy you a drink.'

'Well, that's very kind, but let's say it's also on the house.' He turned and poured himself a Jamesons – good choice if you're into the whiskey. We clinked glasses.

I think the Rose and Crown is going to do quite well.

Thursday 23rd May

India and Pakistan acting like a couple of teenage boys threatening to punch each other's lights out, and saying things like 'Oh, yeah? You and whose army?' Except of course they do have armies, and nuclear weapons to go with it. You'd think they would have sufficient problems with poverty not to spend money on advanced nuclear missiles, but there's no explaining things to some people. Appears to be a political thing on one side, and religion on the other, and with a million soldiers on their borders all it needs is one little incident to start a real war. Which is pretty much how the first world war started.

The latest government wheeze over here is to combat illegal immigration by sending Royal Navy warships to patrol the Mediterranean.

Wot, both boats?

The good news is that the football world cup in Japan and Korea is promising to be fun for all the family, whether you like football or not. An Irish player has been slung out of the Ireland team for criticising his boss just once too often. That and swearing at him, and suggesting that his fellow team mates weren't of his quality.

Cameroon look like they're going for the record of taking the longest time to get to a world cup ever – starting off with the team refusing to leave until their world cup pay was guaranteed, and then having to take a detour because their plane had not been cleared to fly over Cambodia, Vietnam and the Philippines. So far they're five days behind schedule and counting.

I imagine the poor person organising them must be sobbing into his beer.

The Swedes have belied their peaceful image by having a full on brawl amongst themselves during training. They even managed to do it in front of assembled reporters armed with cameras, who probably thought Christmas had come early. I wonder if anyone asked the Swedes for a repeat to get a better shot.

When the England team read that news they must have fallen off their zimmer frames laughing. If there's any player on the England side who hasn't either already got an injury or is prone to anything from achilles tendon to hamstring to groin weaknesses, then they aren't mentioning it. Maybe it's a secret plan. Just when the opposition expect England to come on with crutches and elastic bandages, send on a player who can walk unaided.

And of course there's the shaggy-dog story, except the dogs aren't shaggy; dog meat is considered a speciality in Korea, and some people are quite upset about this. These are not vegetarians, but people who are quite happy to eat lamb chops and rabbit pie, so I'm not sure how well their mental processes are wired up.

To complete the picture all we really need are a few car chases and a romantic interest. There's a story that the Brazilians were due to receive a consignment of pornographic magazines, but they deny it, and I can't see that qualifying as 'romantic'. But I remain hopeful over the car chases. Maybe even a riot or two. After all, the Japanese and Korean police have been training so hard for so long it seems a shame to waste it all.

The only people who think England have a snowball's chance in the fiery regions are the English media, but I suppose it's only natural that countries will concentrate on their own teams. If someone had asked me this morning to name five countries in the cup I would have struggled, so I've made a note. It should come in handy when I want to bore someone to tears.

Group A are France, Senegal, Uruguay and Denmark. Group B are Spain, Slovenia, Paraguay and South Africa. Group C are Brazil, Turkey, China and Costa Rica. Group D are South Korea, Poland, USA and Portugal. Group E are Germany, Saudi Arabia, Ireland and Cameroon. Group F are Argentina, Nigeria, England and Sweden. Group G are Italy, Ecuador, Croatia and Mexico. Group H are Japan, Belgium, Russia and Tunisia.

Looking at that list is interesting in a way. You kind of wonder how the hell the US and China got in, and what happened to countries like Holland and Australia. I must have missed that.

Mrs Gladstone apologised for having to cancel our bridge game today, due to Miss Melly being under the weather. I wasn't aware that we were going to have a game today, but that's not unusual. I've never been able to remember appointments other people make for me. But I took the chance to assure her that Jimmie had promised to sit in if required, and the game was duly on. She only knew Jimmie by sight, which rather helped. He said nary a word as we sat down and organised the cards and score sheets, merely nodding politely at Janice's idle chatter. Behind the chatter I could see her gearing herself up for a bit of subtle mental distraction, and Mrs Gladstone had that look in her eye which suggested that taking prisoners wasn't on the menu.

Jimmie dealt the first hand and thus took the first bid.

'One spade ... ' he opened. The combined flak started.

'What do you understand ... ' Mrs Gladstone began.

'I do enjoy ...' Janice joined in, about to pat my hand.

'... feck,' Jimmie finished his bid with a timing which couldn't be bettered. Mrs Gladstone's mouth remained half open in surprise, Janice's patting hand stayed in mid pat. I beamed in friendly fashion.

'I believe it means he's got an opening hand, and strength in spades,' I told Mrs Gladstone brightly. Then I patted Janice's wavering hand with friendly warmth. 'I do so enjoy a good rubber,' I assured her.

After that it was all downhill for them.

Jimmie said 'feck' at odd moments, such as when Janice, after hesitantly deliberating for a while, started to pick a card to play, and then immediately pushed it back, no doubt wondering whether that "feck" was significant. They could hardly object to personal mannerisms, not in this place. There was no more patting of hands, and Mrs Gladstone even gave up asking me what I understood of Jimmie's bids.

In fact Jimmie's bidding was very good, and his play totally unorthodox, so established players like Janice and Mrs Gladstone hadn't a clue about his strategy. Nor did I, though that didn't matter since I had been making it up as I went along anyway.

In the end we took three rubbers against their one. Mrs Gladstone was magnanimous in defeat. She congratulated us and told how she looked forward to the next session. But the look in her eyes suggested that we weren't going to have it so easy next time. I think "fair play" in her book means anything short of knives and guns, and possibly even those under certain conditions. No doubt she and Janice are going to have a few words.

Funny how people can become obsessed by something so trivial.

Jimmie seemed to enjoy it considerably. He seemed much more cheerful than usual, almost smiling. It's obvious he's a good bridge player, something I would never claim for myself, though where a corporal, or ex-corporal learnt to play that well is a bit of a mystery.

I sure as hell ain't going to be playing poker against him anytime soon.

Monday 27th May

'According to the papers,' Colin announced, 'a rugby player used his hand in a scrum to pull the ball back to his own team, which, according to the laws of rugby, is illegal. The ref didn't notice it, but the TV cameras did. And the player has now stated that although it was a foul, he was not cheating.'

I ran that through my head a few times as we strolled through the garden.

'Come again?' I asked finally, ignoring Colin's beam of triumph.

'He claimed that, although he had broken the rules, he wasn't cheating.'

'Right,' I said. I tried to grasp the concept, but it was the mental equivalent of trying to catch an eel in an oil bath.

'This chappie of yours, he didn't have a bad tackle or something? Hit his head against a post? Someone thumped him with a brick?'

'Not as far as I can see. He just seems to have a kind of moral dyslexia.'

'Ah, is that what it is. Sounds like the latest illness. This year's blackout, as it were. I can see,' I added as we perched on the sunny wall, 'the scene now. Your friendly tea-leaf in the dock, bang to rights, saying to the judge, I knew it was wrong to nick the money, your guvnership, but I suffer from this moral dyslexia, like, you see. And the judge saying, that's truly terrible my lad, off you go then, and be more careful in the future.'

Colin didn't seem too over enthusiastic about the proposed drama.

'It's not funny, you know. It shows a definite lack of understanding of right and wrong. And these rugby players tend to be from the upper and upper-middle class. If that's how they're thinking, what can we expect from anyone else?'

Poor Colin does tend to have this illusion that somehow there's a class of wealthy people who are upright and honest and treat life as a game of cricket. A fair game of cricket, that is, not the ball tampering stuff that must happen in another world. Not that their wealth came from anywhere but honest toil and good breeding, god forbid.

'And what sort of treatment has this mental dyslexic received from the media then?'

'Moral dyslexic. He's been giving a good pasting, and serves him right.'

'So what's the problem? One burk shows how stupid he is, and gets roundly hammered for it. Shows that things are working. After all, do you know any people who would do that sort of thing? Would you?'

'Of course not. I've never cheated in my life. And I have no intention of starting now.'

'There you go then,' I replied, and concentrated on The Times, one story of which had now been ruined. I mean we all know that there are people who cheat and lie and rob, but we aren't among them. Which is the important bit.

Isn't it?

Well, when I say cheated and lied, I mean really cheating and lying. The serious stuff.

Tuesday 28th May

The mother who gained her fifteen minutes of fame by being locked up because her kids played truant once, or several times, too often, has emerged from chookee to declare that she has seen the light, that she was wrong to have let her girls slip the leash, and that she deserved her, now reduced and spent, sentence.

Apparently the sentence has had an amazing effect on parents throughout the land. One mother turned up, dragging her seven year old to school, declaring that she was not going to prison for him. I think they've omitted the words "you little tyke". Elsewhere schools are seeing pupils they'd forgotten existed turning up in their droves.

So it seems that the measure has had its effect, though I can't help but wonder about the rightness of it all, if I can put it that way, without using the word "morals", a word with which I have several problems. If jailing single mothers achieves the aim, are we to accept that the aim justifies the means? And will the mother feel the same way once she has got over the humiliation and indignities of prison?

You wonder what conversations she had inside. 'I'm in for shoplifting'. 'I'm in for burglary'. 'I'm in for killing me husband'. 'I'm in for rape'. 'What you in for, Patty?'

'Er, I let me kids play truant.'

'God, that's disgusting. You're a pervert you are. Your own kids and you let them miss out on an education what I never had before. You should be ashamed of yourself'.

Shades of Arlo Guthrie and Alice's Restaurant.

I still think they ought to consider some form of public humiliation for minor offenders. Maybe not the stocks – or possibly even a version of the stocks – for half a day. Better than locking people up in overcrowded prisons, wasting taxpayers' money, getting no insight into how their crimes are viewed by other people, and probably learning some other nasty habits. The mother in question said that she hadn't realised the damage she was doing to her kids, and somehow I doubt whether she would have listened to any teachers or social workers, but a spell in jail doesn't normally result in clear headed thinking.

I think I'm beginning to sound like Colin.

He seems to have got over the major's "ossifiers only" place-labels. In fact the major is looking almost haunted by them. They've had zero effect, and are now looking a little tattered and forlorn, and I don't think he can see an easy way out, such as quietly binning them and pretending that nothing happened.

Of course he hasn't noticed that someone has written "Catering Corps Only" above the message "Officers and Ladys Only" on the far side of the labels.

I don't know where this childish behaviour comes from.

Saw Jimmie and Tonique chatting together in the garden. Or at least I assume she was chatting to him. I presume she's got used to his rather limited vocabulary. I think she might be losing her fear of the fruitcakes, which is a good sign. I'm sure she could do quite well if she only realised that other people are just as human and frail as her.

Of course, compared to the indomitable Ms Dervish or Matron, Tonique must feel rather left out in the confidence stakes. Matron probably learnt hers through the hard knocks of experience. Ms Dervish – I reckon she was born with it. Or maybe learnt to use it with those eyes of hers. When I asked her if she'd be watching the world cup, she replied "Only if I can find someone to watch it with", in tones that suggested further enquiries were not advisable. I suppose she tends to find herself with the sort of in crowd who only follow football as a fashion.

And would you believe it? Our town – we're just inside the border, so we qualify – has voted in a referendum to have a mayor, in addition to the existing local councillors. 50.05% of the votes were pro, which is enough to give that lot in Westminster the excuse to foist more bureaucracy on us, including one of their chosen appointees as mayor, no doubt. The fact that only 22.03% percent of people actually voted, which leaves the 50.05% as about maybe 11%

of the voting population, as far as I can work it out, doesn't count I'm afraid. Amazing how a phrase like "the bare majority" can turn into some form of surrealist democracy.

It would be nice if someone did something about it. Since I'm not registered to vote there isn't much I can do, but it would be heartening for someone to as a "None of the above" candidate. After all, if Hartlepool can vote a monkey in, I'm sure we could elect the Easter Bunny.

I won't hold my breath.

Wednesday 29th May

The minister for transport, local government and the regions has resigned as cabinet minister. I guess he decided it was only a matter of time and decided to scuttle himself rather than being taken out by the massed guns of the media. Or massed ranks of vultures scenting a dying man possibly. There's no doubt that they were out for him, but it has to be said he gave them good cause. Refusing to admit to misleading parliament when he undoubtedly had was a mistake of ego. All he had to do was go to the Commons and say, "terribly sorry, bit of a communication cock-up, my earlier statement was not actually correct". Instead he decided to play sophist and insist that there was no reason to apologise as he hadn't lied, which isn't the same as being misleading – and then blame things on his senior civil servant, something which didn't do anything for his reputation. British political tradition is that the minister takes responsibility for his department, and does not name bureaucrats.

Was.

What with the football world cup about to start you would have thought that he could have braved it out for a few days. Within a few weeks people will have totally forgotten anything that has gone before. And if England make any headway – admittedly pretty unlikely – most people would be in such a good mood they'd be ready to give him a people's pardon so long as he didn't mess up again.

Would you believe it, the major is making noises about all the television sets being tuned to programmes on whatever the latest royal celebration is, and the flag being flown from the flagpole.

Now this place does have a flagpole, which leads me to suspect that it used to be some form of military barracks. Unlike the United States, where it seems even dogs' kennels' flagpoles have their own flagpoles, Brits don't really go in for those sort of things – which is probably why, when you see flags in times of joy or crisis, they tend to hang from people's balconies. Still, if the major wants the Union

Jack flown, I'm not too bothered. I think the medical opinion here – from the occasional doctor you might see these days – is that it's not good to excite the patients with anything which might be construed as jingoistic. He seems to have settled for a little Union Jack on his breakfast table, to replace the badly written place label, which one of the Omley sisters finally realised had the "Catering Corps Only" addition.

The major was not impressed. Poor chap.

But the television question is much more serious. What he wants is to prevent anyone watching the world cup, pure spitefulness, and, as I told him, shows a definite lack of patriotism. Not wanting to support the national team in the most important sporting event of the year – of every four years – just isn't acceptable to anyone of good British yeoman stock. (Ignoring the fact that Scotland, Wales and Northern Ireland didn't make it through the qualifying rounds, but you can do that with the major.)

It's very much a moot point, since there are three large areas with televisions, and two smaller ones, something specifically designed to avoid this sort of thing. You wouldn't want a full on fight between one set of fruitcakes who wanted to watch Eastenders, and another determined on watching Coronation Street.

There would be Words.

Which is what Matron said. And the major didn't dare argue. I think he's afraid of her.

I don't blame him.

Friday 31st May

Senegal 1, France 0 (zero, null points, eff all, zilch, nada, take that you foreign type French people).

Ok, we're talking football world cup here, so please do not try to adjust your sets.

Senegal were rated as having as much chance of winning as the ex-minister for transport (etc) now has of having a sensible transport policy. France are the current World and European champions, highly rated, likely to win, and, of course, are the evil empire. They gave the world Napoleon, Rousseau and garlic, and we gave them Allo Allo. Fair trade, I reckon.

And apparently you could have got odds of 10-1 on a Senegalese win – just a 100 quid and you'd walk away with a thousand – now why didn't I think of that?

Probably because the only time I bet is the occasional quid on the lottery every so often, and the odds are better there.

I slipped out to the Rose and Crown just after midday, though the match was at half twelve, and lunchtime drinking is not exactly something I enjoy. Or possibly it would be more accurate to say that I enjoy it, but it doesn't agree with me. This year, the world cup being in Japan and South Korea, we get to see all the matches at ridiculously early times in the morning. People go down to their local at seven in the morning. Full English breakfast and a pint.

I'd rather not know what they look like by lunchtime.

I sat chastely drinking shandies – well the first one was a shandy, but it tasted bloody awful, so I moved on to a rather nice ale the landlord, Pete, had managed to acquire. We were convivially exchanging admiration of its colour, texture and body when Ms Dervish walked in.

Now the question of patients popping out for a pint is a grey area. I think the general rule of the doctors is that they're happy so long as they don't know about it. Otherwise people start to ask questions about why their tax money is being spent on people who are capable of going down the pub every day. So I fully expected Ms Dervish to manage not to see me at all – a difficult job, as I was sat at the bar where she would have to come to make an order, but not impossible for one of Ms Dervish's skills.

Instead she came right up next to me, pulled up a bar stool and ordered a white wine.

'Well, I suppose there is one good thing about you,' she said, 'at least you follow football.'

It was a strange remark, but I've long learnt that the best thing with strange remarks is to ignore them entirely. Otherwise you'd go mental.

Funnily enough we had a rather enjoyable time, mostly spent slagging off the Frogs.

The football wasn't really up to much.

June

Sunday 2nd June

The great event we've all been waiting for. Well, possibly not all. I get the feeling that there are a number of people out there who just don't appreciate the world cup.

Honestly, sometimes I despair.

Though having watched England's performance against Sweden I don't blame them. I almost fell asleep half way through. If that's the best they can do I shall have to consider supporting someone else. Ireland, maybe, who scraped a one-all draw yesterday against Cameroon despite all the soap opera of Ireland's ex-captain being sent home in disgrace. Now that they've have got rid of their prima donna they can play as a team, whereas England play as a bunch of hair-dos.

Or hair-don'ts as the case may be.

Germany beat Saudi Arabia eight-nil yesterday. Today South Africa managed to come back from two-nil down to level two-all. I would have loved to have watched it, but ITV showed the second half on what they now call "ITV2", just in case people might think it had any relation to ITV Digital which is bankrupt. We don't get ITV2, so I went into the garden to read the papers, rather than sit and listen to a bunch of would be experts waffling the same waffle they've been waffling for the past three weeks about England's chances. If England make it to the second round it won't be five minutes before they start claiming that "we can go all the way". Then the Republic of North East Podgorvovia will knock them out, and the media will explain how they knew all along that they were useless.

And Argentina beat Nigeria one-nil. Damn nuisance.

Tuesday 4th June

Some royal celebration going on. BBC and ITV were trying to see who could outdo the other with forelock tugging. There was some concert with people who were once considered rebels of society – about a hundred years ago, before their first zimmer frames – who now play nice music for the queen and her peasants. Although the one young lady from Nuclear Kitten (or whatever it was called) was wearing a rather interesting outfit, the top of which seemed to consist of two narrow lengths of silk which threatened to expose her at any moment. I'm told it's all done with sellotape.

Amazing what they can do these days.

Mrs Gladstone and Miss Melly went off to London to join in the celebrations as a special treat, and came back seeming tired and happy. The major was going to go with them, but somehow missed the ladies – probably due to Mrs Gladstone's good eyesight – and ended up going alone. He came back happy and singing "Britons never never will be slaves", which is rather ironic for someone who supports an unelected head of state.

Still it did mean that I was able to watch the footie without any undue distractions, such as a certain person wandering in, looking at the screen, and muttering "hmmph" loudly. On the debit side is the fact that I can't really remember much of it. Maybe I'm already footballed out. Though I recall that South Korea beat Poland two-nil, and Japan levelled with Belgium at two-all, so at least the two host countries South Korea and Japan haven't disgraced themselves.

Wednesday 5th June

Papers are full of sanctimonious cant about how popular royalty are today, and how well the royal jamboree went off yesterday. The PM quoted as saying of the queen, "We don't just respect her, we love her".

Pass me the sick bag.

On the other hand the PM is enough to make you consider royalty as a viable option. I doubt the Queen is naive enough to believe a word he says. If the royalty becomes a liability – and the media can switch sides faster than you can say "Eh?" – he'll drop them down the pan without a second thought.

On a lighter note, there are reports that members of the dear old Labour – I use the word in its loosest possible sense – cabinet are refusing to dip into their pockets to buy a suitable present for the Queen. Apparently there was a deathly silence when he brought the subject up at a cabinet meeting, and much pursing of lips and looking out the window.

The good news, however, is that Ireland drew one-all with Germany, with a stunning goal (did I just write "stunning"?) in the last minute of extra time. Their manager's face was a treat to watch. His jaw just dropped open, bounced off the ground, up and down a few times, and you could see his face go from dejected defeat through puzzled possibility to ecstatic euphoria. Someone tele-texted channel 5 to say that the Irish deserved their win, and it did feel like a win somehow. And they did deserve to win.

I'm sure I have Irish ancestry somewhere.

All civilised people do.

The bad news is that the fanatics in Northern Ireland have decided that this is the ideal time to turn the place into a war zone again.

And a suicide bomber has left eighteen dead in Israel, near Megiddo, also known as the ancient city of Armageddon.

Thursday 6th June

France 0 – Uruguay 0. Looks like favoured France might have a couple of problems. In other news: Denmark 1 – Senegal 1, Cameroon 1 – Saudi Arabia 0.

And in other other news, India and Pakistan continue to rattle their sabres. Britain and the States have warned their citizens to leave both countries. Possibly the French and Germans have done the same, but our media never bother to mention any other countries. Unless there's some schadenfreude is involved.

India has adopted a policy of "no first nuclear use"', meaning that they won't use their nuclear weapons first. It sounds good, but I can't see that it means anything. You see twenty or forty missiles aimed at your major towns and cities, and you aren't going to wait for a radiation count before deciding whether this is the big one.

As has been pointed out, during the Cold War the States and Russia had hotlines available in case something went wrong – "terribly sorry, that missile we just launched was a mistake, can we have it back, please?", Whereas India and Pakistan have no means in place to handle accidents.

I just hope they don't have one before the end of the cup. They're far too close to the goal line.

Friday 7th June

England 1, Argentina zero.

Now that may leave some people cold, but you have to understand that Argentina are now officially enemy number one. We could have forgiven them the Falklands, especially as they lost, but what with the prima donna "hand of god" cheating goal in 1986, and then beating us in the 98 cup through blatant diving and fouls, this was the big one.

And today good honest Englishmen defeated their odious underhandedness. I must admit that I lost my normal reserve. I leapt up, punched the air, shouted something or other, and did an impromptu dance with the person next to me, who was also punching the air and shouting. It was only after a few seconds that I realised that it was the major. We both sort of half-stopped in embarrassment.

'Bloody good goal,' I said, for want of anything else to say.

'Yes, definitely,' he replied, and we sat down to continue the match in polite disinterestedness. As I was turning to sit I saw Ms Dervish watching us from inside the doorway. I can only describe the look on her face as sardonic.

Women are strange.

Apparently the Argentine media have responded very reasonably. La Nacion stated that the Argentine team deserved to lose.

I must start taking that newspaper sometime.

It's not much fun when you beat the evil empire and they turn around and say, "Yup, your guys were better, good game, you deserved to win". Kind of takes the enjoyment out of it.

Oh, and Sweden beat Nigeria two one.

Nice people, the Swedes.

Monday 10th June

Those Russians don't like losing. At least not against the Japanese. After the Japanese beat them one-nil there was rioting in Moscow. Cars set alight, a Japanese restaurant invaded, Japanese music students attacked, some took cover in a Macdonalds – they must have been desperate.

It's at times like this that you find out what other countries' loves and loathes are. The Japanese and Russians have never really got on. The Russians have never forgotten that the Japs won the battle of the Tsushima Straits in 1905 (which brought on the Russian revolution of 1905, a sort of dress rehearsal for 1917), and the Japs still want the Kurile islands back from Russia, who nicked them at the end of WWII. Stalin carefully avoided going to war with Japan while everybody else was fighting both Germany and Japan, until Germany was finished, and the first nuclear bomb was dropped on Japan, at which time he decided to join in the war by invading the Kuriles, which Russia subsequently annexed, and kicked out all the Japanese.

Apparently the two countries never actually signed a peace treaty, so technically speaking they're still at war. Let's hope no one points this out too loudly.

Proud Italy was beaten two nil by Croatia. Which is good. Not that Croatia won, but that Italy lost. So far things are turning out quite well, with most of the favoured teams doing rather badly. Otherwise things would be really boring. Only Brazil is maintaining their reputation.

Brazil. Where the nuts come from.

Speaking of nuts, Mrs Phillips came around with the library books this afternoon. As she said, she always comes on Tuesday mornings except when she can't, so this week it's on Monday afternoon. I didn't understand a word of it, but nodded in that sort of manner that indicates to the person that you understand totally, and to anyone else watching that you think the person is barking mad.

It's not easy. You can get real bad neck problems doing it.

She was bringing me news from the other side. Now to me that means across the boundary wall, but to her of course it means from a place where people aren't still quite alive.

Dead, actually.

She speaks to them all the time. Even occasionally on buses or other public places, she says. She claims that the dead are never bothered by irrelevancies such as the best time to speak to someone who can't see them, and that at one stage she found it rather embarrassing. People looked her as if she were mad. Now they presume she's using a mobile phone. Modern science has its uses.

She was bringing a message from Evdokia. Who Evdokia is, I'm not sure. I've never met an Evdokia in my life. Let's face it, it's the sort of name you'd remember. But apparently Evdokia can foresee the future – which suggests a certain carelessness, seeing as she's dead.

'So what is this message?' I asked Mrs Phillips, hoping that it would be short and meaningless. As lovely a person as she is, I tend to get brain ache after being around Mrs Phillips for too long. In this case she looked a little embarrassed.

'I must admit that I forgot to write it down,' she answered. 'There were so many people clamouring to speak to me at the time. I suppose I thought I could remember it.'

'Don't worry, Mrs P, I'm sure Evodkia will pop back some time.'

'Evdokia. But she might not remember. I wish I could. Something like ... the Ides of March. Only not that. Something similar.'

'The Ides of April?'

'No, no, don't be silly. I mean it was like the warning given to Caesar. Only different.'

'I promise you, Mrs P,' I said, patting her arm soothingly, 'I will steer clear from Roman consuls.'

I left her muttering something to herself about getting old, and starting to lose it. She should take a lesson from us. We started out by losing it. Get it over and done with. It makes life easier.

Tuesday 11th June

Ireland beat Saudi Arabia 3-0 to take a place in the next round. It's funny how everyone seems to support the Irish. It's almost as if you can hear people muttering in an embarrassed way, "Yeah, well, sorry about Cromwell and all that, no offence meant, didn't much like him myself either" – well some people anyway. I doubt if the National Front share the feeling.

According to one of the news reports the Irish fans were all singing "The Fields of Athenry", a song which I have since discovered is popular with Irish football fans, and relates the story of a young man about to be parted from his beloved by being sent as a criminal to Australia during the famine; his crime was to try to steal some corn to feed his family. I can see how such a song would unite all the descendants of those forced to join the Irish diaspora. And you can sing it while drinking pints of Guinness and having a good time. I can't think of any English song which does the same thing. "Gathering nuts in May" hardly qualifies, and "Knees up Mother Brown", well, you'd be embarrassed, wouldn't you? And these days Mother Brown would probably clock you one.

I see the English fans in Japan have actually been praised for their behaviour, and the Japanese are now more concerned about their own young "huurigans" as the papers call them. There were even some awful reports that littering might have been committed. And some of them were caught on television shouting when supporting their team. Some of them were women, as well. Disgusting. I don't know what the world's coming to.

On another planet, the loya jirga in Afghanistan, the great meeting in a German beer tent – no beer, of course – to set the foundation for a peaceful and prosperous Afghanistan seems to be spluttering along. As far as I can see the country's so split into little fiefdoms run by warlords it'll be a miracle if they ever achieve anything peaceful. They'll be lucky if the tent's still in one piece at the end.

And all of these warlords professing a passionate belief in the Koran. Only they seem to have read a different one to everybody else. Still, it was only a few hundred years ago that the Catholics and Protestants here were busy setting the world on fire, depending on which religion the then monarch fancied. So give it a few more centuries and we should be okay.

Speaking of religion, I saw Father Patrick this morning. He's the local priest who pops in from time to time to cater to the spiritual welfare of our flock, those who are, or think they are, Catholics, or who don't mind speaking to a Catholic priest. He used to be Anglican himself, but when the Anglican church decided to ordain women as priests he had a Damascene experience.

Well, maybe not Damascus, probably somewhere closer to Bognor Regis.

I had wanted to discuss with him the recent scandals in the US church regarding certain priests who indulged in paedophile pursuits, and the bishops who turned a blind eye to the allegations. Unfortunately he saw me coming, waved quickly, and disappeared in the general direction of somewhere else. I think he suspects me of taking the mickey, which is a bit hurtful. I admit I did ask him once whether the trinity was a sexual metaphor, a concept he seemed unwilling to discuss, and there was the time when I enquired whether you still needed to believe in religion to become a priest, and possibly I shouldn't have queried why they still wore skirts, but that's hardly any reason to take umbrage.

These things should be discussed.

Thursday 13th June

Big political hoo-haa about corrupt – allegedly – politicians. The labour party chairman has taken the opportunity to accuse the media of being pious and hypocritical. That had me rolling in the aisles laughing.

Dear Mr Kettle, Yours Sincerely, Mr Pot.

England drew with Nigeria nil-all yesterday. If their game with Sweden was like watching paint dry, yesterday's was like watching cement set. The only reason people got excited was that a draw would take them through to the quarter finals, so they're in.

Good news from the India/Pakistan playoffs: India has withdrawn its warships from positions close to Pakistan, and normal diplomatic relations are expected to resume shortly.

Of course a lot depends on their notion of "normal" and "diplomatic".

Bad news: the government are planning a bill to allow local councils to eavesdrop on such things as private e-mail and telephone calls. All in the name of the war against terrorism, of course. Let's hope that one gets kicked into the very, very long grass.

One day we will have a balanced government and opposition, and the prime minister will not be able to ignore parliament, and propaganda and spin will be outed for the nonsense they really are.

It just won't happen in our lifetime.

I see a man in Norway was arrested for barking in public. The police claimed that he was disturbing the peace, but fortunately, in a triumph for freedom of going woof in the open, the court threw out the case. I couldn't imagine a world where people weren't allowed to woof where they wanted. It would be the end of civilised freedom as we know it.

Friday 14th June

Session with Snaffle Sausage this morning. Sometimes I wonder if the man isn't a few hampers short of a picnic.

'Do you not think your arguments with the major are somewhat petty?' he started off by asking.

'What arguments?' I replied. 'As far as I'm aware I don't have any arguments with him.'

'What about the television programmes then?'

'What about them?'

He sighed as if talking to an especially obstreperous child.

'You wanted the football shown on every television.' I gawped at him for a few moments.

'Sorry? When did I do that?'

'That is what the major claims. He merely wished to watch the royal celebrations as a patriotic person, and you asked that this should not be shown.'

'Have you asked anyone else about these strange allegations?' I queried, with little faith in Sausage's ability to distinguish between fact and fiction.

'And then there is the question of the card on his dining room table. Did you not think that a little childish?'

For a moment, despite his ignoring my appeal to fact and logic, I thought I saw a glimmer of hope. 'Of course. Absolutely ridiculous.'

'Why, then, did you write those remarks about this catering corps?'

I don't often go goggle eyed, but this was surely an appropriate occasion. 'Are you accusing me of writing on the poor little major's place card? Are you mad?'

'I think our relative positions should indicate which one of us has a problem with reality,' he replied smugly. 'So you deny that you wrote those comments?'

'Of course I deny it. I've got better things to do than indulge in such idiocy.'

And I'm sure no-one saw me.

'But you did not like it when he put the card on his table.'

'Doc, as far as I'm concerned he can do the tango on his table. So long as he doesn't interfere with me I really couldn't give a toss.'

'Ah, yes, his table. It is interesting – significant – how you people set out your little territorial areas. I was thinking of doing a study into this.'

That was a bit rich coming from someone who only spoke to other people from behind his desk, the contents of which were almost fanatically aligned and squared off.

'However, I have been thinking.' He paused to show how much thinking he had been doing, and leant back and steepled his fingers in front of his mouth, an action I have only every seen in movies.

Patton, The Lust For Glory, if I remember correctly.

'I think, to solve these problems, we need a voice of the patients. I was thinking that we need a patient on the Board of Administrators. This I believe is a good idea.'

He's definitely short of the normal number of marbles. And the ones he's got are rolling around south of the equator.

The so-called Board of Administrators used to be a gathering of all the doctors once a month, during which they would swap gossip, do a bit of back-stabbing, and desperately try to conceal their latest ideas from their fellow shrinks, while generally boasting of how well their latest books were doing, even if they weren't.

Oh, and they'd end up signing the request Matron had sent in for toilet rolls and disinfectant, which is what administration is all about.

Eventually they got bored – or Snaffle put them off too much – and it ended up as a meeting between Sausage, the Matron – who was called in to justify the number of toilet rolls – and Ms Dervish, who was there to make up the numbers.

'Why would you want to do that?' I asked, trying to avoid using a tone which might suggest that I thought it a ridiculous idea.

'To give us an insight into the feelings of everyone here. A guide, as it were. To help us in reaching decisions which are acceptable to the majority.'

'And who were you thinking of as this guide?' I asked out of politeness, wondering what possible input the patients could provide on the number of packets of washing powder required.

'The major strikes me as a responsible person. At least he is used to command. I think he would be well qualified to take part in the decision making process.' God help us. If the major was used as "a guide" we'd end up having morning parades saluting the flag. And pictures of the queen in every room. And I'm sure the only thing he's ever commanded is a standard plumber's wrench. This needed nipping in the bud. Very quickly.

'Have you thought of letting people choose their own representative?' I asked innocently. He frowned.

'A sort of vote, you mean? Hmmm. I had not thought of that. I am not sure that this is the best place for such things.'

'Well, I dare say some people might see it as good therapy. Emulating the world outside. Maybe someone has made a study of it. It would be very relevant in contemporary society.'

'No, I think I would know if such a study has been made. Such a study would indeed be widely known. I would imagine it would be required reading for political academics.'

'And politicians. Like the prime minister.' It was like guiding a blindfolded man off a cliff. I could see his mind imagining the respect and popularity he would receive after publishing a major book analysing modern politics within the nuthouse, comparing it to the apathy and malaise within Western democracies ... senior politicians would invite him round for drinks ... serious newspapers would beg for articles ... television interviews ...

He managed to snap out of it.

'I will give it some thought. And, of course,' he added quickly, 'I shall expect you not to mention a word of this. It can do, ah, great damage if such ideas leak out prematurely.'

'Course not, Doc, my lips are sealed.'

No way am I going to let my name be linked to this daft scheme.

The session ended very shortly afterward, no doubt to allow the great doctor time to plan his new project. It should take a few months, at least. And then I am sure enough will happen to render it totally impracticable. If not, we can always give it a helping hand. Or shove.

South Korea and the US are through to the knock-out stages of the world cup. Portugal, another favourite, is out. So many of the rated teams are out now the bookies must be rubbing their hands in glee. Brazil are still in, though, and everybody seems to think they'll take it. However I'd note the saying that Napoleon should have listened to: keep your eye on the Germans.

Saturday 15th June

Down to the Rose and Crown prompt at midday to ensure my favourite place at the bar with a clear view of the television for the England-Denmark match. Exchanged the usual banter with Pete about his lousy beer and high prices, and he countered with his usual comment about having to be mad to drink in here. I'd just sat down and taken a good sip of a rather wonderful ale when Ms Dervish came in. She was wearing white slacks and a rather tight England t-shirt which showed off her perfectly shaped bosom.

It's at times like these that I wonder whether the burka and voluminous clothing for women might not be a good idea. I don't think they realise the effect they have on poor innocent men.

She pulled a bar stool up while I was quietly choking from breathing in a mouthful of ale, and made herself at home. Pete was up like a shot. He might be happily married, but he still has an eye for good looking women. Especially ones with a quick brain who can give as good as they get. While I was busy choking he complimented Ms Dervish on looking like a million dollars, and she replied by saying that he didn't look a day under thirty. Or something like that.

It felt rather comfortable with the three of us there, even though the place was absolutely crowded within a very short time. Football fever spreads as the competition becomes more important.

We spent the rest of the time until the kick off discussing whether England would manage not to lose too badly, and, if it came to penalties, whether we could get the Danes to take ours for us. To non-football supporters it might seem strange, but I suppose it's the same concept as going to watch a horror movie. You expect to be on tenterhooks for most of the time, but unlike the horror movie, you truly don't know what the outcome will be like.

Fortunately the time came for kick off, and we were able to settle down into a state of terrified expectation.

It's difficult to describe what happened next to anyone who doesn't share the sense of doom and gloom and hope and terror at their football team's ability to cock things up.

England scored within the first five minutes. Or, to be more accurate, the Danish goalkeeper, whose name will remain tactfully unmentioned, managed to fumble an incoming header so badly that the ball, which wasn't going anywhere like close enough, landed up in the goal. Napoleon's dictum about having lucky generals suited England that night.

Not long after another England player proved his worth by turning on a sixpence and slotting in another goal. And then came a perfect strike to take England three nil up. With each goal we were up clapping and cheering and hugging each other, which was, I must admit, a rather enjoyable experience with Ms Dervish.

Fortunately the bar was between Pete and myself.

And this was before half time. Which is where the problem comes in.

You would think that any normal person would then relax, confident in the knowledge that their team is now effectively unbeatable in this game. There is just no way that a team can come back from three-nil down to win at this level. But that would be to misunderstand what ever football supporter knows in his or her own heart. No matter how good your team might be, they are always capable of truly ballsing things up and managing to lose against impossible odds. Snatching defeat from the jaws of victory has nothing to do with it. Here we are talking about scaling the highest mountain, fording the deepest stream, and crossing every byway to find defeat, no matter where it might hide.

So half time came, and we spent the fifteen minutes chatting absent-mindedly about nothing much, during which time Ms Dervish pointed out that my shoes needed a hint of polish, and I agreed but responded that such things cost money, and there were certain priorities, to which she replied that that was probably why I always looked permanently scruffy.

The conversation was a measure of how much we were looking forward to and dreading the second half.

In the end there wasn't much to say for the second half. The Danes tried a bit, but never looked as if they believed in themselves. There were one or two scares, to which England's goalkeeper responded with his usual effortlessness. In the end the score remained the same, and though we cheered at the final whistle, it was a bit of an anti-climax. The game had been won in the first half, and the rest was purely nervous tension at waiting for the inevitable result.

Though it has to be said, I began to wonder if England couldn't go all the way and win it this time. I quickly stifled the thought. Such thoughts are bad luck. I wouldn't want to be the Jonah who gave them the evil eye.

The only black spot during the game was the behaviour of a couple of oiks in the pub who had found themselves a large England flag, which they waved all over the place whenever it looked like England were approaching the Danish goalmouth, obscuring everyone's view and forcing people to duck every so often. It wouldn't have been so bad if they hadn't spent the rest of the time playing with their mobile phones, swearing a lot, and generally ignoring the game. Eventually Pete was forced to ask them politely to put the flag down and stop swearing, something that earned the response of "fucking Paddy" from one, and "fucking-the-c-word" from the other. Since Pete is undeniably English, it seemed a strange reaction.

These are people who struggle to walk and talk at the same time. Actually, they struggle to talk whatever happens.

Their response earned them an immediate exit, and though they argued against it they left after Pete promised to get the local coppers around to have a word. Their leaving was greeted with cheers and applause from the rest of the pub.

Apparently they come from a local estate, the centre of crime and poverty in the area, and a nest of National Front supporters. According to the newspapers, the England flag used to be a symbolic of the National Front, but has now been taken over by England football supporters of all colours and classes. I'll have to take their word for it. Hopefully they're right.

It's been a strange world cup so far. Prior to the start many people were worried about hooligans, riots and damage, yet it's turned into almost a carnival.

And whether or not you like football, that can't be a bad thing.

Sunday 16th June

After yesterday's heart-stopping stroll of England going through to the next round, today the Irish showed how these things should be done.

Spain scored in the eighth minute, and then absolutely nothing happened for the next eighty-two minutes. Well, obviously lots happened, and much sweating was done, but the score-line remained obstinately at one-nil. To be fair to the Irish players, they never stopped attacking, and, much as I dislike the over blown language of commentators, the description of "wave after wave of attacks by the Ireland players" was an accurate one. Despite their energy and enthusiasm, all seemed lost, and the look on the faces of the Irish supporters was that of people regretfully wondering what time the next plane home was.

Then in the ninetieth minute – last minute of normal play – Ireland were awarded a penalty, and slotted it home. The crowd went mad. As I had stayed in to watch it I didn't experience the same feeling around me – sometimes you really miss being there.

It went into extra time, the time of the 'golden goal' – whoever scores first wins. And the Spanish were soon down to ten men due to injury and having used up their substitute allocation. And the Irish attacked again in waves. And waves. And all to no effect.

Extra time having been played without a result, it went to penalties.

I remember hearing a player describe what it was like when a game moves to penalties. The goalkeeper has to walk from the half way line to the goal. The player to take the penalty has to walk from the half way line to the penalty spot. Then goalkeeper readies himself as the player steps back from the ball.

And all of this taking place in front of a present crowd of tens of thousands, and a television crowd of millions, and almost the entire population of your country watching you.

I've always thought they should play the music from that

Western, where the music is set to the background of a fob watch chiming the hour. Ting-ta-ting ... ting-ta-ting ... (drum roll) ...

Alas it was not to be Ireland's hour. They lost three-two on penalties.

But they can certainly go home with their heads held high. They came in riven by disputes, doubtful to get past the first round, and ignored as an opposition by everyone else. Having sent their captain packing, they united as a team, and showed the world what team spirit and giving it your all meant.

I wonder if anything else has been happening in the world. Probably not. It is the weekend, after all.

Monday 17th June

I see the latest great political scandal continues to rumble on. It's almost like watching a soap opera: "Last week on The Latest Political Scandal: the PM climbs down on complaint to Press Complaints Commission, the press claim that their version of events was correct. Claims were made that a certain official had sent a memo to the PCC confirming that Downing Street aides had attempted to interfere with the funeral. This week: Downing Street propaganda machine starts smearing said official, whispering campaign begins to spread rumours that he is a closet Tory."

There are suggestions that the official is indulging in "party politics", a heinous crime. If it is such a crime, why don't politicians walk around with their head hung in shame?

I don't think they can actually see the irony.

A quick summary of football news: with Japan still to play Turkey, and South Korea to play Italy, those through to the quarter finals are currently, England (of course), Germany, Senegal, Spain, Brazil, and the US. It's quite amazing to see the Yanks get this far, but strangely comforting. The better they do the more interest the Yanks will take in a proper sport, then, when they go out in the next round we can patronise them.

After all, it is one thing we can still do quite well.

Wednesday 19th June

Now wifely loyalty is a good thing I'm sure, but someone should explain to the PM's wife that it doesn't mean that, when you see your hubby digging himself into a hole, you should immediately dig yourself into one as well. Though you have to admire the depth and speed of her shovel-work.

Just hours after a suicide bomber killed nineteen people in Jerusalem, including children on their way to school, she publicly commented that "as long as young people feel they have got no hope but to blow themselves up you are never going to make progress". Needless to say this caused a major eruption. Apart from the ever-current question of a prime minister's unelected wife getting involved in political discussions, the suggestion that suicide bombings are justified was breathtaking in the extreme. It took me a few seconds to find my own breath after watching her make the statement on television.

Downing Street went into overdrive on the explanation and apology front. The PM found himself defending his wife instead of answering questions about his planned speech on criminal justice and his meeting with his buddy the Spanish prime minister. A spokeswoman for his wife expressed her regret if the remarks had caused offence. Generally the approach was that the comments had been taken out of context, misinterpreted, she never actually said that, well, yes she did, but that wasn't what she meant, and have you heard the latest football score?

The Foreign Secretary managed to get involved in the furore, and surprisingly also managed to avoid digging himself into a hole – give that man a sweetie! He pointed out that the real offenders were those who brainwashed the young people, and sent them as suicide bombers to their deaths and the deaths of innocent people. The media could have so easily taken parts of his speech out of context, but don't appear to have. Given the current position they probably wouldn't dare to – both sides are just waiting for the other to make a whoopsee.

I've been thinking about this business, and where the difference lies between terrorists and freedom fighters, and where "giving your life for your country" is a good thing and where it's a bad thing. I'd like to bounce a few ideas off Colin, but he's still in "I'm not coming out until the football's over" mode. Jimmie wouldn't be much help. I have a suspicion he lives in a very black and white world; either it's dangerous and you kill it, or it's not and you leave it alone.

Or possibly you eat it.

Once you start looking at this from an objective point of view, taking note of how various people see things, avoiding emotional bias, considering all the viewpoints, you very quickly end up with a headache. In the end it is a subjective matter, and objective analysis is almost impossible. I keep coming back to the old military saying, that you don't win wars by dying for your country, you win them by making the other poor bastard die for his. The point is that we can understand people who are prepared to fight for a defined objective which they hope to live to see, we can't understand people who are willing to kill themselves and others for some mythical idea of martyrdom in the afterlife.

You can negotiate with the former, but not the latter.

Something like that.

Apparently the PM's wife is now very busy and unable to take any calls.

Of course they're able to get away with quite a lot at the moment, with everyone either glued to the football on television, or having switched their sets off for the duration. I have a lot of sympathy for people who find it a bit of a trial. The television pundits invariably use every game as an opportunity to discuss England's chances against Brazil, and if you're the sort of supporter – like most – who awaits a game like that against Brazil with their hearts in their mouths, all this extra waffle about "England can do it" is likely to give you a heart attack. Which, with the said organ already in your mouth, could be highly dangerous.

Just bring the sodding game on and let's get it over with, I say.

On the good news front: the Home Secretary has climbed down on his "snooper's charter", whereby anyone from your local fire department to the street cleaning division of your local council would be able to demand details of your private life without a court order. Apparently his son pointed out to him what a bad idea it was. You would have thought he might have guessed all on his own.

On the really, really good news front: South Korea have knocked Italy out of the World Cup. Now I don't know why this appeals, but I have a suspicion it's to do with wars and the underdog. We always support the underdog – in this case South Korea – mostly because our team is always the underdog, and we always boo a team which comes from a country we have been at war with in the past, which basically means most of Europe. The Korean war doesn't count, because they were on our side – or were we on theirs?

Talking of dogs, I haven't noticed anything about the Koreans penchant for dog meat, stories of which were circulating faster than a wildfire prior to the start of the cup.

Thursday 20th June

Boy, some mothers do have them, don't they? You'd think that, after all the politicians and advisers and some politicians' wives who have caught a bad dose of foot in mouth plus hole digging, the others would quietly keep their heads well below the parapet. Only a total fool would say anything to give the press more ammunition.

Step forward the Home Secretary.

Being obviously aware that relations between Downing Street and the media have been going so well recently, and intuitively understanding that the media generally are kind hearted souls who can tolerate a little bit of justified but positive criticism, he has taken the opportunity to call the press "hysterical", and "on the edge of insanity".

Perhaps he should have asked his son first before opening his mouth.

Needless to say the press are now questioning his sanity. He actually used the phrase "the chattering classes", a sure sign that a politician is losing it.

Poor chap.

I think it's called the tap-dancing method of landmine location.

There's some news about the Church of England choosing a Welshman to be the next Archbishop of Canterbury. Or the current Archbishop of Wales, not sure if that makes him Welsh. I'm sure it's a fascinating topic, which I immediately ignored. Much more important is the news that people are being asked to pray for the defeat of Brazil on Friday. Now that's taking things a bit far. It's bad enough when you find yourself nervously wondering whether some striker's groin will be up to it, expecting us to go to church as well is definitely expecting too much.

And with all these cars you can see going past with England flags flying, it's impossible to escape. So Brazil were one of the best teams in the world. So they took football and turned it into an art, inventing "the beautiful game". I'm sure England can beat them. It's just the waiting that's a problem.

Oblivious to the football, Israel is taking its revenge for the latest suicide bombings by launching helicopter strikes against targets in the Gaza Strip. Or, an alternative view, they're defending themselves by trying to prevent future attacks.

At times like these I think of the Israeli contestant who won the Eurovision contest a few years ago. "She" was either a transvestite or a sex change, I forget which. You just can't imagine something like that coming out of Gaza. I remember at the time thinking that, if they could be that liberal, there was hope for the Middle East. Not much hope there now.

Maybe if they could get into the world cup things would be different. Make Palestine a state, get their football team into gear, and give them something peaceful to cheer about. Just try not to let the two countries meet each other in the knock-out phase.

I'm sure England have a chance against Brazil tomorrow. Brazil just aren't the team they used to be. They really haven't faced any decent teams up until now.

I see the subject of the "fridge mountain" has come up again. They signed up to a European agreement whereby all the nasty things in fridges and freezers – CFCs and whatnot – would be carefully removed before disposing of said white ware so they wouldn't escape into the atmosphere and cause more global warming. Unfortunately they didn't think of the practical side, i.e. how the fridges and freezers were going to be disposed of. So now there are locations around the country to store them until the specialist work can be done. Definitely one for the "they should have seen that one coming" file.

Meanwhile over here people are asking whether a bank holiday should be declared if England make it to the finals. Considering most of us are chewing our finger nails to pieces over tomorrow's game, looking that far ahead is pure masochism. But I'm confident that England can do it. Though I also have great faith in their ability to make a mess of it. On the other hand, the language coming out of their camp is quiet but confident. So I'm pretty sure they'll do it.

Two-one to England, I reckon. Which is not to say it'll be a walkover. But the general mood according to the interviews on the telly is that the entire country is behind the team, and believe that they can do it.

Roll on tomorrow.

Friday 21st June

All the signs are that summer is definitely here. The French air traffic controllers are having their annual strikes, and ETA has begun its usual bombing campaign. Some day soon the French ports will be closed due to strikes, or farmers protesting something or other, and we'll have the traditional shots of stranded Brits showing true grit by making tea next to their cars as they sit in tailbacks waiting to board ferries which can't leave.

Football? What football?

A summary of the great battle with the Brazilians: Brazil were competent, England were useless. The England goalkeeper has been accused of a blunder because he was caught off his line, but the shot was so well executed it's unlikely that the goalkeeper could have saved it anyway. The basic fact is that Brazil were down to ten men for over thirty minutes of the second half and England couldn't capitalise on the advantage. They ran out of steam. Or maybe panted out of steam would be more accurate.

But, considering that a few months ago it looked like England wouldn't even qualify for the world cup, it's amazing they got this far. There's that to think of. When all the fans, now sitting feeling gutted, dazed expressions of shock on their faces, numbed in disbelief, look back in a few weeks time they'll probably say "well, we didn't really do that badly, did we?"

On the other hand, the amount of money they pay these footballers, I think we have a right to expect them to put a bit of welly into it.

Ah, well, maybe next time.

I don't normally read the obituaries, but the phrase "Marxist historian" caught my eye, and, intrigued, I read on. I wasn't aware that you could have Marxist historians, I thought they were all supposed to be ultra objective and analytical and spend their days in dusty libraries wandering around wearing ancient cardigans. But Professor R. H. Hilton, who passed away on the 7th June was apparently an academically famous Birmingham historian whose field was medieval peasantry, and who was indeed a communist until 1956, and a Marxist up until his death.

It's a strange feeling reading the word "communist". Rather like coming across a photograph of a time that was once very important to you, yet you had all but forgotten about those days.

It wasn't that long ago that the Berlin Wall was still in place, and the Soviets were the other, evil, superpower. These days I wouldn't be surprised if young school kids had never heard the word "communist". And how many people would remember the names Burgess, Blunt, Maclean, and Philby, let alone McCarthy?

Then again, Professor Hilton's work included a detailed analysis of the Peasant's Revolt in 1381. I never even knew they'd had a revolt in 1381. I did a little quick research, and came up with the name of Wat Tyler, and it all came flooding back. Summer days in classrooms spent looking out the window and hoping the bell would go soon, the teacher droning on about the perfidious Richard II, and probably also desperately awaiting the sound of freedom.

You can't really mix summer and education.

Monday 24th June

Football update: Spain vs South Korea, and Senegal vs Turkey – who to support? If you apply the underdog/war test, it's quite simple. Korea were the underdogs, and we've definitely been at war with Spain. Maybe not recently, but how could you ever forget the Spanish Armada? And there's Gibraltar; the Spanish have been trying to get it back for ages, something they no doubt thought possible with our current PM, but the Gibraltarians made it quite clear that the answer was "no way, hose", though if I were them I'd keep a close and beady eye on the PM.

As far as Senegal goes, they're were the underdog in that match, and I'm pretty sure we've never been at war with them. On the other hand Turkey joined the wrong side in WWI, and gave a great deal of trouble at Gallipoli, a name synonymous with British incompetence and the waste of Australian and New Zealand lives.

Unfortunately Turkey scored a goal in extra time, so they're through. But South Korea managed to beat Spain on penalties. The Spain-Korea game was notable for dodgy decisions. Spain had two goals disallowed, and a ball ruled out that was obviously still in play.

That's the way it goes, I'm afraid.

You tend to forget about North Korea. Just some crazy outdated communist state living in the past which is best ignored until they come to their senses and adopt a modern democratic constitution (who knows, maybe even this country will do that one day). Now, with the world cup going on in South Korea, just a few miles down the road, you'd think they might let the news get through, but apparently not. The government-controlled media hasn't told the people that part of the cup is taking place in South Korea, nor that South Korea are doing so well. In fact they don't report on any matches that South Korea take part in, so anyone who tries to make sense of a chart of the games will become very confused. Seems rather sad to me.

But they've finally ended the silence with a report on South

Korea's defeat of Italy – which happened five days ago. Maybe it has something to do with North Korea beating Italy in 1966. Or possibly they realised that, with the South Koreans broadcasting commentaries of the matches across the demilitarised zone, the people were likely to hear about it sooner or later.

I can only presume the North Koreans aren't too hot on tourism, or they could have advertised themselves as being an ideal refuge from the world cup.

For sport-phobics, bad news: Wimbledon started today. But then Wimbledon isn't so much sport as a summer celebration, a chance to guzzle champagne and strawberries in cream, to ignore the men's games because they're terribly boring, and to admire the lady competitors' choice of underwear.

And for anyone who has decided to invest in a new television to watch this fest, better do it quickly. Britain is shortly to adopt similar guidelines on the disposal of electrical appliances such as televisions as they did with fridges – so now we'll have used television mountains along with the fridges.

Thursday 27th June

Things are returning to normal now that England are definitely, absolutely, undoubtedly out of the cup, and it wasn't just a bad dream. Jimmie, Colin and I spent the morning soaking up the wonderful sunshine relaxing in garden chairs which Jimmie had filched from somewhere. The chairs were brand new – in their original plastic wrapping – and coloured in bright red and green stripes which made me hope the designer had ended up somewhere safe and secure with a lock on the outside and no access to drawing materials on the inside.

There are so many buildings and rooms around here for storing things which no-one knows about that I wouldn't be surprised if they one day found Lord Lucan living in luxury somewhere, maybe on the second floor, or in the attic. My theory is that it went from being government controlled, where excessive bureaucracy allows the stockpiling of all sort of necessary and unnecessary goods, to being privately run without staff to do inventories, leaving a veritable utopia of goodies for the interested scavenger.

Jimmie lay sprawled in his chair with a silly floppy hat on his face to keep the sun out of his eyes. At least it should have looked silly. Jimmie has such a utilitarian approach to clothes he makes silly things look sensible. Colin was indulging himself in his favourite pastime of searching the newspapers for Schadenfreude, and he didn't have far to look.

'Three point eight five billion!' he said with a gasp. He looked up. 'That's how much they booked to capital expenditure instead of expenses. That would buy a lot of Chinese take-aways.'

It's the latest great capitalist scandal, whereby an international company managed to convince shareholders that it was still making a profit while they were actually heading for bankruptcy on a speed close to timewarp. The auditors who should have picked up this small but rather important point were famous for missing similar obvious facts in the last great capitalist scandal, and then shredding evidence as the accounting authorities were on their way over for a pot of tea, a choc digestive, and some very heart to heart discussions on the finer points of accounting.

'I see the US President has decided to enrol in the Texan approach to democracy by trying to force Arafat out through giving the Palestinians an ultimatum,' I replied.

It's a game we play sometimes. You sit reading your own choice of newspaper and see who can find the more breathtaking example of hypocrisy. The important thing is to acknowledge the other person's story, and then try to trump it with a better one. It's like tennis, only with news stories as balls – some of them in more ways than one. And you don't have the drug tests afterwards. Or upper middle class young women wearing face paint and waving flags shouting things like "Com'n Colin" in a voice which suggests they're trying to shout and be polite at the same time.

'They certainly caught him at the G8 summit with that stetson. Poor chap actually put it on. At least the PM wasn't that stupid.' The G8 summit is a meeting of the leaders of the wealthiest countries in the world at an exclusive gathering in Canada this time. One thing they're going to discuss is poverty in the world. All other citizens are being kept miles away, just in case they might break into a demonstration and upset the world leaders tucking into their caviar.

These meetings where they get together in such tight security, with armed soldiers – including anti-tank, anti-aircraft, anti-everything – remind me too much of a feudal system, with the king and his retainers in the castle, and the peasantry whipped back by chain-mailed soldiers.

'I see that that fire in Arizona is getting worse,' I countered. 'Quite a few towns are being evacuated.'

'I don't understand why they're so excited about who caused it. According to all the reports it would have gone up sooner or later. They should concentrate on why they didn't have the resources to combat it. Oh look, Mugabe's doing his usual impression of maniac dictator. It says here that white farmers have been ordered not to grow any crops while the country's suffering from drought, and having to import foodstuffs. Any idea why Snaflwurst is suddenly fascinated about everyone's insight into modern democracy?'

'He's got a new bee in his bonnet. I'm not allowed to tell you anything. Sworn to silence. Mugabe always was a strange one. Barking mad, really. I see the EU rulings about not being allowed to sell bananas as bananas if they're too curved have been deemed as not applicable under British law. That's a victory for common sense.'

'Cucumbers, wasn't it? I noticed last night that the Evening Standard have started a crusade to get the London mayor out. What is it you aren't allowed to tell?'

'I'm not allowed to mention that Snaffle Sausage is planning a book on democracy in the nut house. I think it was bananas as well as cucumbers. The Evening Standard has always wanted to get rid of their mayor. They really should get some treatment for it. Their loathing is positively unhealthy. The business section here says that property prices are continuing to go through the roof.'

'Only thing that's keeping the British economy going, people spending money they don't have. Did you read the list of questions the Standard wanted the mayor to answer? Number 5 was asking why he left the scene of the accident before the police and ambulance arrived, and number six asked why he didn't speak to them when they arrived. You'd think the obvious answer from number five was that he wasn't there. What's democracy got to do with us?'

'I'm not allowed to tell you that he's planning on having a resident on the Board of Administrators, and intends holding a democratic vote so that we can elect said person. While he sits and makes notes on the process so that he can publish a thesis on it. If the bubble bursts in the economy it's going to be a bad one. Not being held together by much more than misplaced confidence. Who cares if the mayor had a scuffle with someone? He was voted in as mayor, not as St Joan of Arc. I see some papers are trying to raise questions about why there hasn't been a homecoming celebration for the England team.'

'Because they lost. I suppose you're going to support Germany in the final. Why on earth does the man want anyone else on the board? It could be a disaster.'

'No, I'm going to support Brazil. Germany don't have half naked young women wearing feathers supporting them.'

'Feck,' said Jimmie. I fully agreed. Good to see he was keeping up.

'True.' Colin dropped his newspaper and looked across at me. 'This business about Snaffle Wurst, though. He isn't serious, is he? I mean, what if they take someone like the major on?'

'Feck,' said Jimmie angrily. Once that lad gets going there's no stopping him.

'Oh, I wouldn't worry too much. I'm sure that, with a little help, the whole thing will become somewhat of a burden to the Herr doctor. You know how badly these things can go wrong.'

'You mean – sabotage it?'

'Now, really, Colin, that's a terrible accusation to make. I would never interfere in any democratic process. I'm merely thinking that we could highlight the potential weaknesses in the dear Herr doctor's scheme, as an aid to his analysis of the whole project, which I'm sure he will appreciate as it will give him more material for his dissertation on the subject.'

'You do mean nobble it. Excellent idea.'

'Feck,' said Jimmie, a mixture of relief and enthusiasm.

I wonder what Snaffle Sausage's sexual orientation is. I think I might accidentally suggest in a session that the major is gay, and quietly fancies him. That should change his mind about the major's suitability. In the unlikely event that Sausage is gay, he could well make the wrong kind of move towards the major. Especially if the major somehow acquires the belief that Sausage is gay and fancies him. I'm pretty sure the major would be horrified by the idea. All we need now is for someone to accidentally give the major the wrong impression.

This is definitely going to be fun.

Chapter 2: Fighting for the status quo

July

Tuesday 2nd July

'I see the blonde one's out, then' Colin commented, nose stuck in the Sports section. Colin doesn't normally show an interest in sport, but Wimbledon appears to be the exception.

'Who, Cornucopia? I thought she went out ages ago. On the first day.'.

'No, not her, the other blonde one.'

'Colin, you might not have realised this, but there is in fact a cosmic rule about Wimbledon. At least eighty per cent of them must be blonde. In the future they'll probably discover that Wimbledon lies on the intersection of two ley lines which cause this remarkable phenomenon. It is in fact the awesome and subtle controlling force of the natural cosmos.'

Colin gave me a look which showed how little he thought of the idea, and went back to reading about the blonde one.

Personally I don't think it's such a fanciful idea. OK, maybe the phrasing is a little esoteric, but there are certain perennial circumstances which occur for no good reason. Take English players and Wimbledon. Every year they say "this could be his/her year". And every year people get their hopes up. And every year up until this year they manage to win the early games in heart stopping fashion, just scraping through. And every year they've been knocked out before the final. And they're saying it again this year.

Funny to think that in fifty years time they'll still be tucking into strawberries and cream during Wimbledon – and no doubt there'll be another true Brit who just manages to lose every year – and the strawberries and cream will no doubt be genetically modified – and people will say things like, "Sampras? That name rings a bell. Tennis player, wasn't he?" Or, as a schoolgirl responded a few days ago, "Bjorn Borg? That's that singer isn't she?"

And no doubt there'll still be the same argument about how women get paid less to play. But they play fewer sets, so that makes sense. But they attract a larger audience, so it isn't fair. And so on.

Or maybe we'll have aliens taking part. Like they do now in politics.

Another perennial of the season is ID cards. The Home Secretary seems to want to go down in history as the most illiberal politician since Ghenghis Khan. Each year they bring up this subject of ID cards, and each year they realise that (a) it's just not British, (b) the people don't want them, (c) it's going to cost a lot of dosh, and (d) ID cards don't do anything except irritate honest people. They seem to think that by some miracle dishonest people will be honest enough not to forge the things. But the Home Secretary isn't renowned for a great deal of common sense in the "let's not piss off people for no good reason" department, so he's come up with the jolly wheeze of calling them "Entitlement Cards", and insisting that you'll only need them if you want to claim benefit or get hospital treatment or breathe or something.

Another seasonal idiocy due to kick off sometime soon is the marching season in Northern Ireland. I was reminded of that when I saw the major stalking along a corridor, doing his imitation of an officerly walk. My mind put together the words "march" and "idiot", and I immediately thought of strange people wearing orange sashes and bowler hats celebrating a victory which happened hundreds of years ago, their main purpose being to insult their fellow countrymen – and women – of a different faith. As Colin once commented, they might think themselves the master race, they sure as hell aren't the human race.

Trying to describe the major's walk in human terms would be difficult. The closest I can come to is that he resembles a rather moth-eaten woodpecker continually chasing a non-existent tree. And today, his eyes were bright and his tail seemed bushy, as if confident of finally getting to grips with the invisible and elusive tree.

Too late I realised that he was actually going to speak to me.

'You've heard the news, then,' he said with a great deal of enthusiasm which could only foretell bad news.

'The Japanese have surrendered?' I hazarded.

'Japanese? No, what's this got to do with the Japanese? I'm talking about me being elected to the board.'

'You've been elected? I didn't even notice the election happening. When did this take place?'

'Well, it hasn't taken place yet, of course, but it's only a formality. Dr Snaflwurst assured me.'

'Ah, he didn't tell you about the other candidates, then,' I said, nodding my head in sympathy.

'Other candidates? What other candidates? This is about me being elected to the board, there aren't any other candidates.' He was becoming quite angry.

'He didn't tell you?' I cried in feigned sympathy. 'That's terrible. It must be part of the study he's doing. You know it's just a study, don't you? He's going to write a book about it.'

His eyes narrowed in suspicion. 'You're lying. That's what it is. You're just jealous. No wait a moment – you're planning on standing as well!'

I tapped the side of my nose and winked at him. 'Can't say anything. Strategy, you know.' And then I walked away very quickly. Not quickly enough.

'You layabout!' he screamed after me. 'You slacker! No-one will vote for you. And when I'm in power I'll make sure we get rid of all the slackers and layabouts around here! I will, you hear me, I will!'

I walked past Harry who was standing holding onto a polisher with a worried look on his suddenly pale face. As I turned the corner I heard him hurrying after me.

'They won't let it happen, will they?' he asked pleadingly, gripping hold of my arm. 'I won't find another job if I lose this one. I'm not trained. I've dedicated my life to this place. And I've got this bad back. Surely they can't fire me?'

Perhaps I should have pointed out that the slacker the major was referring to was me. Instead I prised Harry's hand from my arm, patted his shoulder, and pacified him. 'Don't worry, Harry, so long as that twit is kept quiet we'll all be okay.' He didn't look too assured by this. And he hadn't picked up on my suggestion that the major be kept quiet. With added emphasis on the word 'quiet'.

Harry knows where the Mogadon is stored after all.

'I don't understand this election business. What's wrong with the way things are at the moment? Why change anything?'

'I fully agree, Harry. That's why we must make sure it doesn't happen. If the major isn't in a fit state to stand nothing will happen, will it?' This still didn't hit its target.

'You're going to stand, aren't you? I'm sure more people will vote for you than him. You are going to stand, aren't you?'

'It'll be alright, Harry.' I patted him on his arm again. 'So long as we all do what has to be done, eh?'

He stood there uncomprehending, and I left him. Hopefully something will filter down to his one brain cell, and he'll arrange for the major to be somewhat dozy for a few weeks.

Me stand for the board? Harry's missed the whole point. The idea is to make sure no one stands for the board.

Thursday 4th July

Independence Day in the US, and everyone there is apparently running around like Corporal Jones out of Dad's Army shouting "Don't Panic! Don't panic!". Or looking mean and thoughtful like Cary Grant while waiting for the bad guys, some might say. Or was it John Wayne? They believe that international terrorists are going to try something, only they don't know what. The bottom line is that they're nervous and guessing. And who can blame them?

Closer to home, some idiot has knocked Maggie Thatcher's block off. Not her own one of course, but rather the head on a marble statue of her. Whatever you may think of the subject of the statue – and to be honest I thought it looked terrible in the photographs, even with the head on – the statue, that is, but not necessarily only the statue – it was an example of consummate skill and artisanship, not something to be subjected to wanton vandalism. The attacker claims that he was "making a protest against global capitalism", and called the statue "an idol", so presumably he belongs to the same school of thought as the Taleban who blew up thousand year old statues. Even though he admits doing the damage, he has stated that he cannot plead guilty to criminal damage as he is not a criminal, a defence which suggests he is hoping to invoke the insanity or extreme stupidity clause.

'I didn't know we had someone here called Jaws,' Colin commented as we sat out in the deckchairs in what should have been lovely July weather, but must have come from north of Russia. Cold, overcast and threatening rain. We were all wearing jackets and jumpers more suitable to winter; Jimmie's hat covering his face was a teasing reminder of the weather that should have been.

'Didn't you know? Short bloke, hardly says anything, always dressed in jacket and tie, looks like an accountant.'

'You mean John Anderson. And apparently he's called Jaws because when you give him a piece of paper he hides behind the coffee machine in reception and eats it.'

'What, the coffee machine?'

'Very funny. Only the first I heard about this Jaws is when Snaflwurst mentioned him. I had to hum and hah and make noises to suggest that I knew what the hell he was going on about.' He gave me an injured look. 'You could let me know when you're going to invent stories like that.'

'Sorry, Colin, spur of the moment thing. He was talking about ballot papers, so I warned him not to give one to Jaws. He asked me who Jaws was, so I ad-libbed a bit. You know, make him just a little nervous. Gradually give him so much to worry about he gives up the daft idea.'

Colin snorted.

'Jaws! You really do let your imagination run riot at times, don't you. And I'd love to know how he's supposed to hide behind that coffee machine.'

The coffee machine in question is a huge and hideous piece of solid iron which theoretically dispenses cups of coffee for two pence a go to anyone brave or foolish enough to try it. On inserting your tuppenny coin it starts to gurgle and vibrate, carrying on for about five minutes with an occasional deep throated hiccup or burp, threatening a rather noisy and messy explosion, until it dispenses something brown and sludgy which tastes more of rusty mud than anything else – and if you're really lucky, it's remembered to issue a cup first, otherwise your shoes and trousers will never be the same. It probably came out of the ark – as you can tell by the cost of the coffee – though I've often wondered whether it was left by an alien spaceship in the style of The Hitchhiker's Guide To The Galaxy.

And as for hiding behind it, it's bolted to the wall.

'Well, yes, technically he couldn't hide behind it as such, but I wanted to see whether Snaffle Sausage knew that. I could have argued that "behind" was relative to the viewer. But I didn't have to. Sausage only walks past the damn machine at least twice a day, but he didn't stop to think that what I was suggesting was physically impossible.'

'You like that sort of thing, don't you? Sometimes I wonder if you weren't a politician in a previous life.'

'Now be fair, Colin, that's a bit below the belt.'

'I suppose so. I was just thinking about that advert the anti-euro lot have come out with.'

'That actor dressed up as Adolf Hitler saying "ein fuhrer, ein reich, ein euro"?'

'That's the one. A load of pro-Euro politicos are wetting their nappies about it. Calling it "offensive" and such. Personally I thought it summed everything up rather neatly. Give up your currency and you hand over economic and political control to a bunch of bureaucrats in Brussels who want to create a European State. At least they're putting forward the real case for not taking up the euro – much better than that "save the pound" nonsense. Who cares whether it's a pound or a groat, so long as we can see who's controlling it.'

'It's a question of visibility,' said a voice, interrupting Colin's diatribe.

I looked at Colin. He looked at me. Then we both looked at Jimmie, but he obviously hadn't said anything. So we looked at each other again, then to the left, to the right, and behind. But apart from the trees next to us, and an open lawn in front devoid of any living being we could see nothing. At least nothing which might have joined our conversation.

Jimmie grunted. 'Feck,' he said, and pointed a thumb upwards, without taking the hat from his face. 'Up there. Feck.'

I got the impression that the second "Feck" was to indicate that he thought we were both blind as bats.

We looked up into the branches of the tree. About twenty foot above us appeared a most remarkable apparition; a tall, lanky man sitting on a branch, wearing a black beard, white shirt, black trousers, black coat with tails, black top hat, and black shoes with five inch soles, the sort teenagers wear so that they can be fashionable and trip over and break their necks.

'You okay up there?' Colin asked solicitously.

'I must admit it might be an idea to come a bit lower,' the man replied. 'I don't like to get too near the ground, but one doesn't want to have to shout, does one?' He gingerly manouvered himself down until he was about ten feet from the ground, and settled on another branch.

'How do you do?' he asked politely. We nodded back – not an easy thing to do reclining in deckchairs while looking at someone above you, more a sort of hitting the chair canvas with the back of your head.

'My associates call me The Professor,' he vouchsafed. We hit the chair canvas with the back of our heads politely. It doesn't do to get too chummy too soon in this place, especially with someone looking like a cross between Abraham Lincoln and an undertaker. 'Or ex-associates, I should say,' he added. 'They're all in jail now.' He raised his hand as if to fend off our sympathetic commiserations. 'don't feel sorry for them, please, it was just what they deserved. Petty criminals, all, not very intelligent I'm afraid. I've no doubt jail is but a second home to them. I, on the other hand, have a mission.'

He waited for us to ask what his mission was.

We waited for him to tell us.

'My mission is to find the perfect crime,' he said eventually. Deciding, presumably that we weren't going to break his pregnant pauses for him he continued, 'And I thought I had finally found it. A crime worth a fortune, with no victims, and one that would never be found out. Or at least, not until so long afterwards no-one would be able to pinpoint the perpetrators. It was very simple, you see. That's the whole thing about perfection, simplicity. People tend to get carried away and invent complex and unrealistic plans, they watch too many films. James Bond gadget syndrome, I call it. JBGS.'

He paused for a moment, as if trying to remember something.

'Where was I? Ah, yes, the plan. Very simple, as I say. There was a gold chalice in a little church dating back to medieval times – I can't reveal the location for obvious reasons. It was inlaid with precious stones, priceless – though the vicar and his congregation didn't realise it. They were using it daily, unaware of it's worth. In other words, part of the furniture, something which people never really look at closely, because it's always there. And that's when I realised my plan.'

Another pause for dramatic effect.

'All we had to do was to gain entry one night, replace it with a replica, depart with equal silence, and no one would be the wiser.'

He paused again – he'd obviously practised – and this time we were interested. No doubt it was a pack of lies, or a fertile imagination, but we wanted to hear how the story ended. Apart from Jimmie, who's face lay impassionately under his hat. Though with Jimmie, when he's not going "feck", you don't know whether he's listening intently, or sleeping.

I wonder if he says "Feck" in his sleep.

'So what happened?' Colin asked after a few seconds of silence.

'Ah,' said the Professor, 'well, that's the embarrassing bit, really. We were in the church, and I had given the necessary orders to my associates, when I noticed the organ.'

'The organ?'

'Yes. A lovely organ, mahogany casing, I think, polished by countless loving hands throughout the ages, gleaming grey pipes disappearing into the darkness of the roof, the ivory keys looking smooth and well used and warm and just ready for the soft touch of delicate fingers, the pedals almost eager for the pressure from a subtle foot to let the music soar out to the heavens.'

'And then?' Colin asked after another dramatic pause.

'I, um, I... well, basically, the nub of it is, I ... I thought to myself, "I wonder if I can play that organ?". You see I've never had the chance before. And I've always thought organ music inspiring to the soul.'

'And could you?'

'Sadly, no. But I could get it to make noises. Which woke up everyone nearby. And they called the police. Who weren't too happy. Come to think of it, my associates weren't too overjoyed either. They are what one might term, to put it bluntly, Philistines. I was in search of the perfect crime. They were only after the money. I wanted to hear the glorious booming of an ancient organ in the early hours of a new day, they only wanted silence in the dark. No spirit, you see. No sense of, of ... art, I suppose you could call it.'

'So how come you didn't end up in the clink like your associates?' I asked.

'I believe that's because the judge understood my point of view. After I explained my mission he appreciated that I wasn't some petty criminal intent merely on depriving others of their possessions, but rather an artist in search of the perfect.'

After a moment or two pondering the far-sightedness of the judge, he added, 'And because I wore this hat.'

We slapped the backs of our heads against the canvas in understanding appreciation. Appearing in court dressed in a top hat could well win the sympathy of a judge. And a recommendation that the person wearing it be sent to a nice quiet place where the rooms are all soft and they don't allow you to play with anything sharp.

'The worst of it – the really depressing part – was when I discovered that the plan has been used before. Not at all original. That was quite crushing.' For a moment he looked like Abraham Lincoln in one of his more depressed moments. 'Still, no use crying over spilt milk. There's always something new on the horison. I hear you're having some sort of election soon.'

'Yes. I don't suppose you could arrange for it to be stolen by any chance? In such a way that people don't realise it's gone?'

'I'm afraid not. Apart from the difficulty, it would be tainting my hands with politics. I really couldn't look myself in the face again if I did that.'

I could see his point. Obviously a man of integrity. Very strange dress sense, but undoubted integrity.

Good thing I always keep my room locked.

Sunday 7th July

Apparently the Professor has a thing about being on the ground.

It was a little unusual to walk into breakfast the day before yesterday to see him sitting contentedly on top of one of the tall cupboards, eating his egg and bacon. A couple of days later it seems perfectly natural to walk into a room to find a tall, bearded man wearing a top hat and tails perched on a cupboard, plate on lap, munching away.

After all, compared to bungee jumping, sitting on top of a cupboard seems to me the very mark of sanity.

He did make the mistake of commenting on the dust when he first ascended – dust is hardly surprising, given the paucity of funds for cleaning staff – a comment which came to the ears of Matron. Ever one with a practical approach, she merely tossed up a couple of dusters to the prof, and told him to get on with it and stop complaining. Ruefully he acknowledged defeat, and the cupboards are now dust free on top. The condition inside them is another question; I think some of them haven't been opened in years.

As today is Sunday, and also the Wimbledon final – the men's final, that is – it is, of course, raining. The rain is expected to let up; presumably the final will go ahead, though I can't remember who's playing. One's an Australian, I think. A Brit isn't the other.

Due to the weather everyone was indoors. I found myself collared into a bridge game as Janice was indisposed with one of her turns. At the table next to us Colin was playing chess against the professor; the prof sat on top of a nearby cupboard and called out his moves. A way away there was a gin rummy session going on with the major, the Omley sisters and a couple of others. Elsewhere there was a confused game of monopoly taking place, with one of the players travelling the wrong way around the board, and another continually throwing the dice and missing the table.

I checked the latest hand of cards I had been dealt. A few half decent clubs, might be worth a shot.

'A club,' I said, listening to the prof calling out to Colin to move queen to king's rook's bishop's four or similar. Colin pointed out something to the effect of the move being illegal, and the prof revised his count and called for queen to king's rook's bishop's elbow's second cousin's five.

'I see our good old Labour PM is over a barrel for having his kids tutored privately,' I commented, partly out of interest, and partly to put Mrs Gladstone off. It's a hopeless effort. If a nuclear explosion went off next to her she'd calmly dust it off and carry on playing.

Watching the PM is a great sport. It's like watching someone on a high-wire, waiting for him to fall, and this time one of his own side kicked the wire. A week ago one of his buddies criticised the opposition leader for sending his kids to Eton. Since (a) it was only one of his sons, and (b) the lad got a scholarship, and (c) the Tories are quite open about supporting private schools, it was a rather meaningless attack. It also meant that the PM's protests that his own children shouldn't be the subject of media attacks sounded exceptionally hollow. I don't think the PM is very happy with his comrade at the moment.

Then again, this New Labour party dumped all their ideals as excess political baggage, but retained the paranoia and self interest of all left wing parties, such as bringing in illiberal laws, and taking over bus lanes for politicians while the peasants have to sit in traffic jams.

'A diamond,' bid Mrs Gladstone. 'All children should go to private schools. My brother went to one, and it was perfect preparation for life.'

'Very successful, was he?'

'Feck. A heart.'

'Up until he was found guilty of fraud, yes. But at least he was prepared for the prison life.'

'A spade,' from Miss Melly.

'Bishop times queen knight five pawn and check,' the prof called out.

'Two clubs. Your brother went to jail for fraud?'

'You can't move the bishop, that would leave you in check.'

'Two diamonds. Yes, he always was a charmer, and he charmed quite a few companies out of their funds for a non-existent venture in Argentina. They weren't too happy when they found out.'

'Two hearts. Feck'

'Bit of a waste of a private education then, surely?'

'You are pedantic, aren't you. Very well, I shall sacrifice. Knight times king's pawn.'

'Two spades.'

'A total waste, I thought. But those were the days when the sons of the family were given everything. Daughters had to hope for a wealthy husband. Of the same class, of course.'

'Three clubs. Do I detect a note of bitterness?'

'Bitterness? Life is too short for such a luxury. Three spades. But enough of that, water under the bridge. I hear you're going to stand in this election the dear Doctor whats-his-name is planning.'

'Feck no bid.'

I would have preferred to hear more about Mrs Gladsone's convict brother, but I couldn't let such misinformation go unchallenged.

'Where did you hear that?'

'No bid,' from Miss Melly.

'Four clubs.' Well, I had four of the things.

'Checkmate!' Colin sounded triumphant. For such a gentle person he can be quite aggressive at times.

'I don't recall. Somewhere or other. Hmmmm.' She studied her cards intently, pausing only to glance at me suspiciously. If she didn't bid over my four clubs we'd get a right walloping. If she did, she'd probably get the walloping.

I was the picture of innocence.

'Four spades,' she decided on finally. 'I've been thinking that I might stand. As the women's candidate.'

'No bid. Feck.'

'Checkmate it is, unfortunately. You were lucky that time. Set them up again and I'll show you what I'm made of. I'm not known as the chess king for nothing.'

'No bid.'

'Nope. How do you mean, "the women's candidate"? I didn't know there was going to be one of each.'

'I didn't mean that. I mean that I shall campaign on women's issues. For example, did you know that there are more conveniences here for men than for women?'

'I thought that there were plenty for everybody. I don't remember seeing queues anywhere.'

'That's not the point. It's the principle that's at stake.'

Jimmie, as player to lead, tossed down the two of clubs. Miss Melly, as dummy, laid her cards on the table.

'I think we should all take part,' Miss Melly said. 'I intend to stand on the question of education.'

Well, as an ex-schoolteacher, you could understand the link, but education is hardly top of the list of the concerns of people around here.

'How do you mean, demanding day-classes for all, or something?' I asked.

'No. I mean education as a concern of our society. The failure of the current government to deliver on their "education, education, education" promise, to such an extent that the socialist prime minister has his own children have top up lessons from private tutors.'

My mind boggled. Mrs Gladstone is going to stand because the men have more loos than the women, and Miss Melly is going to stand because of problems within national education. I wonder who will stand opposing GM crops. And there's the transport question.

Not to mention Defence.

Or the nuclear issue. Not unusual for someone here to go nuclear every so often.

'And besides,' Mrs Gladstone winked at me with a wicked gleam in her eye, 'the more the merrier, don't you think? It will give the dear

Doctor something to do.'

She has a hidden streak of mischievous humour in her, that one. But she didn't make the contract.

Monday 8th July

Woke up this morning to find a handwritten note slipped under my door. "Vote for the silent majority", it said.

I reckon that it's the work of a chap called Roland, someone who suffers from extreme shyness. I remember the time he unintentionally let slip a mild burp one dinner time, and sat there red faced for the rest of the meal until everyone else had left. The fact that there was no-one sitting at the same table, and that hardly anyone had heard, far less taken notice, didn't seem to make any difference. He stayed in his room for the next three days until Matron convinced him that no-one remembered the unfortunate burp. Poor chap.

I see some poor Royal Navy captain has managed to get his boat into trouble. The boat – ship? vessel? – was holed below the waterline somewhere off the coast of Australia, and now the captain is likely to end up being court-martialled. Understandable, I suppose, they don't have many boats left to play with.

Politicians are condemning the assassination of the vice-president in Afghanistan. A vice-president in the transitional administration, he was either a war lord or a fearless fighter for democracy, according to your interpretation. Apparently he was also a Pashtun, which is supposed to mean something out there.

And a story somewhere that claims that AIDS is cutting life expectancy to 26 in Africa. Now I'm sure the Africans are just as chaste or promiscuous as anyone else, so why the disease should be so prevalent there rather than, South America, say, seems a mystery.

Tuesday 9th July

The "failing to learn the lesson" award for this week goes to the Los Angeles police department, members of which were filmed beating up a young black bloke in public. This is the same department which found itself in the limelight a few years ago when they were – cue chorus – filmed beating up a young black bloke in public. Although in that case the four officers were acquitted when they came to trial, so maybe the others didn't see it as a problem.

Apart from the rioting that followed the verdict and left large parts of Los Angeles in flames.

Closer to home the government have once more been shown to be less than enthusiastic about the concept of open government. A number of civil servants' e-mails were obtained under the Data Protection Act – which the government will no doubt try to scrap as soon as possible – which show how the "civil servants" avoid giving out any information. One read "I have gone for a narrow and pedantic interpretation of the question which makes the answer short and easy", another "Fortunately, he has asked his questions wrongly. We should be able to avoid answering them on that basis." Reminds me of the "a good day to bury bad news" comment when the Twin Towers were attacked.

A spokesman – woman? person? thing? – for the Department Of The Vow Of Silence, or DOTVOS as I call it – DOTVOS not vot ve sed – has said that "We recognise that no-one in the department should be making comments about MPs or anyone else. We will be re-issuing guidance to all our staff to remind them of their responsibilities." Which I think translates as "we will remind our staff that e-mail is not a safe mode for discussing things we don't want the public to find out about".

Apparently Snaffle Sausage was working late last night, presumably on his thesis about lunatics and democracy, went to his little coffee maker for a cup of whatever exclusive and expensive ground mud he prefers, only to find he'd run out. As everybody had either gone home or to bed he couldn't rustle anything up from the kitchens. However, remembering the machine in reception which I had so kindly brought up in conversation – I don't think he ever realised what it was supposed to be – he toddled off to put his two pence in. Unfortunately he wasn't aware of the golden rule: if no cup appears, get the hell out of the way as fast as possible.

For once I managed to make Ms Dervish smile in a less than sarcastic way. I suggested that the dear doctor was the victim of an infantry attack.

He'd been hit in the privates.

I hear he's off ill with minor burns for a few days. We've been told it's a sensitive issue.

Wednesday 10th July

Cool morning, but at least the rain has stopped. Autumnal weather, almost, very peaceful. Jimmie had just finished setting out the deckchairs when I got to our garden retreat. I was surprised to find Tonique giving him a hand. She's obviously more sensitive than people think – must have seen Jimmie struggling with three deckchairs and given him a hand. She scampered off when I approached. Funny girl.

The prof was in a tree a while away, very politely not intruding on our little domain. Colin arrived soon after, and was not long short of an news item.

'I see the Church of England is due to lift its ban on divorcees getting married in church so that the prince of Wales can marry whatsherface.'

'You mean his neighbourhood sweetheart?'

'That was a pun, wasn't it?'

'Of course.'

'You should give them up, you're not very good at them.'

'You just don't recognise quality. Anyway, they're not just doing it for Charlie. It's an attempt to stop losing more members, like appointing women vicars was.'

'Only partly. It's also because of Charlie. They're very fond of rules for the workers, but they're quick to change them when they're affected.'

'Oh, look,' I exclaimed, mainly to get Colin away from his pet subject of royal iniquities. It's not that I disagree, just that there's not much we can do about it at the moment. It's so difficult to organise a decent revolution these days.

'The University of the Bleeding Obvious has just released research which shows that working long hours contributes to heart attacks. No, wait a minute, someone from the University of Ignoring the Bleeding Obvious and Flogging the Peasants to Death Is a Good Thing has said that the link hasn't been properly demonstrated, and that more research is needed.'

Colin snorted. He's good at that. Jimmie said "feck" from underneath his hat, and for a moment I thought we might get a symphony going.

'Experts!' Colin said dismissively. 'They always manage to be ever so right until they're definitely wrong. They failed to spot BSE until it was too late, and even then they insisted that a link hadn't been proven until the research was so overwhelming they hadn't a leg to stand on. Now you've got the MMR business, and the government can't understand why people don't trust it when it says that there's absolutely no link between that and autism. Never mind GM food.'

'Ah, I see why you're upset – it says here that we suffer from Seasonally Affective Disease when it rains. You see? After a couple of days of sunshine you'll be back to thinking the government's doing a wonderful job.'

'I very much doubt it. Not with the PM's wife opening her mouth again. This time on why people shouldn't be sent to jail.'

'Well, she is a lawyer, she might have something worthwhile to say.'

'A lawyer is someone who is either trying to put someone in jail, or trying to keep someone out. In her case it's the latter, so I doubt whether she'll be going around cheerleading for more prisoners. It's called a conflict of interest.'

The image of the PM's wife cheerleading was not necessarily an appealing one.

'Well, I don't think prison is the best thing that can happen to someone.'

'Feck,' said Jimmie, with some vehemence.

'It's not supposed to be. The thing is that she's saying the prisons are too full, so criminals shouldn't be sent there. Imagine a judge saying, "well you did commit burglary, murder and rape, but because the prisons are full we're going to let you off this time". It's daft.'

'Well, look at that. The 73rd All-Stars game ended in a tie.'

'Let me guess. Yank. Baseball.'

'Yup. Apparently they ran out of pitchers, whatever that means. The crowd weren't too happy. The Yanks don't like draws.'

'You can always tell when it's Yank sport. The titles are funny, and they sound like the entire world is playing – like the World Series – when it's only them.'

If Charlie married whatsherface in the States I think Colin would have a coronary.

'Looks like their president could be in trouble. There seems to be suggestions that his financial past isn't what you might call squeaky clean. Certain company names keep cropping up."

'But no solid evidence yet. And unlikely to be. Did you see that thing on telly the other day where this French reporter was claiming that the attack on the Trade Towers was organised by the FBI – or the CIA, or someone like that? I've heard of conspiracy theories, but that's a dandy. You know, I've just had a thought – maybe the FBI or CIA or whatever started that rumour themselves, so that people would think it so ridiculous that they'd also ignore more plausible accusations.'

Colin can dream up some strange thoughts. No wonder he's so good at chess.

'Speaking of conspiracies, did you know that we have a resident who collects pieces of paper, marks them, and hoards them in her cupboard on account of how she used to be a school teacher?'

'No, can't say that I know anyone like that.'

'Well, I think we're going to have just such a person. Just so that you aren't surprised when hot-pants mentions it.'

Colin chuckled. 'Hotpants. I like it. Much better than your sausage name. Hotpants, yes, that's a good one.'

Personally I thought 'Snaffle Sausage' was quite good. But there you go.

Friday 12th July

On the really humorous side, Morocco has invaded a Spanish rock. Or, from their point of view, reclaimed a Moroccan rock. Apparently it's uninhabited, and just about large enough to fall off, but a couple of Moroccan soldiers have landed and planted the Moroccan flag, which has sent the Spanish into a fit of apoplexy. It might be uninhabited, and uninhabitable, but by god it's their uninhabited and uninhabitable rock, and if ever anyone's going to fall off it, it'll be a Spaniard.

And whatever you do, don't mention Gibraltar.

All good Friday fun.

And what is Friday evening for, if not a leisurely stroll down to the local hostelry, and the slow quaffing of a couple of pints of finest ale while exchanging witty banter with the friendly landlord?

I got there at the time I like best; the early evening crowd had almost all disappeared – people out for a drink after work, all suits and smart skirts – and the late evening crowd hadn't yet started turning up – your serious drinkers who intend to be there at closing time, whether they're standing up or not.

When I walked in there were only a few of tables occupied, mainly by couples who looked like they might be indulging in a bit of extra-office fraternisation. Ginger was sitting in a corner, all tidily turned out and looking into space. There was one chap at the bar, chatting to Pete. He looked the sort of chap who was used to sitting in bars chatting to people, and not very used to the idea of ironed shirts or pressed trousers.

I exchanged the usual banter with Pete about being charged extortionate prices for inferior ales, at which this chap commented, 'Actually I thought that one was quite good.'

'That's because you're hoping for a free one, no doubt,' Pete responded.

'Seems fair to me. After all, we'll be giving you free advertising.' He turned to me and introduced himself. 'Jim Carney, Local Echo.

We're doing a series on the fine pubs of the area.' He rummaged around in his jacket pockets, until he found a dog-eared card which he handed to me.

"The Newspaper for the People", it read. As opposed to the newspaper given out free to everybody in the district which no-one ever read, unless it had a story of your own primary school or dog or whatever, and people could point to it and imagine themselves famous.

'Do these cards come pre-stressed like this?' I asked.

'Oh, no, takes me ages to get a new lot into the right condition. It's image, you see,' he grinned with a naughty-boy mischievous look. 'People are much more likely to talk to you if they think you're an absent minded bachelor type who isn't able to look after himself. And it pulls the birds. Vegetarians, mainly, for some reason.'

'But it doesn't get them to do any ironing for you,' I commented, taking a pull on the ale Pete had set in front of me.

'No, sadly not. Vegetarians aren't into ironing, I find. There must be a logical connection somewhere, but I've never been able to spot it.'

'I have to admit it sounds like a good job. Being paid to spend your day wandering from pub to pub testing their beers.'

'And ambience too, don't forget that. Use the word ambience and you can sometimes get a free meal as well.'

'Not around here you won't,' said Pete. 'We don't do food, for a start.'

'To be honest, it might sound good but it isn't really,' Jim said with a sad look on his face. 'You can't visit more than two pubs a day, unless you want to be rat-arsed by early evening. And then you can't mention the bad ones – you either have to point out that they're pretty grotty, which can be embarrassing if they advertise in the paper – or you run the risk of some readers going there thinking a place is decent, which upsets them for some reason. And they don't half give you a mouthful afterwards.'

'Not of beer, one hopes.'

'Hopefully not, but I've heard of it happening. No, the only reason I'm doing this is as a space filler. News has been rather scarce recently.'

'What, no rescued pets or babies saying their first words? No discovery of strange shaped vegetables in allotments? Not even a smidgeon of noisy neighbours?'

'Nope, very short on the noisy, strange shaped vegetables as neighbours front at the moment.'

'I don't think you're trying hard enough. I thought you journalists could make up stories without even trying.'

'Go on then, you come up with something then.'

'Well, those crime statistics they've just released, for a start. Must be some to do with the local area.'

'Have you had a look at those statistics? Depending on the way you read them crime has gone up, down, sideways and Dolly Parton is pregnant with quintuplets. We can't afford to take a political stance the way the nationals do.'

He had a point. Possibly not about Dolly Parton, but certainly the statistics just released – two sets, just in case your brain wasn't hurting sufficiently already – appear to have been interpreted in more ways than there are humans on this earth.

'You should do an article on problem teenagers,' suggested Pete.

'Sounds like tautology to me. You having problems with the kids around here?'

'My youngest daughter, mainly. Seems to be in a permanent mood.'

'I don't think that would really qualify as a news story. Otherwise we could double the size of the paper.'

'What about this suggestion that people should have to pay if they put more than two bags of rubbish out in a week? That must be worth a couple of columns at least,' I suggested.

'Three pages, actually. It's our lead story this week, talk about a gift. Pictures of irate householders threatening to dump their rubbish at the town hall if they tried to charge them an extra fiver a week.

Though admittedly it did take a bit of prompting to get them to say that. Most of them hadn't read about it. Actually, I think most of the people we interviewed can't read, but that's life.'

'You do realise that there is actually a special department in Whitehall that comes up with these suggestions? It's called the Department of Silly Ideas, unofficially known as the Department Of Thick Thoughts and Ideas, or Dotti for short. Every time the government are about to release some news they don't want people to notice, and there aren't any towers being bombed anywhere, they get this department to release another silly idea.'

Jim chuckled. 'That sounds almost believable.' Then he looked at me worriedly for a moment. 'You don't, er, seriously believe that, do you?'

'Not really. Sounds too efficient for them.'

'Oh good. For a moment there I thought you might be a conspiracy theorist – one of the loonies from down the road.'

'I am one of the loonies from down the road.'

'Ah. Errm, yes. Um, err, ah, yes.' I think he could have gone on like that for quite a while. Trouble is, it doesn't give you a chance to have a break to enjoy your beer. And I felt sorry for him.

Not that I'd trust him, though.

'Don't worry about it,' I said. 'A lot of people have the same problem. Though now you come to mention it, you could probably do a story on that place. Or on one of the doctors there, anyhow.'

'How do you mean?'

'Well, this is strictly confidential, mind. You never heard it from me, okay?'

'Course not.'

'Well, suppose one of the doctors there was doing some research which could become world famous. That would make a story, wouldn't it?'

'Depends on the research. What is it?'

'Ah, well, you'll have to find out that yourself, I'm afraid. If I told you any more I could get into serious trouble.'

'You're not winding me up, are you?'

'Course not,' I replied. Well, technically there was a story there, even if it was a non-story type story. What I was more interested in was how Hotpants would react when a journalist came sniffing around, asking strange questions – and they would be strange, since I hadn't given him anything to work on. Or at least, hardly anything. You can always rely on humans to misunderstand each other, even when they know what each other's talking about.

And a little of the wrong publicity will make Hotpants drop the election nonsense.

'But whatever you do, don't mention his mother. Or the Sound of Music.'

'Whose mother?'

'You'll know when you meet him.' He shook his head in despair. 'Times like these I know I should have become an accountant.'

A short while later, having consumed my self imposed limit of two ales, I began the stroll back to the residence. Ginger caught up with me at the door, and we walked in companionable silence. Silence, until he actually spoke. Ginger doesn't normally speak.

'You know this election that you and the major are standing in?' he asked.

'No. I know the one the major's standing in and I'm not though.'

'Oh? I heard you were.' He looked at me suspiciously – why do so many people do that? 'What I want to know is why other people can't stand.'

'How do you mean?'

'Well, I don't want to stand, but I think I should have the right to if I did.'

'Who says you can't?'

'Everybody knows that we aren't allowed to.'

People like Ginger, the quiet, silent types, always seem to receive information anonymously, rather like the slave network on the cotton plantations often picked up news before their masters knew of it. And like the slave network, it's often inaccurate. Or plain wrong.

'Well, there's a simple answer. Ask Hotpants. I mean the herr doctor. I'm sure he'll say yes.'

'But I don't actually want to stand. I wouldn't have a chance. Do you think I'd have a chance?'

Don't you just love questions like that.

'That's not the question. And you don't have to stand, just ask hot – the doctor – if you can. And get all these others you mentioned to go with you.'

'You mean a representation in strength? Force him to acknowledge our rights? That would be quite exciting.'

I've no doubt it will be. For Hotpants as well.

Monday 15th July

A surprisingly busy weekend on the news front. I've never worked out how they manage to print these massive Sunday newspapers with almost nothing in them. But things have been busy recently; yesterday – Bastille Day – a supposed neo-Nazi tried to assassinate the French president. Fortunately for him the assassin was pretty incompetent. Took out a .22 rifle in the middle of the crowd, and was promptly jumped upon by various citizens.

The Japanese tested a model in Australia of a supersonic jet which is supposed to rival Concorde when it appears in its full size form. Unfortunately it spiralled out of control, and dived into the ground, narrowly missing a highly indignant kangaroo.

The US is heading for $165bn deficit this year – where do they get the money?

At least 27 Hindus killed in a gun attack in Kashmir.

The Tour de France is in full swing.

The US president still under the spotlight about some of his business dealings.

Passed Hotpant's office this morning. There was an interesting crowd of the silent majority standing around him. He stood in the doorway looking flustered. It was like looking at a victim of the living zombies. 'Of course you can all stand,' he was saying, 'here, here is a piece of paper. I want you to all put your names down on the piece of paper, and then one of you give it back to me when you have finished, Ja?'

When he starts saying "Ja" you know he's feeling the pressure.

He slammed his door shut, and the group crowded around Ginger who was holding the piece of paper. He carefully wrote his name, and passed it onto the next person without a word, who then silently wrote theirs, and so on.

I walked on, feeling an urge to whistle.

I'd promised to spend the morning helping in admin and reception, so I wandered along there. There wasn't much to do, apart from stacking everything neatly, putting the pens and pencils back in their mug – "A Present From Bolton" – trying surreptitiously to log onto the local network or surf the web when Ms Dervish was in the admin room, that sort of a thing.

It must have been about half ten when these two men walked in. Big, burly chaps with cropped heads and strange tattoos, wearing dark green overalls, and looking very nervous. Kept looking all around as they almost tiptoed up to the reception counter.

'Morning, mate,' said the slightly smaller of the two, in an almost whisper. 'We've come for the coffee pot.'

'Coffee pot?' I asked, bemused.

'Yeah, coffee pot. Bloke said it was a really big one.' He looked around in apprehension, as if expecting a really large coffee pot to jump out and assault him. I casually reached for the admissions book to see whether we were expecting two large men in overalls who had a phobia about really big coffee pots.

'I'm not aware of any large coffee pots awaiting collection,' I said casually, as I noted that there weren't any admissions due today. Not that that was an infallible guide. Nutters are notoriously difficult to schedule. 'You sure it wasn't a very, very large teapot?'

'Nope, definitely a coffee pot. Listen, this is the loony bin, isn't it?'

'I think people might agree with your geography though not your terminology.'

'Eh? You wot?'

'I fink he means you mustn't call it a loony bin,' said the other.

'Precisely,' I replied, rather surprised at his comprehension.

'Only, none of them ave got loose, ave they? Only, we saw this bloke in a tree out there, and you know, you don't want to come round the corner and have some nutter bite you in the throat.'

For a moment I had this image of these two hefty chaps turning a corner and being attacked by a flurry of Mrs Neal, who is all of five foot nothing, and uses a zimmer frame. On the other, hand, if their imaginations were already stretched ...

'Don't even think about it,' said Ms Dervish, coming through from admin.

'What?' asked the two, backing nervously away.

'I wasn't talking to you, I was talking to him,' she said, jerking her thumb in my direction.

'What, me? What am I supposed to have done?' I asked in my best injured tone.

'It's what you were thinking about doing, like growling at them,' she said.

That was unfair. Bark, yes, growl no. I don't do growls. In fact, beckoning them forward and suddenly going "Woof!" in their faces sounded favourite.

'The coffee machine you are looking for,' she continued, emphasizing the word "machine" as if for a retarded two year old, 'is what you are currently backed into.'

The pair of them turned around slowly as if it were a time bomb with a rocker trigger installed. Then one exclaimed, 'Bloody hell, haven't seen one of those for years.' He turned around and looked at us in awe. 'That's a museum piece you've got there. I don't think they've even made any of those in the last ten years.'

'Which is precisely,' Ms Dervish said in her best kindly-but-firm-teacher-dealing-with-village-idiot voice, 'why you are going to take it away and replace it with something more modern, preferably one that works.'

The two men looked back at the museum piece. 'Heavy buggers, those ones are,' the first one said.

'I would appreciate it if you restrained your language,' Ms Dervish said. God, but she was putting it on. She probably heard far worse than that in a morning here most days – almost all from the clinical side, as well – but here she was needling them – and she had had a go at me about winding them up.

They looked at each other for a few seconds.

'Woof,' I said.

The two of them looked nervously from her to me.

'Sorry, Miss,' the first one said finally, 'only, it might help if you have a couple of hands – you know, blokes to give us a hand.'

'What about Igor?' I asked. 'He's had his breakfast and sedatives, so we can let him out of his cell for a short while. Just don't,' I continued, with a piercing look at the first man, 'make any comment about his tu-tu.'

'Tu-tu?' they asked in breathless unison, backing again up against the museum piece. Ms Dervish gave one of her "I am irritated but you won't get the better of me" sighs.

'We do not have any dangerous patients here – apart from this one here, and that's only because he leaves confusion and chaos in his wake. And you,' she said, turning to me, 'can help these gentlemen remove the coffee machine.' She exited on high heels of triumph – she does it quite well. And she's got the legs for it.

'Bollocks,' I said. Not quite my normal standard of repartee, but the best I could come up with.

'Feck,' said another voice. The two burly blokes climbed even deeper into the coffee machine as Jimmie walked in.

'Ah, Jimmie. Just in time. These gentlemen require a hand in removing this coffee pot.'

'Feck,' commented Jimmie.

'I'll just get me tools then,' the first man said, sidling towards the entrance.

'I'll give you a hand,' said the second, exiting with a speed you wouldn't have expected.

I'll give them their due. They did actually come back in with their tools, despite a heated argument outside. I can only presume their fear of being bitten in the throat was marginally outweighed by the fear of having to go back and face their boss. Or Ms Dervish's sarcasm.

Once they had unbolted the machine, and closed off the water pipes, Jimmie and I gave them a hand to manhandle the thing outside. It was incredibly heavy. It was only when we were almost at the truck that the first one slapped his head, and remembered that the water tank inside needed emptying – apparently we had just shifted quite a few gallons of totally useless water.

'The new ones don't have a big water tank, you see,' he said apologetically, 'they feed straight off the pipes, more or less.'

So we emptied what appeared to be a small dam onto the parking area. By this time we were getting on a treat – nothing like having to shift a couple of tons of coffee pot for male bonding. At times we had sounded like a chorus of Jimmies, as we bruised and cut our hands one way or another, or acquired shining bruises on our shins.

Fortunately they remembered to take the new machine out of the truck before loading the old one. Even with the water tank emptied that thing still weighed a ton. The new one, on the other hand, was like lifting a feather, though it was roughly the same size as the old one. Plastic appeared to have taken the place of solid steel.

Jimmie and I stood and admired the new machine as they plugged it in, coupled pipes, stocked the various canisters, pushed buttons, and generally looked very efficient. Finally they stood back, happy in a job well done.

'There you go mate, fully functioning, state of the art, latest model. Best coffee machine on the market.'

It certainly looked impressive. Loads of little green lights above lots of different choices – coffee, white, with sugar, without, black with, tea, lemon tea with, black tea without, soup without, quite possibly soup with, and a red light flashing across the front from left to right to indicate that it was working, quietly humming away. It looked a bit like that car in that television programme.

One thing that puzzled me – there was no place for a cup. The first chap put ten pence in – that's inflation for you – and there was a quiet gurgling noise, and a semi circular piece of plastic went 'swish', to reveal a little plastic cup of coffee.

Or possibly little cup of plastic coffee.

'Does it do latte?' I asked.

'Er, no,' was the embarrassed reply.

'Well thank god for that. Can't stand these coffee shops which do everything but a decent cup of coffee.'

'I'm with you on that one, mate,' said the first. He looked at me sideways. 'Look, no offence mate, but what you said about this Igor bloke – you was joking, wasn't you?'

'Absolutely. I'm afraid what Ms Dervish said is quite correct. No violent people around here at all. We're all quite boring, to be honest. Some real nutters might liven the place up.'

Just then Colin wandered in, and stopped to admire the quietly humming, strobing machine.

'Very impressive,' he said, 'must have been a job getting the other one out. Did you get Igor to give you a hand?'

Honestly. Some people.

Chapter 3: When things go wrong

Wednesday 17th July

Spanish troops have overwhelmed the Moroccan defenders of Parsley Island. That's the rock a couple of hundred yards off Morocco that half a dozen Moroccans landed on to plant a flag claiming it for their country the other day. The Spanish call it Perejil, which is Spanish for parsley, and the Moroccans call it Leila, which is Moroccan for parsley, so now we can refer to it in English as Parsley Island, which is English for, well, an island with parsley on it. Which is what the goats eat.

What I want to know is, are these Spanish or Moroccan goats? I think we should be told.

The Spanish arrived with five warships, two submarines, Cougar helicopters, air-to-air missiles, and a couple of battalions of special services troops, so the six Moroccans were quite comprehensively outnumbered. Even so, the Spanish had to wake them up to overwhelm them, as it was only six-fifteen in the morning, which is a bit rude. You'd think they'd give them a chance for a breakfast coffee and croissant, and a bit of a wash-up before carrying out the overwhelment.

Now that the Spanish are once again firmly in control, they have raised two Spanish flags on the piece of rock. That'll show the Moroccans, they only had one.

Colin was rather upset at the reaction of the media generally to the news that the IRA have apologised for all civilian deaths during the troubles. Certainly the right wing press have used it as a chance to have a go at the IRA. I think the word "hypocritical" was used once or several thousand times. "Well, I don't recall anyone apologising for Cromwell, or the deaths caused by the loyalists, or the gerrymandering by the Protestants, or the banning of schools for the Irish, or the execution of Irish fighters after the Easter Uprising" was Colin's reaction – though his list was a bit longer than that. I lost track somewhere.

News in brief: the world stock markets are still as nervous as a cat after an earthquake on a hot tin roof. Coal production at Selby in the north is to stop, with over 2,000 jobs going. Today more than a million council workers went on strike for better wages. And apparently North Sea cod stocks have been so over-fished that they are now "commercially extinct". On the other hand, if such local problems seem depressing, we can look to Paraguay, where two people have died in anti-government protests, or Israel, where seven Israelis have been killed in an ambush.

Colin was most delighted with the news that the chairman – chairperson? – of the Commission for Racial Equality was arrested outside Lords cricket ground. It combines Colin's dislike of what he believes to be politically correct organisations, and also his distrust of anyone who goes to watch cricket at Lords, though I have a suspicion that Colin just thinks that anyone who enjoys watching cricket automatically qualifies as some form of toff, and someone whose name should go on the list for post-revolution re-education. Yet at the same time he manages to believe in some mythical incorruptible 'them' who believe in 'fair play' and can spot something which is 'not cricket' at a mile.

The media have been rather coy about the story, saying only that the chairman and his wife were arrested by the police under "section four of the Public Order Act". My reading is that he and his wife were boozed up and had a go at the coppers, but no-where has any newspaper explicitly said so. If it were Joe Soap in the street, they'd be quite happily printing lurid accounts of a fifteen pint binge, no matter how true it was, but for public figures they tend to be somewhat more circumspect, which isn't to say cowardly, however accurate that word might be.

I'm definitely beginning to sound like Colin.

But it's true what they say about not trusting newspapers or journalists.

I was in reception this morning looking for something or other when I saw Jim Carney come out of an office with Dr Gummer, a doctor who appears for about an hour every month or so. Gummer was going on about how pleased he was that the local media should take an interest in his important research, and how happy he was to be of service even though the information he could give was of necessity limited as the study results were yet to be confirmed blah blah blah.

It suddenly struck me.

That idiot Carney had got the wrong doctor.

He looked up and caught my eye, and I shook my head violently to indicate that he'd got the wrong man. Unfortunately Gummer looked up at just the same time, and I was forced to carry on shaking my head with a smile on my face for a few seconds as if it were quite normal, before putting up a hand to stop it. 'Ah, that's better,' I said, and pretended to carry on with some paperwork.

'Poor chap, classical symptom, classical symptom,' I heard Gummer say as they walked out of reception. I managed to resist the temptation to throw A Present From Bolton after them.

You'd think that even a local reporter like Carney could at least identify Hotpants from my clues. Even a five year old wouldn't have to spend more than a couple of minutes with him to work out that not all his marbles were rolling in the right direction. But, no, not our fearless local journo, upright defender of the truth, democracy and freedom.

It put me in a bad mood for the rest of the morning, and I was even sarcastic to some of the visitors. OK, more sarcastic than usual. A middle aged man waiting to see someone commented on the "lovely new coffee machine", to which I replied that it wasn't really a coffee machine, it was a thought reader. I pointed to the red light moving tirelessly across the front of it.

'See that?' I asked. 'The whole time it's scanning everyone in the room to read their minds. Collects everything and uploads it to this massive computer it's linked to, buried in these bomb-proof bunkers under the North Downs.'

This idiot looks at me nervously, looks at the coffee machine nervously, chuckles nervously, and then sidles away across to a corner in the reception area where the evil red light can't see him.

'And if you put twenty pence in it'll e-mail you your secret sexual desires,' I called out after him.

At which point he scuttled outside.

Some people will believe anything.

Friday 19th July

I see that the Home Secretary is still on a mission to change this country into a police state. The latest whizz is to get rid of double jeopardy – the rule that states you can't be tried for the same offence twice. The long and short of it is that between the police and the CPS so many high-profile cases have been bungled that the HS thinks they need two or three goes to get it right. And he wants it to be "easier to convict" people. Some old fashioned people might think that this should include such things as evidence properly presented before a jury, but this New Labour lot welcome new fashions. And as for juries, well, they're out as well. Too many juries have been coming up with the wrong verdicts, so we'll scrap those and use a judge who can be relied upon to come to the right conclusions.

One of the things that the HS is missing – or maybe he isn't – is that a jury requires people to sit in judgement on one of their peers; it forces them into a position where they, as members of society, must take decisions on issues that directly affect them – in effect they are bound to the whole idea of society and responsibilities. Take that away, and they just become powerless viewers criticising the decisions of politically nominated judges.

Which brings us to another of the HS's plans: take away planning power from local authorities, and invest it in unelected regional bodies, which, gasps of amazement, will be chosen by central government. So if you object to a four lane road going through your village, or an extra runway put in front of your door, tough luck, complain to your MP, who, funnily enough, will probably turn out not to be a member of New Labour.

Because sure as eggs are eggs they aren't going to have new railways being driven through their swimming pools.

At the same time that they're trying to destroy anything resembling democratic freedom, they're still hoisting these unwanted mayors onto towns. You'd think after London they would have lost their appetite for the things. Personally I reckon it's a plan to reduce employment; create all these mayors – jobs for their unemployable buddies – and then you need all the support staff for all the meetings and papers and policies and dinners and trips overseas.

I saw somewhere that Labour have named their man for the mayoral contest here; Arthur Dodsworth, loyal Labour member for thirty years, never made it to any significant post, never known to have actually done anything worthwhile, but has met a number of cabinet ministers at junkets provided by the local Labour branch, doesn't have a beard, wears a tie, can still tie his own shoelaces on most days even when his paunch gets in the way, blah, blah, blah. But it doesn't matter because he won't have any real power anyway.

Freedom once lost is hard to regain, as someone once said. Maybe Spartacus.

It's enough to make you weep in your beer.

Did I mention I was starting to sound like Colin?

Must get out more.

When I reported for duty at reception this morning I found that Sarah Lee or Maggie May, or whoever it was whose absence required my help previously, was back at work, thus making me redundant for the day. Before ambling out into the garden I noticed an addition to the noticeboard – it's quite easy to tell by the colour of the paper. All the older notices have a faded look to them, making you wonder if they haven't been up since the war. World War II, that is. Possibly the Boer War. I've often been tempted to put up some poster such as "Dig for Victory", and see what the response is. Tunnels called Tom, Dick and Harry, no doubt.

The new addition to the noticeboard is the electoral address of the major to the minions. Or, his campaign letter, I suppose, poor chap. Almost every sentence contains the word "change", and there are a number of threats to discipline "laxity", which most people might interpret as incontinence.

Or they will do once I start explaining it to them.

While I was standing there wondering how the major's stimulating words could perhaps be enlivened Harry came up and started to read – I could tell, his lips started moving. He's been off for a few days with his back. Not a very healthy place this.

'Mogadon, Harry,' I said.

'Eh? Wot?'

'I said "Morning, Harry". Not having trouble with your hearing, are you?'

'Er, nah, thought you said something else. Maybe I should have me ears checked though. What with me back and all, wouldn't be surprised if it had done something to me earing.' I carefully ignored that, as you do when you hear something which doesn't make any sense, just in case it makes your head start hurting.

'This stuff,' he continued, jerking a thumb at the major's call to arms, 'you think he's serious? Could cause all sorts of problems. Upset the horse cart, like. Can't see the reason for it, change for the sake of change, innit?'

'I fully agree, Harry. I think something should be done about it. Time to take things into our own hands. Action now, as Churchill used to say.' That left him silent for a few seconds.

'Like wot?' he finally asked.

'Oh, I'm sure you'll think of something, Harry. A man of your experience.'

With that I wandered away, towards the sun garden. I'm sure Harry's a fine bloke, but trying to get an idea into his head is harder than getting a politician to give a straight answer.

Colin and Jimmie were in their usual places, in their usual postures, Jimmie stretched out, Colin with The Graudian in front of him, and my deckchair awaiting me. I sank into it gratefully.

'Have you seen the major's campaign resolutions on the noticeboard in reception?' I asked.

'Indeed.'

'Feck.'

I waited for some further response, in vain. 'You don't think much of them, then?'

'Not really.'

'Feck.'

A few more moments of silence. 'don't you think we should do something about it?'

'Absolutely.'

'Feck.'

I gave up. A conversation like that is like pulling teeth. I picked up the Independent from the pile Colin had brought out, and stretched out.

Away from the HS aiming for Minister Of State Security and General Keeping The Peasants In Line, it seems that the unions are becoming more militant. After the council workers strike on Tuesday, the tube went on strike yesterday, so London was almost closed down. To help engender further confidence, the leader of the Amicus union, a "Sir" and a friend and "ally" of the PM, has been deposed by a former member of the Communist Party, and described as "left-wing". They don't actually say "raving loony militant nutter", but almost as good as. Much talk of a summer of discontent. Though with the current weather it hasn't been much of a summer anyway.

On the other hand, I could never trust anyone with a "Sir" in front of their name, least of all a trade union one.

'You know,' I commented, 'I think I should stand as mayor. On a pledge of doing nothing. Like not having fancy dinners for visiting buddies because they happen to be the minister for bogs, local fleas and sewerage. And not building new buildings for bureaucrats and filing cabinets. And especially not increasing everybody's council tax to pay for the extra filing cabinets.'

'You?' Colin scoffed. 'I can hardly see many people voting for someone in the loony bin.'

'They voted Maggie in three times,' I pointed out.

'Ah, but she wasn't actually in the loony bin, was she. Wherever she might have belonged. A subtle technical difference which might lose you votes. Speaking of which, it says here that they're planning to increase rail fares to deter people from travelling because the trains are overcrowded. Wasn't it last week that they were trying to get people out of their cars and onto public transport?'

'They voted a monkey in as mayor in Hartlepool,' I pointed out.

'Maybe they want people to just stay at home. So that two-jags whatisface can take his wife to the hairdressers in comfort.'

Colin has no faith. OK, it'll never happen, but it would be fun to try.

'And anyway, you need a five thousand pound deposit which you lose if you don't get five percent of the votes,' Colin pointed out.

Fun to try, yes, lose five thousand quid I don't have, no.

'You don't have five thousand quid I could borrow, do you?'

Saturday 20th July

Stocks and shares still falling at the end of play yesterday. The experts keep saying things like "This is not like 1929", referring to the Wall Street crash which caused the Depression of the Thirties, and arguably resulted in WWII; recovery only began well after the war started. What worries me is that these experts all seem to have their fingers crossed when they say these things.

Still, that's what they do when they're buying and selling shares anyway. I feel sorry for the mugs who have been talked into putting their savings into the stock market – the brokers walk away with their fat bank balances, and Joe Muggins is left with a few worthless pieces of paper.

On the political side – why does that sound like a swearword? – the Home Secretary has been quoted as saying he regrets nothing about the decisions he has made so far – is that an echo of Marie Antoinnette or Edith Piaf? – except that he would "have been a little less full throttle" on police reforms. This might have something to do with over 5,000 police officers coming out in protest against his plans to restructure their service. If only Citizen Alf had also come out to protest against loss of civil freedoms. In his thousands. With Missus Alf.

Even politics has to have a fairy tale, I suppose. the leader of the Liberal Democrats, the most admired party in the house – people like them, they just don't vote for them – is to be married to his sweetheart. Even after an interviewer, during a chat with the Lib Dem leader, insinuated that he was one drink short of being an alcoholic, something the interviewer now regrets. You can understand how it happened, though; they like grilling politicians, but the only policy the Lib Dems have is to raise income tax, and after you've covered that one you still have twenty five minutes left in which to find something to talk about.

I see that the United States have been forced to recall 8,000 tonnes of minced beef, which has to be a good thing. Not that I have anything against US minced beef, but if you've ever seen the process of "mechanically recovering meat" as they call it, you'd never touch a hamburger ever again, whether it came from the US or Transylvania. Then again, after BSE and the foot-and-mouth disaster, I'm surprised that the entire population haven't become staunch vegetarians.

Speaking about foot-and-mouth, the official inquiry is due to release their findings shortly, and apparently it reveals "a catalogue of incompetence at the heart of government". Brave people. One of these days the HS will have them locked up for revealing a state secret and weakening a democratic state in the fight against communism. Sorry, terrorism. Things change so fast these days you tend to forget who the current enemy is.

Went into the local shopping centre this morning, about half an hour by bus. I make this mistake about every three months or so. The shopping centre itself is quite modern, had loads of money spent on it by the local council, new pavements, bollards, open space etc, etc. All the major shops are represented, there are numerous shoe shops, health shops, sports (i.e. fashion for kids) shops, fast food places, cinemas; almost every type of shop you might ever need. Theoretically your ideal shopping centre.

But the trouble is, no matter how much effort and money they put into it, it always looks seedy, cheap and downcast. Even the pigeons with their droppings look tatty.

Part of it is the people. You seem to be eternally surrounded by pasty faced single mothers screaming at Jason to shut the fuck up while dragging along two or three other children which obviously never had the same father; or it's the local weirdos who were chucked out of their residential homes during the "lack of care in the community" drive quite a few years ago, and have ever since roamed the streets in a fog of confusion; and there's the winos and hobos sitting in their favourite filthy place close to the main bus stop where they can try to cadge some money for some cheap wine or strong cider.

And in the main open space in front of the library there is always a table holding pamphlets on Islam, and at least one Muslim behind it calling on all to acknowledge that Allah is great, normally with a loudspeaker. More often than not there is also some other chap with his own table quietly calling on the passers-by to come to Jesus. And of course the Socialist Worker lot are usually there, stopping people to enquire if you supported their latest cracked-glass view of society and the government.

Supposing you manage to navigate through these disparate groups of single mothers, screaming children, weirdos, winos and religious or social nutters, you still come up against the roving element, tinkers trying to press tiny bunches of "lucky heather" into your palms for a pound or two, or clean-imaged young couples who stop you to ask if you'd like to join them at a Christian coffee morning.

Every time I make the mistake of going in there I come out feeling frayed and in need of a cleansing shower. But for some reason after about three months all I can remember is that they've got at least one semi-decent bookshop, and the idea of spending a morning browsing through books appeals so much. They used to have a really good second hand bookshop, but that had closed down when I got there this morning. Some shops disappear without notice, but somehow the loss of a second-hand bookshop leaves a hole, especially when surrounded by plastic replicas of other shops, shops which look the same from Aberdeen to Bolton.

So I felt I deserved to relax with a stroll down to the local in the evening. Normally I don't go near a pub on Saturday or Sunday evenings; too often there's a group of drinkers who have been there since lunchtime, and have had just enough to set them in for the duration. Or, to put it another way, are only a drink or two short of becoming loud, abusive and aggressive. And they're determined to have that drink.

But this evening the pub was encouragingly quiet, and the evening drinkers had yet to appear. I sat down on my usual stool at the bar, and began the usual banter about Pete's dubious beer. He didn't take the bait this time, rather asking whether we had a place for him down the road.

'Now why would you want that when you've got your own little asylum here?' I asked. He put the ale down in front of me, and passed over a newspaper, folded at the second page.

'Seems like you lot have much more fun down there,' he commented. I looked at the top of the page. It was the local rag, The Echo. Then I looked at the title of the main story, and groaned quietly. You didn't have to be psychic to get the general drift.

"Local Doctor About To Release Latest Sex Research," it said.

'So is there some sort of queue you have to join?' asked Pete with a smile on his face. I ignored him and started reading.

"Doctor Julius Gummer, who works in the local mental hospital, is shortly due to publish his long awaited report on the findings produced from his in-depth study into how sex can be used to stimulate and maintain a healthy mind and body. Doctor Gummer is confident that the research will supersede all current Freudian approaches, and will result in a new wave of changes to sexual practice within society. He has been helped throughout the long period of research by many of his patients, who have responded well to novel therapies."

And so on. And on. Carney hadn't openly stated that the local home was a shag fest of copulating crazies, but it wasn't a conclusion you'd need to jump any great distance to reach.

'I think I shall kill that little sod,' I remarked, crunching the rag into a ball and throwing it at the wastepaper basket behind the bar.

'What, you mean it isn't true?' Pete asked in mock surprise.

'Very funny, Pete. You know bloody well it's not true. The closest most of the people there will get to a hard-on is rigor mortis.'

'Such a pity. I was working on a plan to get admitted. I was almost ready to start wandering about town in my nightclothes. Howl at the moon, that sort of thing.'

'Well, don't let that stop you. Howling at the moon in your nightclothes is probably very good for you. I wouldn't be surprised if it didn't relieve stress. Yours, not your neighbours.'

'Nah, I'll wait for that research. But if it didn't come from your lot, where did it come from?'

'I don't know. Books probably. His imagination, maybe. Look, this Doctor Gummer works there at the most one hour every three or four weeks, and even that only consists of chatting to some of the other doctors. But of course Carney didn't mention that, because then it wouldn't be a local story, would it? And I'll bet you ten to one that this so-called "sex research" doesn't go further than showing someone a funny picture and asking them what they feel. But that wouldn't make it a story either, would it?'

'Bloody newspapers, eh. Won't your lot complain?'

'I'm sure they will. If this idea gets out too far you'll have all sorts of weirdos trying to get in. In fact I reckon old Hotpants will hit the roof.'

'Hotpants?'

'The nickname for one of the doctors.'

'Tasty, is she?'

No, it's a he. Austrian bloke.'

Pete gave me a very funny look.

'You dead sure there's no funny business going on there?'

Monday 22nd July

Stocks and shares have stopped bouncing along the bottom, and are now digging below. Another global organisation has added to the general air of gaiety by filing for bankruptcy protection.

Yet funnily people in general don't seem to be devastated by the business. Maybe they've become used to these crashes, and are now waiting for things to pick up again. In the same vein, New Labour have their own funding crisis, a shortfall of six million quid or so. Mere spare change when compared to the astronomical figures you see flying around these days.

It's been a quiet weekend for news. They've published a report that pregnant women should take multi-vitamins; a couple of weeks ago the report was that multi-vitamins made no difference. Two weeks before that the story was that multi-vitamins helped stop criminals re-offending. Watch out for the next research which will no doubt show that multi-vitamins do nothing for you, unless you're a left-handed piano tuner born in 1986 with one eye called Bert.

Oh, and the Scottish Parliament has decided that they won't be requiring signs in "the Old Scots" language, which would have included ones such as "wey oot" for "exit". Probably just as well; they already have signs in English, Gaelic and braille. Any more and they wouldn't have the wall space to put them.

While surreptitiously surfing the internet this morning in reception, I discovered that "puckle" is a Scottish word for "a number", or "a few" – well, that's what it appears to be to me. It's one of those things that might well come in handy some time.

Or maybe not.

The reason I was back in reception was that Peggy-Sue or Sarah-Lee or whoever had got over their personal maladies, but now their child or children were down with whooping cough or sprinting sushi or galloping lumbago or whichever illnesses kids have these days. The only things I remember having as a kid were chicken pox and panic attacks. Kids these days just aren't up to it.

I was concentrating on a game on battleships on the computer when Ms Dervish came up behind me. I like to think I can switch between programmes faster than anyone can see.

'You couldn't lend me five thousand quid, could you?' I asked.

'Five thousand pounds? What are you planning on, an extended holiday?'

'I was thinking of standing for mayor. Only apparently you need a five thousand pound deposit.'

'Ah, so that word you used, "lend", what you meant is, give away.'

'Course not. You get it back afterwards, when you've got five per cent of the vote.'

'Precisely. As I said, give away. If you could return to the land of reality for just a moment. When you've finished surfing the net for porn, I have a task for you.'

God, but that woman's sneaky.

'I have never surfed the net for porn, and I have no intention of ever doing so,' I replied haughtily. And also with some truth. I don't honestly see the point.

'If you say so. Now I've created a list of names for this election business that Doctor Snauflwurst is overseeing. It's on the network H drive under a folder called Names. Just so that you can find it easily.'

'Now, now, no need to have a go at me. Wasn't my idea.'

'I'm sure you had some involvement. The doctor gave me a long list of names to type in, but I thought it would be easier just to dump all resident names from the database into a text file, so that's what I did. I'm sure you can format it into something approaching a table with names on one side and a box on the other where the voters will be able to place a tick?'

'No problem. Just one thing, though.' I had opened the file and it seemed perfectly straightforward, apart from one minor point. Included in the list were some names with "(deceased)" after the name. 'do you really want to include those ones?' I asked, pointing at one of the offenders.

'Bugger,' she said, not quite the reaction I had expected. 'I must have dumped everyone's names by mistake. I suppose the staff are also there.' A quick search for "Snafl" confirmed this. The herr doctor was now included in his own election. 'Well, get rid of them somehow. The deceased ones, anyway. I'm not doing another one of those. Took me an hour to work out how to do it this morning already.'

'Hokay,' I said, and with a few key strokes did a global search and replace of "(deceased)", leaving the names intact. 'How's that?'

'Well, it'll do, I suppose. Might be confusing to some people why dead people are standing in an election, but since the whole thing is already daft enough a little extra won't be noticed. Can you get that done this morning?'

'Barring unforeseen circumstances, I should have it ready and waiting in an hour or so.'

'Oh, I'm sure you could overcome even the worst of unforeseen circumstances.' She turned to go, then paused. We had both heard an unidentified noise from the one corridor. Entrance and the reception area form a connection between two of the blocks, and patients often walk through on their way to somewhere, and quite often nowhere. But this was the sound of someone stopping suddenly and muttering. The muttering wasn't unusual, the stopping was.

Suddenly a man whom I vaguely recognised shot out from the one corridor, sprinted across reception, and shot out of sight into the other corridor. We could hear him stop, panting and muttering. Ms D and I looked at each other. Then we stood and leaned over the reception desk in a vain attempt to see into the corridor. As we leaned over, another figure suddenly shot out from the second corridor, and did a reverse sprint to the first one, except this was a women wearing a dressing gown and slippers.

Now it's not uncommon for residents to wander around in dressing gown and slippers, but the operative word is "wander". They don't normally try for the hundred metres record at the same time.

Or the twenty metres record, anyway.

Ms D and I leaned back into our normal postures.

'Is there something I should know?' she asked.

'Not that I'm aware of. Not some special day, is it? Something to do with the Commonwealth Games? An overdose of prunes at breakfast?'

'No, if it were prunes I think they'd still be running. You quite sure you don't know anything?'

'Cross my heart and hope to die. It's probably some fad or other.' I sat down again and addressed the task of creating a voting slip of hundreds.

'Mmmm,' Ms D said thoughtfully, pushing her glasses to the top of her nose, where they were already. She does that when she's suspicious, but can't put her finger on something. Eventually she wandered back into admin, while I got on with the list.

'They voted a monkey in, in Hartlepool,' I called out after her.

About every fifteen minutes a resident would sprint past from one corridor to the other. It seemed quite normal after the third or fourth one. Some even called a hasty "morning" as they whizzed passed. Very polite. I also managed to hand out most of their mail as they came sailing through.

Oh, and I think I did a rather neat job of the voting forms, even if it did end up being three pages long. And the major's name might seem to be a little smaller than everyone else's. And Greta Garbo and Elvis Presley made it onto the list too. Along with Linda Lovelace and Einstein.

Well, I do think voters should have as wide a choice as possible.

Wednesday 24th July

Some transport report has come up with various ideas about building extra runways at airports around the country. Naturally this has really pleased the green lobby no end (not), especially as Heathrow is one of those mentioned, Heathrow being that place where a couple of months ago they received permission to start building a new terminal on the condition that they agreed to abandon plans for a new runway.

What I don't understand is where this extra demand is coming from when the airlines are screaming about their losses after the twin tower bombings. Apparently things are so bad they're about to go bust, yet they can see a time not too distant when people will be falling over each other to fly. They don't have any passengers at the moment, but if something isn't done soon, all the passengers they don't have will be flying to other places, like Paris and Berlin. Which will be really confusing for them when they start looking for the Tower of London.

On the spiritual front we have the appointment – probable appointment – of the soon-to-be Archbishop of Canterbury, the chap in charge of the Church of England. It's accepted that this will be the current Archbishop of Wales, who is also a druid. Or attended a druidic service. Or something like that. But that's okay, because the druids aren't religious, just pagan. And if that doesn't confuse people, you can always reflect of how the new Archbishop is selected; the prime minister of the day is given two names. He takes the top one and takes it to the queen, who is the Defender of the Faith. The current prime minister probably isn't too worried, since he normally goes to his missus' church, and she's a Catholic. Which means she can't marry the heir to the throne, because Catholics aren't allowed to. And it's not because of some sort of ancient custom, this is actually the law.

I don't know about anyone else, but if I were Catholic that would seriously piss me off. Not that I would ever want to marry the heir to the throne, of course. Who would want to marry a sponger like that? After all, what would the neighbours say?

Amazing scenes in the breakfast room this morning. The two Omley sisters talking in loud and slurred voices, discussing some youth they had known many years ago, who apparently had very fine legs. The major sitting between them, looking more and more embarrassed, until finally the one fell asleep in her porridge, the other slumped over her chair. They were taken back to their rooms to sleep off what was presumed to be a mistaken excess of their normal medication. I think I was the only one to notice Harry quietly slipping away with the sugar bowl from their table. Silly Harry, he should have known the major doesn't take sugar. But the Omley sisters do. And did.

Had a session with Hotpants, who was more interested in his "research".

'What is the one thing that is asked every time there is an election?' he asked me. I waited for a few seconds in the vain hope that it was rhetorical. Hotpants' normally are, but on this occasion it was one of those rhetorical questions which required an answer – one of those you know you're going to get wrong whatever happens.

'Er, who won?' I hazarded.

'No, no, of course not. Who wins is obvious. The real question which is always asked is why is the turn-out so low. This is the big question. This is what the analysts always ask. This is what they write many columns about. I have here ' – he waved a folder full of newspaper clippings – 'collected the thoughts of many professional political commentators and analysts, and none of them can reach agreement on why elections in modern democracies have such low turn-outs.'

He slapped the folder down in triumph, a silly beam across his face, as if waiting to be congratulated. I wondered what he expected me to say – "Nice folder"? "Love the collection"? After all, it wasn't as if he claimed to have the answer – and then the penny dropped.

'But you have the answer,' I supplied the prompt.

'No, no, I cannot claim that yet,' he answered in a modest tone which was anything but, 'but because I am approaching the issue using a disciplined, academic approach, incorporating accepted statistical evaluation, I know that I will reach an answer, and it will be the right one. These reporters,' he waved dismissively at the press clippings folder, 'merely chat about the subject, there is no coherent thought, no strategy. Now you have to ask yourself one question.'

He stopped suddenly, and I was left time to ask myself several questions, all of them concerning Hotpants and none of them polite. He waved a list of names in boxes at me, and I recognised my work on the putative ballot paper.

'You see this? This is a list of those here who wish to stand in this election I am organising. I have checked and counted this personally, and I can tell you without revealing any confidential information that it includes almost everyone of the residents. Almost everyone wishes to join. Almost everyone!'

And some, I thought.

'And you have to ask yourself why it is that here, where you would expect apathy and a lack of interest, here almost everybody wishes to take part.'

Including some from beyond the grave.

'And why do you suppose this to be the case?'

I studied the ceiling for a while before replying. 'Organisation,' I decided finally. 'Strong organisation and closeness of the people involved.'

'Well, yes, of course my organisation must have had some influence,' he said, almost blushing, 'but I would not want to stress that too much. As you say, the closeness of the people is also important.'

'And trust,' I added, to lard things a bit more. 'People believe they can trust in the election.'

'Yes, this too is a factor. Of course.' Though he said it as if it were obvious, he stopped to make a note.

'You should put a note about that on that paper, the one with the names, you know, the, er, ballot paper, about what you said about checking it personally. Put your signature next to it. I know it'll only be a photocopy in the end, but it'll be a sign, something people can trust, if they see you've checked it personally.' He looked at the three page ballot paper for a while, as the thought trundled round his brain looking for something to latch on to.

'I shall think about that. I can see the point. People will obviously trust my name. It might be a thought. Yes, I will think about that.'

But for God's sake don't actually check it properly this time, I prayed.

'Is it true that the major's gay?' I asked suddenly.

'Vot? Gay? Nonsense. It vould be in his file. I would know.'

'Ah, sorry, just something one of the other doctors suggested once.'

'Other doctors? They are fools. They know nothing. I am constantly having to correct them,' he said as he waved me out.

Which could be why the other doctors don't turn up so very often these days. I know I wouldn't, if I had the choice.

'Good session?' Colin asked as I slumped into my deckchair, closed my eyes and let the sun warm me up a little.

'It's like being locked in a room with a paranoid knife thrower with a twitch in both arms. And a hundred hysterical chimps as his assistants,' I said.

Sessions with Hotpants always leave me feeling drained.

'And two hundred hedgehogs with sharpened spikes on drugs,' I added. 'The hedgehogs, not the spikes. And angry with it. Along with a thousand of those springy balls we used to have as kids, which bounce all over the place at vicious speed.'

'Ah, well, cheer up, it won't last forever. Look, see here? An asteroid is going to hit the earth in 2019, devastating life as we know it.'

'Oh, good. Do wake me up for that.'

'No, no, it's actually quite amusing. You see, members of

parliament are about to vote themselves a pension increase – you know, our money, their pension – so if we get hit by an asteroid in 2019 they won't be able to use it. That would be so unfortunate.'

Sometimes I wonder about Colin's sense of humour.

'On a totally different note, I don't suppose you've noticed that people seem to be using reception as some sort of race track?' I asked.

'Yes, I have. "The Archbishop of Canterbury elect, has condemned any possible attack on Iraq by British and US forces"', he quoted from some headline.

'And you wouldn't happen to know why people have suddenly to taken to the short sprint? And be willing to divulge that information to me?' I added quickly, in case his answer was just "yes".

'Apparently someone told them that the new coffee machine is a mind reader. They're trying to avoid having their brains scanned as they go through reception.'

'Nah! Go on. Who would come up with such a daft idea?'

'I wonder,' he said, in that tone that suggested the words "though I can guess" were included.

'Amazing what rubbish some people will believe,' I chuckled heartily, if you can actually chuckle heartily.

'So have they given a time for that asteroid then?' I enquired.

Friday 26th July

The Commonwealth games start today, which is rather fortunate. The doctors presume that the patients doing the reception sprint are somehow acting out some fantasy inspired by the television lead up. Just so long as the docs themselves don't get into the act.

Talking of misperceptions, research conducted at the University of Wales has found that one of the things asylum seekers find attractive about the UK is Maggie Thatcher – apparently they believe that Britain is a powerful country because of her. Good thing they don't know about our current PM then. It's a good "story", which the media have picked up as such, but since the research was based on only 65 interviews, I think we can drop it into the "amusing but irrelevant" bin.

Back in reception today. At this rate I should apply for the job full time. I did suggest that to Ms D, but she said that no matter what happened I wouldn't be getting a £5,000 advance. I pointed out that if it were my money I sure as hell wouldn't be wasting it on frivolities.

Mrs Phillips turned up this morning, trolley full of library books in tow.

'Morning, all,' she said, very bright and breezy. I was about to reply in kind when I heard the ominous patter of feet speeding up.

'Er, Mrs Phillips, could you move your trolley -' I began, but too late. A figure came hurtling out of one corridor, shot straight towards the book trolley in the middle of reception, and hesitated for a split second before hurdling it in a display of athleticism a professional gymnast would have been envious of.

'- out of the middle of reception, please,' I concluded. She looked a little flustered as she quickly pulled the trolley out of harm's way.

'Don't tell me it's some new therapy,' she said. 'Always changing their therapies, this lot are. One minute it's psycho-this, the next it's shrinky-that. No wonder people have such problems.'

'Not to worry, Mrs Phillips, at least it gets them fit.'

And indeed, after only a few days there were reports of much better health, people sleeping more soundly, improved appetites – most of them had even started doing a run up in the corridor to get up speed, and then using the other corridor to slow down in. The panting was much reduced.

I do hope they don't start thinking of using it as standard therapy. You wouldn't get me running around like that. It's not healthy, you know.

'So, Mrs Phillips, how are you this bright and sunny morning?'

'Bearing up, bearing up. Quite well, really.' Someone came flying out of the second corridor, obviously forewarned about the dangerous trolley, and vaulted an obstacle which had already been moved out the way.

'And the young Evdokia? No more messages of doom and gloom from her?'

'Evdokia? Evdokia. Hmmph. She's emigrated. To Australia. Said she preferred the climate.'

'Emigrated?' I wondered if we were talking about the same person.

'Yes, would you believe it? Born and raised not fifteen miles away, never went further than London in her whole life, apart from a day trip to Calais for her honeymoon. She's even buried in her own village graveyard. Now suddenly it's not good enough. Oh, no, has to go gallivanting around the world. This place isn't good enough for her any more.'

'Well, fancy that,' I said, trying to get my mind around a spirit world where people decided to emigrate to the sun. Footloose and fancy free.

'Can't say I hold with it. It's not natural. Suddenly moving from where you've lived your entire life to a totally strange country where you know absolutely no-one.'

'Shouldn't be allowed,' I agreed. 'There ought to be a law against it.'

'And who's she going to find to talk to her over there? That's my question. Who's she going to find to talk to?'

'Good point. They speak foreign over there.'

'Well, can't stop chatting the whole day, must get these books on.'

With which she dragged the trolley off towards the day room, carefully checking for flying fruitbats before moving into the corridor. Ms D appeared silently beside me, as she was wont to do.

'Evdokia?' she asked. 'Friend of yours, is she?'

'No, I don't think you could put it that way. Especially since we've never met. She's one of Mrs Phillips' friends from beyond. And now apparently she's down under in more than one way.'

'Doesn't it ever worry you that you can actually have conversations with people like that as if what they were saying was perfectly normal?'

'Nope. What would worry me is if I had conversations with people who said things like "praise the lord", and thought that normal. You know, the sanies.'

'You are a complete cynic, you know,' she said, and disappeared before I could reply. I shrugged my shoulders and held out a letter for Mrs Perry, who grabbed it with a rushed "Thankyou!" as she shot past. She's the one who has one shoe longer than the other, or one foot shorter than the other, so her footsteps sound like "perlap perrrlapp perlap perrrlapp plap perrlap plap perrplap" and so on.

After a while you can recognise everyone by their footsteps. Apart from Mr Goldstein, who never manages to put on two shoes from the same pair, and quite often not even on the right feet. It's very irritating. You'd think he could at least try.

Sunday 28th July

'I find that morally very, very dubious.' Colin was deeply absorbed by some article or other

'Well, I've warned you about page three before, you know,' I replied.

'Very funny.' He was not amused. 'I am, in fact, talking about this civil suit against people suspected of the Omagh bombing.'

'What's dubious about that?'

'The idea that – and I quote, here – "a lower standard of evidence is required for civil actions". Shades of Blunkett's aim to make it easier to convict people. Why don't they go the whole hog and just say all that's needed is the word of an honest copper and anyone can be banged up.'

'Well they do need to have a little veneer of civilisation.'

'Veneer's right. That's all there is.'

I left it at that. Colin was in a picky mood. From time to time he would raise another angry protest at some or other news item, and occasionally Jimmie would respond with a "feck!", either through agreement, or a readiness to show willing.

Sometimes you wish that there could be just one day a year when only good news happens.

The Rose had a look of having gone through a minor war itself, when I ambled along there this evening. Broken table and chairs stacked in the corner, along with a couple of bar stools. Ginger was sat in his regular place, only instead of the normal sturdy table, his pint stood in front of him on what looked like a rickety old card table. I perched myself on one of the surviving stools and requested details from a rather angry Pete.

'Those bloody yobbos from the estate,' he said. 'Came in here already pissed and looking for trouble. Which they found.'

'I thought you barred them.' I checked the supplied pint of ale carefully, making sure there were no cracks in the glass.

'Don't worry,' said Pete, 'the broken ones are all in the bin. I'll probably have to break out the plastic ones for tonight. If anyone comes in, of course.' He sighed. 'Yes, I did ban them. And everyone knew it. Including bloody Tamsin, who was looking after the place, and who allowed them in.'

'Your daughter?'

'Yeah, the seventeen year old. She knew she was to call me if that lot showed up, but did she? No, decided they were okay despite what I told her, and now look at the result. And to top it all she's now sulking in her room because I gave her a right bollocking, and the missus is angry with me because Tamsin is sulking in her room. As if I didn't have enough problems.'

'Well, it could be worse.'

'Really? And how would that be?'

'Well, you might have to rely on having a bunch of loonies as your regulars.' He frowned, and then chuckled, before leaning his elbows on the bar and rubbing his face with both hands.

'There is that, I suppose,' he said finally. 'No, you're right. I've seen much worse than this in my time. I suppose it's just the kids. They're at that age when they just seem to do anything and everything to annoy you. And it always succeeds.'

'Cheer up, Pete. Tell you what, I'll buy you a round. Impoverished as I am, your need is greater than mine.'

'No, put your money away.' He turned to pour himself a large Scotch, dropped a couple of ice cubes into it, and raised it in salute. 'The insurance will pay for this one. And your next.'

'Well, that's awful kind of you, Pete, a man after my own heart.' We clinked glasses and drank to the insurance, though I can't say I shared his confidence in their co-operation.

'Might even get enough to redecorate the place,' he commented.

'Well, it does need it. Been ages since the last time. Looks a bit dark and dingy.'

'It was done when we first moved in and you know it, you cheeky sod. Still, that was the wife's choice. This time I'll decide.'

'You sure? Sounds a bit brave.'

'Well, I won't have any choice if she isn't speaking to me, will I. Have to move fast though, she forgives too easy.'

'Don't you just hate that. Nothing worse than a forgiving woman.' I drained my glass and handed it over for a refill.

'It's the truth. I think they do it deliberately.'

He's a perceptive man, Pete is.

Monday 29th July

Breakfast papers were full of a story about some conservative MP who has openly declared that he is gay. They seem to think it's incredible news, while the rest of the world yawns and says "and?". Reminds me of when Clinton was being hounded by that chap Starr, aka the Witchfinder General; the Republicans were so engrossed by their sense of outrage and righteousness they didn't notice that most people were getting seriously annoyed that their politicians weren't concentrating on doing their jobs properly.

From Zimbabwe, stories that Mugabe's lot are preventing food aid from getting to anyone suspected of supporting the opposition.

Another company is the latest to admit that its accounting practices were possibly not quite as accurate as they could have been in an ideal world – or, in other words – they seem to have added over a billion dollars to their profits by mistake.

As you do.

In one of those rare incidents of people power asserting itself, passengers on a budget flight due to leave from Nice to Luton refused to move when the company decided that they should get off in favour of passengers from another plane which had developed technical problems. Eventually the company had to give in and let the flight continue as planned. Good on them. You wonder who was in the other aircraft who was so important.

Hot today. Hot and humid and sultry. Massive dark clouds rumbling and threatening, teasingly suggesting an imminent downpour to cool everything down, but without so much as a drop falling.

It's the sort of weather that causes sleepless nights, and makes most people tetchy – Ms D was more acerbic than usual. I merely remained cool and calm in reception as usual, though admittedly it wasn't the best time to point out her spelling mistakes. People never like that sort of thing.

We were sitting in front of the computer screen in reception, trying to reconcile the monthly accounts using some godawful piece of accounting software which had been designed by sadists on steroids. I've seen some bad pieces of system design in my time, but this one could only have been created by a team whose brief at the start was to make it impossible for any normal human to actually use it. And things weren't being helped by having Ms D's knees right next to mine. I'm only a weak man, after all. She should know better than to sit so close. And not put her hand on the armrest of my chair.

She was convinced that the only reason the company had bought it was because the salespeople from the software company had given the board of directors a box at Wimbledon for the season.

We were fruitlessly trying to locate a missing invoice for something like £8.99. So far we'd gone through the paper records twice without identifying the rogue amount. Personally I thought we should just bung it under "petty cash" or something – the "I can't be bothered to waste my time on such a small amount" accounting approach – but Ms D insisted that that was just the sort of thing the accountants loved to find, and if we didn't reconcile it now we'd only have to do it when the bean counters came for the audit.

Makes you wonder how these international companies manage it.

I was seriously considering pointing out that when I had originally volunteered to help out in reception it was only meant to be an occasional thing helping with visitors and minor paperwork, not getting involved in something that smacked suspiciously of real office work. If I wanted to be both frustrated and bored to death I could have stayed working in the city.

It was at that moment that the prof wandered in. We both looked up, surprised to see him ground borne. He raised his stovepipe hat graciously, and bid us good morning. We mumbled something in reply.

'Oh, look,' he said, 'just what I was looking for. A machine that makes tea. I'm dying for a cup, and it's so long until morning tea – it's the weather, you see.' He emitted a sudden gasp of pleasure.

'Lemon tea! It actually makes lemon tea. How lovely. Of course, it should properly be called Russian tea, but that became unfashionable because of the communist thing. And when they stopped calling it Russian tea they also stopped making it the way it should be made – and served in a glass cup, naturally. I wonder how it tastes out of a machine.'

Absolute shite, of course, what do you expect out of a machine, I was tempted to respond, but Ms D pre-empted me.

'I don't think anyone's actually tried it,' she said. 'It isn't the sort of thing most people here would go for.'

Why is it she's always polite to everyone but me?

The prof sighed. 'People can be so conventional. Very well, let me be the first.' He extracted a little purse from his coat tails – I hadn't realised that's what they were meant for – and made his choice. The machine did its usual soft "whish-whish" thing a few times, and presented him with a little plastic cup. Ms D and I watched in fascination as he carefully lifted it, considered it critically, and slowly breathed in the aroma. I don't think either of us had ever seen such an elaborate approach to what was – let's face it – a cup of tea out of a machine.

He took a little sip, and a grimace slid slowly across his face. He shuddered delicately and smiled. 'Lovely. Absolutely lovely. Not, sadly, as good as the Hilton, but considering its source I think definitely acceptable.' He took another sip, and another graceful shudder passed through his lean frame. 'I think I might pass this way more often. When circumstances allow. Whoops.'

This last because a body had come flying through reception and narrowly missed him. I think Ms D and I were too fascinated by the prof to notice the tell tale patter of little feet making a run up.

'I see it's still as dangerous down here as it ever was,' the prof commented.

'So what's brought you down today?' I asked. 'Out of your tree, as it were.'

'Can't you feel it? The electricity in the air. It drives the forces underground. For a short while I can walk the streets without fear, for there is nothing the forces dislike more than the energy of a coming storm.'

And you'd have to be seriously mad to sit in a tree with thunder and lightning cracking overhead, I thought, but decided not to mention this obvious point.

'Have you ever considered stilts?' I enquired.

'Stilts?' His face puckered in thought. 'Stilts? You know, you may well have an idea there. I wonder why I haven't thought of that before. It would greatly enhance my mobility. Do you know, I think I shall investigate the option immediately. Wooden stilts, I think. With rubber ferules. Most indebted to you for such a good suggestion.' He raised his hat once more in bidding adieu, and swept away, as far as one can sweep away while wearing shoes with six inch rubber platforms, and trying to avoid another body coming flying through.

'Stilts?' asked Ms D in disbelief. 'I hope this doesn't mean we're suddenly going to have everyone running around on stilts. Honestly, you and your ideas.'

'Well, it's an interesting point,' I replied, raising my voice very slightly so that it would reach the audience I suspected was just around the corner, about to make a bid to beat the brain scanner. 'You notice the prof wasn't worried about being scanned by the machine?'

She groaned. 'Oh, good grief, no, I can't listen to it, you're going to tell me he's protected by the electrical force field or something, aren't you?'

'Don't be silly. It's the top hat he wears. He believes it prevents the beams from reaching his brain.'

She closed her eyes for a few seconds, then opened them, looked to the ceiling, sighed deeply and said, 'Eight pounds and ninety nine pence. And I don't want to hear any more about brain reading coffee machines, electrical waves, metal detectors, little green men, flying saucers, dancing geraniums, or any similar weird and wonderful apparitions which might try to escape from that overactive imagination of yours.'

'Don't blame me. I'm just saying what I've heard,' I said with an injured look on my face. Okay, technically I hadn't heard that stuff about the prof's hat. But it could be true, and when something could be true you don't want to let little minor technical points get in the way.

It's not lying, it's just letting the truth out a little early, before it becomes fact.

'Eight pounds and ninety nine pence,' Ms D repeated, with an almost religious determination. Mrs Perry shot past.

'You know, it might not be that,' I said, suddenly realising something.

'Eight pounds and ninety nine pence or I will kill you right here and now,' Ms D said through clenched teeth. 'And no jury would convict me.'

'Now, now,' I said soothingly. I was tempted to pat her on the knee to calm her down, but guessed that that might make things a tad worse. 'Who says it has to be eight pounds and ninety nine pence?'

'The computer says. There, on the screen. At the bottom. Where you can see the figures eight, nine, and nine, with a little dot there between the eight and the first nine, which in my world, and I believe in the world of most people, means eight pounds and ninety nine pence!'

The final "eight pounds and ninety nine pence!" was drawn out very slowly and forcefully, indicating that Ms D was perhaps not overwhelmingly at one with peace, harmony and happiness.

'What I meant was, it's a total. We've been looking for one invoice with a total of eight ninety nine. What if it's two invoices which add up to that amount? Or three or four?'

There was a quiet silence while she took in this rather obvious fact which we had totally missed during three hours of scouring through little pieces of paper. She then said something under her breath, some of which contained words I believe rhyme with "cluck" and "beach" and a mention of mother, lifted the file of invoices with a horrible determination, and said 'right, one by one then'.

We found the little beaches in the end. But I think in future I'll have a diplomatic illness whenever end of month accounts appear again.

Wednesday 31st July

Amongst the many sudden decisions the government made to do with the war on terrorism was one to spend millions on a smallpox vaccine, just in case anyone started indulging in biological warfare. The fact that they chose not to put the contract to tender, and that the company which received the contract was owned by a New Labour supporter who had just given them a £50,000 donation was a pure coincidence. Of course.

The bacon now landing at runway three is not stamped Danish.

Now it appears that the vaccine they've ordered is for the wrong strain of smallpox. The Yanks have ordered a vaccine for the right strain, part of which will be supplied to them by a different British company. The government here however insist that they have ordered the right stuff, according to advice received – advice which they have refused to publish, thus irritating the scientific community, opposition politicians, people in the vaccine producing business and, well, most people concerned. The general public don't seem too concerned. Except possibly for those who already doubt the government's position on things like the MMR vaccine, and are left wondering about the government's trustworthiness in medical issues.

Presuming, of course, that the reports in the media are accurate. The debate about whether a journalist is more trustworthy than a politician is a fine one indeed.

The advice, incidentally, was received from "a committee of scientific experts". Which, given the verbal gymnastics politicians are capable of, could well have been composed of the tea ladies from the department of health and a few of their kids who had received chemistry sets as birthday presents. Or possibly any ten year old who has ever pulled the wings off a fly.

From the "what idiot decided to research that?" file: British scientists have discovered why lobsters go from dull and dingy to bright pink when boiled alive. I can't remember the explanation, but it had something to do with hot water.

From the "University of We All Knew That Before": as much as 60% of on-the-job training is inadequate. Anyone who has every worked knows that all "on the job training" means is that you're the one who gets to make the tea and clean up afterwards.

And finally from the "you got that half right" file: they've discovered that people who do early morning physical training are more susceptible to infections than others. The bit they missed out is that any form of physical training beyond a good walk is bad for you. And the good walk only applies when there's a decent pub at the end of it.

'I think we should do the lottery,' Colin announced this morning. We were sitting in the shadow of the trees to escape the heat. The downpour that had threatened the day before had moved North, and devastated a number of towns and villages by dumping the equivalent of a month's rainfall in a couple of hours.

Since Colin has a panic attack every time he goes too near the gates, and would never be able to actually move outside, I'm not sure what good having a few million quid would do. But you have to put these things diplomatically.

'OK, let's say we won a million quid. What would you do with the money?'

'Buy a place somewhere in the country. Maybe in Ireland. Far, far away from anywhere else. Far from the madding crowd.'

'Not too far. You'd want someone around to pop in and clean every so often. Maybe cook as well.'

'I think I'm able to cook and clean for myself. I used to be quite good at cooking, as it happens.'

'Well, what about a nice, quiet country pub down the lane? Have to have one of those.'

'You'd have to have one, you mean. I'd be quite happy without.' Colin disapproves of too much drinking, which means anything more than half a shandy at Christmas.

'So what's brought on this sudden urge for hermitage?'

'Oh, I don't know. Every day you read the papers, it seems like

185

just more and more bad news. Never seems to end.'

'So you wouldn't want a news-agents close by to deliver the morning papers, then?' He had to stop and think about that one.

'Maybe just a small one. And you can have a small pub.'

I didn't respond to that one. It sounded too much like Colin was thinking that we'd all move into this halcyon hermitage of his. It would be a good way of discovering very quickly how much we didn't have in common. Cooking and cleaning are admirable things.

In other words, there to be admired, not done.

'What about you, Jimmie?' Colin asked the recumbent form, face hidden underneath his cap. 'You in for a go at the lottery? Pound a week?'

'Feck,' said Jimmie.

'Well, that's three of us then. I'm sure some others will want to join – Mrs Gladstone, Miss Melly. The more we have, the better the chances.'

Bringing it down from one split atom's distance away from absolutely no chance at all, to just one atom away from not in a million years. Still, if others are going to do this sort of thing you have to join in. Don't want to be the only one left here while all the others are in Bermuda ritually burning coffee machines.

August

Friday 2nd August

The National Audit Office has released a report detailing some of the problems the British army had in exercises in the desert last year. Amongst them were tank air filters which lasted only a few hours, shutting down the tanks, and boots which melted – leaving the soldiers hopping mad, presumably. In a funny way this is reassuring; at least they're identifying problems. Watching propaganda newsreels from the late thirties you'd be forgiven for believing that the British army, navy and air force were unbeatable, which as it turned out, they weren't.

I think the British – and probably most Europeans – are a sceptical lot. Experience has taught them that something always goes wrong; they never feel comfortable unless they can point to what it is. And even then they know there's another bloody something coming towards them.

A UN report into Israel's incursion into Jenin has concluded that the Israelis did not commit a massacre, but both sides were to blame for putting civilians in harm's way. Those who have adopted an anti-Israeli report stance have rejected the report. Not even a flock of angels could convince either side that there was anything positive to say about the other.

Hamas have exploded a bomb in Hebrew University, which, not only being a seat of learning, also admits students of every race, religion and nationality, and is arguably one of the few places where the next generation can get together to form bonds which will be required for a peaceful process. Which is presumably why Hamas bombed it. The Israelis have moved tanks into Nablus in retaliation. And so it goes on.

Uruguay is suffering from riots and strikes.

The Mexican government has abandoned plans for a new airport after months of violent protests by farmers.

Pakistan is making changes to its election laws primarily to ensure that someone they don't like is kept out of the running.

The Italian Senate has passed a law which some say is designed to ensure that their prime minister won't end up in court on charges of corruption.

And here's us poor peasants believing that the law is inviolate. No doubt the political lawmakers will still be there on the day of judgement, passing new resolutions, trying to ensure the right people go to heaven.

Still, they don't have it all their own way. Here, a court has ruled that the Customs and Excise boys have exceeded their remit in the way they handle suspected smugglers coming back from the continent. Effectively they were making their own minds up as to whether someone was smuggling or not, confiscated their goods and vehicles, and then disposed of said goods and vehicles without recourse to trial – last year it was over 10,000 vehicles. It's one of those anomalies created by the EU: you can bring as much in as you like for your own "personal consumption" – but who is to decide how much a person can consume?

Continuing with the law, a law student has sued his university for the quality of teaching, and won £30,000 in an out-of-court settlement. One might be tempted to reach the conclusion that perhaps they had taught him too well, but on further investigation it looks like things were so bad that even a non-lawyer could make the case. The university agreed to the out-of-court settlement with "no admission of liability". Which, naturally, we believe.

In Nottingham two teenagers have been arrested for throwing eggs at the queen's car. Quite why has not yet been disclosed. It would be nice to think that it was a statement of republican enthusiasm, but the general tenor of reports seems to indicate they were just having fun, which would be a bit of a waste of eggs.

A letter writer to The Times has helpfully pointed out that, contrary to the answer to a question in a quiz in the newspaper, Magna Carta was not signed in 1215, in fact it was never signed, it was sealed. I am sure we are all grateful, and more knowledgeable, now that this distinction has been pointed out. On the other hand it makes one yearn for the days of the death penalty.

I'd better make sure it wasn't Colin before I say anything.

Somerset Maugham once wrote a short story called Rain, if I remember correctly, in which people are driven to uncharacteristic behaviour by the continual drumming rain and their enforced proximity to each other. It's been raining here almost continuously for the last two days, and I'm beginning to understand the feeling. It's a large place, but wherever you go you seem to be have been beaten there by someone else and a cloud of steam. Even reception was a no-go area, with Lee-Anne or Pom-Tiddly or whoever back at her post. She always gets very irritated when she knows I've been working at her desk; claims I upset her "system".

What system? She isn't here often enough to develop a system.

At least I have a system developed years ago; when a requirement arises, put it in a green file, and drop the file on the "things to do" (i.e. everything) pile. If someone asks after it, take it out of the pile, swap the green file for an orange one, and throw it back on the top of the pile. The next time the issue arises, do the same, but replacing the orange file with a red one. The fourth time, pass it on to someone to get it done. Or just pass it on to someone.

Every week or so, throw the contents of the green files in the bottom half of the pile away, because they obviously aren't important.

To be honest, it isn't original: a similar system was used in the plotting rooms during the Battle of Britain to identify plots of raids which were no longer valid.

And why is it that, whenever you see shots of fighter pilots during the BoB, it's never raining?

By the time early evening came the rain had finally stopped, and I used the opportunity to stroll down to the Rose for a quiet, meditative pint. If I had to spend any longer cooped up I would have gone stark staring raving.

Pete barely acknowledged my cheery greeting and insults. He

seemed to be miles away, lost in his own little world of misery. Great, I thought, I've exchanged one lot of depressives for another.

'A horse walks into a bar,' I said, 'What's with the long face? asks the barman.'

Pete smiled grimly. 'Very Funny. Well, it was the first time I heard it, about twenty years ago.'

'Come on, Pete, you look like you've go a dental appointment with your bank manager.' An almost smile almost passed across his face as he placed my pint down.

'Sorry, problems on my mind.' He sighed, and leaned on the pumps. 'Know that daughter of mine, Tamsin? Didn't come home last night. Haven't seen hide nor hair of her since yesterday morning. The wife's going mental, tried all Tamsin's friends, but no joy.'

'Have you called the police?'

'Yup. They said she'd probably just run away for a few days, and would return soon. Told us not to worry too much. Trouble is they've got so much on already.'

'That's nice of them. Give them another call, and tell them to get their backsides into gear.'

He looked even more worried. 'You don't think she's been abducted, do you?'

'Nah, course not. She's old enough to take care of herself.'

'She's only seventeen. She's just a kid.'

Interesting description. Tamsin can break concrete slabs without breaking a sweat. And she'd use customers as a hammer.

'Tell you what you should do – phone the cops and tell them you're going to talk to the newspapers. That'll shift them.'

'What, a sort of threat? The police?'

'Don't be daft, Pete. You know better than that, you being a publican. Just call to see if there's any news, and accidentally mention that you're planning on speaking to the local paper, maybe thinking of putting an ad in the Standard, or possibly one of the nationwides.'

'Well, it's worth a try, I suppose,' he said hesitantly.

'Your choice. I reckon she's out there just waiting to be told mum and dad love her, and will she please come home.' That decided him.

'Right. Won't be a tick.'

He took his mobile out of his pocket, wandered down to the end of the bar, and engaged in animated conversation with some invisible plod. I was ready for the next pint when he came back, much more positive.

'Well, that seemed to do something. Bloke I spoke to had his sergeant on the line very quickly, and then some other high up straight after that. The sergeant's coming around as soon as possible. I think you deserve a free pint for that.'

'Well, if you insist ...'

'Mind you, seems I'm paying for more of your beer than you are. I'll bankrupt myself at this rate.'

'Not at your prices, Pete. I'd just like to know what you're doing with the fortune you're amassing.'

'Fortune? Skint, that's what I am.'

And so we exchanged the usual insults for a short while, before a flustered looking police sergeant with WPC in tow came through the doors.

'Blimey, that was quick,' muttered Pete. I could hardly disagree. Five minutes door to door, if that.

'Mr Finney?' the sergeant asked Pete, and he acknowledged his identity. 'Somewhere more private we can talk?' the sergeant asked, and they moved off to the end of the bar.

I stayed long enough to finish the pint, and wished Pete good luck on leaving.

The sergeant and WPC gave me a look which suggested that they knew I was guilty of something, and were only trying to remember precisely what. Coppers are trained to do that.

All in all, not the best of days. And I think I'm catching a cold.

Sunday 4th August

In Africa, Angola to be more precise, Unita have officially disbanded their army, theoretically bringing a final end to their civil war. Not to worry, though, rebels in Niger are getting ready for attacks by government forces, so there's no reason to fear that peace might suddenly break out on the continent.

Elsewhere things seem a little more positive: North and South Korea have agreed to talks, an improvement on a month or so ago, when their navies were busy shelling each other. Turkey's parliament has lifted some restrictions on the Kurds, and also abolished the death penalty – admittedly only because they want to join the EU. How Turkey manages to be in "Europe" is another question. Maybe they'll rename the EU to "Union of countries sold down the river by their politicians".

Another suicide bomb on a bus in Israel.

Stock markets continue to cause alarm amongst stock brokers.

Neighbours feud over hedge; in the end one chops down the hedge.

Typical. Two humans have a disagreement and the hedge gets it.

The police paid a visit this morning. We were settling gently into a relaxing Sunday morning outside, with the sun finally showing its face – settling gently in more ways than one, as the ground was still soft enough for the deck chairs to gradually sink in as far as they could – when Tonique appeared, looking flustered, with a couple of plods behind her.

'These, er, these, er, officers, want, er, would like, er, they, er,' Tonique started off, flapping her arms vaguely. Sometimes I think she's on the wrong side of the fence here; she'd do better as a resident.

'We'd like a word with you, if we may, sir,' said the one, quite politely. I recognised him, and the WPC with him, as the two from the pub last Friday. The WPC was looking distinctly nervous. Probably expecting hordes of zombies to appear out of the trees intent on taking over the planet.

'Of course,' I said magnanimously, reclining ever lower into the deckchair as the legs sank even deeper into the mud-based lawn.

'Is there somewhere private we could talk?' the sergeant suggested.

'Of course, of course.' I struggled to get up out of the deckchair, but it became easier when I realised that it had sunk so far I was actually sitting on the grass. 'Let's go for a walk,' I said, when I was finally standing upright. Normally I would be rather nervous when approached by one of her majesty's plods for a quiet conversation – was it about the tax return five years ago when you didn't enter that ten quid you won in a bet? Was it the goldfish you had accidentally killed in the dentist's waiting room, and hidden behind the radiator? – but when you start off with your backside in the mud, nervousness seems a bit of an anti climax.

'It's about this girl who's gone missing, the daughter of the landlord at the Rose and Crown' the sergeant said as we strolled in the open, the WPC keeping close by. 'We understand that you know her.' I considered the point for a few seconds.

'I think that would be somewhat of an exaggeration. No, come to think of it, not true at all. I saw her around a couple of times, and she served me once, and that's it. I wouldn't call that knowing her.'

'So you wouldn't know where she might be now?'

'At a guess, holed up with a friend whose parents are away on holiday, hoping her folks are in tears and blaming themselves for driving her away.' A thought suddenly struck me. 'I hope that question wasn't suggesting what I think it might have been suggesting.'

'I wasn't suggesting anything, sir. We're interviewing everyone who drank at the pub in the last couple of weeks.'

'In other words you're fishing.' A slight grin almost passed across his face.

'We're following every possible avenue of investigation, sir. Why do you think she's run away? As opposed to being abducted? Or any other possibility?'

We'd fallen into a slow measured pace along the path that goes around the buildings. No doubt there were eyes at every window, peeking out carefully. This isn't the sort of place a policeman would be welcome. People have enough problems with their imaginations, let alone a real copper. This pair would be lucky to get away without a dozen people confessing that they nicked some lollipops from a sweet shop forty one years ago, and could they please be arrested?

However I had no intention of mentioning the goldfish.

'Probability, I suppose. With all due respect to the young lady, she's not exactly what one would call petite. I reckon she could give someone quite a hefty blow if they tried anything. So the abduction theory is unlikely. On the other hand she's got a chip on her shoulder the size of Everest. I've seen grown men wait until her dad came back before ordering a pint, rather than face her.'

'Strange, her father describes her as being the most kind, generous and defenceless soul on earth.' The half smile slipped quickly across his face again. 'And when did you see her last?'

I thought for a few moments. 'About two, three weeks ago, I suppose.' Funny how you don't realise how long it's been since you last saw someone. You just presume they're somewhere around.

'So she might have been missing for a few weeks as far as you're aware?'

'Eh? You aren't saying – you don't mean Pete might have – I can't believe that.'

'As I say, we're following every possible option at the moment, sir. As it happens we know she went shopping with a friend on the day that she disappeared, so that option is extremely unlikely.'

Never mind fishing, they didn't even have any bait. 'And what is the most likely option at the moment?'

He rubbed his chin slowly. That's body language for 'I'm now going to say something which is true if you listen carefully'.

'I'm afraid we haven't enough information at the moment, sir, but your line of thinking is one of the many lines of enquiry we are following up. Well, thank you for your time. If you hear anything, or remember anything, please let us know.' Translation: we also think she's done a bunk, but we have to make the effort.

'Of course. Anything I can do to help, give a shout. Pete's a good bloke.'

'We'll be conducting a search of the park close to the pub, if you want to give a hand. Tuesday, probably, if we can get the bodies together.'

'I'll be there.' I watched as they walked back to the car park in front of reception, the WPC still looking around nervously. The dark clouds were rolling back in again from the south, heavy with the promise of more thunder, lightning and downpours. Somewhere a chilly breeze was beginning to stir, the first signs of approaching winter. And it's only August.

It's this global warming, we'll all freeze to death because of it.

Tuesday 6th August

Nine Hindu pilgrims have been killed in Indian Kashmir, in what appears to be an attack by what are referred to as "Islamic militants".

Six people shot dead at a Christian missionary school in Pakistan.

Israel are having another go at Gaza City using missiles fired from helicopters.

The Ugandan army has recaptured a refugee camp from rebels.

Sometimes you wonder if you should be keeping score.

Two nursery nurses – ex nursery nurses – in Newcastle have, after nine years, been cleared of all allegations of sexual abuse of children in their care. The judge found that the four people who had compiled the report which claimed that the pair were child abusers had been "malicious" and "dishonest". So the good old witch hunt is alive and well.

On the bright side, the royal celebrations have come to an end at the Edinburgh Military Tattoo.

'Five hundred copies?' I asked Ms D incredulously this morning.

'That's about the number of names on the list,' she replied. 'doctor Snaflwurst wants one copy per person.'

'But over half of these people went to their happy hunting grounds ages ago,' I pointed out. 'And at least another hundred are staff members who left years ago.'

'Yes, and there's also one or two who have never heard of this place. And Michael Mouse isn't a real person either.'

'Course he is. Look, there's Hotpants' signature saying he's checked it, and he wouldn't lie, would he?'

Ms D pursed her lips in her best school-teacher-tolerating-no-nonsense manner.

'Five hundred copies. Some time this morning, preferably.'

'What's the magic word?' I asked, accepting defeat.

'Morning!' Mrs Perry strolled past wearing dressing gown, slippers and top hat.

'Morning Mrs Perry. No post today, I'm afraid,' I replied cheerfully. I turned back to Ms D. She had a look on her face that suggested she had thought she had seen it all, but now she realised that she hadn't. Or maybe now she had.

'Tell me that Mrs Perry wasn't wearing a top hat,' she said finally.

'Mrs Perry wasn't wearing a top hat,' I said dutifully. I try to help. Some people don't appreciate it.

'She was, wasn't she?'

It's a woman thing. They say something like "tell me it's not raining", so you do, and then they complain when they go out and get wet.

I sat in silence. It's called self preservation.

'Well?' she asked finally.

'Well what?'

'Did Mrs Perry just walk past wearing a top hat?'

Someone appeared from where Mrs Perry had gone, and disappeared in the opposite direction. It was a chap called Roger Kimble, and he was wearing a top hat. Probably the same one Mrs Perry had worn. Obviously some form of time share.

'That wasn't Mrs Perry, that was Roger Kimble' I pointed out helpfully.

Her lips moved silently for a few moments. For some reason she seemed to be counting. I couldn't help but notice that they looked rather attractive. I wish she wouldn't do that.

'Let me guess. Something to do with the coffee machine. And laser beams. And top hats.'

'Yes, sad, isn't it.'

'That is one way of putting it.'

'Really sad. If only they knew that the top hat they're sharing isn't as strong as the professor's. Doesn't stop all the beams, you see. They move too slowly. A slow trot would help.'

After all, the exercise has been good for them so far. Wouldn't want to lose that.

Ms D has these wonderful green eyes which can look at you

quite expressionlessly, yet still contain something about them that could make a weaker man nervous.

I looked down at the ballot paper. 'Five hundred copies, eh?'

'Five hundred copies,' she confirmed.

'Well, may as well make a start, then.'

'Please.'

'There you go, that's the magic word,' I said. She gave me a final withering look as I disappeared down the corridor towards the photocopier.

I pretended not to notice.

Whenever I have had to use a photocopier I have always wondered whether I could get a research grant to prove that they are not, as the companies would have you believe, a great time and labour saving device, but actually generate more work and fewer results than ever. It's based on a general theory which I call "less labour equals more work". A better example is e-mail: in the days of the typewritten memo, people put a lot of effort into getting the memo right before distributing it; was it required? Were the necessary points made properly? Was it going to the right people? Were there, God forbid, any spelling mistakes?

These days people whack out an e-mail in seconds, don't think things through, don't put forward a coherent question or argument, and then send it to hundreds of other people, most of whom haven't got the slightest thing to do with the point in question. These hundreds of people create their own incoherent replies, copying in a few more people for good measure. Ultimately they all have to get together and have a meeting to discuss what the original e-mail meant. Which no one can remember anyway.

I was thinking these thoughts as I watched the marvel of modern technology in the admin office spewing out five hundred copies of a three page ballot paper containing more names of dead or non-existent people than live. There's a certain monotonous hypnotic effect of watching a machine going through the same process time and time again, as it burps out a stapled set of three pages every few seconds or so, so I didn't realise that the major was in the area until he was almost next to me.

'I hear you're organising a search,' he barked into my face, 'for the young girl that's gone missing.'

I regarded him dispassionately. He has that sort of effect on me – I have this urge to pull his moustache and knee him somewhere impolitely.

'The police are organising a search,' I said slowly. 'Of the park down by the Rose. For possible clues.'

'The police, eh? Of course. Much better idea. Leave it to the professionals to organise, takes experience. When are they starting?'

'Tomorrow, probably.' The plan for today had been postponed due to water logging. A hundred pairs of untrained boots would have re-landscaped the park with a result that would have consisted mainly of mud.

'Tomorrow? Excellent. I'm free tomorrow. And Mrs and Mrs Omley. We thought we could give a hand.'

'I'll let you know, then. When I have more information.'

'Excellent. Excellent. Must do our civic duty, eh?' He nodded a goodbye greeting in the best of officer-to-subordinate manners, and turned and marched away. Idiot.

The photocopier had finished producing half a ton of waste paper, and I put it into a large box to carry back to reception. My thoughts were concentrated on Pete and the delightful Tamsin. More than ever I was convinced that it was a game of revenge on her part, though despite appeals on the radio and local television no-one had come forward with a sighting.

It's at times like these that I really appreciate being on this side of the wire.

'Where would you like these?' I asked Ms D once I had got back to admin with a ton of paper. I was tempted to drop the box on the end of her desk to see if I could make the other end bounce. Purely out of scientific interest of course. I reckon I could have made it jump at least a few inches.

'Storeroom K,' she replied, without looking up.

'Storeroom K? That'll be the one right at the back of the main block?'

'That's the one.'

'The one that only has an external door? So you have to walk right round the outside of the block to get to it? Carrying two tons of photocopied whatsits? In the mud.'

'Alternatively you could put them in the bottom drawer of the filing cabinet over there. The one I've just cleared out.'

It took a while for the penny to drop. 'You were joking. About storeroom K.'

'You aren't the only one with a sense of humour, you know,' she said, standing up. 'But for your efforts I'll even buy you a cup of coffee.' She paused on her way out. 'I was tempted to let you lug that stuff around the block, though.'

'Any chance of a cream bun with that coffee?' I called after her as she disappeared in the general direction of the coffee machine.

I'm not sure I like Ms D's sense of humour.

Wednesday 7th August

There is a minister in the Foreign Office who I don't think will ever reach the top in his profession. This is not to say that he is not capable, possibly even efficient; for all I know he might be the best going. But he is the Foreign Office minister chosen to go for tea and scones with Mu'ammar Gaddafi, Libyan dictator and general world pariah. That sort of thing never looks good on your CV if you're a politician, even if, as a result, world peace breaks out, all known diseases are eradicated, and England win the world cup – all people will remember is that you're the one who went to speak to the evil one.

I presume they drew straws, and he lost.

Though say what you like about Gaddafi, he certainly has staying power. He gained control via a coup in 1969 at the age of twenty-seven, and he's still in there, despite supporting a number of dubious organisations like the PLO and the IRA (though of course they got a lot of support from people in that land of democratic virtues, the good old US of A), the killing of WPC Fletcher which resulted in the breaking of diplomatic ties, the bombing of Tripoli by the Yanks when he upset them, the Lockerbie bombing and the handing over of the two suspects associated with that, and god knows what other matches he's been playing with in his time in the dynamite factory of world politics.

Now he's given up trying to reunite the Arab world, and has decided to become the champion of African unity, though I think he'll have the same success with them that he had with the Arabs i.e. they won't trust him further than they can spit the Eiffel Tower.

The BBC website lists the names of his ministers, among whom is one Husni al-Wahishi al-Sadiq, who is, apparently, "People's control apparatus minister". The mind boggles.

Just think; Gaddafi took control at the height of the days of flower power and the swinging sixties (which probably passed Libya by), the anti-Vietnam protests, and held onto the reigns through punk, heavy metal, rap, garage, living room, kitchen-diner and whatever other delightful forms of music the West has indulged in. If only he played a guitar, he could have been an icon. The only other political leader to have demonstrated such longevity, that I can think of, is Castro in Cuba.

And soon he'll be gone as well, no doubt.

You have to feel some sympathy for Labour supporters. After eighteen years in the wilderness, eighteen years of defeat and disaster, of Foot and Kinnock and Scargill, they finally managed to gain power, only to find that they'd voted in the New Tory party, and instead of a Labour government, they had a presidential administration which makes the Tories look liberal by comparison. You'd think that the government would be a tad bit embarrassed at having stolen every single decent policy the Tories had, and most of their indecent ones too, but not a bit of it. The Health Minister has publicly stated that they must "seize the policies of diversity and choice from the Conservatives" on health issues, just as they did with crime and the economy. So when you next vote you might as well do it on the basis of their haircuts as their policies, unless you want to vote for more taxes with the Liberal Democrats.

The economy, as everyone knows, is stagnant, with companies having to lay off staff, pleading poverty, begging government assistance, etc, etc, etc. So it may come as a surprise that the Royal Bank of Scotland has announced a 15% increase in interim profits. Or possibly not. Maybe the reason that people are still merrily spending on their credit cards is that they don't believe the cries of woe from the business arena, interpreting such noises as merely the bleatings of salesmen down to their last few million.

Staying in the financial world: a woman whose debit card was stolen found that the balance had gone up by £291.40. The thief had used the card to lay two £50 bets on the gee-gees, not realising that the winnings would automatically be paid into the credit card account. And of course the betting shop were able to identify the man who had made the bets, so he was down in more ways than one.

When I had volunteered to help with the search party the plods were organising, I had the idea that it would be just myself, and possibly Colin and Jimmie if they felt like a walk. When I walked out into the area in front of reception this morning I was amazed to see about twenty or thirty people waiting in the sunshine, mainly just leaning against walls sunning themselves. They looked like a perfectly normal bunch of ramblers, if that isn't a contradiction in terms. Mrs Gladstone and Miss Melly were wearing what I presume they called "sensible" footwear when they were at school – boots which, while not large, had an aura of hobnails and steel toecaps – and they each had a stout walking stick of the type used not for aid in walking, but for chastising any misbehaving bull which might mistakenly try to charge them.

Colin and Jimmie popped up as I stood there checking my watch.

'Hello, you two, joining in the fun?' I asked. Jimmie gave an affirmative "feck", while Colin looked longingly towards the gates.

'I'd like to,' he said nervously, 'but I'm a bit busy at the moment. You know, things to do, people to see.'

'Oh come on, Colin. It's a gorgeous day, just right for a stroll in the park. You'll enjoy it.'

'No, no, I'd love to, but as I say, things to do, busy, you know.' With that he turned and disappeared rapidly back into the building.

I felt quite sorry for him. He obviously wanted to come along, but the fear of stepping outside the gates was just too much. The world out there was still too dark and dangerous; the worst thing is that the longer he stays in here the harder it becomes for him to move out.

'Well, we'd better get along then, I suppose,' I said to no-one in particular. I raised my voice. 'Time to move on out, then,' I said to the assembled army, and started walking.

'Yes, fall in everyone,' said the major in a surprisingly soft voice. I tried to imagine him on a parade ground speaking like that, but the image wouldn't come. As Jimmie and I came out of the gates we looked behind to check on the loony army. The major was at the back, Omley sisters in tow, bringing up any stragglers. So he is good for something, I thought. I caught a glimpse of Colin at a second floor window, looking, as far as I could see at that distance, bereft. Anyone would think we were all going for good, leaving him alone and cast out, I thought. Or maybe he was realising that the chances that he might one day walk out had all but disappeared.

It was a pleasant little stroll to what is called the park, hardly twenty minutes in mild sunshine. The ramblers description definitely fitted; all ages and shapes and sizes, but mainly wearing walking gear and old clothes – or maybe we looked like a bunch of refugees from Oxfam. The one distinguishing thing was the absence of voices. Hardly a few sentences were exchanged, yet everyone seemed happy enough.

Strange people.

I caught sight of my friend the sergeant as soon as we came up to the park, which was fortunate. I wasn't looking forward to leading the gang silently around in circles through assorted normal citizenry – three or four people you know well is a manageable amount, but controlling a group of twenty odd – and I mean odd – individuals is another matter altogether. What if some of them were kleptomaniacs? Or had a fit at the sight of red? Or had come along to spread the word of the second coming? It was beginning to dawn on me that perhaps I had taken on a little more than I had intended.

Let's put it this way; no doctor at the clinic would be mad enough to do this, and they're the professionals.

'Ah, it's the loony brigade,' said the sergeant as we came up, quietly enough so that not too many people heard him, though the look on the face of his WPC shadow was one of surprised shock. I have this feeling that the sergeant doesn't think much of political correctness.

'Morning, sergeant,' I said, 'anywhere specific you'd like us to be?'

'Well, I'm not in charge of this junket, but if I were you, you see that large oak over there to the left? Where the cordon tape starts? I'd take your lot down there, and spread out about a foot apart along the line of the tape. That's the starting point. If you go now you can stick together, otherwise everyone will end up mixed up all over the place. And believe me, some of the people here this morning, you don't want to end up next to them, unless you really enjoy being chatted to death.'

'Cheers, sergeant, we'll take your advice. Right, you lot, follow me.' I lead them off to the oak tree the sergeant had indicated. One thing I definitely did not want was for the group to split up. I hadn't asked them to come, and they weren't technically my responsibility, but I was pretty sure where the finger would be pointing if this business went from consisting of one missing teenager to one missing teenager and a dozen or so missing maniacs wandering the streets staring vacantly into people's lounges. Admittedly everyone seemed normal at the moment, but they weren't in the clinic because of their stability. I was grateful to notice that, apart from the major, Jimmie was also doing an imitation of a sheepdog, if only in that he was constantly looking around and checking on where everyone was. He might not say much, but I doubt if he misses much.

I think everybody had heard the sergeant's instructions; it was easy enough to get them down to the oak, and then lined up roughly a foot apart in front of the tape, all standing looking straight ahead like immobile soldiers facing the enemy.

'Okay, relax everybody, just try not to move around too much,' I called out. 'We'll just wait here until they're ready to go.' Above all I didn't want them maintaining their fixed-gaze poses. It made me nervous, I wouldn't like to see what it would do to the normal citizens gathered in little groups about fifty or so yards away. As it was they were adopting the positions of people who, having seen others do something, think that they should do the same, but haven't received any orders to that effect; those sitting stood up, those standing straightened up, stamped in circles, looking for whatever mystery signal had caused our lot to take the lead. There were a few glances in our direction which had a query in them.

Possibly the plods had finally got themselves organised, or maybe we had galvanised them into action, or our group had brought the numbers to an acceptable level; shortly a dozen or so coppers in overalls began to chivvy and move the scattered groups of people down to the tape on our right. It took about twenty minutes, if not more, before they were all in line, excluding one old chap who finally managed to get a copper to understand that he had only been out walking his dog, and had neither the time nor intention of joining a search party, thank-you very much.

A voice came through a megaphone, and, after a little gazing around, I identified the speaker as a grey haired copper with silver scrambled egg on his shoulders.

'I'd just like to thank you all for coming here today to give your time and help. I'll hand over to Sergeant Gilmore who will be co-ordinating the work today.' He handed the megaphone over to a sergeant – not the one I new – and stood there listening.

'OK, everyone, just a few points,' the sergeant's voice came across with that strange mechanical effect that megaphones tend to bestow. 'When we start off I want everyone to stay in line as far as possible. I know it won't be easy, but try to slow down or speed up as required. Now the main aim of this search is to find anything which is out of place – anything man made, a piece of paper, a scrap of material, anything like that. But, and I want to stress this, do not – do not – pick anything up. When you find something, stop, and raise your arm, and one of the constables will come to you to pick up whatever it is you've seen. Apart from the question of contaminating evidence, you might contaminate yourself if you pick up something nasty. Does everyone understand?'

'Amen!' called one of our group, and I thought, please god, no, just a yes will do.

'And one final point. Don't try to search any hedges or bushes or trees. You don't have the equipment. There will be constables behind you with the right equipment to do that. Good. Right, let's get on with it. Constables!'

With that the constables at the various points of the tape cut it loose, and we started a slow, heads-down walk. I was trying to keep my eyes not only on the squelchy ground, but also on my newly acquired charges. I wished I knew where the "Amen!" had come from. I knew there was at least one resident so damaged by religion that "amen" meant "yes" to him, but on the other hand there were at least a few at the clinic who wandered around each day praising the lord wherever they went. I hoped they'd stayed behind today.

'Ooh, look, balloons,' came a cry from one of the Omley sisters. 'Some children's party, poor things.'

'Well spotted, Miss Omley,' I called. 'Just stay there and raise your hand for the constable to come and collect them.' The major alongside the Omley sisters was looking a little embarrassed, and I partly sympathised. Even at that distance I could recognise used condoms. What they were doing in the middle of the park, away from any cover whatsoever, was another question.

'A farthing!' called Miss Melly. 'Goodness, haven't seen one of those for years.' She raised her hand without prompting. At this rate we weren't going to get very far very fast.

'Feck!' said Jimmie next to me, raising his arm, to reinforce my feeling. To my astonishment he was peering at a syringe, intact with needle. What the hell went on in this place, I wondered.

As the constables behind us rushed up with gloved hands and plastic bags the line slowed down. The constables had to hurry to keep up with a flood of sightings – probably mostly useless, but I was impressed at the way our group seemed to be able to spot anything larger than a pin – well, including a pin, as Mrs Gladstone proved. They might have been warned not to touch anything, but no-one had said anything about going down on hands and knees for a closer inspection, and it began to show. A quarter of the way through there were mud patches on knees. Half way, and stains were appearing where hands had rested. By the end some people were beginning to resemble Red Indians wearing war-paint.

The other groups had long finished by the time our lot reached the road which bordered the park. The sergeant from the pub came up came up as everyone caught up, and made a comment about how he'd never seen a more thorough search in his entire police career. The group looked self consciously proud at that. In their position they can spot honest compliments, no matter how sarcastic the tone.

But then it was probably the first determined thing most of them had done in months, if not years, and they didn't have the distractions of chatting to their neighbours about little Timothy's visit to the dentist, or how Jenny had started learning the violin and the neighbours were complaining.

I fell in with the sergeant as we strolled back to the starting point, where a mobile police canteen had appeared, dispensing tea and coffee to searchers now aimlessly milling around.

'So, do you think we managed anything positive?' I asked. He grinned.

'About a shilling in old money, and ten quid in assorted change. I reckon if your lot did the whole area we could probably pick up a few hundred quid. And at least there aren't any syringes or other nasty things left for anyone to accidentally step on. Oh, and the remains of enough joints to make up a few decent spliffs, but don't tell anyone that, they'll all want one.'

'No ancient Roman villas, then. Or hoards of civil war loot. Pity. Next time we should bring metal detectors along. But apart from that, nothing to do with the reason we're here?'

'The girl? No. Can't say that I find that surprising. I still think she's comfortably tucked up with some boyfriend her folks don't know about. Still, we have to do these things no matter what our instinct tells us. Coppers have been known to be wrong in the past.'

'No!' I exclaimed with a mock gasp, 'you're joking. A copper admitting he's been wrong?'

'Now I didn't say anything about admitting it, did I?'

'So what's the next step?'

'We'll be spending the afternoon going through the stuff from this morning. Then tomorrow we'll probably do the open area down by the allotments. You can bring your merry men along again, see if we can get the savings account up to twenty quid.'

'Will do,' I said, and he moved off with a half salute, as Jimmie came up with a couple of cups of tea.

'Where can we get a dozen metal detectors from, Jimmie?' I asked him.

'Feck?'

'Not to worry. Thought we might search for buried treasure while we're doing this. Ah, well, just a thought.'

'Feck,' commented Jimmie, kicking a muddy divot loose. He was right. Any buried treasure would have been found long ago.

People would have fallen over it while injecting themselves. Or doing something else. For which they had already fallen over.

I watched the others standing around, hands cupped around their plastic cups in front of their faces, watching, saying nothing, but looking quietly pleased with themselves. That is, to someone who knew what he was looking at. To normal people I suppose we looked like a bunch of depressed, suspicious and downright moody souls; certainly there were a few suspicious glances from some of the sanies, but I thought little of that.

I was happy enough. Especially when we made it back without losing anyone.

Thursday 8th August

Wall Street has closed higher, so they say. Traders are concerned that it might just be a "dead cat bounce", a phrase referring to the fact that even a dead cat dropped from high enough will bounce. What can you say about a group of people who can come up with such a phrase and think it suitable? Well, what polite thing can you say, apart from pointing out that they are a bunch of merchant bankers?

The Blairs have ended the British part of their holiday – being rained on in Cumbria – and have now moved on to the French part – staying at a wealthy friend's chateau. The bad news is that they're planning on coming back.

Keeping bad news to a minimum, around the world in brief: Saddam Hussein has given a defiant speech on television promising that Iraq would not bow to pressure from outside. In Bogota Alvaro Uribe has been sworn in as President of Colombia, amidst the sound of rebel mortars going off, at least 13 explosions. ("Could you keep the noise down, I'm trying to swear!") Talks on a truce in the Middle East have broken down.

More trouble in Zimbabwe as Mugabe continues to handle the drought crisis by taking farms off white farmers and giving them to his cronies. I don't know why this government dislike Mugabe, they've got so much in common. Oh, sorry, cancel that, when wealthy New Labour supporters give money to the party, and then suddenly receive government help or contracts, it's a total coincidence. My fault, I'd forgotten.

Locally the hunt goes on for the two ten year old girls missing in Cambridgeshire. The more time goes by without news the less hope there is.

House prices are still going up; an "average house" in England and Wales now costs £133,247, a rise of 13.5% over the year. House prices pop up in the news about once a week; in theory the bubble should have burst by now, as it did last time – resulting in a lot of "negative equity" (i.e. what you'd paid a fortune for a few months previously was now worth less than your entire mortgage, a chilling reminder of how these things rely on confidence) – but prices just keep increasing anyway. In certain areas, of course. You wouldn't get much for £133,247 in Kensington.

This whole world seems to run on confidence. If you could bottle it you'd make a fortune.

Wonder if that should be "£133,247.99"?

The International Monetary Fund has agreed to lend Brazil thirty billion dollars to cope with their current economic crisis, which should be sufficient for a small pad in Chelsea.

And finally a story to warm the cockles of Colin's mistrustful heart. The media's previous reluctance to explicitly state that the former chairman – chairperson? – of the Commission for Racial Equality, was fissed as a parrot when he assaulted a policeman has evaporated now that he pleaded guilty to being duurnk and dislorderly, and was so found by a court, and fined £500. He has now resigned his position on the CRE. However, what has many people not very happy is the £115,000 the Home Office paid him for leaving early. In other words, our money has been used to pay off someone for admitting assault while drunk. As a number of the papers have pointed out, this smacks of "one rule for them, another rule for us".

I'm reminded of the Post Office employee who was summarily fired because he was caught on camera during a punch up after a football game between Arsenal and Galatasaray in Denmark. He claimed self defence, he wasn't tried, nor found guilty of anything, but he was fired just the same, sans penny or payoff. His job was that of a counter clerk. Perhaps if he'd been chairman he could have claimed a bob or two.

The last I heard of the case was that an Industrial tribunal had found that he had been dismissed unfairly, but the post office – now renamed "Consignia" – had refused to accept the ruling.

We can only presume that the Commission for Racial Equality believe that some people are more equal than others.

211

And the next time Tony Blair and his sycophants bleat on about people not trusting politicians, they can think about that case.

I suppose the question is, at what point do people get tired of the lies they hear, and decide to evict the politicians?

The search group were quite chatty this morning when I walked out, or comparatively so. Periods of silence were broken by the occasional comment such as "those syringes, disgusting" followed by a "tsk, tsk" of disapproval. No mention of condoms, though. Just because you're mad doesn't mean you aren't middle class. The sun was shining, it was a glorious day, and everyone seemed to be living on the same planet. Until the sergeant from the pub turned up, with the usual WPC in tow. I saw them walking up from the gate, and wondered idly if maybe they had something going, they always appeared together. Without putting it too crudely, she was extremely attractive.

'Come to give us a personal escort?' asked Mrs Gladstone cheerfully as they came up. I could swear the others were almost smiling, an unusual event.

'Not quite, no,' said the sergeant pleasantly. 'I'm afraid the search is probably off for you today. We have what we call in the business, a situation. I need to speak to whoever's running this place, after which I'll get back to you. But don't go out, or anywhere near the gates for the moment.'

'Why ever not?' asked Mrs Gladstone. The others had crowded around, and the sergeant was beginning to look nervous.

'Nothing to worry about, just a very minor problem. A technical issue. Now if I could get through ...' A reluctant path was cleared for him and the WPC to get to reception, and we watched them enter the building with a rapidity which belied the sergeant's "nothing to worry about".

'What on earth is he talking about?' Mrs Gladstone demanded. 'Telling us we can't go near the gates. Who does he think he is?' No-one replied. We were all as confused as each other. An idea struck me.

'Wait here, you lot,' I told them. 'Jimmie, come with me.' I walked slowly down the long driveway towards the gates, Jimmie close on my heels, trying to see if I could make out what this "situation" was, without getting too close to it, just in case it was something unpleasant – a crocodile tied to the gates for instance. You never know.

Coming round the slight curve in the driveway I could see through the closed gates. There was a group of people on the far pavement, holding placards. I couldn't see what was written on them

'Can you read what's written on those placards?' I asked Jimmie next to me.

'One says "Perverts Out"' replied Miss Melly from behind my right shoulder, making me jump. I looked around to find everyone crowded immediately behind me.

I should have guessed that telling them to stay behind was a waste of breath.

'Perverts?' asked Mrs Gladstone. 'What are they talking about?'

'Some sort of demonstration, I would say,' Miss Melly replied. 'Can't see who they're protesting against. Maybe there's someone behind the wall.'

'Whoever it is, serves them right,' said the major fiercely. 'damn perverts ought to be shot. Would never allow anything like that in my command.'

A shout came from one of the demonstrators, something which sounded like 'There they are!', one of them pointing at the gates. The others broke into a chant, "Perverts out! Perverts out! Perverts out!"

'They seem to have seen whoever it is they're protesting against,' Miss Melly said, 'but I can't see who it is.'

'Perhaps we should join them,' suggested Mrs Gladstone. 'Show that we care too. We can spare half an hour, I'm sure.'

'I wouldn't protest, I'd horsewhip them,' the major blustered.

'Everybody come back to the building now,' said a voice behind us. It was Hotpants, looking irritated.

'If you could do as the doctor says,' suggested the sergeant alongside Hotpants.

'What's going on?' demanded Mrs Gladstone.

'We'll explain everything back inside,' promised the sergeant, who had moved with the WPC between us and the gate, and was in the process of herding us back towards reception. Hotpants' face suggested that he wasn't too interested in wasting his time explaining anything to patients.

'Those protestors,' I said as we walked back, 'they're protesting against this place, aren't they? Against us.'

'Don't be silly,' said Mrs Gladstone, 'what on earth would they have against us?'

'Ask the sergeant,' I suggested. The truth was in his face.

'They're calling me a pervert?' exclaimed Mrs Gladstone. 'By god I'll give them pervert!' She lifted her industrial strength walking stick threateningly, and made to turn around.

'Now, now, Mrs Gladsone,' I said, taking her arm. 'I'm sure it's all a misunderstanding, and the sergeant here is going to sort everything out as soon as he can, aren't you sergeant?'

'Of course. Nothing to get excited about, just a little misunderstanding.'

'And he's going to explain the misunderstanding to us now, aren't you sergeant?'

'Er, in a little while.'

'Now, before the ladies here take their walking sticks to have a word with the protestors down there.'

'Okay, okay.' He sighed.

He obviously wasn't having a good day.

'There was this article in the local paper a week or two ago which might have been interpreted to infer that – how shall I put this – certain, er, well, sexual therapies of a dubious nature were being practised here.'

'I read that!' Mrs Gladstone exclaimed in disgust. 'Load of rubbish. Journalists making trouble. If you read it properly you'll see that the miserable worm who wrote it didn't explicitly connect any of his fanciful imaginations with this clinic. All suggestion and smut, that's what it was.'

'Absolutely,' I said. 'The hack who wrote it should be locked up, making up stories like that. He must be pretty sick even to imagine the idea.'

Ever had that feeling that the stone you'd idly tossed up a hill was now heading back in your direction as an avalanche?

'Be that as it may,' the sergeant replied, 'I'm afraid those people out there have a different view of things, and until we can sort this mess out we need you to stay out of sight. We don't want any unfortunate incidents.'

Mrs Gladstone snorted. 'I'll give them an unfortunate incident. Why should we hide ourselves? They're the ones protesting, causing a disturbance.'

'Protestors, scum of the earth,' the major commented helpfully.

'I'm not asking you to hide yourselves, just to help us keep things under control. You see some of them have a theory that someone here is responsible for the disappearance of the missing girl, and there are rather wild ideas being passed around about breaking in to search for her.'

We had stopped outside the entrance to reception. We stood in a group, everyone looking bemused, apart from Hotpants, who was looking at his watch in irritation.

'I have much work to do. I can leave you to look after this situation, yes?' he asked the sergeant.

The sergeant looked a mite surprised. 'Er, yes, sir, I suppose – ' he began.

'Good,' said Hotpants, and promptly disappeared in the direction of his office. The sergeant stared after him in amazement, then around at us in trepidation.

'Okay,' he said finally, holding his hands up in surrender 'How do you want to play this?' I was surprised. With an approach like that he should have been chief inspector. Passing the buck on to others.

'We have a right to walk the streets without being intimidated,'

Mrs Gladstone declared, in a manner that suggested she wasn't quite likely to do be the one being intimidated. You wouldn't want to be caught in a narrow alley with Mrs G and her walking stick if she was in a bad mood.

'Precisely!' the major piped up, 'we do have rights. Those protestors should be locked up. And they should bring back National Service.'

Somehow I don't think the major will be terribly helpful in a crisis.

'Well, I'm afraid there's not much I can do about National Service,' the sergeant grinned ruefully, in his best lost-little-boy-look. He should have been an actor. 'I'm afraid the bottom line on this is that we can't do anything until we've had legal advice. The law about the right to protest is, well, maybe not a literal minefield, but it's not a bad description. And even when we get the go-ahead we don't have the people at the moment, they're all working on this missing girl case, you know? All I can do at the moment is try to keep things under control, and for that I need your help.' He looked at Mrs Gladstone's walking stick. 'If you were to go out and belt seven types of different hell out of them, well, it wouldn't help much, to be honest.' There was a silence as everyone digested this.

Quite neat, really. He had effectively told them that they were in control, to control them.

'Very well,' said Mrs Gladstone, 'twenty four hours then. And if they're still there we are going to teach them a lesson about civil liberties. Right now I could do with a cup of tea.' And she swept imperiously away, into reception and towards the day lounge, where tea was imminent. The others gave the sergeant a glare to indicate that they fully agreed, and also swept imperiously away, though for some it wasn't something they were used to. Most really.

Which left the sergeant, the WPC, myself and Jimmie. Jimmie was staying very close to me for some reason. I don't think he liked the police uniforms.

The sergeant took his cap off and wiped his brow. 'Close call, that,' he commented.

'So what now?' I asked. He paused and thought.

'Sounds like a really good time to have the flu,' he replied. 'But I believe that option is only open to senior officers.' He looked at the cap he was holding morosely. 'You tell me. I'm got nutters out there who want to come in here and take the place apart, and your lot in here who want to go out and take them apart. It isn't your average day-to-day event around here you know.' He sighed. 'In a funny way I'd like to see your lot – especially that old woman – give those idiots a good thumping.'

'You don't suppose that's what's called rather more information than we need to know?'

'Possibly. Strange that. For some reason I trust you. Why is that, do you suppose?'

'Genetically inherited naivety?' I suggested. He laughed.

'Growing too old, that's what it is. Look, I'll do you a deal. Keep them quiet and I'll try and sort out that lot down there.'

'And how do you propose to do that?'

'A special technique called boring them to death. Works most times. Come on Sandra.' He and the WPC called Sandra began to walk away.

I rubbed my jaw reflectively. I do this when my thought processes haven't caught up with reality. Normally you find a section where you haven't shaved properly, which makes you wonder how you missed it. A few thoughts later you've forgotten what the original question was.

'What do you reckon, Jimmie?' I asked.

'Feck,' he replied, after a pause for thought.

Obviously he had also shaved properly that morning.

Friday 9th August

Worldcon, the company famous for managing to misidentify billions of dollars as profit has discovered a further three billion that it accidentally put into the wrong column. This is the sort of thing that gives capitalism a bad name. However the stock markets in Asia and Wall Street have ignored this set back, and are continuing to climb slowly.

Apparently Saudi Arabian newspapers have stated that Christian fundamentalists are just as much of a danger to world peace as the Islamic brand. On one level you could argue that all fundamentalists are dangerous, on another that Christian fundamentalists haven't been spotted flying into buildings or blowing themselves up. The bottom line is that all religions contain fertile ground for maniacs. Ban religion and bring back hippiesm.

Only problem with that is that sinners will be flowered to death.

Most Christian clerics seem to be against the idea of invading Iraq, and the trade unions are reported to be allegedly planning to use upcoming party conferences to challenge any notion of an invasion. According to the press, the United States military aren't too much in love with the idea either. Saddam Hussein has chosen this moment to pour troubled waters on troubled waters by announcing that any attack will fail with many casualties amongst the attackers.

Three people have died after a grenade attack on a Christian missionary hospital in Pakistan.

It's being suggested that Mugabe is in hock to Gaddafi; Libya supplies most of Zimbabwe's fuel, and there are question marks over their ability to pay. One report states that the farms currently been stolen from white farmers may well end up being owned by Gaddafi. And while the drought continues in Southern Africa, more white farmers have been told to leave their farms without compensation. Most are staying on, hopeful that an appeal to the courts will be upheld.

The rains seem to have left us and headed for Russia, several areas of which have had flood alerts declared.

And the latest research discovery from the University of the Bleeding Obvious: bigger babies and those from "higher' social classes" do better in life. Just in case you thought been born healthy into a wealthy family was a setback in the great road of life. Our thanks go to the Institute of Child Health for this information, though what we really need is research that proves that people who pay a lot of money to a political party seem to do much better when that party is in power. Apparently, and I have this on the word of President Blair, money does not buy influence.

Danish premium coming in to land at runway five.

A rather strange day. Stranger than normal, anyway. At breakfast there was almost a palpable air of keyed up energy, with people still around who normally would have long finished by the time I turned up. Instead of the usual monastic silence there was a low hum of voices, and I caught phrases like "direct action", "if they won't do something about it we will" and "take the matter into our own hands".

I don't think I've ever seen such amounts of energy in this place.

After breakfast I went up to the second floor, from where you can get a view over the wall of the road down below, or at least of the opposite pavement where the protestors were. They were still there, about twenty or so, and though it was quite a way away, I'm sure I recognised many of them as people from the search party a couple of days ago. Strange, one day you're working side by side, the next they're at the front gates demanding our heads.

From the look of it they were settling in for the duration, sitting on camping stools, thermos flasks at their side; a very middle class, middle age protest. Vauxhalls to the left of them, Vauxhalls to the right, into the valley of insanity protested the twenty, maybe twenty-one ... Two policeman were standing in front of the gates, looking rather bored. Rather them than me. The protestors might look like they had come from a parent-teachers association meeting, but I wouldn't fancy having to face up to a gang of Marks and Spencers clad vigilantes if they turned nasty.

Most of the women carried handbags. I wondered if any of them had protested at Greenham Common when they were younger.

Probably not.

From there I wandered down to reception, where my presence was required as Anna Kay or Jenni Jay or whatever had decided that it was too dangerous to come to work while all those people were outside. They might have thrown a tea muffin at her.

There wasn't much to do, as hardly any visitors turned up. There was a small piece on the protestors on the local news this morning, and though it was pretty low key it probably put most people off. Wait until the national media get hold of this. The tabloids will have a field day.

So I was mildly surprised to see someone coming through the front doors, and even more surprised to find that it was Doctor Hamilton.

'Morning Doc,' I said cheerfully, finding that I was pleased to see him. After having to put up with Hotpants I think I'd be happy to see the Ayatollah Khomeini. 'Where have you been hiding? Coming back to save us all?'

'No, no, just have to see someone briefly. You're looking well. I would have thought you would have been out of here ages ago.'

'Three square meals and all my laundry done? You're joking, aren't you Doc. Only other place close to it is the army, and you wouldn't want to join them, they're mad. Make you do sit ups and press ups and run around the whole day.'

'Good to see you haven't lost your sense of humour. I hear you're planning on standing as mayor.'

Mayor? I wondered what he was on about. Then the penny dropped.

'Ah, yes, mayor. Well, I was thinking about it. The thing is, people don't really want a mayor. They'd rather the councillors do their job properly. And having a mayor will mean increasing council tax to pay for this mayor and all the staff he'll need, not to mention parties he'll be throwing for his buddies in government. So I'm pretty sure that I could run as mayor on the promise that I'll do nothing. I think it would be a real vote winner.'

'It certainly sounds possible. Apparently they voted a man in a monkey costume in as mayor in Hartlepool. So I'm told.'

'Precisely, that's what I've told the others, but they think it's a crazy idea. Doesn't make any difference, though. You need to put a five thousand pound deposit down, and there's no way I could find that sort of money. So there you go. They talk of democracy, but they make damn sure poor people can't get in.'

'Five thousand? Yes, that would be a lot. I might have an idea though.'

Someone ran past, holding their regulation top hat firmly on, which put the doc off his stride for a moment.

'Er, where was I? Yes, an idea. You see I have access to a fund, money from the EU, which is given for treatment – therapy, basically. Now I could probably get some of that if we say that your running for mayor is therapy. How does that sound?'

'My goodness, Doctor Hamilton, that is a generous offer,' said Ms D, who had appeared beside me miraculously, out of nowhere, in that rather unnerving way she has. Her voice was overflowing with that sickly sweetness that women use when they're taking the mickey. I wondered what I'd done to irritate her this time. Maybe having people jog through reception wearing top hats all the time was getting to her.

I might try to see if I can convince them that straw hats will be better. Boaters. There's something about boaters.

'Yes, yes,' the doc said in a strangely nervous tone. Probably the protestors outside had upset him, though I would have thought he'd be the last person to let such a thing affect his normally laid back approach. 'I'll get that organised then, shall I? Yes, I'll look into it straight away. Better be off then, quite a busy day ahead.' And with that he was out of the door.

'Have a nice day,' Ms D called after him in waves of syrup. Must be that time of the year, I decided, and resolved to keep my mouth shut as far as possible. 'Isn't that kind of him,' she cooed to me, and I carefully ran her words through my head to see which one was a verbal grenade which was about to explode if I reacted to it.

'Very kind,' I agreed finally, and quickly changed the subject. 'Tomorrow's Hotpants' great election day, isn't it?'

'It's Monday, and I'm sure you'll do very well.'

'Me? I'm not standing.'

'Your name's on the list, remember?'

'Well, yes, but that's just because everyone else's is. I'm pretty sure most people will get one vote each. They'll just see their name and presume that's what they have to tick.'

'Oh, I don't know, I think you'll be surprised at the result.'

With that she gave me an overly sweet smile and disappeared back into admin, as silently as she had appeared.

I must admit to a certain feeling of nervousness. People were acting very strangely, and I didn't like it.

The major claimed to have heard Kerry singing. "Something important is about to happen" he declared, my first thought being "Yes, I'm going to thump you sooner or later and you don't need Kerry to alert you to that". To my amazement, Mrs G, in hearing distance, had chimed in with "Yes, I heard her as well. Things are looking ominous".

Someone leaves their radio on and the next thing you know it's messages from the supernatural side.

It was with a sense of relief that I saw the sergeant and his sidekick Sandra come through the doors. At least these two were likely to act normally. I hoped so, anyway.

'Sergeant, good morning to you. And to you, constable. Have you come to let us know the latest details of the great protest rally of, or are you applying for a place here?'

The sergeant grinned, and even the WPC looked like she might have a little smile on her face.

'The second option sounds like a good idea,' said the sergeant, 'but at the moment I'm just checking on the situation. All seems to be nice and peaceful at the moment, fortunately.'

Mrs Perry jogged past wearing top hat and carrying a cane which looked like it had come out of the garden.

'Morning!' she called cheerfully, taking a swipe at the coffee machine as she passed it.

'Morning!' I called back, before continuing the conversation with the sergeant and WPC. They were looking a little bemused.

'So what's going to happen now?' I asked.

'Now? Er, now? Ah, the protest. Yes. Not much we can do really at this moment. Keep the situation under control, hopefully they'll get bored. Er, that was a woman in a dressing gown wearing a top hat who just ran through? Smacked that coffee machine with a stick?'

'I certainly hope so, otherwise I'd be imagining things. First sign of madness, you know, imagining things. Have you tried explaining to those people out there that that newspaper article is a load of cobblers?'

'Yes. A number of times. But they don't seem to believe us.'

'Bad sign when people won't believe the police. What will really sort them out is when you find Tamsin, I reckon.'

He brightened up. 'Ah, now that's the crucial thing. And we've got a little lead on that. Keep it under your hat, but we're following up a suggestion that she might have disappeared with her boyfriend, bloke from the estate down the road. Her father swears blind that she would never go out with someone from there, but we've been getting hints which say otherwise. Although getting information out of the estate lot is like having a chat with a silent monk. And even then, they're the sort of people, if they give you the time of the day you can be sure it's been nicked from somewhere. Still, we're making progress.'

I could hear a slow 'clip-clip' sound approaching, as if someone were walking very slowly in high heels.

'So where is this boyfriend?'

'Nobody knows. Disappeared about the same time as the girl. Gone away on holiday, apparently.'

'Helloooo,' came a voice from the entrance to the left hand corridor, as the prof appearing, on stilts, the smile on his face freezing as he saw the police. 'Hellooo and goodbyeee,' he continued, making an abrupt about turn and heading rapidly from whence he had come. Quite impressive, for a man new to stilts.

'A bloke wearing top hat and tails on stilts?' asked the sergeant in disbelief.

'That's the way I see it,' I replied. Suddenly he clicked his fingers. 'The professor!' he exclaimed.

'You know him?'

'Not personally. But word gets around in the force. He got out of a jail sentence by appearing to be insane. Claimed he was trying to introduce quality control into crime, amongst other things.'

'Well, playing an organ in the middle of the night during a robbery isn't exactly the height of level headedness, is it? If that story's true.'

'Oh it's true all right. What the judge didn't know at the time – and we haven't been able to prove fully – are the three times he broke into various places through tunnels. The seven times he lifted jewellery from hotels by pretending to be a porter. The two times, at least, when he was short of cash and went through a train claiming to be a ticket inspector, and took ten quid fines off those who hadn't valid tickets. And the plans we discovered in his mansion to paraglide on to the millennium dome to lift some diamonds on display. Some other lot got there first, though.'

'Mansion? Tunnels? Funny, he hasn't mentioned those.'

'Well, he wouldn't, would he? Hasn't been done for them. He's not stupid; careless talk costs a real jail sentence. Still, at least he's value for money. Most of the buggers we nick are thick as planks. The prof's got style.' He sighed at the lack of quality criminals. 'Ah, well, must be off. Check on the Ikea protestors.'

'You don't want to see anyone in charge? Keep the doctors up to date?'

'No thanks. That Doctor Sniffle watsis gives me the creeps. Something funny about his eyes – you know, I'm sure I've seen him before somewhere. He's not famous for anything is he? Been on telly or something?'

'Not that I'm aware of, but it's possible. I wouldn't worry too much about him. All he thinks about is what he calls his research, which is a polite term for seeing whether he can come up with theories which are even more weird and wonderful than anyone else's weird and wonderful theories. Reality is just an irritating interruption to his life's work.'

'Sounds a bit of a nutter. Tell me, are there any normal people around here?'

'Well, the groundsman is pretty normal considering his situation.'

'And what situation's that?'

'He died two years ago.'

The sergeant rolled his eyes. 'Come on, Sandra,' he said, 'let's go see the loonies on the outside.'

I watched them go, idly wondering whether there was something we could put the prof's talents to. He must be pretty bored here. Unless he's busy digging a tunnel.

Must be difficult digging a tunnel when you're stuck in the trees the whole day though.

Someone ran through reception, giving the coffee machine a good whack with their top hat.

I think the peasants are revolting.

Saturday 10th August

Most of the media are concentrating on the search for the two girls missing up North. The police are working on the theory that they're still alive, but that seems unlikely.

Apart from that, being a Saturday, they fill the papers full of stories of things which may well be a week old, but presented as if they happened yesterday.

Such as the story that New York has agreed, for the minute, not to clamp cars with diplomatic plates. Apparently they're got so tired of diplomats who park illegally and don't pay their fines, they were planning to take the cars hostage. Egypt is supposedly the front runner, owing one million six hundred thousand dollars in unpaid traffic fines. You can see how that might upset the locals. On the other hand this is said to be a regular story, and has been going on for decades.

ETA exploded a bomb last night in the tourist resort of Torrevieja.

Iraq gets a few mentions, mainly along with the word "war", as does Israel.

The good news – depending on your point of view – is that today is the start of the football season. Some may feel that this is very bad news indeed.

Further in sport, this time rugby (union): a suicidal South African spectator ran onto the pitch during a game between New Zealand and South Africa in Durban and attacked the referee. The spectator was forty-six and overweight. The two rugby teams who, er, chastised him, weren't.

And a truly "warms the cockles of your heart" story: Leina, a three-year-old German girl, miraculously escaped death when she fell from her parents' car as it was moving at seventy miles an hour on a motorway in France. Nicolas Laberthonniere, a French lorry driver behind the parents' car, noticed what had happened, and managed to bring his vehicle to a stop just metres away from the child. Then he and a fellow trucker used their vehicles to block the motorway, until the paramedics could arrive. Young Leina has survived with only burns and bruises.

Nice to see some good news. I hope no-one mentioned the war.

A hot, humid, muggy day. The energy levels are definitely down on yesterday – there was a piece on the local news this morning which raised only a few jeers, though admittedly the way it was presented did rather take the mickey out of the protestors.

They had some local pompous ass with balding head and a grey moustache ranting on about how they would "stay here until the government meets our demands, every second of every minute of every hour of every day of the year" – he had to pause for breath a couple of times – "come rain or shine, winter or snow" – I liked that bit, snow isn't unknown during summer – "until this den of iniquity is closed down for good".

Just in case they closed it down temporarily, and then, while no-one was looking, whipped in a couple of fruitcakes undercover.

I admit I was intrigued by their placards. In this day and age you would have thought they could have organised some professionally printed A3 size sheets, but they had opted for the handwritten approach, and some of the handwriting wasn't exactly from an arts college. Perhaps it's some form of chic; I've never understood fashion.

The sentiments written on the placards were pretty unimaginative, though. "Perverts Out", "Paedophiles Out" and "Bring back the death penalty" were the only three variations, and since there were about two placards to each protestor it did come across as rather boring repetition. I had an urge to pop across and offer some more varied suggestions about what they could do with them.

Funny how every time the cameras turn up the banner brigade are shouting and enthusiastic, yet otherwise they just sit there and drink tea. Doctor's orders I suppose. Might get a hernia otherwise. "Mrs Jones, you can only do ten minutes of loud shouting today, otherwise I cannot be responsible for your health. And be careful of your bunions."

Spent the rest of the morning sitting outside in the shade with Colin and Jimmie. Colin is rather irritated at the moment; he doesn't go out there to bother anyone, and doesn't like it when people out there try to come in to bother him, which seems a reasonable idea. Jimmie appears to be more keyed up than normal, but you'd have to know him to appreciate it. He still lies back in his deck chair with a cap across his face, but if you pay attention you can see his eyes roving around every so often. And his posture is much more tense.

On the other hand, maybe we're just all more alert to these things. The prof seems happy enough in his favourite tree. Some day I must find out why he prefers that tree.

After lunch I decided I'd had enough of been cooped inside, and slipped down the pub, looking forward to a couple of quiet pints exchanging repartee with Pete. Well, as far as is possible under the current circumstances. I worked on the premise that Pete is a pretty straight-forward sort of bloke, and wouldn't be influenced by the current nonsense going on.

Apart from having a missing daughter.

I used a little gate at the back of this place which comes in handy when you don't want to casually stroll out in front of a group of people who apparently want you immediately terminated with extreme prejudice. I don't normally resort to this option – it isn't often that the enemy are at the gates, so to say – and I noticed, in that sort of half conscious way you do, that the path looked a lot more trodden than it used to be. I half wondered who had been using it, but dismissed the thought.

At the end, for a few yards, the path brings you out at a point still just in view of the protestors, and I wasn't overly anxious to meet them. When I reached the point of exposure I checked carefully to ensure that no-one was looking my way. Indeed, no-one was. There was no-one at the protest point.

I checked once, twice, three times. Not a hide nor a hair.

Emboldened by this obvious surrender and retreat, I went on my way with a whistle and a jaunty walk. The only obvious answer was that they had seen the media coverage of their protest, and had capitulated in the face of derision.

Thus ignoring the well known fact that people only ever see what they want to see.

I strolled into the pub, and sat on my usual stool at the end of the bar. Pete came up with an anxious look on his face.

'Are you mad?' he whispered in a mixture of anger and frustration. I contemplated the point for a few moments.

'Yes,' I said finally. 'And now, I shall order a pint of that rather disgusting ale you force on an gullible public at extortionate prices.'

'Damn you. Do you know who those people are?' He half gestured at a group of people sitting at the tables at the other end of the pub. I took a good look at them.

'No, fraid not. Celebrities? They look a bit old for that? Conservative Youth Group?'

'They're the protestors from down the road. Your place. There'll be murder in here if they find out who you are.'

'Protestors? They don't look like protestors. No banners, for a start.'

'I made them leave them in the gents. Place was beginning to look like a scene from the Russian revolution. You've got to leave.'

'Not at all, dear landlord. As you said, they don't know who I am, do they?'

'Yes, but, if they find out – '

'Which they won't. I'm just a – let's say I'm just a plumber from the local estate. They won't talk to me then. And I'm still waiting for that pint.'

He stared at me in an agony of indecision before reaching for a pint glass and beginning to pull.

'No normal person would believe that a plumber would live on that estate. Not with the money they charge. Then again, that lot aren't exactly normal. Daft as brushes, they are. If you listen to them you'd think they were involved in planning Operation Desert Storm. Don't think I've ever heard the word "logistics" used so often.'

'Logistics as in who's going to supply the tea and sandwiches?'

'That's about it.'

'What about strategy?'

'Oh, yes, strategy is another one. They've got more strategies than a battalion of generals.'

'Well, you need strategy. Otherwise the tea and sandwiches might end up in the wrong hands.'

'Or the wrong person will get the cheese and ham.'

'Could be dangerous. Give a vegetarian the cheese and ham and you could have a situation on your hands. Next thing you know it's invading Poland time again.'

He laughed. 'You're a daft beggar. How are things in the nut house?'

I described how everyone was getting worked up, and we chatted about how strange things had worked out. I asked him how things were going with him and his family, and he admitted to being tired with lack of sleep, but said he wasn't feeling as depressed as before, as the police had more or less convinced him that Tamsin had run away, and was bound to reappear once the novelty had worn off.

I decided not to pursue any discussion of teenagers living on the streets of London. It didn't seem a good topic to bring up under the circumstances.

During a break while Pete was looking after another customer I left the bar to attend the call of nature. It was while washing my hands afterwards that I noticed the placards stacked in the far corner, and remembered that Pete had ordered them here to avoid the "Russian Revolution" look. I wondered whether a revolution theme might not be an idea for bringing in trade, but I suppose mixing anarchists and alcohol probably isn't the best of combinations.

Idly I wandered over to inspect their handiwork. It was hardly what you'd call professional; two sheets of A3 stapled together at the corners, a estate agent type pole shoved between the sheets, front sheet stapled to the pole. And the handwritten message using a marker pen of some sort. Protestors around the world must have been hanging their heads in shame. Even the Civil Rights bunch in the Sixties were better than this, and they didn't have modern computers and printers at home.

It wasn't until I was back on my barstool and halfway through the second pint that the idea came to me. Or maybe it had slowly matured over half a pint.

'Say, Pete, you haven't got a marker pen I could borrow, by any chance?' I asked when he next came in range.

'Marker pen? I think there's one somewhere around here.' He fished around in a large mug of assorted objects. 'Here we are – black okay?'

'Black will be just fine. How about a stapler?'

'A stapler? What on earth do you want a stapler for?'

I tapped the side of my nose. 'Ask no questions, get no lies,' I told him. He shrugged, and turned to search a drawer behind him. Finally he came up with a heavy looking stapler, which was ideal.

'Very kind, Pete, I'll return them to you before I leave,' I said, and slipped them into my jacket pocket. I think Pete was about to ask some awkward question, but fortunately a customer came up to the bar to order a round. Even better, it was one of our friends from the tables of protestors.

'Ere, you one of them protestors, aren't you?' I asked, laying on the accent with a trowel. The other man looked at me suspiciously, and nodded. I could see Pete close his eyes in disbelief. It's amazing what you'll try after a couple of pints of that ale.

'Saw you on the telly, this morning,' I continued. The man almost blushed with pride.

'One tries to do one's bit,' he said modestly.

'Bloody right too. But you know what your problem is, doncha?'

'Problem?'

'Organisation, mate. Leadership. That bloke this morning, him with the moustache, not very good on the telly, was he?'

'Well, I hadn't thought about that, really ...'

Maybe not, but you're going to start thinking about it now, I thought. I drained my pint.

'These days you gotta have the right people in control, know what I mean? Proper leaders, not some committee sort of thing.' I nodded emphatically, and left to go back to the gents. I'm pretty confident that dropping words like "leadership" into a group of people like that will result in quite a few petty feuds which should last a couple of generations.

Never mind the arguments over who should talk to the television cameras.

Once back in the gents I carefully pulled out three of the placards from the centre of the stack, and locked myself into a cubicle. What I was about to do relies on human nature; people tend to see what they think should be there, not what is.

I quickly pulled the staples holding the A3 sheets together out, reversed the sheet with the blank side out, and restapled them. Then I wrote new messages with the marker pen, being careful to match the size and style of the original. The first was easy: "Prevets out!!!" I wrote. Even if they did glance at the writing they'd unconsciously correct the spelling. The second was no problem either: "Bring back the deaf penalty!!!". The third was probably a result of a couple of pints of ale. "My aunty shags fishies!!!" didn't match anything in their arsenal of demands, not even closely. But what the hell. You have to take a chance sometime.

No-one had come in while I was busy, and I unlocked the cubicle door and quickly put the redesigned placards back in the middle of the others. Outside the gents I picked up the public telephone in the passage, and fished out Carney's card from my wallet. Handkerchief over the mouthpiece, I dialled his mobile number. He answered within two rings.

'If you want a story get yourself down to where they're protesting outside the clinic,' I told him, 'and take a camera with. Television camera be even better. Be patient, you may need to wait awhile.'

'What? Who is this? What are they doing?'

'And did you know one of the loonies is standing for mayor?' I added for good effect, in a cross between accents. I really must be careful; running for mayor could be hard work.

I'll need a really good excuse to get out of it.

I put the phone back on the hook, and slipped out of the side door, walking briskly back.

If Carney did as he was told he would get there to find out that "every second of every minute" etc etc didn't include time out down the pub. And with a little luck they would turn up lugging their placards to find the press waiting, and be in too much of a rush to get the things staked out to notice the improvements I had made.

But just in case they were more alert than I thought, I made sure I was out of sight as soon as possible. People can be quite unpredictable sometimes.

I had intended taking a grandstand view of the proceedings from the second floor, but decided that I would wait until I heard their approaching voices. I went back to my bedroom, opened the window wide, and lay on the bed listening.

And fell asleep.

Possibly they had turned up, and their voices didn't carry as far as I had thought, but it seemed an awful long time, and the day was even hotter and muggier than before, and one minute I was awake and alert, and the next I was in the land of nod for a couple of hours.

I awoke about half an hour before supper, threw some cold water on my face to shake myself out of it, and stumbled up to the second floor. The protestors had returned at some stage, but were reduced to about twelve, and there appeared to be three different groups, judging by their body language, but apart from that there wasn't much going on, so I wandered back down to the meal room. Almost all the residents were already there, watching television and waiting for din-dins.

'Come to watch the latest news?' enquired Colin as I sat down.

'News? Oh, yes, see what the latest score is.' I'd forgotten that there was a local news slot early evening Saturdays. I sat back and concentrated on the television.

'Protestors nil, residents nil,' Colin replied.

'I blame the referee, personally. What's this rubbish on now?'

A couple of people turned and shushed us vehemently. Obediently we put a finger over our lips and sat in silence until the rubbish ended and the new began with the rather silly intro they've come up with. It's supposed to be "modern", to attract younger people. You'd expect the BBC of all people to realise that news can never be "modern"; it's facts, and the minute you start trying to jazz it up you're colouring the facts and turning it into show business. "Dumbing down", I believe the phrase is.

But there you go. Can't trust anybody these days.

God, I do sound like Colin, don't I?

'Good evening,' said the presenter, 'tonight we bring you the latest on the nutty protestors, as they have become known.' Cue loud music as emphasis for something or other. 'This afternoon local journalist John Cardy discovered that the protestors' promise to maintain their vigil without break does not hold true when the pub is calling.' On came a clip showing the deserted protest site, with the protestors appearing in the distance towards the end. A few jeers came from our audience.

'On top of this, there appears to be a power struggle amongst the group.' Now it was a clip of two red faced men jostling each other to stay in the camera's view, moustache man from the morning, and my friend from the pub.

'... a planning meeting, essential to the organisation ...' moustache man was trying to say in a breathless voice.

'... delineation of responsibilities and important questions of command ... ' hoarsed his opponent.

'And it appears that some protestors might not be taking the effort seriously. While one can excuse a spelling mistake ... ' – cue a shot of a placard saying "Prevets Out!!!" – ' ... another message could be regarded as a disturbing result of the subconscious ...' – cue a shot of a gentleman holding up "Bring back the deaf penalty!!!" -'... and there are some things about people's family life which we really do not need to know', and the camera zoomed in on a raucous middle aged man whose message to the nation was "My aunty shags fishies!!!".

I didn't catch the next bit. Our audience were clapping and shouting, and there were even a couple of whistles. There were comments which, in present company, would normally be regarded as "unprintable". I looked at Colin. His face was beaming. And then a hint of amused suspicion entered his eyes.

'You have a smirk on your face,' he pointed out.

'You have a bloody big smile on yours,' I replied.

'You had something to do with that, didn't you?'

'Now you wouldn't want me to lie, would you?'

'Of course not.'

'Good, then I won't,' I said, turning back towards the screen.

There wasn't much else on the news, or little that interested us, apart from a promise of even hotter weather tomorrow. A few minutes after it finished Tonique appeared next to me.

'There's a telephone call for you. In reception,' she said.

'Me? You sure?' She nodded.

'In reception,' she repeated, and walked away. I stood up, puzzled, and made my way to reception. I spotted the receiver lying next to its base in the half light that they leave on when no one is on duty, and picked it up.

'Hello?' I said, in an enquiring tone.

'I've been watching the news,' said a low, husky voice. Female, so not Carney.

'I see,' I said after a pause. I'm not terribly good at speaking to anonymous women over the phone. With husky voices. Which sounded like they'd being enjoying a pre-dinner aperitif. Or two.

'So how did you manage that one?' she asked.

'Me? How do you mean?'

'You're not going to deny that you had something to do with it? I thought it was rather good.' Suddenly I recognised the voice.

'Ms D!' I exclaimed. 'Er, how are you?'

'Very well, thank you. And it's Fi when I'm off duty. Short for Fiona. "Ms D" sounds terrible at the best of times.'

'Ah, yes, um, of course, absolutely. Lovely name, that, Fi, that is.'

Well, what could I say?

'So you're denying any involvement at all, then?' she asked.

'I think I might have to take the fifth amendment.'

'Pity. I'd love to hear the story. I'll see you on Monday. And the fifth amendment doesn't apply here. Only in the States.' There was a click, and then the dialling tone.

I put the phone down, feeling a little surprised, and also somewhat pleased, for some strange reason. For one thing, I suppose, the protestors might be able to get over a little infighting, but I can't see them returning after their friends and neighbours have videod the late news for repeated enjoyment.

And someone's aunt is going to be very, very angry with them. The fishies probably won't be overly happy either.

Chapter 4: Sunday night, Monday morning

One thirty, Sunday morning.

Same planet I think possibly same year. Whatever.

Woken up by some explosions about an hour ago. Shouting and yelling coming from the road. Went to reception to find out what was happening. Joined by some of the others who don't take sleeping tablets. Sirens after a while, at least two or three cop cars. Some policeman finally turned up to find out if we were all okay. Turns out that there were still a couple of protestors, joined by a bunch of young blokes from the estate who had just been chucked out of their drinking hole at closing time – must have been past closing time. Turned up with firecrackers and started throwing them over the wall. Shouting that they'd burn the place down. Coppers collared a couple when they turned up, but most got away. Apparently the remaining protestors were quite shaken up. Maybe now they'll piss off and leave us alone.

Bill Dughaille

Sunday 11th August

The Earth Summit is due to start in Johannesburg shortly. Michael Meacher, the UK environment minister, has been in the news recently, partly for suggesting that the UK government is not environmentally aware as it should be, and partly because he was allegedly dropped from the party due to go the Earth Summit. Apparently the government didn't want anyone to think it was just a junket for hundreds of politicians and assistants, so they dropped the minister for the environment, arguably the one person who ought to have gone.

Various environmental organisations have offered to pay for Mr Meacher's ticket, resulting in a government decision to take him after all. The end result of the brouhaha being that most people now presume that the Earth Summit is a junket which doesn't even require the presence of the environment minister.

Most heads of government will be at the Earth Summit, the main aim of which is to concentrate on "sustainable development", especially in "developing countries". One who won't be is George W Bush, who has more important things to concentrate on, such as planning a sustainable invasion of Iraq.

Either that or he doesn't know where Johannesburg is.

I think there's one in Arkansaw. That may have confused him.

In the continuing war on terrorism, news has emerged that Iran has handed over members of al-Qaeda to Saudi Arabia. On the surface this could look confusing: Iran is one of the countries Georgie Bush (Jnr) has accused of being a member of 'the axis of evil'. Saudi Arabia is of course a dear friend of the US. However most senior al-Qaeda members come from Saudi Arabia, most notably bin laden. And the exchange took place back in June, so it has to be asked why this has suddenly become news.

The US has played the whole issue down; you can't help wondering whether the "war on terrorism" is just an excuse to settle old scores.

Speaking of old scores, a long-standing family feud in Egypt has left 22 members of a family dead, shot by a rival family. The victims were on their way to attend the trial of two of their family members who were accused of killing one of the rival family members earlier this year, in revenge for one of their own who had been murdered – eleven years ago.

A comment made by the BBC was "blood feuds and honour killings are common in parts of the Arab world".

No shit.

Over here another good old "political correctness" story has been uncovered by our journalist bloodhounds: the story goes that the Metropolitan Police Force is going to drop the crown from their badge because it has a cross on top, which might offend some Muslims. There's the usual outrage, and already a Tory politician has been wheeled out to splutter about "political correctness gone mad". The fact that the politician quoted is from the Greater London Authority rather than the main Tory party gives an indication that this is the standard August-no-news-so-let's-create-some part of the year.

Or maybe it's a smokescreen for another little story; while the peasants have to struggle with outdated, overloaded and dirty commuter systems, special trains are being laid on for delegates to the New Labour conference in Blackpool. The supplying company has denied that it is granting any special favours, as it is doing the same for the Tory and Liberal conferences – which is probably why those parties are keeping stum – quietly ignoring the fact that they are only doing this for politicians. Their main "customers", your normal commuters, mustn't expect any special favours, a half decent commuter service for example.

After all, if the politicians had to use the same services as the peasants we might find the services suddenly improve rather radically, which would require both the politicos and the transport companies to do their jobs properly, and you wouldn't want that, would you?

In Munich a commemoration service has taken place for the

Israeli athletes who were murdered at the Olympics in September 1972 by the Palestinian group Black September. Yesterday an Israeli and a Palestinian died after an attack on "a Jewish settlement".

And finally the weather: Russia, Central and Eastern Europe, and China; floods. Vietnam; floods and drought. Other areas of south and east Asia, Southern Africa, South and North America: drought. The conditions are attributed to the "El Nino" effect, and are said not to be as bad as the last time El Nino surfaced, four years ago, which probably isn't much comfort to those affected.

There are claims by some scientists that it is related to global warming, something which isn't extremely helpful either, since most people's eyes glaze over at the mention of the phrase – they've just heard two many prophets wildly exaggerating both for and against the concept to be bothered anymore.

Woke up this morning wondering if I'd dreamt what had happened in the early hours of the morning. Caught the early morning news, and there was mention of some "drunken youths" from the local estate throwing firecrackers over the wall, so it wasn't just a dream – though it sounds more harmless than I remember. "Firecrackers" sound like little things that make a small cracking noise; what I remember is massive explosions and lights in the sky. Possibly a result of waking up to the sound of them.

It was a bit surreal, thinking back on it. A group of us in the darkened reception looking out, trying to make sense of what was happening. Mrs Gladstone and Miss Melly in their dressing gowns, hobnailed boots on feet, heavy walking sticks in hand, and a seriously not very happy expression on their faces. And they weren't the only ones; the major was carrying a rather evil looking length of piping, and several others were carrying sticks, bits of rail, and various assorted implements which under different circumstances might be considered quite innocent, but not last night.

One old dear even had an iron, which she dangled from its cord. I wouldn't like to get caught by that if she started whirling it around her head.

Another group were standing in the passages, unwilling to get to close to the mind-reading coffee machine. I wasn't aware of them at first, until Mrs Gladstone said something about "doing something about this", and a murmur of agreement came from the darkened passages. Occasional light was reflected off our faces as the firecrackers went off – it was like some scene from a weird movie.

One of those French ones with subtitles.

You have to give the protestors some due – there were still about five of them out there this morning. You'd think they'd have given up by now. Not only lampooned in the local media, but having their night time vigil invaded by a bunch of drunken yobbos should put anyone off, but not them. Tenacious, that's the word.

Stupid, but tenacious.

While most of central Europe seems to be suffering from the worst floods in a century, the weather here is almost perfect, possibly just a touch too warm. Colin, Jimmie and I took our usual place in the gardens, along with the monstrosities called the Sunday newspapers. Half a Norwegian forest per copy.

We were thus ensconced, a scene a million miles from the night's madness, when my friend the sergeant turned up with PC Sandra.

'Battle of Britain,' he said. 'It's 1940 and the fighter pilots relax in their deckchairs as they wait for the Hun to appear. All you're missing is the gramophone playing We'll Meet Again.'

'More like Dad's Army, I would have thought,' I replied. 'What's happening down there this morning? Don't those people know when to give up?'

'Doesn't look like it, does it? I heard about what happened last night – they tell me your lot were all ready to go into battle armed with pikes and axes.'

'Well, I didn't notice any pikes or axes, but if that lot down there know what's good for them they'll stay on their side of the wall. Tell them, if they're not careful, we'll set the vampires on them.'

'Vampires, eh? I would have thought zombies would have been more appropriate.'

'Oh, zombies, no problem. We can do you a good deal on zombies at the moment. Hundreds of them. All man-eating. Nothing can stop them, not even holy water.'

He chuckled. 'Okay, I'll pass that information on. With that lot, who knows, they might even believe it.'

He and the young Sandra went off to alert the few remaining protestors of their dangerous predicament, and Colin tut-tutted.

'Zombies, really! You don't seem to realise that some people will actually believe things like that.'

'Ah, yes, but only the stupid ones,' I replied.

'Those are the ones we have to be afraid of,' he replied, and buried his nose in his newspaper.

Shortly before we adjourned for lunch the Sergeant turned up again, a broad grin on his face.

'You'll be happy to know that the siege is at an end. Protestors all gone home, and everything back to normal.'

'How'd you manage that?' I asked, 'Turn the water hoses on them?'

'Nope. We found dear little Tamsin. And her boyfriend. And a rather large amount of naughty and illegal tobacco, otherwise known as cannabis, amongst other names. Though when I say "we", I should point out that I am referring to our friends in Customs and Excise at Dover. The two tearaways were just coming back from a little holiday on the continent. They don't appear to have realised that every copper in the South East was on the look out for the dear girl.'

'Well, I suppose that's what you'd call good news. Possibly not for them, though. How's Pete taking it?'

'Apparently his initial relief has been replaced with a certain determination to commit murder, firstly of the boyfriend, and then probably his daughter. Fortunately they're still locked up at Dover, otherwise I wouldn't like to lay any bets on their immediate future. But I did have the immense pleasure of letting the loonies over the fence know, and they appear to have decided that they're probably on a hiding to nothing. Carrying on a protest when your original reason for the protest turns out to be a drug smuggler doesn't appeal to them.'

I sighed. 'These middle class people, just aren't what they used to be, are they? No staying power these days.'

'Thank god for that,' he replied. 'Should be able to get home for a quick pint and a late Sunday lunch now. Didn't think I was going to see home at all this weekend. Well, I'd love to stay and chat, but that pint is calling.'

Rather an anti-climax, I thought. A peaceful summer Sunday's afternoon, the sun blazing overhead – I could almost hear crickets chirruping, and the low sounds of a lazy river slowly flowing by.

As the nearest river is a mile away this would suggest incredibly good hearing, but it was that sort of an afternoon.

And there were strawberries and cream for dessert.

You know, that Kerry should stick to library books.

Monday 12th August

The sky was beginning to lighten this morning when Ms D turned up. I was leaning against a police car, face streaked with the black from smoke, cigarette in hand, trying to decide whether I looked more like Clint Eastwood or Charles Bronson. Maybe Indiana Jones.

Pity I didn't have one of those hats they wear, the old beaten up ones which always seem to retain some style, no matter what they go through. Trouble is, whenever I wear a hat it looks like a reject from Oxfam, no matter how new it might be.

'You okay?' she asked, and I could swear she actually sounded concerned. Time to take as much advantage as possible, it doesn't happen very often.

'Sure am,' I drawled, and took a long puff on the cigarette. She patted me on the back as I broke into a bout of violent coughing.

'I didn't know you smoked,' she said.'

'Gave it up years ago,' I gasped, 'last night seemed like a good night to start again. Everything else was doing it.'

'So I see.' She looked around. The fire brigade had done their business, but it seemed you could still see palls of smoke here and there in the early morning light. Very early morning light.

'So, are you going to tell me what happened?'

'It's a long story,' I said, after thinking for a while.

'It's going to be a long day. So I've got the time,' she replied.

So I told her what had happened. Or most of it. Leaving out names and places to protect the guilty involved. And any minor details which might have got in the way of an understanding of the overall picture.

Or might have incriminated innocent people merely trying to defend themselves.

What actually happened started about midnight last night. Or midnight this morning. Whichever.

Seems like a different age.

Everyone was abed, with the lights long switched off. The evening news had carried an item on the arrest of Tamsin and her boyfriend, along with a shot of the protestor-less road outside, and there was a general feeling of security, a feeling that the story was over and we had won. There were even some suggestions of regret that an opportunity had been missed to "teach them a lesson or two" – of the "if you hadn't held me back I would have thumped him" variety.

It was probably the sound of cars racing along the road which first woke me. I would have turned over and gone back to sleep, but the growl of revving engines, screeching of brakes and screaming of tyres continued, as if they were using the road as a racetrack. Then came the sound of drunken voices shouting threats.

I couldn't tell what they were saying, but they weren't there to sing Happy Birthday to anyone.

I slipped on some trainers and hurried up to the second floor for a better view. In the rather dim streetlight, and in car lights, I could work out that there seemed to be about five cars in the road below, one monotonously racing down the road for about a hundred yards, doing a handbrake turn, racing back for another handbrake turn, and endlessly repeating the exercise. Around twenty drunken yobbos hung around the other cars, cheering the driver on, drinking from tins and bottles.

As I stood watching in the darkness Colin and Jimmie came hurrying up. My attention was diverted somewhat by their dress. Jimmie was wearing t-shirt, trainers and shorts, pretty much the same as I was, whereas Colin was impeccably attired in slippers, pyjamas, and dressing gown with one of those funny cord things as a belt.

He reminded me of a sort of English Hercule Poirot.

'What's going on?' asked Colin breathlessly.

'Boy racers just out of the pubs, I reckon,' I replied. There was a rattle of hobnail boots and Mrs Gladstone and Miss Melly joined us, carrying their extra-strength walking-cum-battle-sticks. I wondered for a moment if we would ever get back to normal at some stage, or whether we should organise things properly, and have everyone out each day, drilling and learning basic military concepts in the use of bludgeonware.

'Can't have just got out of the pubs,' said Mrs Gladstone, 'they would have shut ages ago.'

'Not the one on the edge of the estate – the Nag's Head or whatever it's called. They don't believe in normal opening hours.'

'Can't say I've had the pleasure. Bit of a dive, is it?'

'You could say so. Sort of spit and sawdust, without the sawdust. I made the mistake of popping in there once. Not what you might call a welcoming place. And the beer's probably been banned under several Geneva Conventions.'

'Hello, what's going on now?' asked Colin. Somewhere someone in the building had unwisely switched on a light, and it had attracted the attention of the yobbos in the road. They crowded the gates, shouting and waving their fists, apart from one who was relieving himself against one of the cars, and another who was lighting something. The second threw whatever it was over the wall, and we could see a trail of sparks flying through the air. It landed on the lawn, and blew up with an impressive bang.

'Right, down to reception,' ordered Mrs Gladstone, 'the others will be there. Time to prepare to repel boarders!'

We followed her and Miss Melly down the stairs, and I must admit to a certain feeling of trepidation. Standing on the second floor with a squad of trained riflemen picking off targets at a distance would have been acceptable, but down in reception, surrounded by untrained madmen – and women – waving dangerous looking implements, and being unable to even see as far as the gate, things seemed a little more dodgy.

I tried not to think of Rorke's Drift.

I don't look the slightest like Michael Caine.

Besides which I normally get the part of the bloke who ends up as an assegai cushion.

'Has anyone called the police?' I asked, thinking it might be a good idea to hand this over to professionals who are paid to be insulted and assaulted. I'm not racist, but boozed up, drugged up young louts with half a brain cell to share amongst each other aren't my favourite type of people.

'Police? Nonsense. We'll sort these thugs out,' replied the major, adopting a bellicose stance in a light blue silk dressing gown with navy piping on the edges.

'Be fair,' I said, 'you have to give the idiots a chance to surrender. Standard military practice.'

'I'll do it,' said Miss Melly with a certain irritation, and pushed her way through to the reception counter where the phone lay.

'Military practice!' exclaimed the major. 'Exactly. We need to split up into units. Platoons with platoon commanders.'

My head reeled somewhat. 'So you can take a platoon round the side and hit them in the flank?' I asked sarcastically. In the semi darkness I could almost see his face beam.

'Excellent idea! Excellent idea! Out the back, along the side, and hit them in the rear! I'll take twelve people.' And to my disbelief he began to select a suicide squad.

'Now just a minute -' I began before being interrupted by Mrs Gladstone.

'The rest of you follow me,' she commanded, advancing to the entrance doors. She had just put her hand on one of the handles when we saw a light fly over the wall, circling in a strange way, and then hit the ground about fifty yards away from us, breaking out in a spread of fire. No explosion, obviously a dud.

'Feck,' said Jimmie quietly.

'The police say they'll be here in an hour or so,' said Miss Melly. 'They're rather busy at the moment.'

'Their problem, they can pick up the pieces,' said Mrs Gladstone, and yanked a door open.

'Feck! With me,' said Jimmie, pulling at my arm and dragging me away to the right side passage.

'Jimmie? What's the problem? Not now, we've got a riot on our hands. Two riots.'

'Feck!' he insisted, and dragged me past a group of night-gown arrayed, weapon carrying figures hiding in the passage from the mind rays, muttering to themselves. We got to the French windows opening onto the lawns, and I followed him across the lawn, having given up on trying to get back to the others. They were to our right, a band of people in dressing gowns, night gowns and pyjamas, mostly white, walking slowly but purposefully towards the front gates, sticks and stakes and poles held at the ready, like an avenging horde of ghouls.

You never have a camera with you when you want one.

Jimmie led our way silently across the lawn, lit only by the distant street lamps, moving quickly from the shade of one tree to another. I followed his example. He was good at it.

For some reason we were headed, in a circular fashion, towards the front wall, the one keeping the barbarians out. The ones who apparently wished to do some nasty things to us. I was about to point out this salient fact to Jimmie, just in case he hadn't noticed the implications, when a noise of metal crashing against metal came from the direction of the gates.

'Feck! Down!' whispered Jimmie, and we crouched down in dark shadow, trying to work out was happening. The band of ghouls – platoons two to five, Mixed Company – on their way forward had also halted, about thirty yards from the gates, a column devolving into a wider group as the ones behind moved out sideways to get a look at what was in front. And they had halted for good reason. We could just see a car reversing from the gates it had obviously just smashed into, and it looked like it was about to have another go. Taking on a car was something they had apparently not foreseen.

But their mood seemed to indicate that it wasn't necessarily something they'd object to.

Just as soon as they'd worked out the how.

We watched in stunned silence as the car disappeared out of our view, screeching backwards to a halt, and then reappeared in a blaze of smoke, hitting the gates with another sound of metal crunching against wrought iron. There was loud drunken cheering from beyond the wall. It was obvious that the gates, sturdy as they might be, weren't going to last much longer.

I'll bet that isn't his own car, I thought to myself.

'Feck, c'mon,' said Jimmie, in a hurry. He leapt to his feet and raced off towards the wall. I followed him, wondering what his plan was. Hoping he had a plan.

As we ran, another object flew over the wall, about forty yards to our right, glinting strangely in the street light. Out of the corner of my eye I noticed it explode on the ground and send what seemed like a sea of fire out around it.

Puffing badly – I was, anyway – we reached a lone tree growing close to the wall, and Jimmie fished around it for something. Looking back I could see the others still stood watching the car attack on the gates. Back at the entrance to the buildings I noticed another group of mostly white-clad residents trying to drag something out, almost like a battering ram. They were shouting and singing, and some were dancing, and I thought to myself that it was a good thing they couldn't see the gates, because they were going to need a serious battering ram when that car got through.

'Feck! Here!' said Jimmie, and I turned back towards him. He was holding two bottles of clear liquid with something solidifying at the bottom, one of which he was handing to me. He dragged me back to a point about fifteen yards from the wall and the tree.

'Feck! When I say "now" throw like this,' he said, and demonstrated a sort of stretched over arm throw I'd only previously seen in bad war movies. I looked sadly at the bottle he'd given me and thought, at a time like this he wants to have a water fight. Poor chap. He'd even stuffed the mouths of the bottles with cotton wool to stop the water escaping in flight. The thought occurred to me that shards of glass could be quite dangerous out there, and maybe this wasn't a good idea.

'Feck!' he said, 'ready?' Without waiting for an answer he

brought out something looking like a lighter, which proved to be a lighter, as he flicked it, and applied a flame to the cotton wool on his bottle, then to mine, and I suddenly realised that the petrol smell I'd noticed wasn't coming from outside.

'Er, Jimmie, are you sure this is legal?' I asked.

Well, it's the thought that immediately strikes you when you're about to launch a petrol bomb, isn't it?

'Feck! Now!' he said, and threw his bottle in a gracious movement, the now merrily burning fuse describing a perfect parabola towards where the louts would be, about thirty yards over the wall to our right.

I flung mine.

All I can say is that I haven't been trained for this sort of thing. I think any ordinary person finding themselves holding a burning petrol bomb in their hand is quite likely to adopt the "let's get rid of this thing very, very quickly" approach. So when I say that my throw wasn't exactly Olympic level, I'm sure you'll understand. To be honest, it did a sort of "whoop-whoop" through the air, bounced off the branches of the tree in front of us, and flew downwards to the right.

As it bounced it let off a few flames, illuminating the professor, sitting high in the tree.

I don't think I will ever forget that sight. A top-hatted, tail-coated figure in black, sitting with his feet dangling, and one arm stretched out to keep his balance, vaguely illuminated, almost a silhouette, watching the situation like a devil from the vast infernal regions. I shall have nightmares about that.

'What now?' I asked Jimmie, in a voice that seemed to come from somewhere outside of me. Everything had gone into slow motion.

'Feck. Run?' He suggested.

It seemed like a good idea, possibly one of his best, until I heard, from somewhere over the wall to the left of us, the major's high, piping voice scream 'Charge! Charge now! Attack! Attack!'

'Oh, sweet Jesus,' I murmured to myself, 'come on, let's see what the silly bastard's up to now.' I grabbed a low branch and pulled myself up, branch by branch until I could sit on the wall. Jimmie followed me.

To the left the major was charging up in his blue silk night wear with navy piping, followed by about twelve white clad harpies, all bearing various building items of daily use with evil intent.

The charge of the Night Brigade.

To the right, where the cars first began, one was on fire, presumably a victim of Jimmie's aim. Further to the right the car battering the gates had just started it's latest attack.

Which is when the driver must have noticed something going on to his right, and taken his eye off the ball. Or the gates, in this case. He swerved violently, and managed to catch the gates with one side of the now largely crumpled bonnet, and the wall with the other. The car was undoubtedly wrecked. As were the gates. They came tumbling down with a rasping crash, and the way was open for the thugs. Ironically, with the car now out of action, the way was also open for Golf company, Ghouls Division. While the yobboes stood in confusion, the car beginning to emit smoke, their minds were addled not only by the drink but also by the sight of a band of nightclads coming in from their right led by the major, Golf company realised their advantage.

Someone let yell a whoop – I couldn't tell who – and surged forward. The others took only a second to follow suit, and suddenly there was a wave of white nightwear headed towards the broken down gates. Looking back quickly, I could also see the group at the building entrance; they seemed to have given up on their battering ram, and were now dancing around it, singing and shouting.

I decided our reserves weren't going to be much cop if they were needed, and concentrated on the battle below. I noticed that the major, on our left, was on a blind collision course with one of the louts dragging himself out of the bushes after presumably relieving himself. At least that was what I hoped it was. The girl behind him suggested otherwise.

'Major!' I shouted, 'watch your left. Your left, watch your left!' He looked up, puzzled at this voice from above, caught a glimpse of me – okay, I was standing on the wall by now, hanging on to a branch for support – waved, and looked to his left as he charged, so that when he suddenly came upon the yob his arm was up and ready to strike. Fortunately, or unfortunately, he was too close, and had to head-butt the thug, who threw his hands up in astonishment, and fell back onto his girlfriend, back into the bushes.

I was most impressed.

The major gave me a thumbs up, and carried on, shouting 'Get the cowards! Get the bastards!'

The yobs weren't looking too certain of themselves by this stage. Decidedly nervous, in fact. If it wasn't for the booze in them they might have recognised defeat and legged it sooner.

It was only when Golf company suddenly poured across the broken gates and into the road that some of them realised that they had now been outmanoeuvred, and that they were faced with two sets of murder driven, nightclothes wearing, very unhappy madmen. Who were largely women. And some of those were large women. And the ones that weren't looked even more evil.

I felt absolutely terrible. I almost stopped grinning for a moment.

I noticed that the spin out of the gate entrance had slowed down as everyone tried to adjust to the streetlights, and a change in alignment.

'Mrs Gladstone, lay into them!' I yelled as hard as I could. 'Go! Go! Get them!'

Look, I'm not saying I'm proud of it, but you do get carried away with the excitement.

And I didn't sound a bit like the major.

Under this encouragement Golf Company seemed to collect themselves, and looked towards the yobboes in a hungry way. I could have sworn the whole group actually snarled in unison.

'Oh, shit!' I heard one of the yobs say, and I don't think he was alone. Then they did something they should never have done. They began to break and run. And Golf company sprang after them. Though to be honest, with the major and his nightclads coming up fast from behind, they didn't have much option.

Amongst Golf company I saw a charging figure impeccably dressed in cream dressing gown with matching cream pyjamas, and a shiny cyclist's helmet adorning his head. He was brandishing a rather nasty looking hockey stick.

I don't think I shall ever be able to look at Colin in the same light again.

To his right I could see one of the thugs in a red t-shirt trying to hide behind the far side of a car bonnet.

'Colin!' I yelled at the top of my voice. 'Other side of the car! On your right.'

He stopped uncertainly, saw me, and waved. Then he turned, leaned over the car bonnet, and his eyes met the thug's eyes at the same moment. I think the thug cried a helpless "Noooo" before Colin's hockey stick came flying over, and hooked the young sod behind the neck. With an impressive display of force and determination Colin dragged him slowly over the bonnet, towards himself, as red t-shirt's nails scratched uselessly across the car bonnet, desperately trying to get a grip. When he was half way across, and the bonnet paint ruined, Colin suddenly let go, reversed the stick, and brought the head straight into red-t-shirt's forehead. He toppled slowly backwards, his eyes wide open, a stream of blood starting to issue from his forehead, and fell into a bundle on the road.

Red t-shirt will probably never find out, but it was payback time – and he had inherited some rather heavy debts from some other thugs. Colin watched him for a moment to make sure he wasn't about to get up, turned and raised the hockey stick in acknowledgement, and pressed on determinedly.

I was even more impressed.

At almost the same time the remaining young thugs suddenly

turned and ran as if the devil himself was after them, which isn't too far from what they were facing. They ran towards the major's group, probably on some primordial calculation of numbers, and in a way they were lucky that that was exactly when Mrs Gladstone's group hit them, because it allowed most of them to escape northwards. There were three unfortunates lying on the ground in the foetal position, crying loudly, but the majority were suddenly legging it up the road back towards the estate.

They could have tried out for the national team.

One poor unfortunate ran right underneath our position, or he would have if Jimmie hadn't dropped on top of him. Jimmie's feet hit him right in the shoulders, a trick you won't see on Blue Peter. They fell apart, and Jimmie leapt up, gripped the youth by his shirt collar and trousers, and threw him – someone twice his size – threw him straight against the wall, face first. I think he was rather angry.

The youth bounced off, crumpled, and begged for mercy.

'Get up, feck,' said Jimmie, dragging him up by his shirt front. He forced him against the wall.

'Feck! Protstant or Cathlic?' he demanded.

'Eh?' cried the confused youth.

'Eh ye Protstant or Cathlic shitball?' demanded Jimmie.

'Protestant! Protestant!' screamed the unlucky one.

'Feck! I hate Protstants!' Jimmie yelled back, raising his fist.

'Catholic, Catholic, I'm Catholic!' the youth screamed.

'And I hate fecking Cathlics too!' Jimmie shouted, and launched a haymaker to the side of the religiously confused one, who sank into a heap.

Maybe if he'd confessed to being Jewish, or having a budding interest in Buddhism he might have avoided retribution, but somehow I doubted it. I don't think Jimmie's very hot on religion.

Mrs Gladstone and the major looked at the fleeing enemy, and then turned towards me and raised their hands in triumph and salute, a touching gesture, which I acknowledged with an ironic wave. Which is why too late I noticed that the foot soldiers hadn't taken on board this concept of a battle won, and were pursuing their quarry up the road, nightskirts flying.

'Oh, shit,' I said. 'Oh, bollocks.' I didn't want to even think of around fifty assorted crazies in nightwear roaming the streets saying "vengeance is mine saith the lord" to potentially innocent dog walkers. I jumped down to the ground, not something I would normally have considered – not a twelve foot drop, anyway – and felt something give. I should have taken Jimmie's option, and used a passing lout to break the fall.

'Mrs Gladstone, Major, we've got to get them back,' I called. They came up to meet me as I hobbled on what I presumed was a broken ankle.

'When the enemy is on the run you pursue,' said the major enthusiastically, but somewhat breathlessly.

'Serves the buggers right,' agreed Mrs Gladstone.

'We can't let them wander around on their own,' I pointed out, 'they'll lose touch with each other and we'll have them all over the place in ones and twos.'

'Point,' said the major after a few moments thought. 'duty to the troops and all that. Need to round them up and prepare for a counter attack.'

'Come on, let's go,' I said bitterly. I really wasn't looking forward to roaming the streets. Roaming the streets looking for people who couldn't remember their last known address, while some rather ugly thugs might be reassessing the situation and thinking of revenge on any individuals they might encounter.

As I took a step forward the ankle said hello and goodbye, and I staggered, muttering curses.

'You're in no shape to go anywhere,' said Mrs Gladstone disapprovingly. 'You stay here and we'll sort this out.'

I breathed deeply. The pain was quite excruciating. 'Bollocks,' I said.

Well, I was I bit tired for the repartee side of things.

'Jimmie, take him back,' ordered Mrs Gladstone.

'Absolutely,' said the major. 'We need you at HQ, organising things, not wandering around here. Classic problem of officers come up through the ranks, don't know when to let the chalk face go. Come on, Mrs Gladstone, let's round the stragglers up.'

And with that they turned and left me. I can't explain it, but somehow I really thought I should be with them.

I must be mad.

'C'mon, boss,' said Jimmie gently, taking my arm, 'feck, need organising back feck there feck.'

'I'm not, I'm not,' cried the heap of youth to our side, weeping.

'Feck, a second, boss,' said Jimmie, took a step towards the heap, and put a boot in. 'Come beck here an I'll feckin kill you,' he promised the heap.

And then he gently helped me limp back towards the fallen gates, and back up the driveway.

As we came around the curve of the driveway we caught sight of the group at the building entrance, dancing around something like some sort of cross between an Indian war dance and a pyjama party. As we got closer one of them noticed us, and gradually, one by one, they fell silent, and stood there looking sheepish. When we finally got close enough to identify the object of their celebrations I could understand why.

There was one coffee machine that was never going to issue coffee ever again. It's panels were beaten in, and around lay plastic cups, teabags, and occasional patches of milk powder and instant coffee.

'It fell,' said one of them defensively. The others immediately echoed this idea with varying degrees of enthusiasm, making a sort of verbal Mexican wave.

'Fell, yes.'

'Fell!'

'Fell! Just fell!'

'It fell! It fell! It fell!'

I waved my hand to quiet them. 'I believe you, I believe you,' I said. I limped on painfully with Jimmie supporting me. 'Pity, I could have done with a cup of coffee just now.'

'Feck,' he said in agreement as we got into the reception area.

The first thing I noticed was darkness; normally there would be a side light on somewhere. The second was that my feet were getting wet. I could hear water sloshing around somewhere. Like around my trainers.

'Am I imagining things, or is the floor about an inch deep in water?' I asked Jimmie.

'Feck. Half an inch,' he replied. 'Here, boss, you sit down. Feck.' He guided me to the end of the reception counter, where there was a space low enough to sit on, but high enough to keep my feet out of the water. He lit his lighter to give some light on the area.

'There's a torch behind the counter somewhere,' I told him. 'Bottom drawer, far left.' I heard him rummaging around, and there was a click, and the reception area was suddenly revealed in those weird shadows a torch can give off. The coffee machine assassins were standing at the entrance doors, peering in, eyes wide. A slight rise in the floor towards the doorway had prevented the water from escaping their way. Where the coffee machine had stood there was now a blank space, apart from a pipe which was gaily dispensing water. Jimmie sloshed his way over to it.

'Feck. Tap,' he said, and the water suddenly stopped.

'Well spotted Jimmie,' I said, 'though I think we can be rather grateful that the fuse had already blown.' He looked down. The plug from the coffee machine was still in its socket, about a yard of cable trailing in the water, the socket blackened around the plug. That probably explained the lack of lights and any general electrical activity.

I looked at the people at the doors.

'You could have pulled the plug out first,' I remonstrated. 'Oh, well. Well, don't just stand there. Get some mops and buckets, and start cleaning this mess up.'

'Mops?' said one.

'Buckets?' queried another.

'Squeegee!' said a third enthusiastically, and they all nodded. 'Kitchen!' he added, and they all nodded again, and traipsed in, some holding their dressing gowns delicately away from the water. 'Mops!' said one as they moved off in a group down the passage towards the kitchen. 'Buckets!' responded another.

'Feck. Kitchen's locked, boss,' said Jimmie as I rubbed my face and wondered when I'd wake up to find that this was a dream.

'Know how to open it?' I asked.

'Feck, yes. Have to break the lock though.'

'Well, needs must. Off you go, otherwise that lot will stand around in a confused huddle for the next few years.'

'Hokay, boss,' he said, and hurried off after them.

I shall have to train him out of the "boss" bit; it sounds too much like responsibility. And he could have left the torch behind. I was sitting in darkness again.

It was amazingly quiet. A sort of surreal quietness in the darkness, as I could see out beyond the doors the reflected light of the burning cars, and could distinguish the black smoke rising in a pall. It was a bit like the scene from Gone With The Wind, only without the noise and the horses and the music and Vivien Leigh. And with wet trainers. At least the trainers could come off.

I had just finished taking them off – one of them very carefully and slowly – and was holding them in my hands when I heard a suspicious noise just outside the door, and a silhouette appeared slowly, the sort of slow movement of someone who wasn't about on a mission of good and kindness to the world. I looked around in the darkness, hoping some outline would suggest itself as a weapon, but failed to find anything before the figure was fully in the doorway. Stuff it, I thought to myself, and threw the first thing I had to hand – a soggy trainer.

Everything considered, it was a good shot. I heard the flat slap of wet trainer hitting someone's cheek, and a cry of shock.

Well, how would you feel if a wet shoe had come flying out of the darkness to attack you?'

'Who's there?' a man's voice quavered. Stuff you sunshine, I thought, if you think I'm going to let you know where I am by opening my mouth you've got no hope. I balanced the other trainer, ready to send it after it's companion. 'This is the police,' continued the voice, 'identify yourself.'

Hah, I thought, you don't expect me to fall for that one, and took aim. I was about to let fly when a wavering torch beam lit up the area from the passage, and Jimmie reappeared. He stopped when the beam fell on a nervous looking figure wearing a policeman's uniform. I quickly put the second trainer down.

'Who threw something at me?' he asked imperiously, the effect somewhat damaged by a quaver in his voice.

'I did,' I said, 'and you were about to get the second instalment. Aren't you lot supposed to have torches?'

'It doesn't work,' he said miserably, 'they never do.'

The cleaning squad trooped in bearing mops and buckets, led by someone proudly bearing a squeegee.

'Who are these lot?' asked the copper, backing off slightly as squeegee man began sending small waves of water outside.

'Cleaners. Can't you see the mops and buckets?'

He took off his peaked cap and wiped his brow. It was a warm night, but he was sweating more than normal.

'Seems like you've had a bit of trouble here.'

'You could say that. We phoned your lot over an hour ago. And they send only you?'

'My partner's in the road checking the cars. Two are burning, you know.'

'You're joking! Burning? Well, well, that is a surprise.' I could see that he wasn't sure if the mickey was being taken.

Obviously not Brain of Britain material.

'Why don't you make yourself useful? Get an electrician sent out to sort out the power?'

'I'm a police officer, I'm not here to find electricians for you.'

'Okay, your station should have an emergency contact for this place. Get them to give the contact a bell and get them round here sharpish.'

'Don't you have the number here?' he asked petulantly. I sighed.

'Funnily enough, yes, there's a list on the computer.'

'Well, look it up then.'

I looked at him for a few moments. I don't think he could see the look in my eyes, because he hadn't turned to dust.

'Him big chief computer machine needum electrical power to run on,' I said, 'which just so happens to be what we don't have now, understand?'

'Feck. Fuse box. I know where it is, boss. Feck,' said Jimmie.

By this stage the cleaning squad had finished most of their duties, and were arranged around the edges of reception, silently following this exchange.

'I'm an electrician,' piped up one of the cleaning mutes.

'Well, go along with Jimmie here, and fix it, okay?' I said with some irritation in my voice.

'I don't like electricity,' he whined, shrinking back. I closed my eyes and counted to ten, to stop the sudden urge to throttle him. With a length of twin flex. And then beat him to death with a fuse box.

'Okay, I tell you what,' I said, sliding down from my perch, 'we'll go together, you tell me what to do, and I'll do it, how's that?' I grimaced at the pain as my bad leg touched the ground, and thought once again about murdering the phobic electrician. Slowly.

'Feck, no, boss, you stay here,' said Jimmie. 'You, come with me, feck,' he told the electrician in his inimitable way of stating that "No" was not an option.

We were left in the darkness. Caught between a constable with the intelligence of a newt, and a bunch of silent coffee machine killers, I couldn't see much chance of social or intellectual chit chat.

'He's taken the torch,' said the constable in a whining voice, as the connection between light and dark managed to permeate his brain.

'Yes, that's because he works better in darkness. He's trained to kill people in uniforms, you see, and he prefers it to be dark when he sneaks up behind you with a stiletto. Or a garrotte. Very partial to the garrotte, he is.'

'Whatcha mean?' asked the constable suspiciously. 'I wuz told none of you loonies were dangerous,' he snickered, and then suddenly screamed.

A light flickered on behind him.

'Quite right, Constable Greeves,' said a voice, and Sergeant Gilmore from the search appeared in the doorway. 'And you were also told to be polite to people, but you don't seem to have taken that on board either. Perhaps you could tell me why you are here?'

To be honest I would have preferred the other sergeant, with WPC Sandra in his wake, but I was beginning to quite like old Gilmore.

'Trying to ascertain the facts,' PC Greeves said, hastily straightening himself.

'And how long have you being trying to ascertain the facts, Constable Greeves?'

'Er, I've only just got here Sarge,' he stuttered.

'No, you've been here – in this area, if not in here – for over half an hour now. I've been here for five minutes and I already know the facts. You see, Police Constable Greeves, I have interviewed a witness. Did you think of that unlikely option?'

'Er, yes Sarge, of course, but er, I – ' He was saved by the squawking of his radio. 'Sorry, Sarge, I'll just take this,' he said, and slid out through the doors. Sergeant Gilmore came into reception.

'You found a witness?' I enquired nonchalantly.

'Not a very good one, I'm afraid,' he said with a grimace, 'but he was out walking his dog, and did see those thugs trying to ram the gates.'

'Thank god for that,' I replied, 'it was quite frightening. There must have been about a hundred of them.'

'A little bit of an exaggeration, I think,' he smiled back. Of course it was an exaggeration. There's a bloke in jail called Martin, and he's in jail because he killed a burglar in his own house. I didn't want to know what the sentence would be for lobbing petrol bombs at people trying to kill you – probably life on Devil's Island at least, strapped to a rack and flogged daily. I was getting my excuses in first.

'I've got another four men at the front,' he continued, 'so you can feel a lot safer now. We've also picked up six of the young thugs. Drugged out of their minds, I'm afraid. One of them seems to have tripped and smashed his face in. Kept swearing that he wasn't a Catholic or a Protestant for some reason. And the others wanted protective custody. It's the drugs, they start hallucinating.'

'You think four is enough?' I asked, with a hint of panic in my voice. When it comes to the trial I want everyone to be convinced that I was petrified, in fear of my life.

Okay, so I was, but you have to lard these things a bit.

'For the moment it's all that we have. We are under pressure on Sunday nights – or Monday mornings perhaps I should say.' I glanced at the clock on the wall. It looked like four o'clock. That couldn't be right I thought. I noticed young PC Greeves slink back in.

'Er, Sarge?' he asked tentatively.

'Yes? Come on, what is it?'

'It's the area car, Sarge. Um, they seem to have had an accident.'

Gilmore exhaled slowly in controlled anger. 'An accident? I hardly have enough officers to cover an old Tom's respectability and now you tell me that they've had an accident? I've just lost an area car because someone can't drive properly?'

'Er, there's more to it, Sarge ...'

'Well? Go on,' he said, recovering his poise in a rather unsettling way.

'Er, they want to know if there's a revolution of sorts going on.'

'A revolution, Greeves?' He closed his eyes, and I could see him counting to ten. 'Apart from the minor fact that revolutionaries are unlikely to personally contact me with their plans, what with my being a police officer, and, as some might see it, a representative of the state, what the FUCK are you talking about?'

For a moment I even felt sorry for Greeves. And at the same time I suddenly became aware of a strange noise, a sort of measured 't...t...t...t'.

'Er, from what he said, er, Sarge, the reason he had the accident was that he was, er, turning an um corner, and ...'

'And?'

'And found himself facing this platoon of people marching.'

'A platoon. Of marchers. Carrying machine guns presumably? Anti-tank cannon? Flags flying? Couple of nuclear weapons hanging from their belts? One or two signs saying We Don't Like The Government Too Much?'

The noise was growing louder, and seemed to be accompanied by a flippity-flop sound. 't ... flippity ... t flopppity ... t ... flippity ...'

'Er, no, Sarge, he says they were dressed in pyjamas.'

'Pyjamas?'

'Though most of them had dressing gowns on top.'

'Ut ... flippity ... ut ... floppity ... ut ... flippity ...' It was definitely coming up the driveway.

'Dressing gowns? Dressing gowns? With machine guns? Or were they carrying dangerous dusters?'

Just then there was a sudden whirring as the power came back on. The reception night nights flicked on, seeming far more powerful than usual. And one after another other lights came on.

I think Jimmie was flicking all the switches he could find. The lights illuminating the lawns and driveway sprang into life, and I could see behind PC Greeves a sight which I don't think the sergeant was going to enjoy. The major had formed up his escapees into a three rank platoon, and was striding alongside them, calling the pace.

'Left ... left ... left and a right and a left ...' he was crying. With every step their plimsolls and slippers made a sort of flip-swoosh sounds. And with the sudden light on them they seemed to brace themselves and raise their effort.

It was quite impressive.

Sergeant Gilmore turned and gaped.

'Well fuck me gently,' he said softly.

'It's some residents,' I explained quickly, 'they ran off in the confusion, and we're trying to get them all back.'

'I see,' he said. 'That explains a bit.' He turned back towards me. 'We tried to raise that Doctor Snufflewarts of yours, but he wasn't interested. Said we were better qualified for solving a civil problem, and put the phone down on us.'

'That's good old hot – er, Doctor Snuffelwarts for you,' I said enthusiastically. 'Man's a complete academic, doesn't understand real life.'

'And he's your doctor?' he asked in disbelief. 'Wonder how any of you cope.'

Badly, I thought. But we're still hanging in there. Just.

'Squad ... squad ... halt!' came the order from the parking area as the major brought his platoon to a point rather too close to the building for comfort, with a sound of out-of-step feet smattering down, plop-plop-plop.

And one final "plop".

There's always one.

Didn't seem to worry them too much, though.

'Not bad, not bad,' enthused the major. 'Takes practice, always practice. Now hold the position before I give the order to fall out. Hold that position!' he commanded, as he snapped to attention, facing them.

I could barely get a glimpse as the two police officers and the sanitary squad crowded the doors and windows to watch.

'Squad ... squad ... remember what I've told you ... squad .. DEESMISSSS!' he bellowed in a squeaky voice, and they obediently turned right – most of them – and stomped a few paces, before breaking up, looking very pleased with themselves. They headed towards us.

'Why are most of them carrying sticks and, er – pipes, it seems? One of them has a garden fork,' Gilmore pointed out.

'Hoarders,' I said quickly. 'Can't leave anything lying down for a minute and they'll have it for their collection. They'll pick up anything. One of them collects clods of soil.' I just hoped he didn't ask for any names, or someone was about to find their cupboard full of earth.

'Right, well, er, very interesting,' said Gilmore. 'I must get off and visit my men, though. I'll leave you with – ' He looked at Greeves, and changed his mind. 'I'll send someone up to make sure you're okay. Greeves, come with me.'

He slipped out before the entrance became too crowded with Night's Pyjama Army. They ignored him, chatting and talking as they flowed in.

'Okay, okay, just a minute,' I bellowed above the noise. They paused briefly before ignoring me as well. The major swept in and came up to me.

'Ah, general,' he said – general? Man's as potty as a rhubarb too long in the sun – 'as you can see I've brought my men – my platoon – back safely.'

The squaddies had stopped to listen.

'Excellent, major,' I reassured him. 'Good work. Wish I could have been with you.'

'Yes, I know, I know that feeling, but someone has to command, to co-ordinate, and none better than tonight.'

Right, I thought, and I want some of the pills you're on.

'If you could just take everyone to the day room,' I suggested. 'We'll see if we can't organise a spot of tea.'

'Excellent idea,' enthused the major, 'I'm sure we'd love one.' And he shooed his platoon towards the day room. If ever he really was in the army he probably got fired for being too nice.

Somewhere amidst the shuffle Jimmie forced his way through, followed by, of all people, Tonique.

'Toni!' I exclaimed, 'what are you doing here?'

She looked nervously at Jimmie.

'I heard there was some trouble. I thought I'd come to help,' she said, looking at the ground. Poor girl, terrified of being around people like Jimmie, yet still brave enough to come out and help us. I gave her a pat on the head, hoping that it didn't appear too patronising. She flinched.

Don't you just hate it when people don't trust you?

'You couldn't do us a favour, could you Toni?' I asked. She nodded, still looking at the floor. 'We need to organise some tea for the resistants. I can get some people to help you,' I promised.

'Feck. I'll help,' said Jimmie.

'Okay,' said Tonique, and they scampered off before I could say anything. I made a mental note to send someone else after them as soon as possible. I didn't want Tonique worried about being alone with Jimmie any longer than possible. Personally I reckon Jimmie's a fine chap – apart from some strange aversion to religion – but people get funny ideas when you're living in this sort of setup.

But just at that moment I was alone on my perch in reception. I looked at the clock on the wall, and it did say four twenty five. About an hour and a half to dawn. I felt my cheeks, the stubble now apparent.

How come these actors in movies either have perma-stubble, or are permanently well shaven? Remember the scenes where the hero is interrupted in the middle of a shave, wipes the lather off half his face, and that's shaven as well?

Must be some sort of towel they have.

The early hours of the morning are not the time to go into deep thought; I could quite happily have dozed off, apart from the fact that it would have resulted in falling on the floor. I contemplated going off to my room – hopping off to my room – and falling asleep. Peace, bliss, it seemed so close.

Which is when Mrs Gladstone turned up.

She was Bouddica to the major's Caesar. Instead of columns of marching troops she and Miss Melly led a rabble of bloodthirsty and undisciplined peasants, a sight to strike fear into any conqueror.

Well, I wouldn't have liked to have to face them in anger, anyway.

'The others are in the day room,' I told her as they flooded into reception, if twenty odd people can be said to flood anywhere.

'Off to the dayroom, you lot,' she ordered.

'And tea will be ready shortly,' I added.

'Tea!' said one stout looking woman, 'just what the doctor ordered. A nice cuppa to restore civilisation!' There were murmurs of agreement as the motley band floated off, leaving myself with Mrs Gladstone and Miss Melly.

'That the lot, then?' I asked.

'Don't know,' Mrs Gladstone replied briskly. 'The major was doing another group. He beat us to it, did he? Bugger. I was hoping to show him up.'

Well, I suppose a little healthy competition is a good thing.

'You brought more back than he did,' I said in compensation.

'Good. I shall accuse him of desertion, then. That'll get his little moustache all aquiver. How's the leg?'

'Only hurts when I walk on it.'

'Well, don't then. We'll have to get you a medic.'

'Great. I love doctors,' I replied with some feeling. 'Give you a pill and tell you to come back in a week so they can give you a different one. Anyway, that can wait. How do we know there isn't anyone still out there?'

'Take a roll call,' she suggested. I was about to point out that I didn't have access to a list of patients when a thought suddenly struck.

'Hang on,' I said, got off my perch, and hopped around to the other side of the reception desk. I picked up one of the voting ballots and waved it. 'Not brilliant, but it's something to start with. Let's pop along to the day room, shall we?'

They each put an arm around me, and we did a version of the three legged walk, or possibly five legged walk. Even without pressure on it the damn ankle felt like it had a knife shoved in it with every step I took.

Inside the day room I nodded to the tables at the end, where Tonique and Jimmie were dispensing tea. Everyone was standing around chatting in a lively fashion, and I rather suspected that several tall stories were being exchanged, which would get taller as time went on.

In a year's time it'll be the Battle Of The Thousand, along with German paratroopers disguised as nuns.

I perched on one of the end tables, and Jimmie came up with a mug of coffee, which was a bit of a surprise. I enjoy tea, but coffee is more my drink, especially in the early hours of the morning. And I can't stand these poncy little cups with handles you can hardly get a finger through, and which break off if you do. I must have mentioned it at some time, and Jimmie had remembered. He's a soft little cuss at heart, I thought to myself as Tonique brought tea and biccies for Mrs Gladstone and Miss Melly.

'Cheers, Jimmie,' I said. 'Everyone okay?'

'Feck, yeah. Enjoying themselves, feck.' I looked around. He was right. This room isn't used to such lively chatter. Well, let's get the boring bit over with, I thought.

Bed, I thought, I want to go to bed.

'Okay, everyone, can I have your attention for a few minutes, please,' I called out in my best I-am-a-crap-public-speaker voice.

'Quiet, everyone,' Mrs Gladstone boomed, in her best do-as-you-are-bloody-well-told voice. In the middle of the room the major started shushing everyone.

I sat up a little straighter. I could get used to this power thing.

'Right,' I continued once I had everyone's attention, or at least that of those still awake. A few had fallen into quiet slumber at the sides of the room, except for one chap who was snoring heartily. 'I want to take a roll call to see if anyone's missing. I've got a list of people here, but it includes everyone who has ever been here, which means some who have left, or have passed on to greater things. So when I call out a name, just let me know whether it's you, or someone no longer here, okay?'

There was a murmur of assent. The thought of others having gone to greater portals had cooled things down a bit, I thought.

'Right, let's get it over with then. Archibald, George?'

'Here!'

'He's here!'

'She's here!'

I looked down at the paper. If I tried to sort the responses out we'd be here all night. All day. And despite the confusion over George Archibald's gender, it appeared that he or she was definitely here.

'Atton, Sheila,' I carried on.

'I'm Here!' trilled a voice

'She's here!'

'He's here!'

Atton Sheila got ticked off.

And so it went on. I missed out the obvious pretenders, but couldn't avoid the deceased. However they didn't present a problem, apart from when Sergeant Gilmore poked his head in at the back, to hear what might be construed as a very strange conversation.

'Callow, Charles?'

'Dead!'

'Bloody good send off. Sherry and mince pies.'

'Cooper, Jean?'

'Dead!'

'Still owes me five quid!'

'Crewe, Adam?'

'Dead!'

'Copped it while shagging old big-tits!'

'Really, Mr Jenkins, there are ladies present!'

'Not when he was around, they weren't!'

'Daley, Anne?'

'Here!'

'She's here!'

'He's here!'

I noticed the sergeant withdraw his head quickly and disappear. I'd love to know what he was thinking about this apparent slaughter of the innocents, and some not quite so innocent. With my thoughts elsewhere I carried on.

'Dervish, Fiona?' There was a short silence, and someone called out, 'Girlfriend!' and everyone laughed.

'That's Ms Dervish,' pointed out Miss Melly.

'Oh, of course, not concentrating,' I replied, and ticked her name off.

'You should know!' called out someone, and there was another general laugh. I wasn't sure what they were on about, but they seemed happy enough, so I carried on.

We got through the D's without too much bother, and the E's, but hit a snag on the F's.

'Ferris, James?' I called out. There was no response.

'Come, on, James Ferris? Anyone know James Ferris?' There was a whispered muttering, and I heard the name "Ginger" being mentioned.

'Okay, okay,' I said to quieten them down, 'I'll put a question mark next to him for the moment.' Ginger was no doubt sitting somewhere quietly, looking into space and trying to remember all the Chelsea players since the Battle of Waterloo. 'Now, Fulton, Graham?' I continued.

We got through the rest of the F's and then on through until the W's without anyone missing in action, managing to remember not to call out Linda Lovelace's name.

She probably owed someone five quid.

'Wood, Colin?' The room was quiet.

'Colin Wood, who knows Colin Wood?'

'Feck, Colin!' said Jimmie, and I suddenly realised which Colin we were looking for. Surnames aren't a big thing for most people here, and I hadn't recognised his.

The last time I had seen Colin he was brandishing his hockey stick as he charged down the road, cycling helmet shining under the streetlamps.

'Feck! I'll go look for him,' said Jimmie, ready to go out.

'Sit down, Jimmie,' I told him. 'He's probably gone to bed. Let's get the rest of the list done before we do anything.'

'Feck, I'll check his room,' said Jimmie obstinately.

'Okay, okay. Take someone with you who knows Ginger Ferris, and see if he hasn't had an early night as well.'

'I'll go, I know Ginger,' said someone in front.

I watched the two of them march off, but didn't hold out much hope. We had already had several people identified as being firmly tucked up and in the land of nod, so I doubted whether Colin or Ginger could have sloped off without anyone noticing.

'Wotham, Peter?' I called, and his presence was acknowledged in the now standard manner, if a little more subdued. I carried on to the end, trying not to think about Colin and Ginger.

I couldn't help think that it wasn't fair that it should be two people out of all of us that I liked. With so many people I hardly knew, why those two? I tried to put the thought out of my head as being uncharitable.

'Right, that's the lot then. Thanks for your time and patience, all, you can get back to tea and biscuits now.'

'What about Ginger and Colin?' called a voice.

'Let's see whether they're in bed first. If not we'll decide then.'

There was a general muttering of reluctant acceptance, and people began to chat amongst themselves, but with a heavy air of unease.

'We'll get a search party together,' said Mrs Gladstone as the major came up to us.

'Precisely!' agreed the major. 'Street by street search. My men will volunteer.'

I held up my hand to stem the flow. 'Hang on, let's not get carried away. First we wait to see whether they are asleep, okay?'

They nodded dubious assent. 'And if they aren't, we'll need to do things in a planned fashion. We don't want to lose anyone else. We can only take those who aren't half asleep or totally knackered.'

'We're all half asleep,' pointed out Mrs Gladstone.

She was right. I hadn't really noticed the smoke-stained faces, the night clothes which had developed tears and rips here and there, the nervous high voices caused by an excess of adrenaline – somehow all that had seemed quite normal.

Well, normal in the context of what had gone before.

'She's right, you know,' confirmed the major. 'But you've got a point as well. Can't expect the troops to do more than is physically possible. But as I say, mine are still ready and willing. The others we can leave here to recover.'

Mrs Gladstone bristled. 'That's because your lot only strolled around for ten minutes doing nothing. My people were out much longer. And they'll be ready to go when I give the word.'

'Okay, okay, that's enough,' I said. The last thing we could do with was a pitched battle between the majorites and the Gladstonites. As it was some of them were listening in, and looking like they were getting ready to defend their reputations.

'If – and I stress if – it's necessary to go out and look for them, we'll take everyone I say is fit to go. And we will co-ordinate it with the police. It's about time they did something useful for a change.'

'Damn the police,' boomed Mrs Gladstone.

'Agreed, useless bunch. We didn't need them before, and we don't need them now,' said the major.

'Look, I will use anyone who can possibly help,' I said angrily. 'Whether it's the police or the local sea scouts.' That stopped them for a moment.

We're miles from the sea.

Jimmie and Ginger's friend came in. Everyone fell silent as they watched them walk up to us. Jimmie shook his head.

'Feck. Sorry, boss, they aren't there,' he said apologetically.

'Okay, Jimmie, not your fault,' I told him. I rubbed my face. I was tired and needed time to think. Which this lot weren't likely to give me. If we didn't do this right we'd have a neighbourhood of loonies in dressing gowns wandering the streets calling "Coooeee!" and frightening the horses.

'Okay, let's think about this,' I told them. 'It's – what's the time now, it's going on for five o'clock. Daylight won't be for another half an hour or so. No use in doing anything until we can see properly. So,' I decided, 'use the time to get your search parties ready, okay? And don't choose anyone who isn't fit enough, right?'

'Right. No walking wounded,' agreed the major.

'Yes,' agreed Mrs Gladstone in a voice which said "No". They moved off to muster their troops.

I sighed as I watched the room break up into three groups, the majorites, the Gladstonites, and the sanitary squad. The sanitary squad came up to us silently.

'We want to search too,' said one. The others nodded their heads mutely. I looked at them.

'Okay,' I said, 'first of all make sure you're all wearing decent footwear. Those slippers will fall to pieces before long. And once you've done that, choose a leader amongst yourselves, someone to co-ordinate things.' They looked at each other, nodded quickly, and silently disappeared to their rooms to put on proper shoes, not noticing that most of the others were clad in slippers and plimsolls.

By the time they had managed to decide which shoes to wear and choose a leader it would probably be lunchtime. I certainly hoped so.

'What do you reckon, Jimmie?' I asked quietly, hoping for some inspiration.

'Feck, don't know boss,' he replied.

'I wish you wouldn't call me boss, Jimmie.'

'Sorry, boss.'

I sighed. Yes, repeat no. No use in flogging a dead horse. I watched Mrs Gladstone and the major weeding out the injured and unfit.

It looked like their definition of unfit was anyone they couldn't shake awake. Or kick awake.

Or if that proved impossible, carry.

'Jimmie, there's an A to Z of this area in reception, somewhere next to the computer I think. Could you get it for me, please?' If we were going to do this we might as well do it properly.

'Right, boss,' he said and shot off, narrowly missing Sergeant Gilmore as he came through the doorway. Voices dropped as Gilmore walked in, and eyes followed him as he came over to the table I was sitting on.

'Seems a little frosty in here,' he commented.

'I don't think your lot are flavour of the month at the moment. Most of these people don't like authority at the best of times, but they weren't too chuffed at your response times tonight.'

'Yes, well, sorry about that. Lack of resources, you know. And it's Sunday night, when everybody gets legless for their Monday hangover. We've been stretched all over the place. But,' he brightened up, 'we'll make amends for it. I've got every man and car I can lay my hands on coming over to look for the bodies.'

'Bodies?'

'I heard you calling out the names. Terrible, terrible. How many? Sounded like at least five or six. But we'll get the bastards who did this.'

I looked at him. It was so tempting. A little bit of winding up and we could get the local plods running all over the show. If only I hadn't been so tired. And with Colin and Ginger missing it didn't seem like the right time.

'What are you talking about?' I asked.

'I was talking about those names you were reading out, and the ones that people seem to think are dead.'

'Oh, that,' I laughed. 'That's because the only list I could find had the names of everyone who had ever been here, so we had to work out who should still be here.'

He groaned. 'I've just sent an area message saying ... oh, god, I don't even want to think about it.'

'Well, we've still got two people missing, you know.'

'Thank fuck for that!' He suddenly looked embarrassed. 'Well, you know what I mean. I'll, er, I'll go see how my lot are doing, um yes, good idea.' He scuttled off, once again narrowly missing Jimmie as he came back with the A to Z.

Sometime I must tell him not to do that, or Jimmie is likely to thump him one. When he isn't looking.

'Here you go, boss,' Jimmie said, handing me the map book.

'Ta Jimmie. Let's have a look.'

I was interrupted by Mrs Gladstone making an announcement.

'My people are ready. I think we've got enough to cover the whole area.'

'My men are more than ready,' countered the major in a shocked voice, 'and we are much better trained. Your lot can't even march properly.'

I groaned as the two groups spread out to face each other. Down the middle I could see the doors, and wondered if I could make a run for it before World War Three broke out. Someone on one side was hitting the ground with a walking stick, or piece of wood or something, and everywhere people were brandishing their chosen weapons and making threatening gestures. There were strange noises coming from them.

'Now cut it out, you lot,' I shouted.

'That bunch of old women there started it,' yelled back someone from the major's side. At the back.

'Old women?' screamed back one of Mrs Gladstone's warriors, 'I'll give you old bloody women you bald headed old coot. We'll give you the same whipping we gave those lager louts, while you were running away.'

'That's enough!' I yelled. The two groups were getting a little bit too close to each other; one misjudged move and the feathers would fly. More than feathers. I'd seen what these people could do when pissed off.

'Running away? How dare you! We were way ahead of you. Did the job before you even got out of the gates, hiding away like you were.'

'I'll give you a hiding, you skinny legged old fart!' A curtain rod went up and was about to come crashing down when the doors burst open and two grimy, smoke-stained figures came in. They staggered in carrying something heavy between them, put it down to get a better grip, and then hoisted it onto their shoulders.

'Bloody hell,' I said as I recognised the two. 'Ginger! Colin! Where the hell have you two been?'

They didn't answer, but staggered slowly between the opposing tribes, who made a path for them. There was some whispering, and then someone shouted 'The Nag's Head!' They got the Nag's Head!'

What they were carrying was the heavy wooden sign from the Nag's Head, which up until recently had swung outside the local of the thugs who had tried it on tonight. In old days victorious armies would parade their enemies heads; Colin and Ginger had acted on an instinctive understanding of the requirement for trophies of war.

In a few seconds they were surrounded by members of the opposing tribes, dancing and clapping, cheering them on, slapping their backs. The two managed to make their way to where I was sitting.

'Thought you might like a present,' Colin said modestly.

I grinned back at him. 'I think it will look rather splendid on the mantelpiece over there, the one in the centre.'

'Yes,' he agreed. 'I rather think it would. Come on, Ginger.' They staggered away to the mantelpiece with their prize, some of the others clearing a place for the war booty. I looked at Jimmie, who shrugged his shoulders and smiled.

'Feck,' he said simply.

'I couldn't have put it better myself,' I replied. We watched the party around the mantelpiece. Very soon they were going to discover how tired they were. I certainly was. It felt like the long night was over.

'Come on, Jimmie, give me a hand. I need to tell that copper that his services will no longer be required. And I'd rather he didn't have to come in here to find the Nag's Head sitting on the mantelpiece. There might be Questions Asked.'

'Okay, boss,' he said, and I wrapped an arm around his shoulders, and we made the hop walk slowly out to the car park, the others oblivious to our going.

Dawn was breaking as we got outside, that strange mixture of electric and natural light as night gives way to day. There was a police car sitting in the parking area, and Jimmie helped me hobble over. I leaned against the bonnet with my good foot on the ground as the sergeant inside finished talking on his radio, and got out.

'I'm afraid we won't be needing your services after all,' I told him. 'The missing two have just turned up.'

'Turned up? From where? I haven't seen anyone coming in.'

Good lads, I thought, Colin and Ginger must have sneaked in the back way. 'Well, it's a big place this, you know.' I waved around to point out the lawns and trees, just in case he had missed them. He sighed, and leaned his forearms on the car roof.

'A long night,' he said quietly.

'You can say that again,' I replied. He straightened himself, and took a pack of cigarettes out of his pocket.

'Not supposed to smoke in uniform in public,' he said, taking one out.

'This is hardly public, is it?' I pointed out. He offered me one. After a second's hesitation I took it. 'For medicinal purposes only, of course,' I made clear. He flicked his lighter on, and for a brief moment I had an image of bottles with cotton wool in their necks. I took a deep drag and tried to forget about it.

And then Ms D turned up.

'And that's the whole story,' I finished.

Except for the bit about the petrol bombs, of course, she wouldn't want to know that. And the names of anyone involved in any physical violence. If pressed I shall claim that it was far too dark,

I was too far away, etc, etc.

'Sounds like you did a good job,' she said. I thought about that for a while.

'Old Abraham Lincoln said something once, can't remember the exact wording, but –'

'I confess not to have led events, but to have been led by them?' she quoted.

'I'm impressed,' I confessed, 'not only beautiful and intelligent, but well read as well.'

'Don't try your charm on me,' she smiled, 'I'm impervious to it.'

'I suppose so,' I sighed, 'you must be used to it.'

'And that didn't work either.' She looked at my leg. 'I think it's time for you to go to hospital.' I looked down. My ankle had turned a rather interesting purple colour, and had swollen to a gross extent.

'Yuk,' I said feelingly. It did look gross.

'Exactly. Come on now, I'll drive you there.'

It sounded appealing.

'What about that lot in there, though?' I asked. 'They're going to be buzzing for a while, and we don't want the mother of all battles to erupt.'

'Matron will be along soon, any minute now. I phoned her before I left. Of course,' she added, 'you can always wait for her if you prefer. She could take care of you.'

That decided me. Matron's a lovely person in all departments, except for one; the sympathy vote. With Ms D I wouldn't get much sympathy, with Matron there'd be precisely none. I think she's seen two many ill people to be impressed by a mere broken ankle.

'Okay, let's go then.'

'Right, let me put my arm around you.'

'That's the best offer I've had all year.'

'That's the only offer you've had all year.'

Don't women just love having the last word.

And that was about it, apart from a four hour wait in Accident and Emergency, where apparently you have to be dying to be seen immediately, and a broken ankle is quite low on the scale of things. On the other hand I was told that the swelling had to come down first, and they applied all sorts of things to do that. Ms D kept me supplied with newspapers, and we spent the time slagging off all and sundry, or at least I did.

Everyone has to have a hobby.

She stayed with me the whole time, making regular calls to the clinic to ensure all was quiet on the home front. Apparently most of them needed pills to calm down, and then tried to fall asleep in odd places. Once my leg had been wrapped in plaster, with some steel thing in for good luck, and I had been given a pair of crutches, Ms D drove me back, and helped me get to my room, where I promptly fell asleep.

I was awakened in time for a shower before dinner by matron knocking on my door. She chivvied me all the way to the shower, and showed me how to tie some plastic above the plaster cast to keep it dry, and then gave me a short lecture about the dangers of slipping in a shower.

Refreshed to a certain extent, I hobbled into the dining room on my crutches, to be greeted with an ironic cheer by those there.

'Hail the wounded hero,' called out the major, and I waved back briefly, discovering the hazards of trying to wave while walking on crutches. They might give you an air of wounded hero, but they're a real pain in the whatsits. Trying to carry a tray of food is impossible, but Jimmie was there to give me a hand. Tonique was behind the food counter, which meant that she had been on the go for over twelve hours, more like fourteen. I hoped she had managed to get a few hours kip in along the way.

From various comments I overheard it appears that matron has been looking after her brood with a firm but gentle hand. It seems that she told the doctors that everyone was too tired for sessions today. Even Hotpants had to give in.

I've just remembered – his exercise in democracy was supposed to be today.

Oh, well, too bad, there you go.

Ms D has been standing shotgun in reception ever since we got back. Not even the police were allowed in. Carney tried it and got a ear-wigging for his troubles. Good. He was responsible for this mess, he should hope I don't catch him in a dark alley sometime.

And now I intend to sleep for about twelve hours. Maybe twenty four. And then we can decide what story we're going to spin to the plods.

I think we can make their lives reasonably interesting.

Bill Dughaille

Chapter 5: Clearing up

Bill Dughaille

Friday 16th August

Roy Keane, who we last encountered being thrown out of the Ireland football team at the World Cup for describing his boss in language rarely used even after the nine o'clock watershed, has reappeared in the news. Apparently and allegedly and seemingly he deliberately fouled someone called Alf-Inge Haaland during a match between Manchester United (R Keane, captain) and Manchester City (A Inge-Haaland, victim). Haaland's knee ligaments were damaged, and he has hardly played since.

A number of things make this interesting; the "allegation" appears in Keane's autobiography, so we can probably dispense with the "allegedly" (etc). Secondly Keane appears to show no remorse, boasting how he stood over the injured Haaland while taunting him. Thirdly he has stated that the tackle – attack is more accurate – was a result of a perceived slight he had received from Haaland three years before.

The BBC can now no doubt extend their comment to read "feuds are common in some parts of the Arab and Western worlds".

Why does the name "Bush" suddenly spring to mind?

Incredibly enough, some football supporters of Keane are attempting to play the whole thing down, saying that "such things happen in football", which is rather like saying that corruption "happens in politics", so maybe we should accept it.

I think this story will run and run. Into the law courts.

Roy Keane, however, should not be confused with Robbie Keane, who, from all accounts, is a generally nice all-round guy, who was somewhat of a hero as a player in the Irish squad during the world cup.

Yet who, for some bizarre reason, seems to want to play for Spurs. Arsenal would be a much better choice.

School results are out; there is a marked increase in the number of pupils getting good results, resulting in the traditional "standards-are-falling" cries. Typical August stuff, happens every year. If the results dropped it would be "why are our teachers so bad?" Maybe next year the figures will be the same allowing both the cries of falling standards and the criticism of teachers. Or perhaps fallen teachers and the criticism of standards.

Prague and Dresden are among European cities struggling to cope with floods.

Elvis fans from across the world are getting together in Memphis to commemorate the 25th anniversary of his death. Strange people.

Mugabe continues his attempts to emulate Idi Amin.

According to the BBC, millions of web site addresses have been abandoned after their first two year purchase period; the original explosion in web site mania has disappeared, leaving unused addresses such as refffffffffffffffffffffffereeeeeeee.com. Or so they say. It's difficult to imagine anyone actually registering such an address, but on the other hand it's quite easy to believe it.

Finally, also in the "I wonder if that's true?" category, a story in the Times relates how four teenage boys were trapped in a loft for 27 hours after they had gone into the loft to get the food and alcohol for an illicit party while their parents were away, only to find they couldn't get the trapdoor open again. It took them those 27 hours to realise that they were supposed to pull the trapdoor rather than push it.

Just think; Ali Wood and his friends from Gillingham, Kent, will now forever be known as the Trapdoor Gang.

Strange few days, which is only to be expected, I suppose. Tuesday was uneventful. Wednesday the sergeant with WPC Sandra managed to get through the defences with a few of his bods, and tried to interview everyone. He looked relieved when he came across Colin, Jimmie and myself sunning ourselves.

'Ah, relatively sane, people,' he said with a grin.

'How much money do you want to put on that?' I asked. He thought for a while.

'Bugger all, I suppose. But you can't be any worse than the

others. That woman over there – ' he gestured towards where Mrs Gladstone and Miss Melly were sitting on a bench – 'all I could get out of her was the fact that you can't get decent hot chips any more. Just went on and on and on about it. Suggested that it was my duty to investigate.'

'Well, she's right, isn't she?'

'What, you want me to investigate a lack of old fashioned chippies?'

'No, she's right about hot chips. Where can you get decent, proper sized chips, freshly cooked, with salt and vinegar, just the way it should be, not this "fries" rubbish you get these days. . When I was a kid they'd put them into paper bags, and you could nibble off a bottom corner and suck the juice out. Lovely!'

'Still used newspaper when I was a nipper,' he ruminated, 'but I remember being a brand new constable when they brought the paper bags in. You wouldn't know anything about those days,' he told WPC Sandra. he turned to us. 'All bloody kebabs or whatever it is these days. Isn't the same.'

'I heard there was a place off the High Road which still did them,' I said. He shook his head.

'Greek bloke. Closed down and went back to Greece, more's the pity. Then a Chinese bloke took over, tried his best but the environmental department closed him down because of the rats. Turns out in the end that there'd always been a problem with rats, only the Greek bloke knew how to sort the sanitary people out. Some councillor getting a few quid in a brown envelope. Poor Chinese bloke didn't know the scam. Or wouldn't pay up.'

'You can't trust anyone these days,' I said. I was prepared to run the clichés through for as long as it took, through gritted teeth and mental anguish.

'So I'm not going to get nowt out of you lot either, am I?'

'What have you learnt so far?' I asked, ducking the question.

'That you can't get decent chips anymore. Oh, and one of my constables is being taught the Foxtrot, and another found himself forced to investigate some problem with someone's car, only it turns out the car doesn't exist. They spent an hour looking for it before I enlightened the silly bugger.'

'Well, we'd be no good in the witness stand, if you think about it.'

'I know, I know. I only really wanted to know for my own sake. Satisfy my suspicions, as it were.'

'What about the little sods you arrested?'

'Yes,' he said, sighing, 'what about them? Let me see. One claims to have been ambushed by the IRA. Then apparently some loyalist thug kicked him in the guts. Had a deep Belfast accent, so he says. Another assures us that there was a vampire in the trees, breathing fire. I thought that was dragons, myself, but that's modern fiction for you. The others more or less agree that they were just walking past when a hundred thousand zombies attacked them, out of the sky. They want contracts with the X-Files. And they don't know nothing about five stolen cars which just so happened to be in the street where they were walking, innocent as the day is long.'

'So, no chance of prosecutions, then?'

'I wouldn't say that. Okay, these kids get good lawyers – one of them's National Front, so our greasy little lawyer turns up pronto – but we've got their fingerprints on the cars, and the steering wheels, and on one of those petrol bombs they threw in here. And we've got the old codger walking his dog who's prepared to say he saw them throwing the petrol bombs, including the ones that backfired and bounced of that tree there. We've got prints on those, but can't find the buggers. Skipped town, I reckon.'

'You don't honestly expect to get convictions?' I asked, hoping that they hadn't actually worked out how a petrol bomb could bounce thirty yards off a tree. He shrugged.

'I've been in this job a long time. Even so, I remain hopeful. We did get blood samples off them – someone had his brain in gear – so we know they were both pissed and high. On the other hand any decent lawyer is going to say that any statements they might have made were under duress, purely because they were stonked. I hate lawyers.'

'What happens now, then?'

He fixed his cap firmly on his head and looked directly at me.

'I know something happened that night. And I know you were involved. And the others. And I don't believe this run around with hot chips and non-existent cars and foxtrots. But you know what my problem is? I can't prove a thing. Squat. Zilch. I'd like to see those gormless little bullies locked up for the safety of society. Or at least, the safety of the old people I have to deal with when they get mugged. But I can't. So the second best thing is that they had the shit kicked out of them, and I can't prove that either.'

'Sergeant, really,' I said, 'you must watch your blood pressure.'

He grinned back.

'Six months and it's retirement for me. The world can go hang. I've done my bit.'

And off he went. I wondered what WPC Sandra thought about it. She's a bit young for retirement.

Nothing much happened yesterday. Well, around here that is.

Today we finally had the Great Election of. The ballot box – some cardboard box, carefully sellotaped with a hole cut out of the top, and the name of some industrial detergent on its side – was placed in reception where Ms D could keep an eye on it. I made some witty comment about it when she was setting it up, being in reception at the time. Jo-Lee or whatever still wasn't back, but apparently I need to take it easy and recover, and they can get along without me – that's gratitude for you. Anyway, she replied with some comment about being sure the best person would win, and followed that up with something about everyone supporting the wounded hero.

'Bollocks,' I replied. My stunning repartee muscle seems to have atrophied somewhat.

Again.

'We'll see,' she replied sweetly. She's been ever so polite since

Monday, it's unnerving. Almost sweet. Considerate. Very unnerving. She stuffed some of the precious ballot papers into the box, and I couldn't help noticing that the top one appeared to have a tick close to my name on it.

'Early voters?' I asked.

'Some people left them here straight after breakfast,' she replied. 'I'm just putting them where they should be.'

Now I'm sure Ms D could fool most people, but I'm pretty sharp at spotting an untruth, and she had the air of someone who was telling them. Slightly shifty, answers too fast. I grunted.

'Well, I suppose I'd better be off then. Catch some rays while they last.'

'Off you go, then. I'll bring you a cup of coffee at elevenses.'

'It's okay, Jimmie always does that.'

'Ah, well, mustn't interfere with the loyal batman then, must we,' she replied huffily, and did her sweeping-away-into-admin trick. I might have tried the same thing, only I can't normally – and on crutches it's impossible. So I stood there for a few seconds, trying to grasp an idea that was flitting around my brain, desperately dodging my consciousness. Acting on instinct I leaned over the counter, and quickly appropriated a thick wad of the ballot papers. They had about five times as many as they needed, a few wouldn't be missed.

And I doubt if General Franco will be around to sign his.

Then I made a hasty if somewhat unco-ordinated exit.

I hate bloody crutches.

Out in the garden Jimmie and Colin stood up to give me a hand sitting down as I dropped the papers down carefully, face down. Initially I had tried to insist that I didn't need help, until I found out just how difficult it was parking yourself down in a low slung deckchair without the aid of one foot, which you have to keep hanging in the air.

'The gorgeous Ms Dervish doing well?' asked Colin enthusiastically. I haven't seen him smile so much over the past few days as I have in aeons.

'How do you tell, with women?' I asked in response as they took their seats, or deckchairs.

'True, true,' replied Colin.

'Feck,' said Jimmie. I'm afraid he's beginning to relapse into his old method of communication.

'Jimmie, you really must try to expand your vocabulary,' I remonstrated easily.

'Feck, sorry boss,' he replied.

'Well, it's a start I suppose,' I sighed. 'Apparently the voters have been out in force in the early hours of the morning. Even anonymously, so I am led to believe.'

'Well, I put my vote in straight after breakfast,' said Colin. 'Ms Dervish was saying how some people had even put their papers in before she was ready. She was busy stuffing them into that soap box.'

'Well, well, what a coincidence,' I said a trifle sarcastically, 'seems like so many people prefer not only their votes but also their selves to be anonymous today. Strange that.'

'What on earth are you going on about?' asked Colin, unfazed.

'I'm talking about something called stuffing the ballot boxes.'

'Ah, no, you can't be serious,' Colin said angrily, and picked up my pile of papers. 'Ballot papers! You want to rig this, don't you? I would have thought that would be below even you.'

I thought the "even you" was a bit much. I raised my hand imperiously.

'Now just a minute Colin, what do you think I'm talking about?'

'You want to rig the vote. You just said, "stuff the ballot boxes", even if there's only one.'

'And why do you suppose I would want to do that?'

'I don't know,' he said after a while, 'I know you don't want the vote, but the logic is irrefutable.'

'Irrefutable? Colin, you do come out with such long words,' I teased him. 'Tell me, did you notice whose name had been ticked on those ballot papers the delectable Ms D was busy shoving into the soap box?'

'I didn't look, naturally,' he bristled, and then looked a little embarrassed. 'Well, I didn't mean to look, but it could have been your name. I don't see what's wrong with that. A lot of people want to vote for you.'

'Including the Fabulous Fiona,' I thought out loud.

'Who?'

'Colin, let me put it to you this way. When I was in reception Ms D was also stuffing papers in which had arrived too early. And they also had my name ticked. The logic, as you say, is irrefutable. Ms D is stuffing the ballot boxes, and I'm the target.'

He paused.

'Yes, that makes sense,' he said finally.

'Precisely', I replied bitterly. 'She's trying to fit me up. I must have made some comment that upset her, so this is her method of revenge. Women are like that.'

'Er, boss ...'

'Yes, Jimmie?'

'Er, feck, boss.'

'Precisely. Irrefutably, in fact.'

We sat for a while contemplating the unknowable ways of women, until I picked up one of the ballot papers.

'But I have a plan,' I said, 'and you two are going to help me. It's called – ' I paused for effect – 'pre-emptive stuffing.'

'Feck, can't be pre-emptive if she's started it, boss,' said Jimmie unhelpfully.

'That's not fair,' Colin remonstrated excitedly, 'you want to set up some other poor sucker. Just to get out of things. It's – it's unethical.'

'That depends on who I'm setting up, doesn't it?' I asked. I carefully ticked a name on the list, and held it up for them to see. There was silence for a few moments.

'We're going to need more papers than those,' Colin pointed out.

'Feck. Watcher so she don't see,' said Jimmie.

It's all about politics.

We gathered in the dining hall this evening shortly before eight to hear the results of the great election. There was a good turnout, and a general air of happy chatter. One or two people waved to me and held a thumb up to indicate that they had voted for me. I resisted the urge to hold a finger back up to them to indicate my thanks.

Finally Hotpants turned up to a smattering of applause, carrying a stuffed briefcase, and with an armful of papers. He took up position at the serving end, and began a speech.

I'm not very good with listening to speeches. I struggle to stay awake.

From the occasional moments when my concentration managed to latch on to what he was saying, he was thanking everyone for taking part, boasting about how important it all was, and claiming that, although he hadn't actually calculated the figures, there seemed to be a big turnout, possibly as high as 90%, way above any normal democratic result.

Of course, depending on which basis he uses for his figures, he could probably get a figure of about 500%. God knows what he'd make of that. Only in a true democracy do the dead get a vote.

Finally he got onto the results, and, as I expected, there were a number of people with one vote, almost undoubtedly their own. Mrs Gladstone made a very respectable fourth place, the major was one vote ahead in third, I came in second with more votes than people in the room, and then Hotpants got to the victor.

'And the winner is,' he announced proudly, 'Linda Lovelace.'

This was greeted with an initial silence, and then an outburst of cheering and clapping, with a few whistles thrown in. Hotpants stood there beaming, his face bathed in sweat as he enjoyed the enthusiastic response to his work.

'Miss Lovelace,' he managed to call out over the noise, 'where is Miss Lovelace? Is she here?'

'She's gone to bed,' I called out, 'having an early night. Said she had a sore throat.' The room erupted into more noise, including a certain amount of laughter, through which Hotpants stood there, smiling ecstatically, blissfully unaware. I caught the eye of Ms Dervish, standing against a wall behind the others, and she smiled and nodded, accepting defeat.

At least I hope that's what it meant. Otherwise I'm in deep something.

That was when the doors opened and Sergeant Gilmore entered quietly followed by four of his plods. The room went slowly quiet, as people noticed him moving silently around the room. By the time he reached Hotpants you could have heard a pin drop. I doubt if there was a resident there who wasn't expecting to be taken away for a quiet chat and a game of hit-the-truncheon-with-your-head.

And that's when it happened.

They took Hotpants away.

After a whispered, one sided conversation where Sergeant Gilmore was the only one speaking, two coppers took Hotpants' arms and guided him unresistingly to the doors and out of the room. Gilmore stayed behind to give a short speech on staying calm and nothing to worry about and could he speak to the head of admin?

While he and Ms D were involved in a secretive tête-à-tête I slipped quietly outside. Well, considering the circumstances, I crutched out without too many people making any comments. I made my way to reception, from where I could see a police car moving off with Hotpants in the back, a constable either side of him. Then I went outside and waited by Gilmore's car, leaning on the bonnet, enjoying a cigarette, which I am going to give up again, any day now.

It must have taken him about twenty minutes to make his way out.

'Sergeant Gilmore,' I said enthusiastically as if his appearance was the most welcome thing in my life. It was, at that stage; standing on one leg kills you after a while, even when you are leaning against the bonnet of a cop car. 'Why have you taken away our dear, highly regarded Doctor Hot – Snuffelwurtz?'

'Sorry, can't tell you, I'm afraid,' he replied, getting into the car.

'I promise not to mention it to a soul,' I promised, crossing my fingers.

'Can you keep a secret?' he asked, winding down the window. I know that trick. When you say "Yes", they say "So can I", and drive off. Which would leave me lying on the ground.

'Seems a bit unfair on us, keeping us in the dark.' He didn't seem to me the sort of person who would be too long bothered by the idea of unfairness. He started the engine.

'I've explained everything to your Miss Dervish,' he said.

'Well, second hand information is the curse of communication, you know. Starts all sorts of rumours.'

He looked at me with a twinkle in his eye. 'And she asked me not to tell you lot anything. Especially you. She was quite – emphatic – about you. Doesn't seem to trust you much. Now are you going to get off that bonnet, or shall I just reverse and let you fall off?'

'Sod,' I said, hobbling away from the bonnet. 'No respect for the wounded, that's your problem.' He smiled, waved goodbye, and did a quick reverse and turn before speeding off down the driveway.

Some people.

I called all sorts of curses down on him as he went down the driveway, but none seemed to work. Reluctantly I crutched myself back into reception, went around the counter, and leaned on the door to the admin office, where Ms D was going through some files.

'So, what's happening?' I asked in my best I'm-not-really-interested tone. She looked up.

'What are you doing there?' she asked in feigned concern. I could tell it in her eyes, which had that look of a schadenfreude enjoyment about them. She came towards me. 'You should be resting with that leg, you know what the doctor said. Now be off to the dining room, have a cup of tea, and get an early night.'

'Yes, yes, but why have they nicked Hotpants?'

'You shouldn't be worrying about others in your condition. Now go get some rest, I have a few phone calls to make.' With that she closed the door in my face, forcing me to suddenly hop backwards, and nearly ending up collapsed over the computer.

Worry about others? She knew I was consumed with curiosity. I wouldn't be able to sleep. The leg would itch like hell into the small hours.

Grumpily I crutched my way back to the dining room, hoping someone had overheard something, but no joy. There was much speculation, and quite a bit of "I always knew there was something wrong with him" from people who had happily told him their life stories in confidence.

But, as to hard facts, zilch. Colin and Jimmie, whom I can rely on to provide solid intelligence, were just as dumbfounded as I was.

Which means not being able to find anything out until tomorrow, at least.

And the damn leg has started to itch.

Tuesday 20th August

So much going on in the world, it's difficult to keep up. Looks like Haaland is going to sue Keane over what the press continue to refer to as a "tackle". The football season is now in full swing, so it's a sort of added spice to make things interesting.

Israel has promised to withdraw troops from Gaza and Bethlehem if the Palestinians take responsibility for security – can't help but feel we've been there before.

While Mugabe continues his policy of destroying his country; Zimbabwe have had to hand over the deeds of their London embassy to Gaddafi, being in hock to the Libyans for oil they can't pay for.

Zambia, meanwhile, is refusing to accept US emergency food aid because it comes from genetically modified crops. Difficult choice; if the GM projects go wrong the word "disaster" won't even describe half of it. There's a story current in the papers about how some "rogue" seeds got into one of the test sites somewhere in the UK, and government ministers are desperately trying to pretend that there isn't a problem.

Most people would prefer "Mutant Ninja Turtles" to remain a fictional concept.

Bush's desire to invade Iraq is still high on the agenda; General Norman Schwarzkopf, who was in charge of the allied forces in the last bash has apparently stated that a unilateral invasion of Iraq is not a very good idea. Over here back bench politicians are also calling for some restraint on the rush to war.

The Pope's in Poland, so the woods are clear.

A fourth person has died of Legionnaire's disease in Cumbria.

Trouble in Chechnya.

A British man has been arrested after "allegedly" becoming violent in mid-air on a flight to Florida. Seems he had polished off two bottles of whiskey, which reminds me of a story from a few years ago about the man who had been picked up wandering around naked after having drunk over three bottles of whiskey. A police report said that he had progressed from being alcoholically poisoned to merely blind drunk.

That sort of thing might tempt some to consider Muslims' rejection of alcohol as an option, until you read about Amina Lawal, a 30 year old Nigerian woman who has been found guilty of having a child out of wedlock, and condemned to death by stoning. The Muslim court in Nigeria has graciously decided that the stoning won't be carried out until the baby is weaned.

Maybe they should have a look at bombing Northern Nigeria instead of Iraq.

The Argentinian economy seems to be improving; more deposits than withdrawals have been made into bank accounts since the crisis began.

Moving to the "that'll be an August regular" story then: Oxford University has been criticised for not accepting a deaf girl who is a "brilliant maths student", getting several zillion A's in the recent exams. Every year they trot out a similar story – "Brilliant single child with one arm longer than the other called Dingle of single Welsh black Jewish one-legged mother student rejected by elitist university".

Actually, last year's, if I recall correctly, was a girl, rejected by Oxford (or maybe Cambridge), who wanted to study medicine, and eventually received a scholarship grant from Harvard about five times the size Oxford could offer, so I don't think she was too overly bothered.

In the "good news" section: a hippo feared lost from a Prague zoo during the floods has been found alive. Eighteen year old male hippo Slavek was said to be rather bad tempered but otherwise unharmed. Now I'm as fond as animals as the next man, but dealing with two tons of unhappy vegetarian hippo sounds a bit beyond the call of duty. I mean, you hardly tickle it behind the ears and tell it everything's okay, would you?

Well, I suppose some people would.

Once.

And in the "I don't believe it" pages: Mr Les Johnson of the Isle of Sheppey is being sued by a burglar he apprehended when he and his wife returned home to find said burglar and another unidentified criminal looting his home. The burglar claims that Mr Johnson caused him physical harm when Mr Johnson executed a citizen's arrest. I think the vast majority of people who have suffered burglaries privately think that Mr Johnson obviously didn't apply sufficient force. That and the belief that the law's an ass.

Politicians are planning on making the use of a mobile phone while driving a car a crime. Opponents of the measure are asking why the plan doesn't extend to people eating or smoking while driving.

Well, precisely.

And the nugget of the day is: Ian Duncan Smith is backing Steven Norris as the Conservative candidate for the next London mayoral election. Apparently it's to do with projecting a more liberal, people-friendly image for the Conservatives. Purely logically speaking, Norris could fit that description; he acquired the nickname "Shagger Norris" due to his predilection for keeping a number of "mistresses" on the go at the same time.

So that'll be the young female vote then.

The fact that the current mayor, Ken Livingston, fired Norris because he is – or was, could well still be – a director of Jarvis, one of the contenders for the privatisation of the London Underground, something which Ken opposes, and saw as a conflict of interests for Norris, will not escape the attention of Londoners. Or maybe it will.

That's a long, convoluted sentence. Others seem to have the same problem when talking about Norris.

I read somewhere that Nixon lost an election to Kennedy because of a poster showing Nixon with the question "Would you buy a used car from this man?" Funnily enough, Norris used to be a used car salesman.

But IDS, as Ian Duncan Smith is being called by the Tories – presumably hoping to catch some of the reflected glory of FDR, JFK and LBJ, though it won't work in the UK – faces two problems which, combined, are insurmountable. Okay, three, if you add the fact that he's boring and grey.

Four, he's a politician.

The first of the major two is that he can't adopt any right wing policies, or he'll be perceived as a right wing nutter, much as old Labour was stereotyped by the "Loony Left" image before Blur took over and redefined them as anything you want them to be. The second is that, even if he threw caution to the winds and adopted the most right wing stance you could imagine, he would find that Tory Blur had beaten him to the punch.

Well, we found out why the plods wanted to have a word with old Hotpants.

Strangely enough it was Jimmie who found out first, and even managed to explain it in a pretty straight forward manner, if you ignored the liberal sprinkling of "fecks". It sounded a bit unlikely – not that I was doubting Jimmie, of course – so I decided to get some confirmation from another source when I saw Sergeant Nameless and WPC Sandra the day after, busy supervising the removal of various goods and artefacts from Hotpants' (ex) office.

He confirmed what Jimmie had told us, and a very strange tale it was.

The sergeant had previously remarked on how he had thought he had seen Hotpants on television at some stage; the idea stayed and niggled at his mind at odd hours, like that word or name you know you know, only you just can't get the blasted thing to surface. Until one night when his wife was talking about a holiday they'd had a year ago, spending a couple of weeks in France. She reminded him of his attempt to learn French by watching television – 'actually I was checking the talent out on a rainy day', he confessed to me – when he had stumbled across a French version of Crime Watch.

And that's where he had seen a mug shot of Hotpants, eyes bulging, and looking like the sort of person who can clear a railway carriage just by being there.

The sergeant got in touch with Interpol; initially they were a bit dubious about the matching of someone up with a picture seen a year ago on holiday by some lowly plod, until the sergeant managed to procure a photograph of Hotpants, and send it to the Frog police. Even then it required the particular coincidence of someone in the know happening to be shown the photo purely by chance.

And the someone in the know had recognised the face.

Turns out that Hotpants really does fit in well into a mental home. Only preferably inside, in a padded cell, with no sharp objects in reach, and a large dose of sleepy-bye tablets administered on a regular basis.

He was a student in Munich about fifteen years ago, trying to major in both psychology and political science, when he had a disagreement with one of his professors, a disagreement that developed into a heated disagreement, then a passionate disagreement, and finally led to things being resolved with the aid of a rather sharp bayonet which Hotpants – or rather, Hans Smidt, as the university student's name was – kept tucked in his boot for "protection", pulled out and applied with what sounds like could literally be described as overkill.

After a month on the run the German police caught up with him, and he was quickly consigned to a padded cell in a high security hospital. There were doubts as to whether he had flipped because of what had happened, or whether he was basically a couple of hampers short of a picnic even before the argument, but as far as I'm concerned anyone who carries a bayonet around with them is either attending a very dodgy university or is already suspect in the sanity stakes.

For the next ten years – bar a couple of times when he went awol from high security institutions, which proved that he wasn't stupid, however unbalanced he might be – he spent the time trying to get his doctorate in psychology.

Unfortunately his threshold for criticism was non-existent, as had already been proved, and the initially difficult problem of finding people willing to assess him became almost impossible after a few tantrums, until all contact was through a strengthened glass screen.

Even then he would go into a rage at the slightest suggestion by any visiting academic that his work was anything less than perfect.

The funny thing was, he never once lost his temper with anyone else. The warders, or whatever they're called, were more than happy with his behaviour, considering him a harmless loon who had probably suffered a brain implosion from too much study.

Which is probably why he managed to slip away for the third time. But this time he had no intention of staying anywhere anyone might recognise him, so he set off for somewhere other than the fatherland.

It took a few months for the Germans to put pins in a map where he had been sighted, and find the general line pointing straight towards France. Coupled with the discovery of some Teach Yourself French books found in his room, the Germans put two and two together, and came up with three. By the time the French were informed, and showed his face on television, Smidt was long gone, almost undoubtedly in England by that stage.

They seemed to have ignored the rather blatant fact that Smidt had long been able to speak fluent English, Spanish and French apart from his native German. Blatant to them, that is, since the facts were apparently on his file, though strangely enough he had never mentioned his language abilities to anyone around here.

The hospital where he had been a guest also kept copies of his correspondence, and found letters to and from a respected psychologist named Doctor Adolf Snaflwurtz in Vienna. They promptly hot footed it around there, found the Herr Doctor in perfect health, if somewhat confused by their appearance, and just as promptly forgot about him, probably at about the same time that Smidt turned up on our doorstep and convinced the Board of Directors that he was the eminent Viennese Doctor Snaflwurtz.

God knows how he managed it. A raving fruitcake he may be, but talented with it. Though it also explains why the other doctors around here gradually lost interest in actually being here – I doubt whether Smidt was the most conducive of colleagues.

'Hans Smidt,' the sergeant commented, after he had finished his tale, 'that's the same as John Smith over here, so they tell me. I wonder if that had something to do with it. Maybe he felt he had to rise above such a common name.'

'I doubt it,' I replied. 'But then, who knows why people do things?'

'I thought that's what your precious doctors were here to tell us?'

'God, no. Bunch of loonies, that's what they are. Apart from the ones who are in it just for the money. And they're probably missing a marble or two.'

'Makes me yearn for your average criminal,' the sergeant mused. 'Nice, simple, straightforward motives. They may not be rocket scientists, but at least when you show them the evidence they don't try to tell you it's all because of a deprived childhood and inner mental anguish – though, that's what the lawyers will come up with.'

'So how is the investigation into the paranormal cum IRA cum loyalist incident coming along?'

'Hah! I think you can forget that one. We've got two of them the CPS are willing to go for – aggravated car theft, I think it'll be – but I doubt they'll get more than a slap on the wrist. Apart from that, case closed.'

'Well, there you go. I suppose we'll just have to live with it then.'

He gave me a sideways look. 'Yes, I can see you're gutted,' he said, and went off to where a van load of Smidt's effects were waiting.

In a way I'm a bit sorry to have seen Hotpants go. Things aren't likely to be as peaceful around here anymore. They'll probably bring in someone who will Ask Questions.

And Expect Answers.

Part Two: Advance

Chapter 6: Not bloody likely

Saturday 24th August

India has refused to consider normalising relations with Pakistan until Pakistan ceases all support for Islamic terrorists in Kashmir. No change there.

Nor in the Middle East, where deaths continue on a daily basis, both Palestinian and Israeli.

Though as far as the Kashmir situation goes, there is a little dark humour in the news that a chocolate company had to withdraw their advertisements which used a joke about Kashmir to sell their products. You can only conclude that they didn't realise people who are dearly trying to kill each other might not be amused by a joke about the fact.

That's the problem with foreigners, no sense of humour.

In the Philippines the army are trying to hunt down one lot of Muslims who beheaded some missionaries, and another lot who have kidnapped four others.

Neil Lennon has decided to stop playing as captain of the Northern Ireland football team after a loyalist threat was made against him and his family if he continued to play for the national team. The reason for the threat is that Lennon is a Catholic.

Mugabe has announced that criticism from Western states is a racist campaign to undermine Africans.

I don't think Mugabe needs any help from the West in that extent.

A state of emergency has been declared in central China due to flooding.

House price increases have slowed down. The question is, are they going to go into reverse like last time?

Usual annual nonsense about how girls are doing some much better at school than boys. Doesn't seem to carry on into life post-school, and no doubt there are more than enough theories about that.

David Attenborough has officially revealed that he is now one of the old fogeys by criticising the BBC for showing too much "trivia". You can hear the words now, "Wasn't like this in my day ..."

Looks like the war against Iraq has started prematurely: some Iraqi "dissidents" took over the Iraqi embassy in Berlin, along with a few hostages. Their principle weapons seem to have been some pepper gas and probably Shouting Loudly. Once the German police received permission from Iraq to enter the embassy, they walked in and the "liberators" gave themselves up peacefully. The group call themselves the "Democratic Iraqi Opposition of Germany"; the "Iraqi National Congress (INC)" who are allegedly the main Iraqi freedom movement have condemned the action, stating that they "do not condone violence".

No wonder Saddam is always smiling.

Wonder if Bush agrees about the "not condoning violence" policy.

Greenpeace have staged a demonstration at a nuclear plant near Cape Town, South Africa to protest at the use of nuclear power in the country. It can only be related to the Earth Summit taking place in Johannesburg, since the interesting thing about the nuclear reactor is that it's the only one in South Africa, and in fact – following some careful research – I find, the only one in Africa.

Plenty more nuclear reactors closer to home.

Though I guess the weather's better over there.

Finally, the way ahead, as seen by people wearing strange glasses and taking pills they shouldn't have (which probably means the news source exaggerated a little): Marks and Spencers are thinking of putting microchips into their garments which will not only warn the householder when they are popped into the washing machine at too high a cycle, but also tell them when their clothes clash. So, after she's listened to her clothes screaming in the wash, there will be Ms Smythe at a cocktail do, when her little black piece starts chatting to Ms Jines' jacket; "put me on at 30 degrees when my label clearly said 25, and, oh, my dear, have you seen those awful pearls she's wearing, and that nose stud, at her age!"

I doubt the idea will catch on. A bit like those devices in cars they mooted some years ago which would prevent you driving if you'd had too much. Would you really want to be reassuring a machine that you'd only had one pint, honest, and would it mind switching the ignition on?

Then you finally get home and your fridge tells you it's time for a diet and won't let you at the Fosters.

We sat outside enjoying the end of the summer, Colin, Jimmie and myself. A bit overcast, so we were wearing clothing to match – there is something eternally English about pretending that summer is still with us, even if it's never appeared for the year.

Colin was engrossed in a critique of the newspapers' coverage cemetery manners.

'Local vicar's been complaining that people have been eating chips in the graveyard,' he said. 'I would imagine people have eaten chips in the graveyard for centuries.'

'Well, ever since they were brought here from the Americas and fried,' I replied. God knows whether that amounts to "centuries". Fortunately I was saved by the appearance of Mrs Gladstone and Miss Melly. Or so I thought.

'Local Echo,' she said, brandishing a copy of that awful rag. 'Latest update on the loonies,' she declared.

'Let me take a guess,' I said, 'we've been working on a nuclear device and they want the army to move in and level the place?'

Her face brightened. 'That would be fun, wouldn't it?'

I think my and Mrs Gladstone's ideas of fun might not be compatible.

'But, no, sadly not,' she continued, dragging out some reading glasses and applying herself to what was undoubtedly Carney's latest miss on the truth. 'According to this – and I quote – "the doctor at the centre of the fantastical revelations of sexual therapies turns out to have made everything up in his own mind" – that will be the poor Mr Smidt, no doubt.'

'Fantastical revelations?' I asked with disbelief. 'Carney made the whole lot up himself.'

'Carney?'

'Er – the so-called reporter – I presume it's a bloke called Carney, seems to write everything in that excuse for a newspaper.'

I didn't really want anyone knowing why I knew it was Carney. They might start asking Questions. Again.

She checked the byline. 'Yes, you're right. Jim Carney, it says. Now you come to mention it, you're right, I hadn't noticed, but he does seem to be involved in all the articles. In one way or another. Hmmm.'

Phew.

'However,' oh bollocks, 'he does add a very interesting item at the end of the item.'

Werewolves at the local loony bin?

'He states here: "and we are led to believe from a totally reliable source that one of the patients is planning to stand in the imminent mayoral election. And why not? The current contenders don't appear to have many marbles, someone who has obviously lost his own will be a great antidote to the hypocrisy and cant that the various parties have put forward so far." You know, I fully agree with him. I think you'll make an excellent candidate.'

'Eh?'

'As mayor. I said to Miss Melly as soon as I read it, "There's only one of us that could be". Of course the major huffed and puffed a bit, as he normally does, but deep down he agrees.'

The major? He couldn't stand as a scarecrow in a birdless rocky mountain. On the other hand I have no intention of being caught up in running around kissing babies and pretending to like my fellow humans.

Then again, "Major Mayor" could sound like a lisped take out from Catch-22.

'Well, I did think of standing at one stage,' I said in all modesty, 'I have this feeling that most people don't really want a mayor – they know that all that will happen is that their council tax will go up to pay for jamborees for the usual snouts at the trough. I was planning on standing as a "none of the above" candidate.'

I paused, realising that I was sounding a little too enthusiastic.

'But it's too late now, I'm afraid. That business with the hooligans, and now with a broken ankle, well, not much we can do about that now, is there?'

'Tosh!' replied Mrs Gladstone.

She really does define things rather sharply.

'I agree,' said Miss Melly. 'Things have been rather boring since our last escapade. We need something to concentrate on. I think it would be just the sort of thing to get everyone going again. We could get out there and campaign for you.'

What, a sort of Blue Peter campaign? I wondered.

'Exactly!' declared Mrs Gladstone. 'I take the point about the ankle, but that will heal, you know. In the interim, we shall work on your campaign. Leaflets, stuff like that.'

'Err, I ...' I began, but they had swept off.

Great. Some people are born to power, etc, I seem to have been hijacked.

'Feck!' said Jimmie.

I looked at him carefully. There had been far too much enthusiasm in that "feck" for my liking.

'Er, boss,' he finished off sheepishly, and pulled his cap further over his face.

'It will never work, you know,' said Colin, retreating back into his copy of the Independent.

'Of course it could work,' I replied, 'if my leg wasn't wrapped in plaster, and hardly any time left for proper planning. But there's no reason why it shouldn't.'

'Right,' he said, meaning "wrong".

Some people have no faith.

As we were packing up for lunch Colin announced that he was going out this afternoon. We looked at him in a sort of stunned disbelief for a moment.

'Want anyone to come with you?' I offered. I couldn't imagine Colin gaily strolling about outside on his own. More likely to have a panic attack and end up hiding in some bushes waiting for nightfall so that he could race back and escape humanity.

'Er, no, that's all right, um, I'm just going down to the village market with Ginger,' he said in a rather embarrassed manner. 'He says they have a couple of good second hand book stalls along with all the rest.'

'Really? I'll have to make a trip down there sometime, when this leg is better. They closed the one in the shopping centre, you know.'

'Yes, you mentioned it. Sad when that happens. Almost like the death of a part of civilisation, it seems. Oh, well, better get back for lunch I suppose.'

We carried the folded chairs and newspapers back across the lawn. I couldn't help but wonder at Colin's news. I presume he was embarrassed because he felt it looked as if he was deserting us for his new found friend Ginger; the strange interplay of emotions that humans display when affected by group and peer changes.

I should become a sociologist.

Funny to think of Colin going outside, though. Almost like watching someone growing up and getting ready to fly the nest.

Ms D caught me this afternoon and demanded my signature on a piece of paper. I rarely look at these things – apart from a pathological hatred of paperwork, I presume Ms D knows what needs to be signed, and anyway, if I accidentally sign the wrong thing it will never stand up in court. On this occasion I had just finished signing it with my usual flourish – I don't think I've ever used the same signature twice, and no-one seems to have noticed, not even when I use a credit card – when I caught a glimpse of the title, the start of which read something like "Application for". Now to my mind "Application for" sounds too similar to "Volunteer for" for my liking.

'Just a second, what exactly is that thing?' I asked as she whipped it away and tucked it into a folder.

'The paperwork for your political career. You can't just turn up on the day, you know.'

Oh, great, I thought, another excuse gone west.

'Great,' I said, smiling enthusiastically, 'I'm terrible at that sort of thing.'

'I know. That's why I made sure we have all the i's dotted and t's crossed. You won't need to worry, I'll take care of the administrative side.' She smiled at me encouragingly – at least that's what I think it was meant to be – and left to get the creaking bureaucratic side of things rolling.

Watching her walk away I began to wonder about this whole thing. So far I had everyone else doing the work; under those conditions I could possibly see a way to enjoying the whole thing.

Maybe that's what leadership is all about.

Wednesday 28th August

Milosevic's trial in the Hague for war crimes has restarted after a month's recess. Milossa-who? I can hear people ask. All seems so long ago now.

There's a report that members of the Saudi royal family – "senior members" – paid bin laden £200m not to attack targets in Saudi Arabia. Wonder how true that is.

The US has criticised Russia for bombing Georgian villages – that's Georgia, eastern Europe, not Georgia-on-my-mind Georgia – in their battle with the Chechnyans. Apparently they're concerned that the Russians are violating Georgian sovereignty. The words pot, kettle and black spring to mind.

Most newspapers are highlighting the contrasts at the Earth Summit in Johannesburg – champagne and lobster at the summit, open sewers and poverty a few miles away in the township of Alexandra.

Violence in Spain as police charge people protesting against the banning of the Basque separatist party, Batasuna. The government claims that it is directly linked to the ETA terrorist/guerrilla group.

A division of views on the upcoming attack on Iraq. The countries around Iraq certainly don't seem to be too happy at the prospect – at one level this isn't surprising, but it could be thought that they would be rather pleased at the prospect of getting rid of Hussein, considering his penchant for invasions.

Only when encouraged by the US, though.

Rabbi Jonathan Sacks – "Britain's Chief Rabbi" – has said that Israel's attitude towards Palestinians goes against the tenets of Judaism. Or that's what the newspapers are reporting. No doubt there will now be a barrage of support and complaints. There isn't the same sort of response when Muslim leaders state that suicide bombings are against Islamic beliefs, possibly because Islam doesn't appear to have a "Chief Imam".

Participants in the Miss World contest are threatening to boycott the event, as it is being held in Nigeria, where Amina Lawal has been sentenced to death by stoning for having a child out of wedlock. The counter argument is that this is exactly what the Islamic groups want, having called the Miss World contest an "abomination".

Talk of a written constitution for the EU; the "UK government thinks that a simple, written constitution will help ordinary people to warm to the European Union".

Babblefish translation: "speak slowly to the simple people so they vote yes when we have the referendum for joining the euro".

What on earth makes the UK government think that the EU could come up with a "simple, written constitution", god alone knows. They'd take five years and come up with something which would confuse everyone, make flatpack assembly instructions look like sensible coherent English, and keep the lawyers busy for generations.

A conservative MP in Australia will be spending a day in the service of a brothel in Kalgoorlie, Western Australia. Apparently the madam, Mary-Anne Kenworthy, won Barry Haase in a charity auction, and intends to put him in a frilly apron and set him to cleaning, to show the high standards of hygiene expected of her brothels. The words "Australia" and "brothel" do not normally come to mind in the same sentence, but according to the report Kalgoorlie, a mining town, has had "an open brothel" for over a hundred years.

Arsenal beat West Bromwich five-two; Manchester United beat Zalaegerszeg five-nil.

Zalaegerszeg?

This being August, it is of course the silly season, no matter how much serious news there is about.

So out come the traditional sightings of "big cats" on the prowl. Panthers, pumas, cougars, almost everything apart from lions and tigers, are out there in the wild, untamed farmlands of Britain, blurred photographs giving tantalising glimpses of feline creatures too large to be domestic cats.

There'll be another sighting of Nessie along in a moment.

In the same category must be the announcement that Roy Keane is planning a coaching career in football. Images of players strewn around a field having been crippled from behind come to mind. "No, Smithy, that's not how you do it, here, give a good kick just in the ankle, like this".

And finally: the Wildfowl and Wetlands Trust tagged six Brent geese to record their 8,000 kilometre migration from Ireland to Canada. One has been found in an Eskimo hunter's freezer, £3,000 tag still attached. The hunter was most surprised when he opened his door to find the researchers asking if they could have the tag back, pretty please.

I'll tell you something about this lot: give them something positive to do, such as forming a private army or organising an election campaign, and they don't half go for it.

And it appears that we have more than our fair share of artists, copywriters, editors, photographers, musicians, actors and generally artistically inclined people – quite often in the same person. But that means we also have the usual arguments and tantrums.

I made the mistake of sitting in on one discussion meeting; from then on I decided that appointed people such as Mrs Gladstone or Miss Melly would bring me the options arrived at in any meeting, and that I would make my choice behind closed doors. Apart from making sure I don't get involved with heated debates over whether using the word "firm" is better than "strong", or the advantages of sky blue over pale blue, it allows me to acquire authority by distance.

People need to create myths around their leaders.

And hobbling about on crutches all over the place is incredibly tiring.

In terms of other resources, Jimmie has become our scavenging quartermaster sergeant.

At some stage – and I'm beginning to think it was as soon as he arrived here – he must have reconnoitred every nook and cranny inside and out. I don't know what he used in place of keys, but there aren't any locks broken anywhere, so he must have some talents he probably doesn't want the world to know about. In any event, if it's needed, Jimmie knows where to find it, if it exists. On commenting that a colour printer would be handy, he disappeared to a storage room somewhere and came back with a brand new colour A3 inkjet, not even out of its box.

According to Ms D one of the doctors had ordered it "for patient therapy" before Smidt had made life so difficult for him that he decided this was a place to avoid.

"For patient therapy" apparently translates as "getting the company to pay for it and taking it home for personal use." According to Ms D it was common practise.

Printing paper isn't a problem either. There's an entire room stacked to the ceiling with boxes of some of the more expensive stuff, including some glossy paper I'm told is for printing high quality photographs. Every month a little more is delivered and added to the stockpile. When I asked Ms D why on earth we were ordering such amounts she let me into a little secret.

'I'm here to make sure this place runs smoothly, and that doesn't necessarily mean efficiently – actually it hardly ever means efficiently. To start off you need to understand how these organisations work. This one has a civil service approach, which means, amongst other things, that you never decrease the amount of goods you order. The people who sign off the accounts understand increased orders, even though they don't like them, but decreased orders worry them. If you tell them that you now only require half of your paper order, the next thing you know is that they've come in to check everything else. And the end result is that you end up under supplied with everything apart from your paper order, which has either stayed the same or doubled. Trust me on this.'

I believe her. I worked for a council once.

Mrs Gladstone, Miss Melly and the major have turned one of the smaller lounges into an operations room, complete with maps of the entire area, broken down into various districts. I presumed that Jimmie had provided the maps, but not so.

'I popped into the council offices,' Ms Melly explained, 'and told them that I was Professor Wittgenstein from Brunel University, carrying out a study of the preparation for the election in order to determine whether it was free and fair. They fell over themselves to help me. Even gave me copies of all their election guides, rules, regulations, you name it.' She gestured to a four foot high pile of manuals, books and documents in the corner. 'They might come in handy as door stops,' she concluded.

I was astonished. 'Ms Melly, since when have you decided to go around pretending to be a long dead philosopher?' She blushed slightly.

'Well, I thought that if poor Mr Smidt could do it ...'

That's the strange thing. When he was a doctor, I don't think anyone would have admitted to liking old Hotpants, but now that he's turned out to be one of us, he's become "Poor Mr Schmidt".

'Man was a raving psychopath,' Mrs Gladstone pointed out.

Well, almost everyone.

My thoughts were interrupted by the sound of what seemed to be a rather loud and long raspberry.

'What on earth was that?' I asked. 'Sounded like someone playing a trumpet very badly.'

'Tuba,' Miss Melly corrected, 'it's the band. I'd better go look after them.' She slipped out the door, and I raised my eyebrows at Mrs Gladstone. She shrugged.

'Musicians,' she said. 'Though I doubt if any of them have played an instrument in the last ten years. They insisted on being able to take part, decided to start a band.'

'And how exactly would we be able to use a band?' I wondered.

'That's what I thought at first,' she replied, 'but I didn't feel up to arguing or upsetting their feelings.' The original noise had been supplemented by several other instruments, not only out of tune, but being badly abused.

'Good for morale, a band,' commented the major.

'Then I thought to myself,' Mrs G continued, ignoring him,

'well, its all about getting the message across. They might sound like a herd of stags on heat with hernias, but they're enthusiastic, and it'll draw attention. After all, we're not pretending to be professionals. One of our main strengths is that we aren't professional politicians. We have to use that.'

Well, a point, certainly, but I think I would like people to see me as professional to a certain degree.

'And Miss Melly has taken them in hand?' I asked.

'Used to be a music teacher. Hasn't done it for a while. Going back to her first love, but that's another story. Come and have a look at the maps.' I hobbled over with them to the wall holding the maps, to a background cacophony which was likely to ensure a visit from the RSPCA.

'Looks very efficient,' I said, nodding at the maps, 'what are the colours for?' They seemed to be coloured in like a children's book, watercolours by numbers.

'We've adopted the red-orange-green approach,' Mrs Gladstone said briskly. 'With tones in-between, as you can see. Red is for waste of time, green is for where we're most likely to pick up votes.'

'Like a traffic light,' pointed out the major.

'This area, for example,' Mrs G said, tapping an irregular section of red, 'upper middle class, Tory voters. Aren't likely to vote Loony. Probably think it bad form. This area,' another red area tapped, 'an estate, mostly poor, aren't likely to vote at all, and probably don't pay their council tax anyway, so our argument will mean nothing to them. This area, on the other hand,' a tap on a green section, 'very arty middle class, like to use the word "irony". Bound to get quite a few votes from people who see us as an argument against global bureaucracy.'

'Um, is that what we are?' I asked, thinking it might be a step too far.

'Course not. That's the way they'll see it, though. Their problem. Bunch of idiots who think modern art is an expression of their individuality. You know, pile of bricks representing the essence of mankind, twenty pence a brick at the builders, sell it for a small fortune.'

'Fools. Total morons,' agreed the major helpfully.

'I've got a group working on something we can flog to them, some sort of lapel badge or something, help to raise funds,' Mrs G said.

That was a question which had occurred to me; at the moment we had managed to find our requirements from the many store rooms here, but sooner or later we would need actual cash to pay for things.

I was impressed.

'I'm impressed. Have they come up with anything yet?'

She snorted. 'No. They're as bad as this lot here,' she said, gesturing at the green patch. 'Keep having arguments about duality and the essentialness of being, or similar codswallop. I suggested something, but they pooh-pooed the idea, so I decided to leave them alone. No doubt they'll eventually come up with the goods, but it's like being at the whole cycle of conception and birth. Very messy and something to be avoided unless you're involved. Anyway, let me explain our plan to you.' She turned to tables laden with leaflets.

'What was your idea?' I asked before she could get started on the plan.

'Idea?'

'For the arty lapel thing?'

'Oh, that! I thought we could have a badge that said "Irony". The idiots would probably wear it quite happily without realising that it was a comment on themselves. Anyway, the plan.'

She picked up a leaflet. I was quite proud of it. I had chosen it especially from the options they had come up with. There was a simple word at the top, asking "More?" Then it went on to explain, in very short, simple phrases, that the choosing of mayor would result in the raising of taxes to pay for bureaucratic snouts in the trough. No waffle, just the basic question of whether people wanted to fork out for others to stuff themselves.

'This is phase one,' Mrs Gladstone continued.

'Phase one,' agreed the major happily. I thought Mrs G might clock him one, but she seemed unperturbed.

I was a little perturbed myself.

'Phase one?' I asked, nervously. Phase one indicated phase two, three, and anything up to phase numpty nine. I was hoping for just one quick phase, requiring limited amounts of energy.

'We haven't got a lot of time, so we've divided things into three phases,' Mrs G elaborated. 'In phase one we put the fear of taxes into them. I'd like to add bureaucracy to that, but we don't have any ideas on that yet, you know, the Brussels approach, all houses will have to be painted regulation colours, that sort of thing. Phase two -'

'Phase two,' echoed the major.

'Phase two we introduce the question of why their local councillors aren't doing the job properly in the first place. Bring into play the thought that a politically appointed mayor will just continue and increase current corruption. Whereas we will play a role in highlighting the corruption, flushing out the bad eggs, forcing the councillors to do their job properly.'

'We will?' I asked. That wasn't on my agenda. Nice quiet life with an annual salary of over fifty K sounded good, flushing out corruption sounded like getting involved.

And it upsets people.

'Absolutely. You get elected, bring us into the job, and we'll sort out those horrible little suited and overweight pompous good-for-nothings. You know that there's only one woman councillor amongst the whole lot?'

'Er, no, I wasn't aware of that,' I replied, somewhat thankful that someone else was going to do the rooting out of evil bit.

Then again, it's all about leadership, isn't it?

'She's the only good one, then, is she?' I asked. Mrs G did her snorting impression.

'Total waste of space. Worse than the men. In the old days she'd have been burnt as a witch, and good riddance. Anyway, phase three.'

'Phase three,' intoned the major.

'In phase three we combine the fear of taxes with good honest feelings of righteousness. It's a combination of phases one and two, and this time we nudge them towards the starting gates. The "you can do something about it" phase. We hit them about a week before the election, just enough time for them to gossip with the neighbours over how terrible everything is, and decide to vote for the man in the cream suit.'

'Right,' I said, rather taken by her energy. Then a thought hit me. 'Cream suit?' I enquired.

'We've decided that you have to wear a cream suit, like that Bell chappy. Makes you look honest and fearless.'

'Er, I think that might be a bad idea,' I said, not overly happy with the "fearless" bit.

There are some nasty people out there. Most of whom probably don't like cream suits.

And the Bell chappy spent a lot of time in Bosnia. Being shot at.

'And why not?' she demanded.

'Excellent idea, I thought,' the major said quietly.

'Um, well, perception,' I replied, floundering. That and the fact that a cream suit makes you an ideal target, and gets dirty very quickly.

I gave up wearing white shirts when I realised my propensity to spill coffee, drop jam and splash gravy on them. 'It's the connotations,' I said, the word "white" raising a thought.

'Exactly,' said Mrs G, 'the knight in white armour. That's the connotation.'

'Or possibly the men in white coats,' I pointed out.

They looked almost crestfallen.

'I hadn't thought about that,' Mrs G said eventually.

'A point, a point,' added the major.

'Get someone to have a look at it,' I ordered.

I'm getting good at this.

'For the moment, however, I have to say, you really have got things under control. Tactics, strategy – the whole shooting match, as they say.' Personally I was feeling knackered. A couple of kind words, and then off to find Colin and slag off the days news, I thought. To my surprise Mrs G softened visibly, and the major almost blushed.

'Well, Ms Dervish has also been a great help,' said the major, 'she's even offered to get a breakdown of the socio-economic groups in the area,' he said. I watched amazed as Mrs G put her elbow into the major's midriff.

'We don't want to advertise the fact, now do we, major?' she asked as the major tried to get his breath back. She smiled at me. 'Ms Dervish is, um, how can I put this – concerned that her job might be at risk if it's known what she's doing. So make sure she doesn't find out that the major's told you.'

'Of course, of course,' I replied charmingly, 'I fully understand.'

I didn't, as it happens, but that feeling isn't unusual.

'I think I'd better do a tour of the various groups,' I said, looking for an exit. 'You know, make them know their effort is welcomed and recognised, appreciated, that sort of thing.'

Mrs G looked at me with some concern in her eyes.

'You're tired,' she said. 'I'm sorry, here we've been prattling on, and you standing there on those crutches with your leg.' She pulled herself together, an imposing sight. 'You get off to your room and relax,' she ordered. 'The major will bring you a cup of tea, and you get some rest. You're going to need it in a few weeks.'

I didn't like the sound of that, but she shooed me out, and the major came along to help me to my room.

I almost smacked him with one of my crutches. He does mean well, I'm sure, but he does tend to get in the way. Once I had stretched out on my bed I told him to get along, and forget about the tea.

After all, in the movies the hero always gets this gorgeous young woman to look after him – I get the major.

It's not the same, somehow.

I drifted into sleep, and half-dreamed that Ms D came into the room with a cup of tea.

I knew it was Ms D. She called me an idiot.

September

Monday 2nd September

Mukhtar Mai, a 30 year old woman from a remote part of Pakistan, has welcomed the death sentences passed on six men who had been involved in gang raping her. The rape had been "ordered" by a tribal court to punish her family because her brother was accused of having an affair with a woman from a more powerful tribe. Ms Mai is quoted as saying, "God has given me justice".

More deaths in Israel, on both sides. Israeli President Moshe Katsav has called for an investigation into claims that Israeli soldiers were becoming trigger happy, resulting in the deaths of innocent civilians. The Palestinians have said that this is a cosmetic announcement, for the consumption of the press and public only.

Debate over whether to build more nuclear power stations. They're more environment-friendly than coal or gas fired power stations, but produce rather nasty by-products, and few people like them.

George Dubya Bush has compared himself to Churchill.

600 passengers were on a ferry which caught fire in the engine room, north east of Great Yarmouth; while the automatic extinguishers doused the fire, the passengers were ordered deck-wards, told to put on life jackets and await further orders.

The good news is that the vessel, ferry Norsea, subsequently managed to re-start engines, amidst what sounds like a veritable plethora of rescue boats and helicopters along with normal sea traffic altering course to be available, and limp its way to Zeebrugge after a journey time of 21 hours.

There's something comforting about the idea of people voluntarily putting all shoulders to the wheel to rescue those in peril on the sea.

Scotland's Environment minister, one Ross Finnie, has apologised to the director general of the Confederation of British Industry for calling him "an English prat". Apparently the remark was made during an official dinner, where one can only presume the wine was flowing rather well. Mr Finnie has claimed that his comment was taken out of context. Difficult to see what context calling someone a prat could make a difference. The CBI director general had, however, suggested that Scottish people had a chip on their shoulders, so it sounds like handbags at five paces.

Arsenal drew one all with Chelsea in a game described as "scrappy", which is putting it politely. Most of the players looked like they'd rather be at home watching the telly. But Patrick Vieira did try to liven things up by getting himself sent off, though manager Arsene Wenger believes it was undeserved.

Taken out of context, no doubt.

A certain Sir Archibald Gwendelynne has been brought in here to "sort the mess out". I think that refers to the fact that this place ran quite smoothly under the control of the staff and patients, without any doctors, for a good few months until the local indignant brigade and the yobbos decided that we were having too much fun.

And we sorted out both lots without any help, thanks very much, but I can't see anyone saying "good job, carry on then".

Colin was very dubious about the appearance of this new character. 'Never trust anyone with an unearned title,' he commented. Personally I think he's being a little unfair; I'm sure Sir Archibald paid a lot of money for his.

I was planning on dubbing him "Wendy", until I had a session with him this morning. For some reason he's decided to meet everyone for a few minutes, god knows why; he isn't qualified in any branch of psychology or psychiatry, though I understand that he does have an MBA.

I can only presume it's some reflex action from the many directorships he seems to hold in various companies, only he hasn't cottoned on to the difference between staff and residents.

I duly crutched into his office this morning and took a seat. He didn't look up, but rather muttered something, and began to read from a list of handwritten questions.

'The vampires keep you awake at night?' he asked.

I considered this question. Maybe we had acquired someone whose fruitcake factor exceeded that of the recently departed Herr Smidt. Then again, if he believed in vampires, who was I to criticise? I was about to respond that my vampires were very well behaved during the hours of darkness – apart from the one which suffers from hay fever – when he looked up, possibly impatient with my lack of response.

He had very nasty eyes.

I'm not talking about mad eyes, raving eyes, doom-is-nigh eyes. I'm talking about cold, light blue, dispassionate eyes. The type that understand everything and feel nothing.

Suddenly I felt nostalgic for old Hotpants.

'No, I can't say I'm bothered by vampires,' I replied neutrally.

He ticked off number one on his list.

'Mind beams? Radio waves? Feeling unbalanced?'

How do you answer that one? 'Haven't noticed any of those,' I said. Another tick.

'Blood seeping down the walls at midnight? Any religious revelations?'

'Nope.' Another tick.

'Are you Napoleon or any other historical character?'

'Not that I'm aware of.' I was beginning to understand, I think. The others interviewed before me had presumably seen a large fish with open mouth, and thrown in bait with gay abandon, hook attached. As he ticked off that one I tried to think what I could add to the list. Fairies?

No, maybe not. Too many connotations.

'Boiled eggs giving you constipation?'

'Not that I've noticed, no.'

'Genetically modified salads eating away at your left breast, or indeed any part of your anatomy?'

I would have paid to find out who had planted that one. I hope they offered a viewing.

'Nope.'

He ticked again, and frowned.

'Any part of the food which gives you cause for concern?'

'Not really. Seems pretty good, all things considered.'

Another frown. I hadn't come up with anything on the list, so obviously something needed to be added. I racked my brain desperately for some weird and wonderful affliction, but for once I was at a loss. Being stalked by the aspidistra? We don't have an aspidistra. An imaginary aspidistra?

'How do you mean, "all things considered"?'

I waved my hand vaguely, as you do under such conditions, and then tucked it firmly under my arm.

'Small kitchen, minimal staff, limited budget. A variety of dietary requirements, that sort of thing. They seem to manage rather – heroically, really.' I added the word quickly, because I could see in his eyes that when the word "budget" was mentioned he automatically thought of the word "cut".

'Interesting. Interesting.' He studied a file for a few moments, mine presumably. 'So what is wrong with you?'

Now that's a very rude question to ask around here.

'Wait a minute,' he said suddenly, 'you're the one who wants to become mayor!'

I could see that he'd found a pigeonhole to put me in.

I rather wondered how he'd classify the other "normal" people standing as mayor.

Probably the same way.

'I'm standing for mayor,' I corrected. I doubted whether he would see the difference.

'Why?'

Well, you have to give it to him. No beating around the bush. So I gave him a summary of how I thought that people didn't want a mayor, didn't want their taxes increased, so I would be standing as a "do-nothing" candidate.

'Interesting,' he said in a bored sort of a way, meaning "you're a nutcase".

'People are tired of politics,' I carried on, even though I knew I shouldn't.

What is this human urge to defend yourself against people who aren't worth it?

'Politics is irrelevant,' he replied, closing the folder, and I thought, Hello, you've just said something you shouldn't have. He had that in common with Herr Smidt; a total disregard of people he thought didn't count.

'People don't want the standard options. They want a chance to say no. Electing a mayor who does nothing is a statement,' I pointed out, valiant to the last in arguing a case I half-believed in against someone – or something – that didn't give a toss.

For some reason it worked. He paused, and drummed his fingers on his desk awhile.

'A mayor who does nothing?' he quoted, seemingly lost in thought. It wasn't reassuring. I'm sure Himmler responded the same when he said, "Zyklon B, eh? It's better, is it?" The cogs of his mind were moving inexorably in some world of his own.

I was beginning to wonder how I could terminate the whole interview when he suddenly smiled and looked at me in the most charming way possible.

'You know, I hadn't thought of it that way.' To say he morphed – a rather ugly word which Colin would no doubt rant against – would not be far off the truth. Suddenly he was Mister Charming of the new century. And he was good at it.

'Good therapy, is it?' he asked.

'Absolutely,' I replied.

If he'd asked me whether it was good for the ducks I would have said yes.

'Any problems at the moment?' he asked, all concern, which didn't fool me. Frightened me witless, yes, fooled me, no.

'Money, I suppose,' I answered noncommittally, wondering whether I could touch him for a fiver. It was one way I would leave this room with a little self-respect.

'Money, of course,' he said in a way that suggested that, yes, he had heard of money, but didn't like to talk about it. 'Money's very tight at the moment, I'm afraid.'

This is a bloke who is director of numpty five companies, I'm pretty sure the first thing he says on becoming director of a new company is "Money is tight" just before sacking half the staff.

I bet when his wife told him about needing new school uniforms for the kids he replied "money is tight", and then charged the cost to his latest company.

There wasn't much I could say to that statement, so I didn't say anything. We looked at each other for a few moments. It was like looking into a snake's eyes. Except that this one tried to smile.

'Well, yes, I wish you the best of luck,' he said finally. I dragged myself to my feet, and hoicked my crutches towards me. He looked back in surprise.

'You've hurt your leg?' he enquired.

'Broken ankle.'

'But won't that – won't that be a problem in, er, your campaigning?'

'I was thinking of going for the sympathy vote,' I said ironically.

He looked at me blankly, then nodded. 'Of course, the sympathy vote.' He nodded seriously, and made another note.

I made my exit.

This guy is a serious weirdo.

And not a very nice one.

Somewhere I could hear the band. They'd managed to master a rendition of something, which if you closed your eyes, blocked your ears and held your nose while hitting your head against the wall, might be recognised as "Yankee Doodle Dandy".

Why, I have no idea.

Chapter 7: Well, thinking about it

Thursday 5th September

Tony Blair has promised to publish a dossier giving overwhelming evidence of Iraq's involvement with developing "weapons of mass destruction", or WMD as the newspapers are calling it. The general belief is that it will be simply a rehash of old facts and general guesswork. Meanwhile Blair is ignoring calls for an emergency session of parliament to debate the issue.

Israel is due to expel the brother and sister of a suspected Palestinian militant, a move called by some a war crime. Senior Israeli judges have debated the issue, and decided that it is permissible under international law. On the Palestinian side, calls to end all violence against civilians, such as suicide bombings, have been firmly rejected by radical Palestinian movements.

Amnesty International has claimed that the UK Anti-Terrorism Crime and Security Act, brought in swiftly after the twin-tower attacks of 11 September 2001, is a contravention of basic human rights. The Special Immigration Appeals Commission has already ruled that the detention of nine alleged international terrorists contravened the European Convention on Human Rights. The main areas of concern are detention without trial and abuse and intimidation while in prison. The case of Lotfi Raissi has been used as an example: he was held for five months until a judge ruled that there was no evidence against him.

Signing of a final declaration at the Earth Summit in Johannesburg has been delayed due to a disagreement on a paragraph concerning women's rights.

Fire-fighters in the UK are on course to go on strike, the first time since 1977. They've been offered a 4% increase – well above inflation – but are demanding a 40% increase. Many people are concerned that the increased use of strikes to hold employers to ransom is a sign of a return to the "winter of discontent".

The foxhunting issue has popped up again, with new research indicating that banning fox hunting will have no effect on the fox population.

A Greek consumer organisation has declared a recent boycott of shopping a success. The Greeks were protesting against price increases which appeared as the result of the introduction of the euro. They claim that businesses have used the euro as cover for increasing prices, and the Greek government is in general agreement.

Roy Keane has been charged by the Football Association on two counts of bringing the game into disrepute.

Following on from the report that Marks and Spencer were planning on putting microchips into clothing so that your trousers could warn you if your tie was too loud, a new report has announced that flat-pack furniture of the future will be equipped with microchips to warn you when you have put the wrong sections together, or even tighten screws too tightly.

The general response of the person in the street to this news has been that (a) instructions are usually incomprehensible, so why would the chips be any different? (b) There is almost invariably a piece missing in a flat-pack, how would you handle a missing chip? And (c) it would be better to have smart chips in the warehouses so that you don't have to wait two months after paying for something that turned out to be out of stock.

A more disturbing thought is that your clothes might end up talking to the flat-pack as you try to assemble all the bits and pieces. It could well be a little off-putting if your new MDF cabinet agreed with your shoes that you really shouldn't be wearing corduroy trousers with silk shirt, and there was no need to put the boot in so hard.

Ms D arranged an interview for me at the local radio station, due date this morning.

That woman is wasted at this place. Her efficiency knows almost no bounds. I just wish she wouldn't practice it on me. Radio interviews weren't part of my original idea. It was only when she mentioned the word "television" as an alternative that I reluctantly agreed.

I did put my foot down, though; I insisted on Jack Rimmer as the interviewer, a straight sort of a person who doesn't get a kick out of embarrassing his guests. Ms D immediately agreed, seeing the logic of my argument.

Unfortunately we didn't see eye to eye about the issue of what I was going to wear.

I wanted to turn up in leather jacket and jeans, mainly because they're comfortable – with a plaster cast on your foot baggy jeans are about the only thing you can pull on. But Ms D insisted that appearance is important.

I pointed out that it was a radio interview, people weren't going to know what I was wearing. She pointed out that what I wore would influence the attitude Rimmer would take. I pointed out that Rimmer was a decent bloke who didn't indulge in reacting to people according to what they wore. She pointed out that everyone did that, and anyway, there could well be photographers around, and she didn't want me appearing in the local press dressed as my usual scruffy self.

Scruffy self? I call it comfortable.

I pointed out that I didn't give a toss for what people thought of my dress sense. She pointed out that that was obvious, and that I was going to be dressed smartly if it killed her.

Or me.

So this morning I stood on crutches in reception dressed in fawn slacks, brown jacket and smart polo shirt – all purchased from ye olde Marks and Spencers by Ms D (sans micro-chips, I hope) – while Ms D, Mrs Gladstone and Miss Melly circled me, tugging and straightening my new clothes like a mother and aunts inspecting some kid before their first day at school.

'Look, do you mind?' I asked. 'I'm not a fashion model. People are going to get the wrong idea,'

'Now shush,' said Mrs Gladstone severely, critically pulling the collars of the jacket down in such a way that almost broke my neck. 'We aren't doing this for you. There's a lot more at stake than just you. We're doing this for the cause.'

The Cause? Since when had my decision to make a stand for democracy and a decent salary become someone else's Cause?

'I think we'd better go,' said Ms D, checking her watch for the fifth time.

'Good idea,' I replied, and crutched it as fast as I could outside to Ms D's car.

'Good luck,' called Miss Melly. I half expected her to add, "and play nicely with the other children, now".

'They mean well,' Ms D said as we drove off, 'they do want you to do well.'

I made a snorting noise, and sank into my chair as much as I could, which wasn't much. I've never liked these cars where you feel like you're two inches off the floor, and there's about three inches of leg space in front of you.

'Think of it this way – they're on your side. Wait until you meet the people who aren't.'

'Now there's a cheerful thought,' I replied.

'You'll have to face up to it sooner or later,' she said.

And sooner it turned out to be.

As soon as we arrived at the studios we were hustled through to the interview room. Apparently Rimmer had been delayed by a minor traffic accident and a urgent need to explain a failed breathalyser test to the police. His place had been taken by a person by the name of Mary-Anne Dinkins.

'She's rather new to this,' explained the young girl leading us through the maze of corridors, 'so we'd appreciate it if you kept that in mind.'

'Of course,' I said smoothly, relieved at the idea of facing some young girl new out of university, beaming little face with fresh media studies degree in sweaty little mitts.

Our conversation was interrupted by a man bursting out of a glass-panelled room ahead, shouting something at someone inside. For some reason he had headphones attached to his head, cord trailing down his back.

'I'll sue,' he shouted at the woman who followed, trying to placate him. 'I've never done anything remotely like she was suggesting, not with a sheep or any other animal.'

'Oh, dear,' said Ms D. 'I rather think it might be an idea to cancel the interview. At least postpone it.'

'Um,' said our young girl, clearly confused by the situation.

'Nonsense,' I said, 'what are you talking about?'

Since I'd already gone through all the rigmarole of being fashion dressed, coached, lectured at, and generally bossed around, I had no intention of having to go through all of that again – especially not for little Miss Jenny-Sue.

Ms D was about to say something when the sheep gentleman almost knocked us over as he came storming our way.

'I'm going to sue!' he yelled furiously, stopping in front of us, as his placater nervously tried to remove his headphones from a distance without him realising.

We looked at him in astonishment. 'Get off, woman,' he shouted, slapping away the other woman's hand from the earphones. 'When I'm finished with you, you won't have a radio station left!' he assured us. Ms D and I looked at each other in surprise, and then back at him. He stopped, doubt creeping into his face.

'You don't work here?' he asked, as the woman jumped into the air and whipped off the earphones, before scuttling back to the glass-panelled office. Sheep man hardly noticed.

We shook our heads mutely. I was dying to know about the sheep.

He shook himself, and patted down his jacket. 'Ah, er, sorry about that, just what that – that disgusting person in there was suggesting was just – disgusting, absolutely disgusting.' He smiled suddenly, fished in his inside jacket pocket, and brought out a leaflet. 'John Harper, Green party,' he introduced himself, handing over the leaflet. 'Standing for the mayoral election, you know? You've probably seen my picture on the posters.'

'Of course,' I replied warmly, lying smoothly. 'You're the one who's into animals, aren't you?' I asked innocently. His face turned purple.

'If you're going to go in you'd better do it now,' said the young girl, checking her watch. I decided that being in there was probably safer than being out in the corridor with sheep man, and crutched quickly away before he could find his breath.

I'm sure Ms Dervish placated him with a story about how I had hit my head in an accident a few days ago. I certainly hope so.

Once inside the interview room I sat down and the young girl silently placed a set of headphones on my head, attaching assorted leads, while making various gestures to another young woman on the other side of a desk loaded with assorted mechanical looking boxes covered with buttons and sliders and things.

Mary-Anne looked all of about twelve. Possibly thirteen. She was wearing a white t-shirt without a bra underneath, which was presumably some sort of statement, but only gave you the urge to put a jacket around her and tell her to go home and get dressed properly.

On the other hand she had these red flushes in her cheeks which mirrored the look in her eyes, which, not to put too fine a point on it, put the words "testicles" and "grinder" into the same sentence.

'And now everyone,' she was saying, looking up at me dispassionately, or at least as dispassionately as you can do while radiating murder, 'we have someone described as the man from the real Loony Party. Now I'd love to be able to tell you that he was wearing a silly top-hat with ribbons, maybe a rainbow coloured waist coat, but I'm afraid he's actually rather smartly dressed. You know, if I met him in a pub I might think he was on the make. So tell me, is that jacket real camel hair?'

'Camel hair?' I replied. What's my jacket got to do with anything? What does camel hair look like? Why introduce fashion? What do I know about fashion? Or camel hair?

I don't even know if it comes from camels. Do they breed them specially?

'I'm afraid I don't know. I wouldn't recognise camel hair if you wrapped it in a brick and hit me over the head with it.'

She paused. 'You mean you bought a jacket and didn't even look at the label?'

I shrugged. 'Oxfam aren't too hot on labels,' I replied easily, making a mental note to apologise to Ms D later. The last thing I wanted was a discussion on who had arranged my wardrobe.

'Oxfam?' she asked thoughtfully. 'You believe in supporting charities?'

'No,' I replied, relaxing into the seat, getting the grip of this strange conversation, 'I believe I'm skint.'

She eyed me for a few short seconds, trying to take my measure.

And wondering if the mincer was required.

'So are you serious about standing for mayor? All the reports I've seen indicate that you're a bit of a joke.'

Nothing like a free invitation.

'All the reports? Such as?'

'The Local Echo wasn't very flattering.'

'Sorry, I thought you were referring to serious reports. Do you really consider the Local Echo a font of knowledge? Anyway, that aside, that's one – what other reports are you referring to?'

'So you mean you are serious?' she asked, neatly ducking the question.

Sometimes you have to create a golden highway, as that Chinese bloke said.

'It's a question of simple arithmetic,' I replied. 'Only twenty five percent of the population voted in the referendum. Just barely over a half of those voted Yes. That's just over twelve and a half percent. If you were in a room of a hundred people, and someone said, "Let's go for a pint", and twelve and a half people said yes, would you call that a democratic decision?'

'How could half a person want a beer?'

'They wanted a shandy. So answer the question, do you believe that doing something because twelve and a half percent of the electorate want it is democratic?'

'That's a very interesting question, and I hope listeners will already be dialling in to give us their answers as we take a short commercial break.' She flicked a couple of switches, and I could hear the radio's jingles coming in through the earphones.

'So you are actually serious?' she asked, puzzled, and added 'it's okay, we're not on air now, they can't hear us.'

'Tell me about the sheep,' I begged, both out of fascination and the fact that I would never believe anyone remotely connected with the media if they told me my words couldn't be heard.

'The sheep?'

'That bloke from the Green party who wants to sue you over something about a sheep.' Her cheeks coloured again.

'He's a patronising little shit. Fat, patronising little shit. Called me his "dear little girl". I don't take crap like that. He's pretty stupid too, so it wasn't hard to twist some of his statements into suggesting that he had abnormal relations with farmyard animals.'

I laughed. 'You think it's funny?' she asked, a note of "that wouldn't be wise" in her voice.

'You should have seen him coming flying out with his headphones still on,' I replied, 'it was absolutely hilarious.'

Her face relaxed, and then she giggled.

'It was rather fun,' she admitted. She held up a warning hand. 'We're about to go back on.'

'Welcome back to News and Views, the programme which listens to everyone, and everyone listens to. We've got a whole lot of people out there phoning in, so let's go straight away to Joe on line one. Joe, what do you think about a madman running for mayor?'

They're all bloody mad, would have been my answer.

'Disgraceful,' an old man's voice was saying in my ears. 'I fought in the war to defend democracy, and these young people think it's a joke.'

'Well, what do you say to that?' asked Mary-Anne, a twinkle in her eye.

I think she takes a nasty enjoyment over watching people on the spot.

'I fully agree with you sir,' I said. 'I believe that people who have sacrificed so much are to be especially respected. And that democracy is the most important thing in our culture, and must be respected as well. Which is why I'm standing for mayor. To give people a chance to say, no, we don't want these plastic non-entities that the major parties want to foist on us, especially not for a position they've invented just to give a soft job for one of their buddies. Let's put it this way, what power do you think a mayor will have?'

'I don't understand the question,' said old Joe, obviously unsure of himself.

'Will the mayor be able to increase the numbers of police on the street? No, because the police won't come under his control. Will he be able to increase your pension? No, of course he won't. Will he be able to provide more health care? Again, no. In fact the only thing he will be able to do is to increase our council tax to spend on traffic schemes, or building a new office for him to do nothing in – nothing apart from holding dinners for his friends in politics. Do you really want that?'

'No, I don't, definitely not,' said old Joe. Of course he didn't. Ask the right questions and you get the right answers.

'So don't you think a good democracy should allow people to vote against it?' I asked.

'I, er, I don't know,' Old Joe mumbled. Mary-Anne cut him off.

'Thanks for calling in Joe, now let's go to another caller, Mohammed. What's your take on the barmy party, Mohammed?'

'It's like blasphemy, you know' said a man's voice which sounded like education hadn't featured heavily in his life, and intelligence even less. And he certainly didn't sound like a Mohammed. More like his life had started in some misbegotten part of London, and hadn't improved. 'You know, when people say things about god, and then they should be stoned to death, you know. I'm a Muslim and we believe in the book you know, and we also believe in democracy, and people don't believe that we do, and they should be punished for it, you know.'

'Thanks for calling in, Mohammed, interesting point you've made there,' Mary-Anne said, cutting him off, smiling impishly at me. 'Sounds like the Muslims aren't on your side, the old people aren't on your side – do you really think many people are going to vote for you?'

'Yes, I do,' I replied confidently – whether I believed it or not is another question – 'You can't take just two phone calls as being representative of the entire population. I believe that most people are tired of politics, the reason they don't vote is that they think that all politicians are as bad as each other. So I'm standing to allow them the chance to say so.'

'So where do you stand on women's issues? Or youth concerns?'

'I don't stand anywhere. I'm standing on a promise of not doing anything, above all not increasing people's taxes to line other people's pockets while getting nothing out of it.' I paused. 'But if you really want, I could dedicate part of the day to doing nothing about women's issues. In fact, I could not do anything for several groups all at the same time. I'll be out there multitasking at doing nothing every second of every hour of every day.'

I managed to restrain myself from adding "come sun or rain".

'Very Monty Pythonesque. But what if you find yourself in a position to do some good? Say there's an old people's home which is due to be closed down, and you could save it? Would you?'

Now there was a googly I hadn't expected.

Admittedly I hadn't thought about any such options, mainly because most planning just makes you nervous. Consider the problems and they're likely to appear. Ignore them and they tend to go away.

The others you can make it up as you go along.

'That's a very interesting question, Mary-Anne, and I'm glad you asked it,' I replied suavely.

She gave me the finger for some reason.

'One of the reasons people don't trust politicians is that they believe they will break any promises made in an election as soon as they think it's expedient. So, having promised to do nothing, if I were to suddenly take up some cause or other, I'd be breaking a promise, and I couldn't do that.'

And I'd have a watertight reason not to get involved, either. Some of these people can get worked up over nothing.

'And,' I continued, holding up a hand to forestall interruption, 'you used the word "good". Who decides what is "good"? Most of the time it's a subjective issue – take your example of the old people's home about to be closed down. It sounds terrible, but what if it's riddled with asbestos and needs to come down? You'll always have people on one side with apparently very good arguments for a case, and others with equally apparently good arguments against, and both will claim that they are on the side of the "good". However – ' I had to raise my hand again as she opened her mouth – 'however, if I really considered that there was an important issue which as mayor I felt I could do something about, I would be honour bound to resign and let the people vote again, because to do otherwise would be to break my word.'

I thought that was quite good.

I had just thought of it.

'That certainly sounds impressive, but can you really expect people to vote a very good salary to someone who promises to do nothing for it?'

'That's an interesting point, but not entirely accurate. After all, my doing nothing is doing something. I'm providing an alternative voice, a chance for people to state publicly that they reject party political abuse of the system. And if people are really that worried about the salary side, I don't know, maybe I'll get a broom and sweep the streets. It can't be any worse value for money than anything the others are offering.'

'You'd be the highest paid street sweeper in the country, then,' Mary-Anne commented. 'Well, folks, you heard it here first. And keep those calls coming in, it looks like this might be quite an interesting election after all. We'll be back after this short break.'

The irritating jingles came back on.

'I'm afraid time's up,' Mary-Anne said, 'we've got the Labour Party candidate on next. Personally I'd have preferred to carry on with you, but we have to give equal air-time to everyone.'

'Bit boring, are they?' I asked, taking the headphones off and handing them to the other girl who had reappeared at my side.

'A lot of what you say is true – what did you call them, plastic? Personally I believe in democracy, I believe that everyone should take part, but I can see why so many people are disillusioned. Here I am, the big break, with a chance to get everyone involved, with someone saying things that I'm sure most people feel are true, and what do I get? Two calls, one from the "I was in the war" brigade, and one from some nutcase who sounds like he's sniffed too much glue.'

'Cheer up,' I said, standing up and pulling my crutches into my shoulders, 'I'm sure things will get better when word gets out. Ask the Labour bloke about his position on sheep.'

She chuckled. 'Good idea, I'll try that. What happened to your leg?'

'Oh, got broken during the fracas the other week. Defending the helpless against the mob, that sort of thing.'

'I'm surprised you aren't using it – for the sympathy vote, that sort of thing.'

'Oh, I'm a modest sort of a person,' I replied, winking at her.

'Full of bullshit, you mean. Good luck in the election.'

'Good luck to you too. Though I doubt you'll need it. I think you'll be quite a star shortly.'

'Correction, bullshit and blarney,' she responded. I waggled a few fingers at her and hobbled out, glad it was over. It had been quite tiring.

Ms D met me in the corridor.

'Not bad,' she said critically, 'though I think we've got some work to do.'

Not bad? Personally I thought I had done pretty well, especially having to ad lib the whole time.

'And what particular points did you think I was deficient in?' I asked her. She sighed.

'Come on, now, let's get back and get you a cup of tea or something. No need to get tetchy.'

Tetchy? Me?

On the way back we listened to Mary-Anne giving the Labour candidate a right good grilling. She kept asking him how he could justify New Labour's abandoning of all policy and beliefs, and he kept trying to talk about what the mayor could do, which she ignored.

I like that girl.

Not sure Ms D does, though. She didn't say much when I described what Mary-Anne was wearing. And she's normally very perceptive when it comes to clothes.

Sunday 8th September

Tony Blair has claimed that Britain is prepared to pay the "blood price" in the battle against Iraq. The phrase sounds more likely to have come from a bad B movie involving Bedouins than Churchill, but Georgie Bush has duly helped by accusing Saddam Hussein of "stiffing" the world, along with "crawfishing" out of agreements.

Hopefully someone understands what he's on about.

Maybe it's the recipe for a Texas salad.

Meanwhile some members of parliament are demanding a recall of parliament to discuss an attack on Iraq. Blair is ignoring them, though whether this means he's stiffing or crawfishing is open to question.

The German company Siemens has decided not to call a new range of household products "Zyklon", after various people have pointed out that (a) Siemens used slave labour during the war and is now liable for paying compensation for that fact, (b) Zyklon B was the gas used in the extermination chambers in WWII, and (c) it isn't therefore the best name to use when you're trying to flog things like gas cookers.

Continuing the name calling theme, the head of the train drivers' union Aslef has called the people who will profit from the public-private-partnership deal for the tube "the scum of the earth". This apparently includes shareholders, lawyers and accountants. Getting into stride he also called the members of the Confederation of Business Industry (CBI) "immature". The report doesn't mention what he thinks about well paid train drivers who go on strike demanding more money, in the process making life hell for others who rely on trains and tubes to get to work to earn a lot less than the striking drivers.

"Friends", one would imagine.

In football, Wales have beaten Finland in a qualifier for the Euro 2004 competition. The results of other teams can be quietly ignored to spare the blushes of other people who get paid a small fortune for achieving very little. Let's just say that a pound either way on the Faroe Islands (population: not many; football team: mainly teachers, cooks, firemen, anyone not doing anything at that particular time; ranked: 123rd in the world) could be a good idea, especially if they're playing Scotland.

The others decided yesterday that my presentation needed some work done on it. All in support of The Cause, no doubt. The first issue on the agenda was the use of the statement, "do nothing". Mrs G thinks it's very negative.

'It's very negative,' she said, 'people will get the impression that you're going to take the salary and do nothing for it.'

I pointed out that this was the whole idea.

'It's not good enough,' she replied, 'people expect something for their money. We need something more positive.'

I restrained the urge to point out that people very rarely got anything for their money as far as local councils went, and that the idea was that they wouldn't end up paying more for more nothing.

'I thought the street sweeping idea was quite good,' Miss Melly said. 'It makes a statement of sorts.'

I can't say the idea appealed to me.

'People don't understand statements,' Mrs G said. 'We need something concrete.'

'I think you should promise to give a good whipping to any councillors who don't do their job properly. Laziest bunch of people I've ever met. I remember when I – '

'Yes, thank you major,' Mrs G interrupted, 'I think we'd prefer to concentrate on something legal.'

'I think he may have an idea,' Miss Melly said. Mrs G raised her eyebrows. 'I don't mean whipping them, but he could keep an eye on them. Promise to keep the public informed of decisions made by their local councillors, that sort of thing. After all, he'll be able to go to all the meetings, even the closed ones.'

This is daft, I thought to myself. Above all it goes against the pure simplicity of my original plan.

And it will involve actual work.

'Now that is an idea,' Mrs G enthused, 'a weekly column in the local paper, maybe a slot on local television. I think it has possibilities.'

'It probably does, and all of them bad,' I said. 'Where do you think the local media gets its money from? I'll tell you; advertising. And who do you think pays to advertise? Local businessmen. And who are these councillors I'm supposed to be giving everyone the low-down on? Local businessmen. Why do you think you never read about politics in the local paper, unless it's some councillor opening a kiddies' play park?'

'Then we'll find some other way of doing it. A weekly newsletter from the mayor. Something like that.' Mrs G is one of these people who always has solutions, especially when you're quite happy with the problem.

'And where precisely do you intend to find the money to do that?'

'Somewhere. I don't know. Maybe there's already a budget for the mayor to use.'

'Maybe we could find it by raising council tax?' I asked sarcastically.

'Shush, now. You're just being negative. You've been standing for too long. Go and get some rest. Lie down.'

'Good idea,' I said, and disappeared sharpish before they came up with any ideas. The plaster cast had come off on Friday, but the leg needs a bit of exercise before it's back in form. Everyone had been very pleased for me, or so I had thought.

'Great news,' Mrs G had said, and I concurred thoroughly. 'Now we'll be able to go out and pound the streets, press the flesh, as they say, let the voters in the High Street meet you.'

Eh? As far as I'm concerned the reason it's good news is that now I can stroll down to the Rose again when the urge takes me.

Admittedly I could have made it there on crutches, but the return journey might have been a little more difficult.

And tonight I had another reason for being there. A strange telephone call from someone who had introduced himself as Simon Legrade-Smith, lawyer, who would like to have a private word, some news to my benefit, or some such, and he readily agreed that the Rose should be sufficiently far from the madding crowd.

Apart from sounding like something out of Great Expectations, I don't trust people who have a double barrelled name. But it gave me an added excuse to pop out for a couple of pints, should I need the excuse – though I didn't mention the proposed meeting to anyone here. People tend to ask awkward questions about such things, and if it's all above board and blameless they make up something else in their imagination.

So, having reached the Rose this evening without incident, and having exchanged the usual banter with Pete, and with a lovely full pint in hand, I surveyed the assembled guests to work out which one was the lawyer with a mission.

It wasn't difficult. Apart from the pub being almost empty, and him being the only one I didn't recognise, he sat alone with a newspaper, and a glass of wine which he sipped at very occasionally with a grimace following each sip. I wandered over to his table and sat down.

'Mr Legrade-Smith?' I enquired. He nodded. He seemed awkward, a fish out of water. His expensive suit seemed out of place in the Rose. Especially on a Sunday.

'I recognise you from your picture,' he said, as if requiring confirmation of who I was.

'Ah, that old police poster. Doesn't do me justice, I reckon,' I replied jovially.

'Police poster?' he squeaked nervously. 'I was talking about the picture on your campaign literature.' He brandished a pamphlet, as if trying to prove that it wasn't a police poster.

'A joke,' I said. Humour didn't appear to be his strong point.

'Ah,' he said, and contemplated the idea of a laugh to indicate that he was fully au-fait with the concept of a joke, even if he had never understood one.

'I'll come straight to the point,' he continued, which I doubted. It's one of those phrases like "I'm not a sexist" which is a prelude to proving the opposite. And if he's a lawyer I doubt whether he'd be capable of coming straight to any point, even if it was about whether it was raining or not.

But he surprised me.

'I represent a group of small businessmen,' he continued, using a phrase which always gives me an image of short people in suits. 'They are most concerned about the role of a new mayor, and feel, as you do, that such a post is merely an excuse for increasing taxes, increasing bureaucracy, and creating even more red tape, under which they are already suffocating.'

I nodded sympathetically. I didn't have a clue what he was on about, or even what he might be on, but a sympathetic nod never goes amiss, doesn't cost you anything, and gives you time to work out where the nearest exit is when confronted by people who might go pop any minute.

Not that he did, but I've been in that position with some football supporters when their team has just lost.

'They have come to the conclusion that they cannot support any of the normal candidates for the position of mayor, and feel that a protest vote is the best option at the current time.'

I ignored the suggestion that I was an abnormal candidate.

'Good to hear it,' I replied neutrally.

'The bottom line is that they wish to support you more actively than merely voting for you. However, they feel, quite naturally, that their positions in the community and the business world prevent them from making such support overt. Hence they have asked me to represent them in an unofficial capacity.'

Quite naturally? They must be strange business people who felt nervous about standing up and saying the whole thing was a load of cobblers, and you might as well vote for the loony over there, but I merely gave another understanding nod.

When you don't know what's going on, let the other person open his mouth first.

'Thus they must limit their support to certain anonymous actions. However the one area where they feel they might be able to show their support is in a financial sense.'

Translation: would you like some money?

Oh, yes please. If you really insist.

'That's very generous of them,' I said smoothly, wanting to ask, OK, how much then?

'However they do wish to be certain of your planned policies. I am given to understand that you have promised not to do anything as mayor?'

I certainly had. Mrs G and the rest of them might be trying to change that, but I decided it was best not to confuse the issue.

Besides, the Causers were not going to do anything that might result in me having to do any work. There was no way I would let them.

'I think the pamphlet states that quite clearly,' I replied, nodding at the pamphlet now lying on the table next to him.

'They were quite explicit,' he insisted, 'they must know that you intend carrying out your promise before they can lend any financial support whatsoever. They could well lose a substantial amount of money if the wrong person were to be elected.'

For a lawyer he was doing quite well in insulting people without reason. I looked at him, taking out my pack of cigarettes – ten only, I'm going to give up again shortly – and slowly lit one, all the while keeping my eyes locked on his. I dropped the match slowly into the ashtray between us, and took a long drag.

You have to use matches. Lighters just don't have style.

'I don't know where you come from, Mr Legrade-Smith, but around here suggesting that someone is lying is not a good idea,' I said in an extremely friendly way.

He shrank back a little. A lot, actually, and had a quick look around the pub in case people were giving him a long look before deciding to beat him up and drop his body in the local sewerage pit.

Old George and Martha probably gave him the shivers. They sat silently in their usual place, looking as if they were viciously about to go to sleep. A few tables away some thin young teenager had pre-empted them, and was snoring quietly in a puddle of beer.

'I didn't mean that,' he said hastily, in a very low, squeaky voice. 'They insisted I must ask that question. You must realise that some people do lie. Though of course I'm sure you're not one of them, naturally, though you'd be amazed what I come across in my work.'

I nodded through half closed eyes. The smoke was getting into them.

'That's as may be, Mr Legrade-Smith, but much as I would love to hear your reminiscences, I am a busy man at the moment.' Well, I really wanted to get away and discuss the football with Pete. 'So do me a favour and put your cards on the table. I'm not a politician and I don't have time to play verbal silly buggers.'

'Er, of course, of course,' he said, sweating at the thought of having to say something simple and comprehensible.

'You're offering me financial support – money, in other words. We need money. How much?'

His eyes opened wide at such a blatant question. He probably spent two hours on getting there normally. This was two hours less to invoice.

'Er, it could be quite a considerable amount you know, I – '

'How much?' I insisted.

'Well, that hasn't been finalised yet – '

'Look, Mr Legrade-Smith, I haven't a lot of time, and you're wasting it at the moment. Why don't I give you my account number and you can pay in whatever you want. We need money, but we aren't going to be bought off. Financial support is most welcome, but we're sticking to what's in that pamphlet, ok?'

'Er, yes, of course. But – your personal account? Don't you have a campaign account? It is most irregular.'

I wondered what Mr Legrade-Smith normally dealt with. Since

his clients appeared to want to remain anonymous they would probably welcome the chance to avoid any nasty accountants who wished to investigate campaign account records. Or anything which might leave a trail leading to them.

'Time's short, Mr Legrade-Smith. We aren't politicians, we lack the usual resources, we don't have anyone who might realise that we might need a campaign account or budget. We need everything and we need it now. Your – clients' – money will allow us to take on professional people. Oh, how would you like to do a spot of pro-bono work?'

'Pro-bono?' he asked, as if I'd used a dirty word.

'Just joking, Mr L-S. We could do with a really good lawyer to point out any pitfalls, but I can see you'd be too busy. Course, if your clients are willing to put up sufficient funds, we might be able to engage your services. It's a nice idea, isn't it? Unrealistic, but nice.'

I scribbled my bank account number on a piece of paper and slid it over to him.

'That's the account number and sort code. Whatever they can spare, we can use.'

He took it gingerly and put it into his wallet as if worried that it might infect it.

'I shall let my clients know the, er, position,' he promised.

But not that some of their money might be used to pay himself, I guessed. On the other hand, if he were the last lawyer left on earth I wouldn't pay for his services. But I wasn't going to mention that.

'I look forward to hearing from you,' I said, standing up. 'Have you parked around here?'

'Er, close by,' he admitted.

'It's getting dark. If I were you I'd get out before the locals start nicking your hubcaps. And more. You're a brave man to come in here alone.' I winked, and gave him a pat on the shoulder.

'Well, I do what the job calls for,' he said, looking ever so chuffed at the idea of his bravery. He raised his glass of wine to his lips.

'I wouldn't drink that,' I warned him, 'industrial detergent, that is. And make sure you get to your car before night falls, otherwise they'll hit you as you open the door.'

'Er, yes, good idea.' As I wandered back to the bar he scrabbled to get his things back into his briefcase, and hastily made his exit.

'You been winding people up again?' asked Pete as he poured my next pint, and I slid onto the bar stool in front of him.

'Now, Peter, really, as if I would. I merely suggested that if he stayed around here after dark he'd be lucky to get away with having his throat slit, and if he continued drinking that sulphuric acid you call wine he'd be grateful for having said throat slit.'

'Great. I should hire you for some PR work. And that wine is good stuff, South African. Not cheap either. Just because you're a Philistine doesn't mean the wine ain't good.'

'Ah, now Pete, I'm a connoisseur. And that wine isn't South African. Pure local swill, I reckon. Put into old bottles. I reckon they got you there.'

He looked at me in concern. And then laughed. 'You're having me on.'

I admitted the fact. Actually the wine is quite good. I've often been tempted to have a glass instead of a pint.

The funny thing is that it's exactly the same wine old whatisface-smith would pay a small fortune for at his local wine bar, and pretend to enjoy it, but here he grimaced with every sip.

People are strange.

Thursday 12th September

The media has one main topic today: remembering "the events of September the 11th", or nine-eleven as they call it in the US. Amongst the topics are "the day that changed the world", "did it really change the world?" and "why nothing has changed".

One question that doesn't seem to have been asked is: if it hadn't happened, would George Bush now be fighting accusations of being soft on big business, with his popularity about ten percent, and absolutely no chance of ever being re-elected?

Instead he's continuing his mission to get rid of Saddam Hussein and install McDonalds in every town in Iraq, along with cheerleader Blair trying to organise support for an attack on the country.

Nelson Mandela has lost some of his popularity by claiming that Bush only wants to go to war to increase oil and arms sales.

Elsewhere in the world: a train disaster in Tanzania which killed almost 300 people has been blamed on human error.

Six inmates of a Brazilian jail have been killed in a riot between two drugs gangs.

French rescue workers continue to search for bodies after flash floods killed up to twenty people.

Two gunmen killed in shoot-out between Pakistani police and militants in Karachi.

At least 100 people believed dead in a train crash in Bihar, India.

Zambia has agreed to accept GM food for refugees, while refusing to distribute it to Zambians.

Uganda and the Democratic Republic of Congo have signed a peace agreement after three year of war.

The rebel Colombian movement, the National Liberation Army, has released ten of twenty seven tourists kidnapped last month, with the others expected to be released soon.

South Africa's Constitutional Court has decided that gay couples have the legal right to adopt children. Previously the Child Care Act had forbidden this, but the new ruling was declared after a couple of lesbian judges had challenged the Act as being unconstitutional. South Africa is the only country in Africa to allow such adoption, the attitude of various other African countries towards homosexuality being notoriously anti. In neighbouring Zimbabwe the cheerful and fun loving Mugabe once referred to homosexuals as "worse than pigs and dogs". How this will affect South Africa's success in international rugby is yet to be determined. Apparently they don't normally tend to mince around the bush.

Back in the UK: the Independent Television Commission has ruled that a beer advert showing a man licking up beer poured by his girlfriend onto various domestic surfaces should not have been shown before the nine o'clock watershed. They decided that there was too much sexual innuendo for it to be shown while children might be watching. Since the advert showed the girlfriend using a trail of beer to get said boyfriend to clean the mess he had created while she was away by licking it clean, perhaps it could have been better banned on grounds of being gross. On the other hand, why a beer company would want its product associated with a lavatory bowl is another question.

Perhaps it's a new approach to advertising.

Good news: Arsenal 1 Man City 0; Bolton 1 Man United 0; Fulham 3 Spurs 2.

Bad News: the threatened strike by fire-fighters might result not only in the cancellation of things such as tubes and trains, because of the loss in fire cover, but also the cancellation of football games for the same reason.

Something tells me that they won't be striking on match days.

It's getting a bit much when you can't take it easy for half an hour in the garden in the late summer sun, especially when it won't be around for long – there's a certain hint of winter around the corner first thing in the morning.

There I was, relaxing with Jimmie and Colin in our time honoured way, when Mrs G and Miss Melly turn up to take me to listen to the band.

Despite my protests that I was letting the leg get a little sunshine to aid the healing process, I was frogmarched off to what is now the music room, and forced to listen to various popular tunes being massacred. I admire their enthusiasm, and Miss Melly has done an incredible job of getting them to play in tune, but I fear that the instruments desperately need servicing, or whatever it is that you do to musical instruments which haven't been used for ten or more years.

Mrs G and Miss Melly beamed as Colonel Bogey was changed from a march to an all-out assault, and I duly smiled appreciation as much as I could. On the plus side, you have to admit that they'll attract attention.

Maybe we could threaten people to continue playing if they don't vote for me.

Miss Melly did admit that "some of the instruments" could do with a little attention. Apparently it involves things like new reeds and such. The trouble is the age old one – money. Jimmie for once has been unable to unearth any replacement parts, and Ms D hasn't yet found a way to fiddle anything through the expenses, as the instruments belong to the residents rather than this place. And apparently these things are expensive enough to be extremely noticeable amongst the other items found on the petty cash list.

If old Legrade-Smith had come through we might have another option, but so far my account looks as woeful as it ever has.

But the band all seem very happy with the results, and it has to be said that they've come a long way, both in terms of playing and their personal approach to life. They do say that music is good therapy, and I'd tried to convince Sir Archie to cough up some money for new instruments, but got the usual "sadly times are tough" response.

Even worse than that, we have a new doctor, and he's very bad news. He believes in something called a "cure", totally missing the point that we're quite happy here, thank you very much.

He'd rather have normal miserable people outside than happy

people with problems on the inside. There have been some rumours flying around that the company want to close this place and sell off the land, and the one thing I've discovered in life is that such rumours tend to turn out to be true.

Fortunately everyone's too busy at the moment to concentrate on rumours, otherwise this place could be renamed Depression Central.

Over the past few days I've been trained up for a debate which took place this evening in the Town Hall.

All the candidates for mayor sitting on stage, each given five minutes to lay out their position, then one minute for each to question the others, and finally questions from the floor. Mrs G, Ms D and the major have been hounding me on the correct questions to ask, the correct answers to give, how to sit, how to stand, make sure your fly isn't open, don't slouch, etc, etc, etc. Normally I would have had a terrible case of stage fright, but after you've had those two fine women on your case for a few days, with the major providing irrelevant comments on the side, having to face an audience can only be a rest cure.

I didn't point out two things which would have made the training redundant; firstly I always make things up as I go along, and secondly the audience would be composed of the sort of weirdos who give up an evening to go along to listen to would-be local politicians talking nonsense. Definitely not our target voters. They probably have long and boring discussions about the difference between a ward and a borough.

I can't see any of them voting for someone whose main point is that he won't do anything.

Ms D drove me over, and took a seat at the back while I made my way front. The others were already seated, looking bored and nervous while trying to pretend that they were overflowing with enthusiasm. The Tory and Labour candidates both wore navy blue suits with ties – New Labour have not only nicked all the Tory policies, now they even dress like them.

Amongst the others were the Green Party chap – I was tempted to make a "baaaa" noise as I walked behind him – the Liberal Democrat, another chap who was standing on the promise to ban fox hunting – not often you see foxes being chased by red-coated men on horses down the roads and avenues around here – there's hardly enough space for double-parked cars – so I reckon he doesn't stand much hope, but best of luck all the same – and finally a bloke standing against the CPZ, next to whom I found myself seated.

The CPZ – or Controlled Parking Zone – is a subject that pops up regularly. The plan is that, in certain areas, you will need a permit to park, otherwise you will receive an instant fine, and your vehicle may possibly be towed away. The theory is that it will stop out-of-towners from using the place as a cheap area to park during the day, while they travel to work by train.

Shop-owners are dead against the idea; they claim it will prevent people from shopping, and I can see their point. Other people are against it because they will be required to pay a hefty whack for an annual permit, without any guarantee to a parking space. So they'd probably end up cruising around for a parking slot in their own street as normal, but with the added knowledge that they're now paying for the privilege. And I get the impression that they don't trust the Council not to give out permits to all their cronies and friends of cronies, gratis.

The ultimate killer is that the people who will issue fines – and tow cars away – are a private company who currently have the job of parking policing, or traffic wardens in other words, and are well known for what they call "aggressive" monitoring, but what everyone else calls extortion. Amongst their tricks are to put up a "towing area" sign in such a place as to make it nigh impossible to see, and then quickly tow away any cars which pause in the general area, charging a few hundred quid for the car to be released.

However the CPZ idea has been mooted about once every two years for as long as I can remember, and then hastily shelved when local residents come to meetings and explain exactly where the council can put its CPZ, so I can't see it being an issue in this election.

I was musing along these lines when the debate chairman arrived, a tubby, pink chap with unruly white hair and whiskers, carrying a brown leather case bursting with all sorts of important paper – the type who loves chairing important meetings, but prefers to be seen as a neutral umpire. I could see him saying things like "paragraph 7, point 4, sub-clause 9, as amended ... "

After a great deal of harrumphing, testing microphones, searching for, and shuffling of, papers and documents, ensuring everyone had water in front of them, confirming people's identities with whispered shouts, along with all the necessary ritual associated with these things, we were off.

I won't go into any great detail about the various speeches. The Tory and the New Tory, sorry, New Labour candidates could have swapped theirs, a lot about schools and health and transport and something called quality of life. The Lib Dem chap gave pretty much the same speech, but included something called "investment", which the other two had avoided, because it basically means "your money". The Green Party bloke was more into the "quality of life" side of things, and mentioned congestion charging – charging people for driving in the central area of town – to reduce carbon monoxide emissions, reverse global warming, create a bright new world for our children, cure all known diseases, etc, etc.

He hasn't got a hope in hell. It'll cost a fortune.

The anti Fox Hunt candidate gave a rant about cruelty involved in fox hunting, which seemed to fascinate the audience just as much as it was entirely irrelevant. By the end of his five minutes he was declaring a class war and calling for the tumbrils to roll. It took the chairman another few minutes to get him to shut up.

CPZ man did an impression of the most boring man in the world. Repeated all the dangers of a CPZ which most of us have heard a thousand times, though his approach was to do it in a very slow, monotonous, droning, sleep-inducing speech. I could see various members of the audience slowly slipping into unconsciousness. I wasn't far behind when my turn came.

Which is why I wasn't quite with it when I suddenly realised that the chairman was inviting me to speak. I had a list of points in front of me, but no prepared speech – lose your way in a prepared speech and you'll never find the way back again.

You can't lose your way in an unprepared speech.

I started off by announcing, 'This is a wake up call – in more ways than one', which got a few smiles. I then went on to make the usual points – democratic choice, increased taxes, etc – without overstressing the bit about only twelve percent of people having voted for having a mayor, because I strongly suspected that everyone in the hall was in the twelve percent.

I did manage a dig at the main party candidates, wondering aloud whether their speeches had been created by the same PR company, and did they get a discount for a bulk order, which got a laugh. All in all, not overly gripping stuff, but hopefully competent enough for the media – a few television cameras were dotted around – to take it seriously.

After my plug the chairman spent a few minutes thanking all candidates for their contributions, and then called on me to start with my questions for the others. I began with the Tory bloke at the end of the tables.

'A simple yes or no question,' I assured him falsely. 'Are you going to increase council tax, yes or no?'

'We have no plans to do so,' he replied glibly.

'It was a yes or no question, so could you answer it with either "yes" or "no"?' I insisted.

'As I said, we have no plans to do so,' he replied with a smile, knowing that his minute was running out.

'Yes or no?' I demanded.

Someone in the audience shouted 'Answer the question you Tory bastard', which I was glad of, though would have preferred the last three words to have been left out. The Tory wriggled in his seat a

363

little.

'According to our current plans there will be no need to increase the council tax,' he said with a fixed smile.

'Yes or no?' I repeated. There were more calls from the audience. The chairman interrupted by banging a gavel on the table in front of him.

'I'm afraid your minute is up,' he told me. 'Please move on to the next candidate.' Certain members of the audience reacted with what could be called negative sentiments.

I turned to the New Labour candidate, who was obviously enjoying the Tory's discomfiture.

'Do you intend increasing council tax, yes or no?' I asked him. He smiled and leaned forward.

'We are confident that our unique relations with central government will allow us to receive sufficient funding to avoid the requirement of an increase in the council tax.'

A nice little piece of blackmail if ever I heard one. Vote for us or our big brother in government won't give you any money.

'I'll ignore the threat. Yes or no?'

'I don't understand what you mean by that – what threat?'

Silly of me, I shouldn't have given him an opening.

'Answer the question: yes or no?' The audience were getting worked up again. Someone – it sounded like the same person who called the Tory a bastard – shouted, 'Answer the question you imitation Tory bastard'. That got quite a few laughs.

'I'd like to understand what you meant by suggesting I'd threatened you,' New Labour insisted. The audience were becoming quite raucous now, yet again the chairman intervened with his gavel to tell me the minute was up, and to proceed to the next candidate. Which was the Lib Dem.

'How much are you intending to increase the council tax by?' I asked him. He smiled.

'Our current plans are that we should be able to institute our promised reforms without increasing council tax by more than the rate of inflation, provided we receive the funds promised by central government to pay for the mayor's projects.'

Neat.

'So are you saying that council tax will increase only at the rate of inflation, or that the portion of the increase required to fund mayoral projects will only increase at the rate of inflation?'

'I'm sorry, I didn't quite get that,' he said, doing a good impression of someone who didn't understand the question rather than someone trying to waste sixty seconds.

'Are you promising that the total council tax bill for each household will not increase more than the rate of inflation?' I pressed him.

'The total council tax bill? That's not what you asked me.'

'I'm asking you now. What's the answer?'

'Could you repeat the question?'

The chairman gavelled again to indicate that time was up, and jeers came from the audience. The trouble is that a minute isn't a lot of time to get decent answers from politicians.

The Green Party was next.

'How much?' I asked.

'How much what?'

'How much are you going to increase council tax by? Apart from the tax you're going to levy on people who drive.'

'That's not a tax, it's a congestion charge. It's important that we create a healthy environment for ourselves and our children to grow up in.'

'Yes, yes, I know, and the sheep too. Just tell me how much you intend to raise council tax by.'

'Sheep? How dare you! I'll sue you! I'll have you arrested! I'll have you locked up!' he shouted as he leapt to his feet in front of a bemused but fascinated audience. The chairman rapped his gavel loudly to get his attention.

'Mr Harper? Are you feeling okay?'

'What? Yes. Of course I am. I'm just not prepared to tolerate suggestions such as he's just made.'

There was a puzzled silence for a few seconds.

'I'm afraid I didn't notice any suggestion, Mr Harper,' the chairman said slowly, turning to me with raised eyebrows. I shrugged my shoulders in innocent ignorance.

'I don't know what Mr Harper saw in my words which could have been suggestive, unless there's something he's not telling us. All I was commenting on was the image that people have of the Green Party wanting to go back to some rural idyll where the sheep graze on the village common and little lambs gambol happily in front of Safeways. Maybe Mr Harper isn't feeling too well.'

'I'm fine, I'm fine,' he insisted, sitting down and mopping his brow. He gave me a look which turned suspicious. 'Do I know you?' he asked.

'You've probably seen my picture on the posters,' I pointed out, resisting the urge to ask him if he had done any good radio interviews recently.

'Yes, yes, good. Fine. Now that that's settled, your questions for the next candidate, please,' the chairman said, fussily making notes on some document or other, and hoping to get beyond discussions of sheep, and candidates who may or may not have a private life better not enquired into.

It was only the anti fox hunt brigade and CPZ man left. I gave the anti fox hunt bloke the standard question on increasing council taxes, determined to keep well away from any mention of fox hunts. I was confident that he could turn it into a rant about oppression by the rich, and would win quite a few votes with that approach.

As it was he managed to condemn taxes, which were "levied by the rich on the working people". Fortunately time ran out before he could nick my point about the mayoralty merely being another job for the boys. So long as he sticks to fox hunting I should be safe.

CPZ man was easier to deal with. I merely suggested that, aside from banning the CPZ, I was sure that he had many other ideas for changes which could benefit the community. He fell straight for the bait, admitting shyly that there were one or two ideas he was thinking of, which allowed me to demand why they weren't in his manifesto, and how could he expect people to vote for someone who might just arbitrarily decide to build a highway through the old folks' home just because he dreamed it up one morning?

His splutters were interrupted by the noise of the gavel. I don't think I have much to worry about from his side.

I would like to be able to report that the others' questions were memorable, but I'm afraid that the main parties' candidates had quickly picked up on the idea of delaying tactics, and the answers to questions could be summarised as 'I'm sorry, could you repeat the question?'.

I would have expected the audience to have been rather irritated at this, and some of them appeared to be, but the majority seemed to be enjoying it as some sort of political fencing, to be admired as a sport.

The chap from the Green party wasn't as experienced in such verbal ducking and diving, and at one point demanded of the New Labour candidate, 'Are you going to give me a straight answer?', the reply to which was, 'That depends on your definition of a straight answer', which brought a brief round of applause.

I could have sworn I heard someone say, 'Oh, nice shot Jim'.

And they wonder why people don't trust politicians any more.

As for we three independents, each of the main party candidates declined to ask us any questions, dismissing us as "joke candidates".

Honestly.

I could understand that attitude towards CPZ man and the anti hunt twit, but they were obviously using it as a tactic to sideline my campaign. You just can't trust some people.

By that stage we had been going for almost two hours; the meeting was only scheduled for two hours, so the time for questions from the audience was limited. Someone tried to force the Tory candidate to give a yes or no answer to my original question, but the chairman ruled that it had already been covered, and moved on to other questions, many of which turned out to be the "when are you going to get rid of the rubbish in my street?" type, addressed to the New Labour candidate. Very important to the person asking the question, but the only real answer starts off with "When I'm mayor ..." which isn't exactly helpful if the rubbish has already been sitting there for some weeks.

I was rather glad when it was all over. My brain felt like it had been assaulted.

On the way back I fell asleep, Ms D waking me when we got back. Before going back in I asked what she had thought.

'I thought you did rather well,' she said, which chuffed me no end. 'I don't think the people there really understand what you're trying to tell them.'

I'm still trying to work out whether that was a compliment or not.

This politics business is hard work though.

Sunday 15th September

The United States has criticised Russia over threats on intervention in Georgia to pursue Chechen rebels who have fled across the border.

The US continues with plans to invade Iraq.

Janet Reno, former US Attorney General and now standing to be elected as the Democratic candidate for the post of Governor of California, has had her request for a manual recount of the votes denied. Voting was interrupted by machines that didn't work, machines that rejected identification cards, machines that reported incorrect results and electoral officials who didn't know how to operate the machines that wouldn't work. After the problems with punch cards in 2000 which saw George Bush sent to the White House, Florida had spent $32 million on setting up the new computerised voting system.

Jean Chretien, the Canadian Prime Minister has accused the US and some other western countries of being arrogant, and partly to blame for the attacks of 11 September 2001.

Bush denies the claim and announces plan to invade Canada.

As soon as someone tells him where it is.

Weekend results: Charlton 0 Arsenal 3; Bolton 2 Liverpool 3; Charlton 0 Arsenal 3; Chelsea 3 Newcastle 0; Charlton 0 Arsenal 3; Everton 2 Boro 1; Charlton 0 Arsenal 3; Leeds 1 Man Utd 0; Sunderland 0 Fulham 3; Leeds 1 Man Utd 0; WBA 1 Southampton 0; Leeds 1 Man Utd 0; Man City 2 Blackburn 2; Leeds 1 Man Utd 0; Spurs 3 West Ham 2.

Oh, and did I mention? Charlton 0 Arsenal 3.

Thank god for Sundays. The one day of the week I can be pretty confident that I won't have my ear bent about some or other refinement of the campaign. Even Mrs Gladstone seems to agree that I can have at least one day off. Or perhaps they're still recovering from yesterday's first foray into town with band and pamphlets.

Actually, I think it all went off rather well, everything considered.

369

Ms D had organised two of those mini buses – the cost of which has been filed under "trip, therapy, for the purpose of" – and a whole group of us set off, including the band and others whose job was to intercept passing voters and force pamphlets into their unwilling hands before they could object.

Originally the band had wanted to dress up.

Miss Melly had suggested a costume based on the era of the Civil War, but that had resulted in the band discussing whether or not they should be equipped with pikes, swords and halberds. I didn't want to even consider the likely outcome if that lot turned out at the shopping centre carrying lethal weaponry. Their music alone probably falls under the terms of one of the Geneva Conventions.

So that was scrapped. Then the idea was mooted that they should organise costumes based on these bands which appear at celebrations in the States, all red and blue and sparkling spanglies. Apart from the fact these things don't really travel well over the ocean, that sort of costume is fine for slim young teenagers, but tends to turn into a clown's attire when worn by people whose midriffs have been expanding for a number of years.

What finally killed that idea off was the cost.

In the end I got them to agree that what we wanted was a "Peoples' band", with everyone wearing their normal day to day clothing, creating an inclusive appearance.

Not that I normally go for words such as "inclusive". But needs must. As compensation, I agreed that we'd all wear little rainbow coloured ribbons; Jimmie had found two boxes – twenty four large reels – of the stuff yesterday. It made things look colourful without being too gaudy.

I still haven't worked out what possible use the Centre could have for the ribbons.

For some reason there was one person in costume, I noted as we boarded the buses. A white rabbit with pink ears, pack of pamphlets in a little wicker basket.

'Who on earth is that?' I asked Ms D as I sat down next to her at the front.

'Tom Perkins,' she replied. 'He really wanted to come along, but he's very shy. So he thought he'd disguise himself as a rabbit.'

'An Easter Bunny. Just what we need. We're trying to show we're serious and here we are, being escorted by the Easter Bunny.'

'Oh do shush,' she said mildly. 'I think it's quite sweet. At least he's trying.'

'As if I'm not.'

'You are. Very. Trying, that is.'

'Oh, very funny.' I left it at that. She was right in a way – at least the bloke was trying to give a hand, and it was one way of dealing with extreme shyness.

I just hoped he didn't pick up a date while we were out there.

We set ourselves up in an piazza-type paved open area in front of the library and social centre. Other groups use it for their Saturday morning harangues – Muslims complaining about everything and insisting that there is only one true god; the odd Christian demagogue with his bible, telling people that Jesus died for their sins; the Socialist Party trying to flog their newspaper and get people to sign a petition against sending criminals to prison, or demanding the establishment of separate schools for homosexual three year olds, or something of that ilk.

There was always the danger the lunatic fringe might rub off on us, but that was a chance we had to take; it was the best spot to catch people moving between the shops.

Folding tables were duly dragged from the buses, tablecloths thrown over, boxes of pamphlets stacked alongside, and a large sign saying 'More?' stuck on to the front of the tables. Jimmie and I watched as Mrs G organised the pamphleteers, giving detailed instructions of where they were to ambush the innocent passing citizenry; Miss Melly was taking the band through a warm up. Ms D was organising the unloading of the buses. Colin was amongst the pamphleteers, which rather surprised me.

The local town centre is not a place for the faint hearted.

Finally all was ready, and Mrs G gave Miss Melly the nod to start. The band launched into a really good rendition of the theme from The Great Escape, which would definitely give us the footballing vote. Mrs G came over to me.

'All ready?' she asked. I nodded.

'Once more into the breach, dear friends,' I muttered, grabbed a stack of pamphlets, and we waded into the middle of the passing pedestrians.

The plan was that I would take the left, Mrs G would take the right, Ms D and the major would man the tables co-ordinating the others, with Jimmie ready as runner, while all the others were posted at various major intersection points along the streets where shoppers might appear. Fortunately it was too early for the usual crush; I wanted some practice before having to face the noon onslaught of shoppers loaded down with bags of ready-cooked cholesterol, dragging screaming kids to the burger bars for lunch. Their interest in affairs political was unlikely to be very high by that stage.

The theory is simple: you stand in front of someone approaching, blocking their path, and ask if they'd like to pay more council tax. Their immediate reaction is to stop in surprise, and then immediately say "no" when they realise what you've just asked them. Then you wade in with the "vote for me and you won't pay any more" spiel.

That's the theory.

The first flaw I discovered was that people don't actually like having a stranger block their path while shoving something in their faces. And their first reaction isn't to stop, it's to try to knee you somewhere unfortunate. I quickly developed a stance whereby I wasn't necessarily impeding the target, and my feet weren't where theirs were about to trample.

And other parts of me weren't in range.

The second thing I discovered is that most people's initial response is composed of two words, the second one being "off". I was quite surprised at the different number of words you could supply before the word "off", but the meaning was basically the same. Other responses were more polite, though just as dispiriting. "Don't vote, mate", followed by a rapid departure.

"Doesn't matter what you say, I ain't ever going to vote Tory."

"You politicians are all the same."

"I don't believe in religion."

"Come away from the nasty man, Tara – look what you've done now, gone and made her cry."

Two instances were slightly different. In the first I spent a good couple of minutes giving my speech to a smartly dressed couple who smiled deep interest, thinking I was getting somewhere, until they introduced themselves as John and Mary, and would I like to join them for a coffee morning discussing Christianity.

I told them to off.

The second was a group of Japanese tourists, who gathered around me to listen to this great democratic speech, their faces alive with concentration, two or three capturing the event on digital camcorder for posterity. I only realised a salient point towards the end, when I asked them if they lived around these parts, a small requirement on achieving voter status. They looked at each other, shrugged their shoulders and smiled back broadly.

'English no good,' they beamed. Then they bowed and went off to take videos of the Easter Bunny, and the Muslim/Christian/Socialist Workers who had taken up their spots and were loudly proclaiming jihad, the end of the world, and revolution.

Mrs G came over to me.

'Bloody hard work this. Time for a tea break, I reckon.' I nodded in fervent approval, and we relocated to the relative sanity of the tables, where Jimmie and one of the bandsmen had just returned from the local coffee shop with a couple of boxes holding polystyrene cups of tea. The band was obviously about to take a breather too, as soon as they finished "Tomorrow Belongs To Me", a stirring if somewhat inappropriate tune. The Muslim was attempting to make himself heard over the music, and over the competition from the Christian and the Socialist Worker. Given that the Socialist Worker had the most powerful megaphone, he was coming second to the band.

Mrs G and I accepted cups of tea from Jimmie and perched ourselves at the end of the tables. I lit a rather welcome cigarette, making the usual ritual obeisance of deciding to give up again soon.

'I don't believe this lot,' Mrs G said. 'half of them don't know that there's an election soon – no, wait a minute, half of the ones that stop don't know there's an election soon. Most of them just mutter something about being busy and run for it before I can stop them.'

'You're lucky,' I said, 'I can't repeat the language I get.'

'Hah, they wouldn't try that with me, they'd get a good slap.'

I was surprised some of them had the audacity to avoid Mrs G's attention, but decided not to mention the thought.

'Most of those who do know there's an election either don't know what it's for, or have no intention of voting.'

A few yards away Tom the Easter Bunny was enjoying himself immensely, shouting 'Vote for your Independent candidate!' while forcing pamphlets into the hands of bemused passers by. Those who had their hands full of shopping had one slipped into the shopping bags.

No-one protested – how could you argue with a six foot rabbit?

I like the slogan, but I have a suspicion people will think he's trying to flog newspapers.

'You know,' said Mrs G, 'the best response I've had is when you tell people a vote for you is a guarantee that council tax won't rise. Anything else is lost on them.'

'That's what I've been trying to point out for the last few weeks,' I pointed out, ignoring the slight inaccuracy of the claim about council taxes. Council taxes are going to rise, just as inevitably as the sun will. Our point is that we won't increase them to pay for another bureaucratic office.

Still, it's all spelt out in those lovely little pamphlets, so they can't say that we're telling any untruths. Not if they read the damn thing. And it isn't our problem if they don't.

'I admit you have a point,' said Mrs G in what I suspect is a rare admission of possibly just maybe appearing to be in the wrong, 'but I would much rather we campaigned on the higher ideals of democratic freedom and standing against established party political bureaucracy.'

'We are,' I said. 'It says all that in our pamphlet. Only you have to highlight different things to different people. Most of this lot have as much interest in democracy as they have in nuclear physics.'

'Funnily enough, that's what one or two have said to me – what good has democracy done for me? And you know what? Both of them were single mothers. Complained about how little state handout they have to get along with. I almost gave one of them a clip around the ear and told her to stop whining and get a job. Stop wasting my bloody taxes.'

I closed my eyes at the thought. I didn't want to imagine what the papers might make of that – "Independent Loony Says Single Mother Scroungers Should Get a Job". And then in smaller typeface, "Clip around the ear the only thing good enough for them".

On the other hand, it could be a winner. If people on the dole aren't going to vote, who cares what we say about them? And the people who are going to vote are tax payers – most of them object to supporting single mothers, no matter what they might say in public.

On the balance, probably not a good idea. Goes against the KISS principle. Keep It Simple, Stupid. One message, clear and concise.

I watched as the pamphleteers wandered back from their various points, partly for a tea break, partly to stock up with more litter. The band had stood down for elevenses, and the religious and social parties were taking the chance to get their messages across.

'We need a slogan,' I said, a thought forming in my head.

'We've tried slogans. You didn't like them,' Mrs G said somewhat ungraciously.

'I didn't like any of the ones which came up,' I reminded her. 'There's a difference. We need to be able to say something like, 'say no to more poll tax, vote – us'? Something like that.'

'Vote for your local loonies? Bit of a mouthful.'

I grunted in acknowledgement. That's why we hadn't come up with anything. It invariably sounded like a five minute speech, or was cringe inducing.

'What are you two looking so depressed about?' asked Ms D, coming back from ensuring that the pamphleteers had been fed and watered – or watered, anyway – and were having a quiet break sitting against the wall.

'We're trying to come up with a short and catchy slogan,' I told her, 'something along the lines of "Say no to more poll tax, vote – something or other". That's the bit we can't work out.'

'It's not poll tax, it's council tax. And I thought we'd been through all this before. You didn't like any of our suggestions.'

'I know it's not the poll tax, but saying "council tax" doesn't have the same ring to it. And "poll tax" suggests Maggie Thatcher. Two blows in one.'

'Isn't that called deception?' she asked, smiling.

'Artistic licence,' I replied. 'And the reason I didn't like any of the suggestions is that they didn't work.'

'True,' she admitted. She looked at my jacket, leaned forward and fingered the loop of rainbow in my button hole. 'Now how about – "Vote for the rainbow party"?' she suggested.

I thought about that. I liked it. I liked it a lot.

'I like it,' I said. 'Only one problem – we aren't called the rainbow party.'

'I'll see if we can get it changed on Monday,' she offered.

'Rainbow Independent,' Mrs G suggested.

'Rainbow Man,' countered Ms D.

'That'll do,' I said, standing up. 'Either one. Tell the others; the slogan is, "Vote no to more poll tax, vote for the rainbow man" – or independent, or something like that. Then slip a pamphlet into their shopping bag, and let them go away worrying about the poll tax.'

'Good idea,' Mrs G said, standing up and trying to ease aches and pains. 'That will save me having to try explain things to the idiots. Right, up and at em.'

That made our lives a lot easier. Only one or two people had any questions, one of whom pointed out that the poll tax was now called the council tax – don't you just love people like that – to which I responded with 'There's a difference?', which caused him to stop and think for a moment, before shaking his head, saying 'No, suppose not', and wandering off, thinking.

No doubt there is a difference, but I would hate to confuse the issue.

By lunchtime we had handed out all the literature we had with us, and the pamphleteers began slowly drifting back. Tom the Easter Bunny had nipped into a shop to buy some revolting sweeties which he handed out to any passing kiddies if their parents let them accept, which was most of them.

Amazing what people will allow a rabbit to get away with.

The anti-fox hunt chap had turned up with a little folding table and small box of literature, and looked at the Easter Bunny with some envy. During a period when no-one was talking to him – most of the time – he wandered over to me and expressed his admiration for such an idea, asking whether we would mind if he used it, only bringing along a fox. Needless to say I very graciously said that he was welcome to use the idea.

Why furry animals seem to pop up in politics god alone knows.

With everyone finally back – including a few who seemed to have gone AWOL, but turned out to have rediscovered the joys of shopping without buying anything – and the buses returned, we loaded up the tables, empty boxes, band instruments and various impedimenta and litter. The band were extremely happy with the morning's work. They'd craftily placed a bucket either side of where they were playing, with the word "donations" labelled on them, and had collected a reasonable amount of pub money. I left it up to them to decide what to do with their collection.

While we were waiting for the stragglers to turn up, I had taken the chance to slip away to a bank machine to check my account, and to my surprise Legrade-Smith had finally come through – a quiet fifteen thousand quid sitting there looking all lonely and asking to be spent. Later on, back at the ranch, after lunch, and when Ms D was about to go home, I took her for a quiet stroll where others couldn't hear, and explained Legrade's charity.

'Sounds a bit fishy to me,' was her first comment.

'Absolutely. But I couldn't care how much it smells like it's being dragged through a fishmongers backwards, it's sitting in my account, it's real – as real as an electronic printout can be – and I want to make sure the little sod can't suddenly change his mind and try to get it back.'

'You think he might?'

'I wouldn't put it past him. There's something in his story that doesn't stack up – why do these businessmen want to remain anonymous? So I just want to make sure that we don't end up owing people money only to find that the pot has been emptied because of a supposed transaction error.'

'You'll have to transfer it somewhere else. And get the bank to confirm that the transaction is correct. Then they haven't any comeback.'

'That's what I was thinking. But transfer it to where? Your account?'

'You'd trust me?' she asked with a smile.

'Of course,' I assured her.

Funnily enough, the idea of not trusting her hadn't occurred to me. And I'm normally a suspicious type.

'I'm flattered,' she said, with a look on her face that I couldn't decipher. Which isn't unusual. 'However I think it would be better to open a new account. Call it a campaign account. At some stage they're likely to want to audit our records; it would be nice to have an audit trail that looked half believable.'

She had a point. Somewhere along the line someone might ask difficult questions, such as who paid for things like pamphlets, leaflets, buses, etc. Having to explain that the paper and buses etc. came from a company paid by the government could be difficult, no matter how often you call it therapy.

And having pretty little invoices will allow us to quietly lose the fifteen grand without actually spending it. If the companies named on the invoices don't exist, well we've got sufficient residents who have imaginary friends, they could handle imaginary companies quite easily.

I didn't point out such a fine detail to Ms D – there'll be time enough for that. But we will be popping down to the bank tomorrow to make certain arrangements. A new account for a holding company or something like that, with myself and Ms D as signatories. I didn't quite follow the terminology.

And Legrade-Smith phoned tonight to confirm the money had arrived. I was pleased to tell him yes, and that it was a good start, which got a response of a startled gasp.

'How do you mean, a good start? It's fifteen thousand pounds.'

'It's an expensive business,' I told him. 'Think of it this way, if we had to hire you, how far would fifteen grand go?'

There was silence on the line for a moment.

'You have a point, I suppose. I'll have a word with the, er, group, and point that out. I think we could probably raise a little more.'

I thanked him graciously, and wished him a happy Sunday evening.

On the way to a well earned pint I wondered whether there were any rich eccentrics we could touch for some more. They do say it's the first million which is the most difficult.

Chapter 8: Turning politician

Bill Dughaille

Wednesday 18th September

Saddam Hussein has agreed to allow weapons inspectors back into Iraq. George Bush has dismissed the offer as a political ploy.

Britain to allow US B-2 stealth bombers to use the island of Diego Garcia as a base.

Blair has suggested that taxes might need to be increased on the better off to meet New Labour's ambitious targets on reducing poverty and invading Iraq.

Some people believe that "better off" means "people who can't afford an expensive accountant to indulge in creative numeric sleight of hand".

North Korea and Japan have started talks to normalise relations. In a related step, North and South Korea have held a symbolic ceremony in which the buffer zone between them, closed for five decades, has been reopened for rail and road traffic.

Here Home Secretary David Blunkett has been castigated for suggesting that immigrants should speak English at home. His statement was condemned by many as "dictating what people should do in their own homes".

The British army's standard infantry rifle, the SA80, will not be abandoned. The SA80 has undergone a £92m upgrade after soldiers complained that it kept breaking down. There are still complaints about the reliability of the weapon, but the Ministry of Defence claims that reliability levels of 17% increased to 85% when soldiers cleaned the rifles properly. Ignoring the fact that losing 15% of your firepower straight off might be considered a worrying amount, the question has been asked as to whether this impressive cleaning regime can be carried out under battle conditions.

You can imagine an ordinary Tommy stuck in a trench as the bullets whizz past over head, saying "Cleaning instructions? I'll give them flipping cleaning instructions".

The first beef to be exported since the foot and mouth crisis began is due to be sent from Wales to the Netherlands. In a cunning marketing ploy it will be labelled as "Welsh" beef rather than "British" beef.

Some NHS hospitals have been found to be routinely "fiddling the figures" in order to meet government targets. The government has expressed surprise.

"Top public boarding schools" will allow their boarders time off to join the forthcoming countryside protest in London, should they wish it. "Public" in this case meaning "private and elitist", but naturally this will in no way suggest that the protest is class based. The campaigners merely wish to fight to retain "traditional rural life", such as chasing foxes with hounds while on horseback – the hunters are on horseback, not the foxes or hounds, which would be far more interesting. Their argument is that they don't interfere with traditional town life, such as having to live in crowded little boxes amidst smog and pollution which will reduce life expectancy, so why should the "townies" interfere with their lives.

In France the author Michel Houellebecq is on trial for inciting racial hatred because he called Islam "the dumbest religion". It's not that he's impressed by any of the others, but he does consider the Koran "mediocre", whereas the Bible, having several authors, is well written in places and merte in others. Since France is a secular country, several people have expressed surprise that an author should be prosecuted for stating his personal views.

In the For Sale section: the Doune Dining Room on the Knoydart Peninsula in Scotland is available for around £300,000. The converted crofting cottage has gained a reputation for being one of the best restaurants in Scotland, despite the fact that it is only accessible by sea, or after a two-day hike, since no roads reach the area.

So what is this "location, location, location" business?

Today was one of those days when you feel like everything's happening at a distance, because nothing seems to make sense.

It started off as I was standing in reception at about ten o'clock with a small group of the others, waiting for the buses to turn up.

We'd planned to do another leaflet attack, but this time in the shopping centre close to the more expensive part of town. Personally I had thought the area a waste of time as far as votes go, but Mrs G reckons that they're probably the best touch for a "don't pay more" campaign.

'Rich people didn't get rich by giving their money away,' was her explanation.

While we were standing there – admiring the overcast gloom outside – Mrs Phillips turned up with her trolley of library books, complaining about how no one seemed to want to read these days. That was fair enough; most of her usual customers were too busy practicing for the last night of the proms, folding pamphlets into shape, or studying the tactics board to work out the next step of the campaign.

'I told George last night, "people are just so busy and rushed these days, they don't have time to read anymore".'

George is her late husband. According to Mrs Phillips he talks to her from the other side. However, from what I've heard of their conversations he doesn't get much of a word in.

'Doing well, is he?' I asked conversationally. Ms D gave me a funny look from behind Mrs Phillips.

'Under the circumstances, you know,' she replied, presumably meaning "not too bad since he died a year ago".

'Any other familiars turning up lately?'

'Familiars?' I don't hold with familiars, you know. That's just superstitious nonsense.'

'Sorry, I meant, um, any of the usual crowd.'

'Oh, I see. Well, do you know, I had a visit from Evdokia a couple of nights ago. She came all the way from Australia for a chat, and to pass on a message.'

'Long trip, was it?' I have no idea how spirit miles compare to the more normal physical ones.

'Well she travelled with Qantas this time, she says the food is so much better. And she feels it's her patriotic duty, now that she's made Australia her home. I'm not sure I agree with her, but it was nice to hear her voice again.'

I thought of pointing out that she could have phoned if that was all it was, but it would probably turn out that Evdokia had a phobia about phones.

I was still trying to work out why the quality of airline food was relevant to someone whose last earthly meal had been many years ago.

'Now what was the message again?' Mrs Phillips asked herself, face wrinkled in concentration. 'She said it was extremely important, I must pass it on. Hmm, memory like a sieve these days.'

I stood there in silence while she racked her brains. I could see the buses turning up, and the rest of the band and others were turning up in reception and flowing out into the parking area. Ms D gave me the raised eyebrow look, meaning "are you going to be discussing chats with the hereafter for much longer, or shall we just go on without you?" I was about to make my apologies to Mrs Phillips when she uttered an exclamation and gripped my arm.

'That's it! I remember now. She said you must keep away from Beatrix. That was it. "Keep away from Beatrix". It was very important. Life and death, she called it'

'Beatrix? Me? Are you sure?'

'Absolutely. I presumed it would make sense to you.'

'Not at all, I'm afraid. I don't think I know anyone called Beatrix. She didn't give a surname, did she? Leave a telephone number? E-mail address, that sort of thing?'

'No, just the name Beatrix. That's the problem with some of these messages they give, as soon as things become important they start talking in riddles. Rather childish, I always think. Like the other night, when I was talking to Agnes, I -'

'Sorry, Mrs Phillips,' Ms D intervened, 'but I'm afraid it's time we were going.'

'Oh? Off on a trip? How nice. Do have a good time, it's always good to get out every so often. Well, must get these books to the others. Enjoy yourselves.' She waggled a hand and pushed the trolley off towards the right hand corridor, making a path between people who were probably the intended recipients of the books she was pushing.

'Sometimes I worry about you,' Ms D said. 'Come on, let's get on the bus.'

'Your name not Beatrix by any chance, is it?' I asked.

'No. You know it isn't.'

'I thought maybe it might be your middle name.'

'No.'

'Pity. Apparently I have to avoid her like the plague. I'm beginning to imagine her now, flaming red hair, shining eyes, thigh length leather boots, big – '

'I don't think I need to know any more about your fantasies if you don't mind.'

'What, not even the one about the –'

'Ah, there you are,' said Doctor Peter Johns suddenly appearing in front of me. He's the new bloke who reckons people are dying to be cured so that they can live in misery elsewhere. He goes around in a white coat, something the others never used to do – even has a stethoscope in one of the pockets. Probably fancies himself as a medical doctor.

'I'll see you outside,' Ms D said to me, and hurried off.

I don't think she likes him too much. Don't blame her myself, there's something about him that gives me the creeps.

'You name not Beatrix then?' I asked him. I bloody hoped not. I didn't want an image of him in thigh length leather boots.

'Beatrix? No, of course not. That's a woman's name. Are you feeling okay?'

'Yes, yes, fine,' I assured him, desperate to avoid any suggestion of another session with him. 'It was just something we were discussing, something from one of those quizzes, you know, where you can never remember the answer, and then after a while you can't remember the question either.'

'Oh, I see, yes. Never had that problem myself, but a lot of people do.'

Smarmy git.

He waved in the general direction of the buses, where loading up had almost finished. 'This all seems good therapy. Everyone's improved quite dramatically. We'll probably have quite a few discharges soon,' he commented.

If he tries to chuck people out before they want to go he'll definitely get a few discharges, only not the type he's thinking about.

'Yes, all very promising. Glad to hear you got your fundraising solved as well.' He gave me a paternal pat on the shoulder, said 'Excellent, yes, very good,' and walked away.

I gave his back the two fingered salute and walked out to the bus where Ms D stood waiting, arms crossed and fingers tapping.

What did he mean about the fundraising? He couldn't have meant the couple of bob the band picked up last Saturday, we'd kept that quiet so that it could be used for a couple of drinks for everyone.

'Quite ready?' Ms D asked sarcastically. 'Anyone else you'd like to have a chat with while we're waiting?'

'After you, oh most gorgeous and heavenly creature from the planet of the perfect,' I said, giving an exaggerated rolling arm gesture to indicate that she should board first. I couldn't see why she was upset because Johns had collared me; she knows I can't stand the idiot anyway.

I took a look around the bus before sitting down next to Ms D.

'Tell me I'm seeing things,' I said to her.

'You're seeing things,' she snapped back, looking out the window.

'Oh good, so we don't now have a rabbit, a lion, a straw man and Pinocchio on the bus then.'

One rabbit was bad enough. We seemed to have collected a menagerie.

'There's another two rabbits on the other bus. And a hedgehog. They're doing their best. They are trying to help, no matter how much you think it silly.'

'Not at all, not at all,' I hastened to tell her. 'You're right, it is rather sweet.' I was about to pat her hand in a reassuring manner, but quickly decided against it, concerned that I might never see my hand again. I folded my arms and leaned back, closing out the world for a while. Between Mrs Phillips' messages from beyond, Johns' strange comment, the assorted animals and Ms D's snappishness it wasn't turning out to be a bright new morning in a brave new world.

When we arrived at the shopping centre the clouds started to break, and the sun came through just where we had planned to set up stall. I think it must have something to do with it being a posh area – they get the Guccis and the sunshine, the poor get pound-shops and drizzle.

One of these days I must find out what Guccis are. Some sort of moccasin I would imagine.

By the time we had finished setting up a couple of tables, unloading boxes and drums and other paraphernalia it was getting on for half eleven. There weren't exactly hordes of locals, but I think some were beginning to stir, having no doubt managed to sleep off their venison and quail, and decided it was time for a round of light shopping before a leisurely lunch.

To be honest, it wasn't as bad as that, but you could tell the difference money makes. In the other shopping centre you had stressed, overweight, poorly fed single mums dragging a brood of wailing brats around; here the mothers were slim and tanned, pushing state of the art prams containing angelic looking babies quietly asleep. Wearing designer nappies, no doubt.

If there was a word to describe the difference I think that word would be "confidence". This place was soaking in it. I doubted we'd be picking any votes up from this lot.

Our first problem began with a thin, ratty looking bloke from one of the designer shops – did I mention the designer shops? – who popped out to complain about the band. Since they hadn't even started playing yet it seemed a bit much. Apparently he didn't want a noisy bunch of oiks creating a disturbance outside his shop.

Sorry, boutique.

Unfortunately he was voicing his displeasure in a very high reedy voice – with fake French accent – to Mrs G, who was regarding him with a sort of disdain that didn't augur well for his future. Even worse, Ms D was coming up on the flank, a look of thunder in her eyes. Miss Melly was in front of the band, almost in tears, which wasn't going to be a point in reedy voice's favour. The band had been ready to start, but now they were holding their instruments in attitudes suggestive of imminent violence.

"Trumpet call" took on a whole new meaning.

I whipped quickly over to Miss Melly. Much as I would have liked to have seen reedy voice having his glottal stop removed, I hate having to explain such things afterwards to the nice men in blue.

'Get them playing,' I whispered to Miss Melly. 'Something quiet.'

'Okay,' she said miserably, 'what do you want?'

'Anything, so long as it isn't Wagner or anything to do with Gotterdamerung or the end of the world.'

'Okay.' She smiled weakly and turned to the band, who obediently – though reluctantly – set their instruments into the playing position. I shot over to where reedy voice was campaigning for his extinction.

'Could I have a word?' I asked politely, putting a hand on his shoulder and firmly steering him out of earshot of the Valkyries. 'Now, what seems to be the problem?'

'I cannot have this noise outside my boutique,' he protested, as the band swung quietly into "In the Mood". Full marks to Miss Melly. And I do love the big bands.

I cocked my head to one side and listened for a few moments.

'I wouldn't call that noise,' I commented, smiling like a double glazing salesman. 'Jazz is the new rock, you know. And they do have permission to be out.'

'Out?'

'Well, you know who they are, don't you? The band from the

institution? You know, the loony bin.'

'The loony bin?'

'Yes, but don't worry, they aren't violent.'

'Violent?'

'Not really. Don't you like jazz?'

'I think I do. Jazz is good,' he said in a voice which suggested that his mind was reversing several cogs to arrive at a new conclusion.

'I tell you what,' I said in my most reasonable voice, 'why don't you go back in your shop – boutique – and let us know if it gets too loud. I promise I'll ask them not to make too much noise.'

'Jazz is – very French,' he said, now smiling happily. 'Very chic. English type chic. After all, we are in England.'

'I couldn't have put it better myself,' I agreed, propelling him firmly back towards his shop. Boutique. He went back in quite happily, having discovered a new chic.

I resisted the urge to help him along into his boutique with le boot up his derriere.

Mrs G had also discovered a new chic.

'Cheek of the bugger,' she said furiously when I returned, 'you should have let him get what was coming to him.'

'I know, I know, Mrs G,' I said, 'but you know how I hate to have to clean up all the blood and bits afterwards. Almost puts me off my din-dins. Now come along and let's get this show going.'

She made a "Hmmph" sound to indicate her take on the matter, and then she and Ms D swept off to get the pamphleteers into gear, in a manner which demonstrated that they were still in charge.

I lit a cigarette and stood there wondering how I had got into this position, and how long I could continue to be this pleasant and reasonable.

Miss Melly turned, caught my eye, and winked happily. Ah, well, I thought, winked back and walked off after the other two.

Fortunately we didn't have any more contretemps with the locals – the band had settled in for a morning of jazz, and it went down pretty well in the autumn sun; quite a few people stopped to listen, some swaying lightly to the music, and a few old couples looking rather nostalgic. I didn't think it would get any votes, but what the hell, it was better than an enactment of Death In The Afternoon, even if it was morning.

Mrs G had forgotten about her temper – she doesn't let such a thing upset her too long, might interrupt with the next person due a bollocking – and Ms D had taken herself off with the other pamphleteers, so things went quite pleasantly for an hour and a half or so, handing out pamphlets while saying things like "vote for the rainbow independent, say no to more council tax". We'd guessed that this lot probably did know the difference between council tax and poll tax. And they'd probably voted for Thatcher. And then Tony Blair when he became fashionable.

The passers by were mostly young mums and young women, with the occasional bloke in a convertible pulling over to park in a bus lane, just to get in the way of the very occasional bus. The mothers tended to pause for a break in their hard schedule between chiropodist and hair stylist so that kiddywinks could listen to the music or admire our collection of animals, busy passing out sweeties and pamphlets in equal measure.

Occasionally they remembered to give the pamphlets to the mothers and the sweets to the kiddies instead of the other way around.

I noticed the anti-fox hunting bloke appear at one stage. He was accompanied by a fox – not a real one, someone dressed up as a fox with waist coat and funny hat. I waved to them, and the anti-hunt bloke waved back. It crossed my mind that this place was turning into a version of some sort of children's fairy tale. I put the matter to the back of my mind to concentrate on the massed hordes approaching me.

Well, perhaps not "hordes"; apart from a group of mums and toddlers listening to the band, there was an old lady approaching on one of those powered wheelchairs. I decided not to try to intercept her, she was moving at a phenomenal rate of knots. Otherwise the place was pretty empty. Obviously the more fashionable walkways were elsewhere.

My attention, or lack of it, was interrupted by the voice of a toddler saying, 'Look, mummy, the fox is going to eat the wabbit.'

I looked around to find it only too true. The fox was advancing on our Easter Bunny, claws raised and mouth snapping. Easter Bunny was carefully stepping backwards as fast as he could.

I don't know what it is about humans. Put them in an animal costume and they suddenly start acting out.

'Oh for – ' I was about to say something, but remembered the toddler in time. I looked down at her sweetly, and finished, 'poot!'

'Poot?' she asked.

'Poot,' I confirmed, but the little one quickly lost interest in me.

'Look, mummy, there are two more wabbits, and a hedgehog.'

I turned around again to find that our other two Easter Bunnies had advanced on Mr Fox from behind, with Henry the Hedgehog in close attendance. One of the Easter Bunnies tapped Mr Fox on the shoulder, whereupon he stopped snapping and turned around.

Now in the real animal world I suppose a fox wouldn't suddenly become nervous on finding himself surrounded by wabbits. Then again he wouldn't raise a paw, waggle it in greeting, and hand out a pamphlet while trying to squeeze past without anyone noticing. And aforesaid rabbits wouldn't give him a cuff across the jaw, followed by the fox legging it, being chased by three wabbits and a hedgehog, all slowed down by the costumes they were wearing.

'Ooh, Mummy, they're chasing him,' screamed the little girl in delight.

'Is it some sort of play?' asked Mummy.

'It's, um, an analogy,' I replied slowly. The anti fox hunt candidate had been engrossed in conversation with a passer-by; now he stood with his mouth wide open as his fox disappeared down the road, followed by the others, plus Lenny the Lion who had suddenly appeared and decided to join in on the fun.

'Ooh, we did those at university,' said Mummy, 'I could never understand them.'

University?

'Still the kids do love them, don't they? Don't you, Mary-Sue?' Mary-Sue gave me the blank look of a three year old who doesn't think much of anything. 'Well, must be off, good luck with the analogy.'

'Cheers, very kind,' I replied. In the distance I could see our Easter Bunnies, lion and hedgehog returning. At least they hadn't chased the fox into the French boutique, though I didn't want to think about where they had chased him.

'Not often you see that sort of thing, is it?' asked Mrs G rhetorically as she appeared next to me. 'Look, they've got his tail!'

'His what?'

'His tail. Can't you see? The middle rabbit – that's Harry, isn't it? – he's holding the fox's tail. Well done Harry!'

I closed my eyes. The Easter Rabbit versus Freddie the Fox, round one to the rabbits. I just hoped Mr Fox didn't have any friends in the neighbourhood. A tactical response by Mr Fox, Mr Wolverine and Mr Leopard might be difficult to contain.

'Do me a favour,' I asked Mrs G quietly, 'ask them to try not to go chasing foxes all over the neighbourhood. It doesn't do our image a whole lot of good.'

'Mmmph! That fox asked for it. I hope they gave it a damn good thrashing. Nasty little vermin. Can't stand the things.'

'Yes, yes, I know, but we don't want to have to go down the cells to bail out three rabbits, a hedgehog and a lion, now do we?'

She laughed. 'Now that would be a sight!' she exclaimed, and went off to bring the returning livestock back into line.

'Feck. Good stew,' commented Jimmie, popping out of nowhere.

'Stew?'

'Feck, foxes. When you're living rough. Make good stew. Bit tough, but farmers don't miss them like they do fecking sheep.'

'No, I suppose they wouldn't.' I hoped Jimmie wasn't thinking of going after Mr Fox to retrieve what was left for a light snack. At that moment there wasn't much that could surprise me.

Not even the police car that pulled up shortly afterwards, the driver calling me over.

'You haven't seen three rabbits chasing a fox around here, have you?' he asked in a tone of voice which said "I have to ask this so I'm going to ask this even though I don't want to ask this".

'Sorry?' I enquired innocently, eyes wide.

'We had a report of a fox being chased by three rabbits,' he said doggedly, emphasising the word 'report'.

'A fox. Being chased by three rabbits.'

'Yes.'

'Just three rabbits?' I asked, trying not to look to where the Easter Bunnies had last been. Hopefully they'd nipped into the loo for a brush up.

The driver rolled his eyes slightly.

'We have to investigate these things,' he said in a it's-not-my-fault manner.

'I understand perfectly,' I assured him.

'Someone taking the mick again,' he said, putting the car into gear. 'Sorry to have bothered you.'

'Not at all,' I told the disappearing car boot, and wandered off to a quiet spot to have a cigarette.

I'll give the damn things up tomorrow.

Ms D floated back in with a few others around about one o'clock, and brought me a cup of coffee, which I sensed might be in the way of a peace offering, but I knew from experience not to say anything. Simple conversation such as "Nice weather for this time of the year" could spark off World War Three in such circumstances.

I still have the scar from the day I innocently asked a young woman whether she was having a bad hair day.

'I saw Sir Archibald and Doctor Johns in that Spanish restaurant down there,' she commented. 'That'll no doubt appear on expenses as a business lunch.'

I nodded. 'Just the two of them?' I asked conversationally, having checked the question for any possibility that it might contain something upsetting.

'Oh, no, looks like and old boys' gathering. Five or six of them. Champagne and caviar while the patients get cut-price mince pie. Typical men!'

She really was in a bad mood.

'You feeling okay?' I asked, deciding to risk life and limb. 'You sound rather tired. Not coming down with the flu or anything, are you?'

'Flu?' She smiled wanly and shook her head. 'I suppose that's what it must be.'

'Shouldn't you be at home then, in bed? You've been pushing things rather hard lately.'

She shook her head and patted me on the shoulder. 'don't worry, just another hour or so. Let's get the rest of the leaflets out.' She picked up a couple of packs, corralled her pamphleteers, and marched off back to accosting strangers.

As I watched her go I caught sight of Sir Archie in the distance, leaving the Spanish restaurant. I recognised Johns, and one other in his party – friend Legrade-Smith. It reminded me of the night in the pub when Smith was so nervous, and I chuckled to myself. On such a small, densely inhabited island people still moved in tribal circles. You could do a study on it.

Then the thought crossed my mind of which tribe I belonged to. I decided it best not to explore that avenue too deeply, and got back on with the business of distributing litter.

After another hour or so we decided to call it a day, and everyone gathered together waiting for the buses as the band played out in the afternoon sun. They finished off with "Jerusalem" as the buses arrived, a tune which seemed to please the small crowd of dallying shoppers, and we commenced loading of equipment. I noticed that the band's "donations" buckets seemed to have done rather well – maybe we should come here more often.

Back on the bus I sat down next to Ms D, and ordered her to go straight home afterwards, have a hot bath, put her feet up, and relax with a glass of wine or something. She smiled, called me a daft sod, put her head on my shoulder, and went to sleep.

In the back the Easter Bunnies were snoring quietly.

Like I said, it was a strange day.

Sunday 22nd September

Two women have gone to the High Court to argue that they should be allowed to use frozen embryos to have children. The relationships with their former partners, the fathers of the frozen embryos, have ended, and the former partners are refusing to give their permission for the embryos to be used. The 1990 Human Fertilisation and Embryology Act states that both partners must give consent before the embryos can be used. The two women can no longer conceive naturally.

Yasser Arafat is pinned down in his West Bank headquarters by the Israeli army. Israel has stated that they are not after Chairman Arafat himself, but want to arrest a number of people in the compound in connection with the latest suicide bombing. The US has urged Israel to act with restraint. Ali Fleischer, White House spokesman, stated: "Israel has the right to defend itself and to deal with security, but Israel also has to bear in mind the consequences of action and Israel's stake in development of reforms in the Palestinian institutions."

German Chancellor Gerhard Schroeder has apologised for remarks made by Justice Minister Herta Daeubler-Gmelin which have been interpreted as comparing Bush with Adolf Hitler. Mrs Daeubler-Gmelin claimed that George Bush was using the planned war with Iraq as a means of diverting the attention of US citizens from domestic problems, adding that even "Hitler did that". There are suggestions that the supposed fury of the US at the comment is aimed at forcing Germany into line to support the war against Iraq. With the Germans going to the polls today Schroeder is walking a fine line, as many German people feel the US is trying to bully other countries into compliance.

The countryside alliance protest march in London has been claimed as a great success by the organisers. What it was about is another question. Some said it showed the level of support for foxhunting. Others said it wasn't about foxhunting. To another group it was not all about foxhunting. Amongst the many things they were apparently demanding was a decent rural transport service, which brought cynical smiles to those who have to use London's overcrowded and unreliable roads, rail and buses every working day. The same went for the call for affordable housing, the closing of Post Offices and banks; people living in large cities, unable to afford increasingly expensive hovels, have seen Post Offices and banks closed in their neighbourhood a long time ago.

The general complaint of the marchers seemed to be the "destruction of the rural way of life", missing the irony that town dwellers, most of whom are the descendants of those pushed off the land during the industrial revolution, have to put up with people complaining about change.

Ian Duncan Smith, the Conservative leader, was near the head of the march, possibly searching for an effective opposition to the government.

During a television programme broadcast during the day, a former Labour politician pointed out that, when the mines were being closed and thousands were losing their jobs, many of which were in in semi-rural areas, the heavily subsidised farmers were no-where to be seen. Now it was the turn of the farmers and their friends to face up to a changing world, and they should not expect any sympathy from others. This was welcomed by loud applause.

A march spokesman promised that the marchers would not leave any litter to make London any dirtier, and that they would, in fact, leave London cleaner than when they arrived, a jibe which suggests they should invest in some better PR.

A woman in the United States, who had become the media's public enemy number one after being caught on a security camera apparently beating her child, has surrendered herself to the police. Her name is Ms Toogood.

Wet. Wet, wet, wet. Drizzle, drizzle, drizzle. You can tell that winter is on the way in; it rains just as much, but it's getting cold.

We were all stuck indoors, central heating going full blast, turning the atmosphere muggy, a guarantee that people will start falling ill with colds and flu shortly. Why is it that no one in companies or organisations has ever heard of thermostatic control? It's that sort of lever you have at home which allows you to make sure that it doesn't get too hot. Shops during winter are the worst; their staff walk around in shirtsleeves while the customers boil in several layers of clothing.

Funny how miserable some people can become in this sort of weather.

We were playing monopoly this morning, Miss Melly, Mrs G, the major, Colin and myself. It's not my game of choice but there was little else to do. I would have preferred Risk, where you can pretend to have no interest in a bordering country, until the player owning that country finds himself at war with another, and promptly invade while his forces are facing the wrong direction.

After all, who wants to be making play money when you can be invading Africa?

Unfortunately the copy we had had was destroyed when a quiet military battle between Iceland and Canada deteriorated into a fist fight, accompanied by the breaking of the board over Japan's head, while Australia sat quietly eating the armies.

This morning I was forking over large amounts of Monopoly money to Mrs G, who seemed to own an incredible number of hotels on exclusive streets, when I noticed a familiar looking chap come wandering by. It took me a few seconds to recognise him.

'Prof!' I exclaimed. 'I didn't recognise you without the hat. And the pall bearer's suit. What's happened?'

'You still owe me another two hundred,' Mrs G demanded.

'I have been cured,' the prof said with beaming eyes. 'Doctor Johns told me on Friday that he felt I was well enough to venture into the world outside, a free man. Tuesday I get my certificate of sanity. Wonderful news, isn't it?'

'If you say so, prof. Personally I think it's a bit dangerous out there. But, hey, if you're happy, that's wonderful. Best of luck to you.'

'Thank you. I shall always treasure my memories of this ... institution. I can honestly say that I have never had such interesting experiences.'

He smiled and walked on.

'Two hundred pounds,' demanded Mrs G.

'Okay, okay,' I said, handing over the money. 'Well, who would have thought it. A real life cured person. It's been ages since I saw one of those.'

'Nothing wrong with him in the first place,' grumbled Mrs G. 'His only problem was a fear of being locked up in prison.'

'Sounds like a perfectly reasonable fear to me,' I commented, and she snorted.

'You know, sometimes,' Miss Melly started, and then hesitated. 'Sometimes I just wish if it could be like this forever.'

'What, you mean wet and chilly outside, and us inside a sauna playing silly games?' I asked. Mrs G shot me a dirty look. Miss Melly laughed.

'No, you know what I mean. Us all together, just enjoying ourselves. Well, mostly. I can't even thinking about moving outside. Losing all your friends, having to live amongst strangers.'

'Won't happen,' said Mrs G, rolling the dice aggressively, knocking down a few of the major's houses. 'They can't chuck you out if you aren't ready.'

I said nothing. We all remembered the famous "care in the community" approach of the Conservative government, which should more aptly have been named "lack of care in the community". Seriously mentally ill people unceremoniously dumped on the relatives and the general public in the hope that someone would take care of them or they would be forced to get better. Our position relies on the company making a tidy profit without having to worry about high-maintenance patients. So long as that continues we should be safe.

'Pass go, collect two hundred pounds,' Mrs G announced triumphantly, making a "give" gesture to the major who was banker, and almost bankrupt as well.

'I heard Kerry sing last night,' Miss Melly said, smiling. 'That means we're going to win the lottery. Or something like that. Something good is just around the corner.'

I felt like banging my head on the table. I managed to resist the urge to ask her if she was awaiting an overdue library book.

'I think I would become an estate agent,' said the major. 'People are always buying and selling houses, you just have to get go around each day opening doors, showing people around. Any fool could do that.'

'Well, that certainly describes you,' said Mrs G tartly. The major looked hurt, poor bloke. Like a little cocker spaniel being chastised without knowing why.

'Damn,' I exclaimed, having rolled the dice and quickly covered the result up. 'Six and one lands me on your hotels again, Mrs G. Haven't got enough to pay you off, unfortunately. Here's my last few pennies anyway.' I quickly handed over the few notes left in front of me.

'I thought that was a five and a four,' said Miss Melly.

'Fraid not,' I said, quickly standing up. 'Just my luck. I'll have to go read a book, I suppose.' I quickly made my way elsewhere. Monopoly is definitely not my game. Bad enough people getting excited about real money, when they turn into rapacious absentee landlords with toy money things are definitely not right.

I should have been reading the newspapers, but those have been cancelled. Officially Johns feels they are bad for peoples' therapy. Unofficially it's a cost cutting measure. And if you start cancelling newspapers – which are supplied at a huge discount – things must be pretty bad. Or, as I rather suspect, someone is trying to make life unpleasant enough to make people want to leave.

Certainly the food has been going downhill. Poor Tonique has to face complaints daily – we can only get fried eggs and bacon on Saturdays and Sundays now. "An improved diet", they call it. In the same way I once got a letter from my bank stating that they were going to close the local branch to "improve services".

Speaking of banks, another twenty five grand appeared in my account on Thursday. It vanished into the new account sharpish, as soon as the bank confirmed that the transaction was correct. Legrade called to make sure I'd received it, and I promised him that it had been well spent on existing debts. I then told him that we would love to engage his services as a lawyer, hoping that he will convince his secret friends to cough up some more dosh to pay him. I even said that we'd discuss a formal arrangement as soon as funds were available.

I wonder if he'll take the bait.

One thing's for sure, he isn't going to see a penny.

Having left the game I wandered around, finally finding a copy of that god-awful rag, the Local Echo. having nothing else to do I sat down and browsed through it. And to my astonishment there was an article on the upcoming election which was extremely favourable to the "Not so Loony Party", as he called us. Carney described the Conservative and New Labour candidates as being "equally shallow, short on ideas, and indistinguishable in what they do say, which is mostly platitudes".

Slipping there, a bit, Carney, I thought; most of your readers probably think a platitude is some sort of Australian animal.

Dismissing the Lib Dem candidate as "another mindless example of Liberal Democrat tax and spend policies", and the Green Party as "the usual idealist pie-in-the-sky nonsense", he went on to describe the "Rainbow independent" as "a breath of fresh air in stale local politics". Also, "a chance for people to reject the mundane offers of established politicians, and for people to demand politicians who have something to say and do."

Well, I liked that. Not a bad bloke, our Jim Carney.

Okay, he's a lying little sod, and I wouldn't trust him further than I could throw Ben Nevis.

In one of those strange examples of synchronicity he was sitting at the bar at the Rose, chatting to Pete, when I popped in this evening to escape the sauna and slake my thirst. Though as it turned out it wasn't synchronicity at all.

'Read the article in the latest issue?' he asked, once Pete and I had finished the initial round of insults.

'Indeed,' I replied. 'I wouldn't have thought your advertisers would have agreed – you know, the people who pay your wages.'

He grinned in that special matey way of his, and tapped his nose conspiratorially. 'There's a lot going on behind the scenes, if you get my drift.'

'No,' I said, 'I don't. Tell me.'

'Ah, well that would be telling, wouldn't it?'

Of course it would be. It's just what I asked him to do.

Pillock.

'All I can say is that there are certain influential people who would like you to win this one.'

I knew. I had forty grand to prove it.

'What I was hoping is, to get some quotes,' he continued. 'Possibly personal stuff. Something for a "fighter for democracy" type article. How you first became interested, that sort of thing.'

The only personal thing Carney is likely to get from me is a raspberry, but I decided it was probably the wrong moment to mention that particular fact.

'You know, thinking about it, I reckon a few revelations about the other candidates would make good copy,' I said, trying to deflect his interest. 'Surely you must know a few stories about them – mistresses, visits to prostitutes, deviant sexual practices, dodgy accounting, that sort of thing?'

Well, every little bit helps.

'Don't worry about that,' he grinned evilly, 'we've got a couple of articles in the pipeline quoting them as denying several things. Never fails. We pretend to be correcting rumours which don't exist, they can't sue, and everyone starts believing the rumours. Oldest trick in the book.' He took a satisfied draw from his pint. 'But at the same time we need a hero story for you.'

'I'll have to think about that,' I told him. 'I'll see if I can get some notes together.'

'Don't leave it long. The election's pretty soon.'

I agreed, and changed the subject, hoping he would leave soon. But Carney's a pub creature; I could see him staying there until chucking out time, and then driving home to a bottle of whisky. So I made my excuses after a pint, and trudged back, irritated. The whole idea of going for a quiet pint is to escape the others and relax, not have to put up with people like Carney.

Still, I've got a radio interview with young Mary-Anne later this week. I must remember some jokes, and we can spend the time slagging the other candidates off.

Bill Dughaille

Chapter 9: Into the valley of death

Thursday 26th September

Miss Melly died last night.

Or possibly early this morning.

No more to face the slings and arrows of an outrageous fortune.

It seems so long ago, yet not so, that she was saying how she'd like everything to stay the same for always. Now, for her, time has stopped.

Maude Melly, spinster of this parish, fifty something, a quiet but constant light in our lives. You will never know how much people loved you, and how much they will miss you. Matron had to send out for extra supplies. John – drummer John, the bloke with the big drum? – he just sat there in the dining hall and beat a single beat every ten seconds or so, until Matron managed to talk him into taking a couple of tablets.

Mrs G refused, as I suppose you would expect. 'I do not need any tablets,' she proclaimed haughtily to Matron, and then: 'I have sufficient of my own, thank you, Alice,' she said quietly, and then marched off to her room, holding the cracks together.

I never knew Matron was called Alice, did you? I suppose you did.

So farewell, Maude. I can only hope that you are up there, relieved from the pain and the suffering of this vale of tears. If heaven ever deserved an angel, I'm sure you're looking down on us now.

Say a prayer for us sinners down here below.

Maude Melly, having been plagued by the trials and tribulations, sadness and sorrow unjustly visited upon her by an unseeing and uncaring deity, was taken from us in this year of our suffering, 2002.

Be happy, Maude. Wherever you are.

Sunday 29th September

The newspapers are having an orgy over the revelation that ex-Prime Minister John Major once had an affair with former minister Edwina Currie fourteen years ago. No one else seems very interested.

The United States is having difficulty getting other countries to agree with the wording of a new resolution on Iraq. Bush wants it to say something to the effect of "let's all bomb it now", but is facing opposition from France, China and Russia in the Security Council. There is a suggestion of political haggling and bargaining going on behind the scenes. Russia, for example, would want a free hand in Chechnya and Georgia in exchange for its support.

In London the Stop the War Coalition and the Muslim Association of Britain, organisers of an anti-war protest march, claim that more than 400,000 protestors attended the march. Reasons for attending the march were diverse: former Labour MP Tony Benn claimed that an attack on Iraq would be "wholly immoral". Film director Ken Loach felt that the proposed war was simply a war to further United States economic – i.e. oil – and political interests in the Middle East. Others were there to campaign for "justice in Palestine". However Yasser Alaskary, of the Iraqi Prospect Organisation – an Iraqi opposition organisation – said that they did not agree with the demonstration; they supported the removal of Saddam Hussein and realised that this would require a "targeted war".

In Washington around 600 demonstrators have been arrested during a anti-globalisation protest.

People have gone to the polls in Morocco, in the first parliamentary elections since King Mohammed VI came to the throne in 1999. Political life in the country has in the past been riven by corruption and royal meddling, resulting in voter apathy. The king has promised not to interfere. As he controls appointments to most important ministerial posts this could be difficult.

An inquiry into the "fiasco" of A Levels – where a number of school students received exam marks contrary to their expectations, some receiving a fail instead of a distinction – has found that there were flaws in the new marking system, but absolutely no-one is to blame. Chris Woodhead, former chief inspector of schools, said that it was "depressingly inevitable" that the inquiry would find no-one responsible.

Russian cosmonauts Valeri Korzun and Sergei Treshchev will receive something else along with the supplies a spaceship is bringing them in the orbiting International Space Station: census forms. Russia is conducting its first census since 1991. Let's hope the tax people don't get any ideas.

Arsenal 4 – Leeds 1; Liverpool 3 – Man City 0; Middlesborough 3 – Spurs 0; Man United 3 – Charlton 1.

The advantage of having to pay for your own newspapers is that you don't end up wasting time on the tabloids.

The disadvantage is that you miss all those pretty pictures.

Had an interview with Mary-Anne at the local radio station this afternoon. I really would have preferred to have cancelled it, but Ms D insisted. Everyone's feeling terrible about Maude, and there are a number of rumours going around. Johns has posted a notice on the noticeboard – a caring way to do things – claiming that Maude Melly died of a heart attack. That might well have become accepted as the truth had Sergeant Gilmore not turned up yesterday on a totally unrelated matter, and decided to do some investigating while he was here.

Funnily enough he had come to see me about a possible death threat due to my standing in the mayoral election. I told him it sounded like a lot of nonsense, and he explained that they had to take these things seriously, as "there were a lot of nutters out there". I pointed out that there were a lot of nutters in here, but they didn't go around threatening peoples' lives willy nilly. He had the good manners to look embarrassed.

I asked him where I stood in the death threat league, and he had to admit that the Labour candidate was top with eight, followed by the anti-hunt bloke with five, the Tory on two, and me on one, which more or less put the matter into perspective.

Though I was a bit irritated at being beaten by the others. After all, my position is more radical than theirs.

While he was there he learnt of Miss Melly's demise, and went off to "ask a few questions". Those questions revealed two pertinent facts, which I managed to force out of him before he left. Firstly, Miss Melly's bottle of sleeping tablets had been found on her bedside table, empty. That of itself could mean nothing, simply that she had taken the last couple of tablets that night. On the other hand, having a supply of required tablets is almost an obsession with most people here; as soon as the bottle reaches half way they insist on a top up, just in case there's a sudden worldwide shortage. On the other other hand, Matron is pretty strict about not allowing people to accumulate dangerous quantities, precisely for the reason that someone might take too many of them when depressed.

The second fact was much more relevant: Johns had told Miss Melly that he considered her well enough to re-integrate with "normal" society, and that he was signing her out. She should get ready to move out in a couple of weeks.

Whether that prompted her to take too many sleeping tablets, or caused a heart attack isn't really that relevant. The ultimate effect would be the same. Everyone knew that there was no way Miss Melly could have coped with the idea. And so everyone believes that Johns effectively killed her.

Fortunately for him he hasn't been around. He's in for a rough time on Monday.

Mrs G has decided that the cure for depression is to do something, and has therefore decided to take over the band, all of whom have been sitting around practising catatonia. Mrs G taking over a band is rather like Maggie Thatcher deciding to run a tiny tots' nursery school. And funnily enough, I think they would both succeed at it simply by the process of pushing people hard enough and long enough until they surrendered.

She was definitely not succeeding at first, despite bullying everyone into the music room and forcing them to start playing. It sounded like a large group of cats with electrodes attached to their privates having a major and extended wailing duel. I caught a sight of her trying to conduct them; it was awesome. She hasn't a clue about music, and her arm movements, while forceful, almost definitely had no relation whatsoever to whatever piece it was they were attempting the destroy.

It was the major who came to the rescue, while hanging around waiting to be berated by Mrs G. In a moment of idle speculation after the destruction of some musical piece which could not be positively identified, not even by its dental records or DNA, he said aloud, 'You know, I wonder what Miss Melly's favourite piece was'. After a few seconds silence someone called out 'A waltz. She loved them.'

That sparked a lively discussion, with a saxophonist pointing out that the first person was a cretin, and Miss Melly had obviously had a lifelong passion for jazz. A third person insisted loudly that the other two were obviously dreaming, they were the offspring of goats, and that the real answer had to be any classical piano work.

There followed an earnest and in depth debate about the truth of this claim, and whether they could somehow include a piano the next time they played out in the open, possibly by attaching wheels to it.

Having neither a piano nor wheels, this might be considered by some as being rather beside the point.

Now Mrs G might not be the best conductor in the world, but she is good at controlling a fight. And in the end they agreed on three tunes – or pieces, or whatever they're called. I can't recall the names, but one was definitely jazz, one a waltz, and the other had something to do with a piano. Which they don't have.

When I last heard them they were playing in tune, and enthusiastically. Full marks to the major. He might be bloody useless at most times, but he does have the ability to suddenly come up with the goods at strange times.

I'm quoting Mrs G there.

I had to leave them to go to the radio interview. Well, when I say "leave them", Ms D dragged me out of the corridor where I had been quite happily listening to the argie-bargie going on inside the music room, without becoming directly involved. It's called delegation.

In the radio studio I noticed that Mary-Anne had given up the bra-less approach, and seemed to have increased in chest size, along with some subtle make-up which made her look rather attractive, and at least twenty-six. She even looked pleased to see me, a broad smile on her face, which I'm prepared to bet is a combination of having been told – or having worked out – that a confrontational approach is not always the best, and the fact that at least I wasn't as boring as the traditional politicians.

On the other hand, maybe my fly was open and she was just having a good laugh.

I didn't think so, but it's a bit difficult checking these things without looking, shall we say, strange. I checked afterwards and it wasn't. Or maybe I'd managed to zip up surreptitiously. I don't think it was.

She started off with an introduction to "the person whose sanity is making this a truly democratic consideration of what politics means to each of us", or words to that effect. I'm pretty sure she introduced the others with similar praise – "the well regarded Labour candidate", and so on – and I confess to a regret that she'd lost some of that aggressive approach which she'd shown to the Green party candidate.

But we had a good time, and I cracked some jokes I'd managed to remember, complimented her on her appearance without crossing the line, being as charming as I could, though it felt a bit like I was on automatic, just trotting out the old stuff.

She asked me what my position on fox hunting was, and I used the question to point out how farcical the situation was.

'Having someone stand on an anti-fox hunting platform for mayor of a town where there aren't any fox hunts about sums up the power the new mayor will have. After all, how many times have you had to wait for the red-clad huntsmen to go clattering past while you're strolling down to the local library?'

'Not that often. Not since the library was closed, anyway.'

'There you go. Might as well stand on a platform for bringing back the death penalty.'

'What for?'

'Littering, I reckon. People who block shopping aisle with their trolleys while chatting. I could make a list.'

'People who park on pavements and force pedestrians to walk on the road,' she countered.

'The makers of those god-awful morning shows on telly,' I added.

'Kids who swear in public.'

'Any non-entity who writes an autobiography. Actually, anyone who writes an autobiography.'

'We could end up with a long list,' she laughed, 'especially when our listeners start calling in. But surely there is something you could contribute if you were elected? Something positive, something which could enhance the democratic process which you say you is so important to you?'

Course not, I thought. Goes against the whole concept. The idea is that I do nothing and they pay me a good salary for it. Showing a finger to the establishment, thumbing the nose at professional politicians.

And then something dear Maude Melly said floated back into focus.

'Well, Mary,' I said, having found out that she disliked her full name, 'I have been giving that some considerable thought. I mean, it's not that I'm asking to be elected just to get a nice salary and do nothing. But on the other hand, my main promise is that I will ensure that the post of mayor does not become yet another bureaucratic snout-in-the-trough post to be paid for by an increase in council tax. So, what to do?'

I paused for effect. And to get my breath and thoughts back.

'A very dear friend of mine who has recently passed away came up with a very good idea, an idea which I have to admit to not – well, I didn't realise its full potential at first. You see, people are dissatisfied with the political process, especially because they aren't told what is going on. They think decisions are being made behind closed doors, decisions over which they have no say. They feel like people in a train stuck in a tunnel, and the driver isn't telling them why they're stuck, or when they might start moving again. So, while I have promised not to do anything, I can still – illuminate, shall we say – the way things are done, by giving regular updates on what is proposed at council meetings. Who said what? Which councillors are in favour of which scheme? What happens behind closed doors? I can reveal all those things to our local people.'

'That sounds excellent,' she gushed, a trifle over the top, I thought. 'But how would you do that?'

'I haven't quite worked out the details yet,' I admitted – well, the idea had only resurfaced a few minutes ago – 'but possibly a weekly or monthly newsletter, maybe a website. A newsletter sounds like the best option at the moment.'

'I shall look forward to reading that. But how will you pay for it?'

Would the bloody woman ever stop asking questions? I smiled back.

'Well, the post of mayor does come with a rather beneficial salary, doesn't it?' I said. 'I'm sure I'd be able to use much of that.'

And there would be a mayoral budget. And if all else failed they could allocate some of their current budget. And raise council tax to pay for it if necessary, sod them. I was tired of this whole business.

'Well, listeners, remember you heard it here first. And it's a big, heartfelt thankyou to the Rainbow Independent for talking to us tonight. We'll be back just after this short break.'

She thumbed a button and the radio jingle came on.

'I think it's a wonderful idea,' she said enthusiastically. 'You know what – we could work it into my show. Regular updates on council planning, that sort of thing. Jazz it up a bit, turn that legalese they use into something people can understand.'

I thought about that while taking the earphones off. I think I contracted some of her enthusiasm

I hate it when that happens.

'Now that sounds like an excellent idea,' I found myself saying. And agreeing with. 'do you think it would really work?'

'We can give it a go,' she said, and waved goodbye as she went back on the air.

Back in the car Ms D was strangely silent. Or maybe she's having one of her moods.

'I thought Mary-Anne was looking rather attractive tonight,' I said conversationally.

'Really.' was her response.

'And she had a great idea about a regular show keeping people informed of council debates,' I added.

'Really.'

I gave it up. Here I was, on the brink of working out a beautiful plan, something which could put a real meaning into what we were trying to do, and all she could say was 'really.'

And it wasn't an enthusiastic "Really." either. More your "I am thinking of cutting out your internal organs one by one very slowly with an extremely blunt object and feeding them to some rather rapacious crows while you watch" sort of "Really".

So I retreated into silence. I'm quite fond of my internal organs where they are.

October

Wednesday 2nd October

The United States has imposed new regulations allowing foreign visitors from specified countries to be registered on arrival, the countries in question being primarily Muslim and largely Arabic. This has not gone down too well in the Arab world, while for many it has overtones of the United States' treatment of Japanese-Americans during World War II.

The Iraqi Prime Minister, Tariq Aziz, has warned Turkey that Iraq could no longer regard Turkey as "a friend" if Turkey allows the United States to use bases in Turkey for an attack on Iraq.

A hurricane named Lili has finished causing chaos in Cuba, and is now on its way to the United States Gulf coast.

Australia's Foreign minister, Alexander Downer, has been holding meetings with the military junta ruling Myanmar, a country known to the rest of the world as Burma.

Stock market values in Europe are up, down in Japan.

Left wing candidate for the Brazilian presidency, Luiz Inacio Lula da Silva, is ahead in the polls, only days before the election due on the 6th. The popularity of Mr da Silva, otherwise known as Lula, has led to a drop in the value of the Brazilian currency, the real.

London has ground to a halt as tube drivers go on strike again. While the tube drivers have rejected a pay offer of almost twice the level of inflation, London mayor Ken Livingstone has refused to condemn the strike, preferring to blame London Underground management. Mr Livingstone was in Brighton for the day, well away from any possible inconvenience due to the strike. He has called on the Transport Secretary, Alistair Darling, to intervene, but Mr Darling is reported to have no intention of getting involved. The majority of commuters struggling to work amidst this unedifying spectacle of buck passing have more chance of winning the lottery than of receiving a salary increase above inflation.

In a related issue, social security staff in Northern Ireland are to strike over what they claim to be an increase in the hours they are expected to work. The Social Security Agency has denied this, claiming that the only change is that offices will be expected to be open to the public until 4.30pm rather than 3.30pm – staff have always been expected to work "normal office hours", from 09h00 to 17h00, also known as nine-to-five. The suggestion is that the staff were using the 3.30pm closing time to quietly leave work early. The "customers" of the social security offices, being unemployed and on the dole or pensioners, are likely to have even less influence in the matter than commuters have in the tube strike

Had a call from Legrade-Smith last night, and he didn't sound very happy, poor lambkin. He started off by complaining that it had taken two days before he could get in touch, as if he expected me to be available any time he felt the urge to call. No doubt the idea of leaving his name and telephone number wasn't something he was anxious to do.

Having got that off his chest he launched into a tirade about the interview I did with Mary-Anne last Sunday. Apparently it was totally against the agreement we had. "Agreement"? His "associates" were extremely angry, and thinking of demanding their money back.

They'll be lucky.

He went on for a while, dropping legal jargon in every so often, which gave me the time to decide on a response. The intelligent approach would be to mollify him, suggest that speaking over the telephone was not secure, but remind him that we were involved in politics, and that what I'd suggested on Sunday had only been put forward as a possibility, which might need to be reviewed in the light of expert legal help, hint, hint, nudge, nudge – and then touch him and his mates for more money for the "expert legal help".

Without, of course, meaning a single word of it.

In the end I decided on the other option. Leading people like Smithy up the garden path was all well and good, and pretty enjoyable while it lasted, but after a while you just want to get away from such people. So I broke in while he was pausing for breath, pointed out that there never was any "agreement", and if his friends wanted their money back he could give me their names and contributions and I would refund, pro-rata, what was left.

Which, of course, was nothing, at least not in my account, but I decided not to overload him with information.

I took the opportunity to inform him that the bank had confirmed the transfers, so claiming they were errors might not look too good. And when the nice people came around to audit our accounts they were likely to find his name on several large payments. Which could be made public. Especially to the Law Society.

I won't say he went quiet, because I could hear some heavy breathing on the phone, but he didn't appear to have much to say for a few seconds. Eventually he managed a threat.

'You'll regret this. Oh, yes, you will regret this.'

'Now then, Smithy,' I said reasonably, and probably confirming his suspicions of the peasantry, 'you and the others thought you could use me. I know it's not nice to be proved wrong, but there isn't much use in crying over spilt milk. After all, I am sticking to the main point I made when I first decided to stand, and I'm sure your associates will welcome a candidate of integrity. And we will probably still need a first class lawyer, if only your friends can come up with the money.'

For some reason that last sentence upset him. He shouted something which contained a number of words, almost all of which could be termed epithets, before slamming the phone down.

Hopefully he won't try anything silly. Since he's the only link, he isn't likely to want any of this becoming public. I'm told that the Law Society can be quite vicious when one of their members is caught doing something dubious.

Today we went out on another litter operation. There are a number of shopping centres we should do, but there's only enough time for two more, and for the penultimate one we chose a mixed area, rich and swanky at one end, pound shops at the other, all in the space of about five hundred yards.

Other countries might prefer to separate the peasants from the aristocracy, but Britain doesn't like the burglars to have to travel too far, it just creates greenhouse gases from their broken-down BMWs.

Almost all of the band were there, a tribute to Mrs G's powers of persuasion. I did jokingly suggest to her that we should swap places, let her become the candidate and I would conduct the band, on the theory that we would each cause less damage that way, but she didn't take too well to the concept.

'We need you where you are,' she said brusquely, 'you're doing better than you think. And while you're about it, I suggest you think seriously of your terrible treatment of Fiona. She does have feelings, you know.'

Eh?

I moved away very quickly, suddenly intent on checking some pamphlets.

There are some things I will never understand in this life, one of them being how you can be blamed for someone else treating you as if you were the source of all the world's woes. So I left her to her energetic arm movements as she warmed the band up, and they pretended to be following her instructions, while resolutely sticking to the original music.

One of the things I had noticed while on the bus was the absence of any domestic animals or wildlife, but I presumed that they were in the other bus. Once on the ground, with tables unfolded and pamphlets in position, I noticed that we had definitely lost our wildlife contingent. I pointed this out to Ms D, who appeared to have decided on the efficient-and-contained persona for today, as opposed to the various others which I had been introduced to in the past.

'They're still coming to grips with Maude passing away,' she said. 'I'm sure they'll manage to recover eventually, poor things.'

"Poor things"? How come they were "poor things" and I was Nero at a fire sale?

'What about that one over there?' I asked, pointing out an Easter Bunny across the road. For some reason the Easter bunny was carrying what looked like a fishing rod holder, one of those long, slim, canvas things.

'Not one of ours,' Ms D said, having taken quick look. The Easter Bunny, noticing our attention, turned quickly and pretended to be browsing in a shop window.

It isn't often you see the Easter Bunny window-shopping for ladies' hosiery.

'A journalist or something, I reckon,' I said.

'I'm sure you're right,' Ms D replied in that sort of tone which suggested that she wasn't paying any attention.

'I'm just wondering why it's wearing a boiled cabbage on its head,' I commented.

'It's not wearing a boiled cabbage on its head,' she replied without looking up from the pamphlets she was stacking, 'it's a perfectly normal Easter bunny about to go fishing, and you're trying to see if I'm really listening to what you're saying, which I am, though I have to wonder why.'

Sometimes you have to admit defeat.

'You know, it's bad enough that you go around looking gorgeous all the time, you don't have to be perfect as well,' I said, and quickly grabbed a stack of pamphlets before walking off to accost the passing citizenry.

Well, you might have to admit defeat, doesn't mean you can't have the last word.

Well, almost the last word. If that was going to be the last word I'd have to throw myself under a bus. Otherwise there were bound to be Repercussions.

The bus sounded like a good idea at that moment.

I got on with the job of trying to convince passers-by that they should go out on election day and put a tick next to the bloke promising not to raise their council tax. In such a mixed neighbourhood it wasn't easy. I've never seen such accomplished ducking and diving. For some reason the locals weren't overly eager to stay and chat, and even less eager to accept innocent little pieces of propaganda.

At one point woman turned up with little toddler in tow. The toddler looked at the band and cried, 'Mummy, they're doing Chwismass carols. You said Chwismass wasn't for aaages.'

'No, Susan, sweetie, they aren't playing Christmas carols, it's a waltz, I think.'

'Is! Is! Is Chwissmass carols! And I been a good girl. And I want lotsfpresents. I want! I want!'

The young woman put a hand over her eyes, holding tightly, as if this was something she encountered on a daily basis.

'No, darling,' she said in a strained, neutral voice, 'Christmas isn't for a while. We've still got Bonfire night before then, haven't we?'

'Do we get presents on bonfer night?' asked the toddler.

I stepped up and put a pamphlet into the young mother's unresisting hand. I think I could have passed her a pinless grenade and she wouldn't have said a word.

'I'm one of Santa's helpers,' I said, looking at the little brat, 'and Santa has asked me to make sure that little girls who claim to have been good have really been good.'

She looked at me in disbelief.

'You doan look like a elf,' she said, looking worried.

'I have a clipboard,' I pointed out. Admittedly it was Ms D's clipboard, which I had picked up by mistake, but there you go. 'And I have to write down the names of all the little children, and whether they've been good or not.'

'Your telling fibs,' the toddler said, unconvinced. 'And you don't know what my name is, so there!'

I checked the clipboard.

'It says here that your name is Susan,' I announced. She went quiet for all of three seconds.

'I bin a good girl,' she wailed.

'Yes, yes, I know,' I said comfortingly – what else do you do with an organism that makes a sound a cross between a fire engine and a mating walrus? Possibly a walrus mating with a fire engine. 'But the question is, do you promise to carry on being good? Between now and Chwistmas? Christmas. Do you promise not to ask your mummy all those questions? Do you promise to be quiet and helpful? It's one of the questions, you know,' I said, indicating the clipboard.

'Es,' she said finally. I patted her head fondly, hoping I wasn't about to lose a few fingers.

'There's a good girl then,' I said. Her mummy gave me a look which combined gratitude and despair, and took the little capitalist away.

'Nice touch,' said Ms D, appearing at my shoulder.

'It must be genetics. Or programming,' I said.

'How do you mean?'

'Well, my instinctive response is to belt the little brat. Instead I end up playing happy fathers. I think it must be some Darwinian response, learned many ages ago, to ensure survival of the species, no matter how obnoxious they might be.'

'There is always the other option. Could I have my clipboard back?'

'Sorry, yes,' I said, passing it back. 'What's the other option?'

'That you're basically a softie at heart,' she replied, taking the clipboard and moving away sharpish.

See what I mean about the last word?

I didn't have time to respond with a reasoned, logical counter-argument before another person appeared to give me a harangue, a short, sharp, incisive lecture about how they should put taxes up, to squeeze the "stinking rich".

My counter argument that it wasn't the stinking rich they were going to squeeze was met with "yeah, well you're all the bloody same".

Hardly the stuff of academic debate.

With a herculean effort I managed to pull myself up and stop a young bloke who didn't appear to be in too much of a hurry. He listened intently while I popped a pamphlet in his unresisting hand and gave him the spiel.

Amazing how quickly you forget such a simple premise: put the pamphlet in their hand, say "say no to higher taxes", and let them go elsewhere to think about it.

When I paused he spoke.

'Hey, Ja, that sounds like great fun, you know,' he said in a South African accent.

'Let me guess, you don't have a vote here, do you?' I asked.

'Ja, well, no, but I work as a builder, been here for six months, do you think I should have?'

'I think you'll have to take that up with the social security office. It's just down the road there, second after Safeways.'

'Good idea, man. I've always been into democracy.'

'Excellent. Let's just hope you've also been into things like paying taxes and being a legal resident.'

'How d'you mean?'

'Have a word with your friends in the building trade,' I suggested, waving him on.

'Hey, Ja, that's a good idea,' he said, moving away while clutching the pamphlet like some message from the The All Seeing One.

God's sakes, it was only the other day he was one of the Master Race.

They don't make them like they used to, I decided in a desperate attempt to raise my enthusiasm.

Please god, don't send me any Australians. Or Kiwis, or Yanks, and especially not any Frenchmen.

Above all, no Germans. No Italians, Danish, Austrians, Congolese or any other arbitrary nationals who might be very nice people but are not required in the current context.

Blonde female Scandinavians an optional.

'I'd give it up now, while you're behind,' said Ms D, once again appearing out of nowhere.

I took a deep breath.

'Just one,' I said through clenched teeth, 'just one person who has the slightest inkling that there might be an election imminent, and who – and this is an important point – who can actually vote in that election. I don't mind if they're true blue Tory or raving Labour, anti-hunt or green as the sky-blue sea, just someone, anyone, who has got half a brain cell vaguely active.'

She patted me on the shoulder.

'Now, now. It sounds like you need a fag break. Coffee's up. Come along.'

I followed her unwillingly. On the one hand one neuron said that it was unusual for her to suggest a cigarette when I knew she was totally anti the things, on the other I had this desperate craving to beat the merry hell out of some passer by.

And I can normally live and let live. Obviously the stress was getting to me. Talking to strangers has never been one of my strong points.

'And no bloody children,' I added, accepting the coffee she passed to me. 'Assorted domestic pets I can just about handle, but I draw the line at anything under voting age.'

'I picked up some polling figures from someone I know,' she said, ignoring my bleating. 'I'll bring them in tomorrow.'

'Not the ones they had on the news yesterday?'

The local television news had had a poll done by Mori or whoever does these things, and the figures revealed that seventy per cent of people didn't know there was an election due imminently, five per cent thought it was a national election – and complained that there were too many of them – and of the rest, only two per cent were planning to vote. I'd worked out the breakdown according to the number of people they'd interviewed, and my calculations showed that the two per cent planning to vote amounted to seven people.

Now if only they could give me the addresses of those seven people we could save a lot of time.

'A combination,' Ms D said, 'I think there have been about three different polls. But the stuff I've been given is all raw data, including notes of comments. Might tell us something.'

'Must be a good friend of yours,' I said neutrally. When you live in an enclosed group you don't like other people intruding.

'Someone who owed me a favour. From a long time ago. Did you see that in the one poll you were ahead of the Tory?'

'I'm afraid that doesn't mean much these days. I'm pretty sure Foxy is ahead of the Tory.'

'You do say the silliest things,' she said easily. Too easily.

'Foxy is ahead of the Tory, isn't he? And he's ahead of me.'

'You know how reliable these things are, why do you think they always get it wrong?'

'Bloody Foxy is ahead of me, isn't he?' I asked rhetorically. 'do we have any dirt on him?'

'I'm led to believe his mascot is afraid of rabbits,' she replied. 'Oh, come on, darling, we haven't much time left. Let's go for a final push, see how many floating voters we can get.'

Darling?

You could have slugged me with a wet mackerel.

I think someone just did.

'Um, many of those pamphlets left?' I asked, in what I hoped was a normal voice.

'No, I'm afraid it looks like we didn't print enough.'

'Used quite a few on the house-drop the other day, though.'

A "house-drop" is where we descend on a certain section of the town and stuff our literature into peoples' letterboxes. While my leg was in plaster, and for a short time afterward, I managed to avoid the duty, but over the past couple of weeks I've been joining in the fun of being attacked by little dogs, threatened by larger dogs, spat at by cats, and even been given a vicious look by a squirrel. It's made me much more respectful towards postmen.

Postpeople.

'I'm sorry,' Ms D said, ' I should have checked how much we had left – I thought it was enough.'

'I wouldn't worry. I don't think the band are up to an extended outing. I'm amazed that they've lasted this long.'

She sighed.

'I should have noticed that as well,' she said. 'I don't seem to be doing too well today.'

'Shush now,' I said gently, unaccustomed to this sudden appearance of Ms D as the less than perfect human being. 'We've all been under a strain recently. Tell you what, let's sort out the rest of this lot and call it a day.'

She was about to say something when we were interrupted by an angry looking man wearing a beard, and a green jumper.

'I don't vote,' he declared loudly.

'Oh, yes, and why is that?' I asked, after a surprised pause.

'I'm sending a message. The more people who vote, the more they think people like them.' He waved his arm wildly. 'You think you're being clever here, but the only thing that works is if people don't vote. Scares them, you see.'

We contemplated this concept.

I was tempted to point out the severe flaw in his argument, i.e. that I'd never heard a politician say "Sorry, not enough people voted so I won't take my seat". Unfortunately this bloke was a version of the drunk bore you find in pubs who tries to force an illogical and totally uninteresting opinion on you. The difference being that this one was sober.

'I see,' I said carefully. 'That's an interesting viewpoint. I tell you what, here's our pamphlet, it's got our address, I'd love it if you could write that down fully, you know, give me time to think about it when I'm not so rushed off my feet.'

He looked at the piece of paper malevolently, and finally, grudgingly, accepted it.

'You won't reply,' he complained. 'No-one ever does.'

I could see him writing angry letters to newspapers who either ignored his letters, or soon learnt to.

'That is a possibility,' I conceded. 'We don't have the money that the big parties have to reply to every letter. But I shall tell our small crew to look out for yours.'

'Might give you something to think about,' he said decisively, squashing the pamphlet into a pocket.

'I'm sure it will,' I replied evenly. "Not", I added mentally. He nodded and walked off.

'Interesting,' commented Ms D. 'He's trying to send a message by not talking to people.'

I was about to agree wholeheartedly, when I realised that this conversation could end up in a lot of hot water.

'His problem is that he doesn't realise that no-one is listening. Hey, what say we call it a day?'

'Okay,' she agreed reluctantly. 'The others are back, and they don't look too enthusiastic about going back into the trenches.'

With an almost unnoticeable flick of her head she indicated the returned pamphleteers lying with their backs against a shop wall.

They looked knackered.

'Buses,' I ordered. 'Back home, a quick pep talk, and then the rest of the day off.'

'Who's going to give the pep talk?' she asked.

'Mrs G,' I replied confidently. 'She's good at that.'

'Looks a bit tired to me.'

I looked at Mrs G. She was still trying to enthuse the band with her energy, but there wasn't a lot left. They weren't looking over-sprightly themselves.

'Oi! Mrs G!' I called, and she looked our way. 'One for the road, and then we're off,' I shouted.

She nodded, an almost grateful look in her eyes. The band seemed pleased as well.

As a final piece they played "Don't sit under the apple tree with anyone but me".

I don't know why.

While we were out, working hard to bring democracy to an eagerly awaiting public, or perhaps not, the Omley sisters were doing their bit for life, liberty and the pursuit of freedom. Apparently they walked into Johns' office while he sat working, went either side round his desk, put a hand lightly on each shoulder, and told him that, should he try signing anyone else out, they would come and find him and neuter him – their exact words, I am told.

Then they walked out.

I hear he hasn't been seen since then.

Who would have expected it from two such quiet and reserved old women?

I think it was quite sweet of them.

Saturday 5th October

British police have raided Sinn Fein's offices at the Northern Ireland Assembly in what they call an investigation into "intelligence gathering by republicans". Northern Ireland Secretary John Reid has stated that it is a police investigation, and has not been interfered with politically. Given that the Ulster police have always been seen as a Protestant force by Catholics, and the fact that a cat's miaow will be interpreted in political terms in that province, such a statement could be regarded as disingenuous at the very least. At the worst it suggests that the peace process is being deliberately undermined now that the IRA have effectively abandoned the "military struggle".

Perhaps that "effectively" should read "allegedly".

Nepal's King Gyanendra has fired the prime minister and cabinet, taking on full powers himself. The decision was made after Prime Minister Sher Bahadur Deuba failed to arrange elections due to be held in November. Deuba wanted to postpone elections due to the threats posed by Maoist rebels. He has called the King's decision undemocratic

US Attorney General John Ashcroft has celebrated the verdicts against "American Taleban" John Walker Lindh and "shoebomber" Richard Reid as "a day of justice". While Reid happily acknowledged his attempt to blow up an air-liner, Lindh was tearful in his admission that he had joined the Taleban before they became the United States' enemy number two. He is expected to receive a twenty year sentence.

The gas company executives who were negotiating with the Taleban over pipelines prior to the bombing of the Trade Centre towers are not expected to face charges.

Problems in Israel at the al-Aqsa mosque.

The UN Committee on The Rights of The Child has criticised the UK for failing to change the law which allows parents to smack their children, or what is known as "reasonable chastisement".

Drivers with the rail company First North Western, serving North and North West Wales have gone on strike for the weekend.

Although they have been offered a 19% pay increase over three years they are protesting against what they call the "strings attached" to the deal, such as drivers having to pick up litter, working on rest days and a six month notice period before leaving the company's employment.

According to the Guardian, executive pay has increased by 17%, despite the fall of the stock market, which has left many pension plans in disarray and people in desperation. Amongst the executives mentioned is Ken Berry of EMI, who was "fired" earlier this year with a £6.1 million pay cheque.

LaughLab, an experiment by scientists to find the world's funniest joke, has come up with the final result. Since the joke they have decided upon is about as predictable as someone stepping on a banana skin, the world's funniest joke has to be: LaughLab and the people who sponsored the project.

In London and the South East women are being warned to take extra care as police hunt a serial rapist suspected of nine attacks over the past year.

In Washington, United States, police are searching for a sniper who has killed five people so far. The killings appear to be random.

The Times has a teensy little article noting that the price of the Guardian has risen to 55 pence, and points out that the Telegraph and Independent have also raised their prices. It coyly mentions that, even after its own price had increased, it remains only 45 pence.

Now that I have to pay for the blasted things myself I am seriously beginning to wonder if they're worth the rain forests they're destroying.

Meanwhile, back on the farm ...

Well, well, well.

What can I say?

Well, well, well.

I suppose I should start, as the Queen said to Alice, at the beginning.

Yesterday was Maude Melly's funeral. The coroner isn't due to report for a while, but they "released the body" for the funeral.

Horrible phrase.

If your life can be measured against the number of mourners at your funeral, then Maude was truly loved.

But let me start at the beginning.

After a shower and breakfast I dressed in my newly dry-cleaned suit. The black suit. I'm rather fond of it, as it's the only suit I've ever had which feels comfortable and makes me look smart. Unfortunately there aren't many occasions when you can wear it. Funerals being one. Wearing a purple shirt with it is acceptable if you're going clubbing, but that's about it.

And if only I had ever learnt to play the saxophone I might have turned up at Maude's funeral wearing a black suit, purple shirt, and playing the sax. But that was left to someone else.

As I walked out of my room I could hear someone softly singing to the accompaniment of a tape.

When I find myself in times of trouble,

Mother Mary comes to me

Speaking words of wisdom, let it be

It was strange – almost unheard of – to hear singing, especially on key. It seemed like the only noise in the building, as if everyone else had stopped moving and breathing to listen. As I walked soundlessly down the empty corridor the singer continued.

Let it be, let it be, let it be, let it be

I got to the end of the corridor and paused at the stairs to listen to the rest. Outside the weather was overcast and gloomy, and the song had a strange quality, both deeply depressing and also comforting. It was like a song for the end of the world.

There will be an answer, let it be

I shook myself and carried on down the stairs. I don't know who the singer was, but they managed to invest a terribly haunting quality into the words. Words which followed me on down.

Shine until tomorrow, let it be

The singer was getting to the final lines as I reached the ground floor, and the last "let it be" was drawn out almost softly, as if the singer knew it was all a lie, but desperately wanted to believe that lie.

Fiona was in reception when I got there.

'You look as if you've seen a ghost,' she said mildly.

'I've just been listening to someone singing a song for the dead. Felt like someone walking over my grave.'

'Ah, that'll be Kerry,' she said.

'Very funny,' I replied.

Ms D shrugged. 'Believe what you want. I happen to know that Kerry exists.'

I decided to ignore the issue.

'You're looking ravishing as always,' I commented. And she was. Black outfit – one of those body-hugging things where the hem was below the knee, but you just knew that when she sat down some lovely legs would be revealed – and a black jacket which gave that element of decorum required for the occasion, with plain gold necklace to brighten things up a little.

'You're not doing too badly yourself,' she said, picking some invisible speck of fluff off my collar.

Why do women always do that?

'Buses arranged?' I asked, in that off hand way you exchange idle conversation in order to avoid the real reason you're there.

The church and cemetery were far away enough to require transport.

'Should be here in a few minutes. I'm going in my car. I can give you a lift if you want.'

'Wouldn't it be easier to go in one of the buses?'

'Well, I was thinking of going straight home afterwards.'

'Not coming down the pub?'

The post-funeral event was to be sandwiches and sherry in the Rose. Pete had agreed to organise a separate area for us, even though it could hardly have been a good advertisement for business. Still, it would only be for lunchtime on a Friday, hardly his busiest time.

'I don't know,' Fiona said uncertainly. 'I'll see how I feel.'

'Okay. I'll come with you then, just in case you get lost.' She made an "Hmmph" sound.

The others were beginning to appear in reception, one by one. Colin, wearing a nervous look and a black suit which showed that he'd put on weight since he last wore it. Mrs G, stern in a black dress and hat. Jimmie, wearing a grey jacket, black trousers and black tie.

He looked like someone the Godfather had sent around to have a word.

We stood around in uncomfortable silence.

'Nice weather,' I said, for want of anything else. Since it was one of those dreary grey days which this country can do so well, I added quickly, 'well, at least it isn't raining.'

The total lack of response to this was interrupted by two travel coaches turning up, to my relief. We went outside and watched the slow procession of people coming out and getting onto the buses. Normally you'd be keeping a continual eye open for someone absent-mindedly going for a stroll instead, or doing something equally daft, but this time there seemed no need. Matron eventually appeared, having chivvied all those who were coming, and we set off.

'Dr Johns,' Fiona said, as we followed the buses. 'You know he's trying to sign people out.'

I thought of the Omley sisters, and wondered whether he was contemplating his position.

'I had a call from the council yesterday,' she continued. 'Some minor question about Ridmore House. That's when I found out the company have applied for permission to move everyone into Ridmore.'

'Sounds a bit silly. Where's Ridmore House?'

'About half a mile before you get to the shopping centre. That eight story building on the left. The one that stands out like a sore thumb.'

'You are joking!' I exclaimed. Ridmore House is an eyesore from the sixties. Weather-stained grey concrete, the sort of place they couldn't use as a prison because it would be deemed cruel and inhumane living conditions.

'I'm afraid not. I didn't believe it at first myself.'

'It's ridiculous! How can they put people in there? They'd go stark staring bonkers within a week. Apart from the fact that it's won awards for bad design and grotesqueness, there aren't any gardens. Just the concrete pavement outside. Surrounded by the sort of neighbours who aren't going to be exactly beneficial to mental well-being.'

'I don't think the patients are their first concern.'

'How do you mean?'

'Our current place is worth millions. Especially if they build houses on it. With the property market the way it is, they'd make a fortune.'

I sat and fumed for a bit. 'We can't let it happen. We'll have to do something,' I said, without having the first clue what that something could be.

'That's what I thought. Then I started to wonder about why Johns was so eager to get people out. I think it's to reduce numbers – Ridmore House doesn't have enough space. And then I realised that if you or anyone starts protesting you're likely to find yourself suddenly well enough for the outside world.'

I sat and thought about this as we pulled up outside the church. Things definitely did not sound so good.

She put a hand on my arm as I undid the seat belt.

'Don't tell anyone else yet, will you? Just in case. We don't want everyone upset if it turns out the council aren't going to give permission. Let's just get through today first.'

I nodded agreement. For today, at least, the problem could wait.

The others were already seated when we entered the church. All the back pews were full, so we had to sit up front with Mrs G and the major. I think we would have sat up front anyway – my personal preference, if I absolutely have to enter a church, is to sit in the very back pew, but I doubt that Fiona would have let me.

In fact it was a very good service, as far as these things can be. There were a number of people there I didn't recognise, and I presumed they were either the church choir or some of these strange people who go to funerals even when they never knew the person.

To my surprise they turned out to be some of Miss Melly's old pupils. Ten years or more after they had last seen her they still remembered her with fondness, enough to make time to come to her funeral. Apparently the news had spread through a website dedicated to re-uniting old school friends.

And the vicar giving the service knew – had known – Miss Melly. She had quietly attended services here almost every Sunday without anyone knowing.

Or at least, I didn't know. She wasn't one to shout about her beliefs.

Mrs G read from the book of something according to someone – I can never remember who wrote what, but I think it was something to do with walking through the valley of somewhere. Then the vicar gave his sermon, making Miss Melly sound like an angel amongst humans, which is what she was.

And then we moved out to the cemetery to watch the mortal remains of Maude Melly being lowered into the ground, as the vicar intoned "ashes to ashes, dust to dust".

It was a bit of a shock when the coffin had been wheeled into the church – as sort of bringing home of the fact that Miss Melly was indeed dead, inside that coffin. Watching the coffin descend into the earth was like saying a final goodbye.

Very final.

Very definite.

Almost all the women had quiet tears running down their faces. Even Mrs G had a handkerchief over her mouth, tear stains denying the set look on her face. I caught sight of Tonique behind a few others, her face pressed firmly into a man's shoulder, her own shoulders heaving quietly. As the others in front shifted slightly I saw who the man was – Jimmie, with his arms wrapped firmly and comfortingly around her.

Well, who would have thought it? I asked myself.

After the vicar had finished John Angerly stepped up to play the Last Post on his saxophone. I doubt you'll hear anything like it in any military institute, but it sounded amazingly apt for this occasion.

Then we went through the ritual of dropping clods of earth into the grave, before moving off. Somehow I've always felt the earth dropping bit to be a little disrespectful, but each to their own.

As Fiona and I moved off I caught a sight of someone in the trees.

'It's that bloody journalist again!' I exclaimed.

'Which journalist?' asked Fiona, trying to see what I was pointing at. The sod had hidden himself as soon as he realised that he was spotted.

'The one dressed up as the Easter Bunny. If I catch him I'll throttle the bastard. You'd think he'd at least have sufficient respect not to turn up at a funeral. Especially not dressed up in that silly costume.

'Forget him,' said Fiona, taking my arm. 'He's not worth the bother. Come on, I think I will pop in for a quick drink.'

I followed her grudgingly, looking back every so often, but bunny the journalist had disappeared.

On the other hand it wouldn't do my image any harm to be pictured looking smart and handsome – well, smart, anyway – at a serious event like a funeral. It would give me a certain amount of gravitas.

I hope he got a good shot.

Back at the Rose Pete had done us proud. Lots of little sandwiches and sausage rolls and spicy Indian things. The sort of thing you pick up because you need to eat something but don't feel hungry, and then realise you've had half a dozen already. Everybody seemed remarkably cheerful, considering the circumstances.

Possibly it was the feeling that it was over, that things could now move on.

Alternatively it could have been the sherry that Pete had stocked up on my advice. Most of those there rarely drank; one sherry would have them nicely mellowed. Just so long as they didn't have more than three. Legless wouldn't even describe it.

There would be Dancing In The Streets, without John Travolta.

The money for the nibbles and drinks came from Legrade-Smith's contribution. I'm sure he would have appreciated it.

I sat with Fiona, Mrs G, the major and Colin. We exchanged the usual chat about how lovely the funeral had been — funny how you can describe it as that. Fiona and Mrs G sat next to each other, agreeing that the organisation and the flowers were marvellous, and I tried to convince Colin and the major that Arsenal would definitely win the double this year. Colin has only a minor interest — such as whether a referee's decision was correct, or the morality of the high prices of supporters' shirts made by child labour in the Far East — but the major unexpectedly turned out to be a Chelsea fan. So I ribbed him about being unpatriotic by supporting a foreign team. Which, considering that Arsenal have their fair share of foreign players, was like giving him a gift.

I'd only intended to have the one pint, but Fiona seemed happy enough to have two glasses of wine, so I went the extra pint. When she announced that it was time to go, I decided that it was time for me to leave as well. There comes a point at which you think to yourself, ah, what the hell, I'll just have another, and then the next thing you know it's five o'clock in the afternoon, you're almost legless and having fascinating conversations with sober people who are doing their best to avoid you.

'I'll give you a lift back,' she said as we walked out.

It's a car-driving thing. It's only a ten minute walk from the pub — depending on your intake — but car drivers tend to offer you a lift even if you're ten yards away from your destination. I got in a little reluctantly, having looked forward to the walk to clear my head a little.

'Damn!' she said as we drove away, 'I've forgotten those figures again.'

'Figures?'

'The ones from the polls they did. I was going to bring them in, remember?'

'Oh, I wouldn't worry too much,' I said, not really being interested.

'I tell you what, I'll make a quick detour to the flat. Won't take long.'

'Okay,' I agreed. I would have preferred not to, but decided that I might as well, if she felt it was that important. She seemed to think so, rabbiting on about the things as we drove.

'Come on in,' she said when we got there.

Well, I suppose it would be a little impolite to leave someone outside while you rushed in to search for some pieces of paper. I followed her in to the flat, which was a neat little half of a terraced house. Very tidy, but comfortable. Strange to see how someone actually lives when you feel you know them so well already.

'Make yourself at home,' she said, indicating a maroon couch, while taking her jacket off.

The dress she was wearing was sleeveless. Very nice, too.

'Would you like a drink? I think I've got some beers in the fridge – real ale, so they tell me, bottles, not cans. Or there's a rather nice bottle of Riesling, should be nicely chilled.'

'A glass of Riesling sounds good,' I said, surprised. I presumed it was automatic for her to make people comfortable. I tried to remember what the drink-drive limit was for wine. I didn't want her to go over it, and I didn't fancy a ten mile walk home.

She put some music on – "The first time ever I saw your eyes", or something – and went into the kitchen while I wandered around the lounge pretending to take an interest in the various objects and paintings which always constitute the make up of someone's home.

Women are always fascinated by this sort of thing – personally I find that it's invariably boring. In the same way that holiday photographs only mean something to those involved, a jug from Amsterdam looks just like a jug from anywhere if you weren't the person who bought it.

I have to admit that Fiona's taste went against that rule. The paintings were the sort which sat on the borderline between art and someone taking the mick – and I was willing to bet that she hadn't paid the ludicrous prices artists can demand. I was admiring one with strange swirly lines which seemed to almost move, when I heard a muttered oath from the kitchen. I went in, to find Fiona struggling with a bottle of wine and an old fashioned corkscrew.

'Cork's stuck tight,' she said, a lock of red hair having escaped its normal position, hanging over her eye.

'Let me try,' I offered, taking the bottle of wine from her.

Masterfully I drew the cork.

Okay, I had to put the bottle between my knees and give it a good yank.

'There you go,' I said, passing the bottle back and putting the cork-laden corkscrew on the kitchen counter. As she took the bottle our fingers touched, and it was almost as if an electric shock passed between us.

That has never happened to me before.

We looked into each other's eyes for a few moments, her lips slightly apart from the strange tingling sensation. Both now holding the bottle of wine.

It seemed the most natural thing to do to lean forward and kiss her. On those beautiful lips, gleaming with lipstick, soft and inviting.

She was a bit hesitant at first, but a bloke has to take control in situations like this. I drew her in and we kissed. Softly, gently, at first, and then her hand pressed down on my neck and things became passionate.

At some stage we must have put the bottle of wine down. Instinctively I must have known where the bedroom was, because we suddenly found ourselves there.

Without going into unnecessary detail, I think we are definitely now what some people would call "an item".

Afterwards I fell asleep, Fiona's head tucked into my shoulder, her body wrapped around mine. The poets try, but they can never describe such a wonderful feeling. If I tried it would sound soppy. I'd have to use the word "love" in there somewhere, and somehow it isn't powerful enough to describe the feeling.

All this time it had been there, neither of us realising it.

I awoke to find her looking down at me. She traced a finger down the side of my face. Her eyes and face were soft and, I have to say, beautiful; the contrast with Ms Dervish The Efficient was impossible to describe.

'Happy?' she asked.

I looked up at the ceiling, trying to find the right words. Eventually I looked into her eyes.

'Paradise,' I said. 'Heaven. Something like that. But better.' She smiled.

'You're full of it, aren't you,' she said, and kissed me.

We didn't get much sleep last night, for some reason.

She drove me back this morning, dropping me off at the gates. As she pointed out, I could get into trouble if I started sleeping out, and she would be fired without doubt. Sleeping with patients is a sackable offence.

Not that I felt like a patient anymore. I had an almost uncontrollable urge to beat my chest and make gorilla noises.

We had a good kiss before I got out of the car. She was a little concerned, but I pointed out that it was Saturday, few staff were around, and no-one could see us from the building. At least that's what I pointed out after the first kiss. Then we indulged in another one.

Eventually I had to acknowledge that I should probably get out and let her get on. I was rather looking forward to a reunion this evening, but she pointed out that my being out two nights on the trot wouldn't look too good, and besides, she needed a good night's sleep. She put the emphasis on the word "sleep".

Personally I was ready to say nuts to the lot of them, but at the moment, as Fiona pointed out, things are at a stage where it would be silly to compromise everything. She promised to take me for a drive tomorrow. In a way I can't wait. There are lots of places around here I haven't seen, and being able to see them with Fi at my side – well, sounds like heaven to me.

I whistled as I walked up the driveway. I couldn't help it. I felt like I had given up all hope of meeting that magical other, and here she was, next to me all the time.

Mrs G was in reception when I walked in. She looked at me critically.

'You look like the cat that's got the cream,' she said critically.

'Sorry, Mrs G, it's a terminal case,' I said, taking her in my arms. 'I think it's called love.'

She slapped my arms away. 'About bloody time, too,' she said, and marched away. Over her shoulder she said, 'And have some respect for those of us with hangovers, if you don't mind.'

I was surprised. I wondered whether she and the major had, shall we say, enjoyed themselves too much.

I smiled as I watched her going, secure in the knowledge that she didn't have a clue. For me the world is as rosy as a rosy thing can be.

Even a dentist would hold no fears for me.

Okay, maybe a dentist. But nothing else.

As I write this, Kerry is singing again.

Let it be, let it be, let it be, let it be

Whisper words of wisdom, let it be

If only Maude could have been here. I'm sure she would have approved.

Sunday 6th October

Only managed to grab a quick look at the headlines today. Weekends are always slow-news periods, so the newspapers bring out huge chunks of newsprint and then decide what to put in them.

The Washington sniper has claimed another victim.

In the Ivory Coast foreign mediators are threatening to leave due to the government's intransigence in signing a deal with the rebels.

The last Rwandan troops have left the Democratic Republic of Congo, after what someone – presumably a weekend journalist with time on his hands – has described as "Africa's first world war".

President Hugo Chavez of Venezuela claims that a plot to oust him in a coup has been foiled.

Bush has stated that war with Iraq might be "inevitable".

The Turks are concerned that Iraqi Kurds might want to set up an independent state after the inevitable war between the US and Iraq. It could encourage Turkish Kurds to demand their own.

The mayor of Paris, Bertrand Delanoe, is recovering after being stabbed while conducting a walkabout during "Sleepless Night" celebrations. He had arranged the festivities as part of a campaign to rejuvenate arts and culture. Entrance to such attractions as the Eiffel Tower and the Louvre were free, and they were open all night. Other attractions included bands and concerts. Fortunately M. Delanoe was not seriously wounded.

Had a chuckle this morning reading Carney's latest piece in the Echo. Apparently I have now "shown my true colours", am as loony as the looniest loon around, and comprise the biggest danger to democracy since Genghis Khan. These sudden revelations being due to the radio interview I had with Mary-Anne. Apparently I have called for the death penalty for motorists who go over the speed limit. Apart from being quoted out of context, I never said that.

If you can be quoted out of context with something you never said.

Something tells me that someone has been having words with

Carney. Just goes to show that you can never believe a word you read in the papers.

While I was admiring Carney's deft footwork – feet of clay, but he doesn't half move fast – I had a visit from Archie, of all people. He claimed that he had just come in to pick up some papers when he bumped into me. That was obviously a lie, and his light blue eyes showed that he knew it was a lie, and that he wanted me to know that he knew it was a lie.

If that isn't too convoluted.

His message was quite simple: Dr Johns had believed that running for the mayor's office was good therapy, but reporting on any council meetings suggested that I was well enough to be kicked out. It was a straight threat: drop the council watchdog business, or go walkies. Dr Johns didn't even enter into it.

He even claimed to be "concerned". No doubt true, but it wasn't my well-being he was concerned with. Quite obviously he and his associates are against the idea of a mayor because it would highlight what the local council is doing.

Now the move of people from this place to Ridmore House is hardly likely to get the local citizenry excited, so I wonder what else is going on that they aren't too keen to have in the public eye.

'Funny game, politics,' I said. 'Seems to me everybody is doing trade-offs of one sort or another. Principles have to be sacrificed for pragmatism on the odd occasion.'

'I knew you would understand,' he said, looking at me with those ice blue eyes, and then left without saying goodbye.

The thing about people like Archie is that they're so used to having their own way they hear what they want to hear. After all, I hadn't said I was dropping the idea. In fact, it sounds better each time I think of it. All I have to do is keep people like Archie thinking what they want to, then once I'm in, if I do get in, they can do what they like. One of the first things I'll do is find out the cost of Archie's mansion – I'm sure he has a mansion – and double the council tax on that band. Tough luck on the others.

I was basking in that delicious thought when Fi turned up, looking gorgeous, as ever, blue blouse, blue skirt, and one of those long almost-winter coats which always look good on other people. I'd made an effort to look smart myself – even borrowed some polish off the major – but I'll always be a short leather jacket person.

'You have a smirk on your face,' she accused.

'Indeed I do. I'll tell you about it when we're away from this place.'

I was dying to take her in my arms and kiss her, but people might have started talking. So we had to wait until we reached a lay-by to exchange greetings properly. I was glad to discover that the passion of Friday hadn't been a result of too many glasses of wine, a doubt that had floated into view every hour or so since we had last said goodbye.

Once back on the road Fi asked, 'so, why the smirk?'

'Sir Archibald is threatening me with eviction unless I drop the idea of monitoring what the council is up to.'

'And you said?'

'Doffed the cap, tugged the forelock, said "yes, sir, no sir", and he went off happy – well, as far as he could ever be happy.'

'Did you mean it?'

'Course not. He and his buddies are in for a big surprise if I get in. I'll make sure that whatever underhand business they're trying to pull off becomes the talk of the town. And beyond.'

'Has anyone ever called you devious?'

'What, me?' I asked in an injured voice. 'I'm not devious. What you see is what you get. Just sometimes you have to handle certain types of people in a certain way, that's all.'

'Sorry, darling, I didn't mean that,' she said, patting my hand, and almost giving me a heart attack.

We were overtaking an articulated truck at the time. If I have to be in a car I prefer the driver to have both hands on the wheel.

'You should read what Carney reckons of me now,' I said, breathing deeply.

'I have. Slimy little piece of work, isn't he?'

'Ah, you can't blame him too much. He's being paid for it. But when I become mayor – if I become mayor – I shall have to seriously consider his license to publish. Pity I won't be able to have him hung drawn and quartered in the public square, but I'll do my best.'

'You think you've got a chance?' she asked.

Oh, woman, ye of little faith.

'Probably not much. Until you look at the opposition. Okay, I wouldn't say I have a very good chance, but it's there, you never know. What is this place?'

We were driving into a long driveway leading to what appeared to be some sort of hotel.

'It's the Hotel Suisse,' she said. 'They do a very good Sunday dinner.'

Now I have the greatest respect for the Swiss, but providing an English Sunday dinner doesn't sound like something a hotel called The Hotel Suisse would know much about. Modern Ironic Dabs Of Sauce With A Lettuce Leaf And a Smidgeon Of Avocado Artistically Arranged In A Random And Humorous Form Just enough To Starve By, yes, good solid roast beef and potatoes, I doubted.

We parked and wandered in. Or at least I did, Fiona doesn't wander anywhere, she Enters. I am sure it will be one of the quirks of our relationship. She will forever nag me about slouching, and I will say "Yes, darling", and continue to slouch.

This is the way the human race is designed.

Inside we were met by an obsequious waiter. He was probably the maître d', but I like calling people like that waiters, it doesn't half get their goat.

'Ms Dervish, how wonderful to see you again,' he gushed. 'Your table is ready and waiting. May I take Mamselles' coat.'

'Thank you, Ernesto,' Mamselle Dervish said, graciously handing over her coat.

'And M'sieur, could I take your coat?'

'No, it's the only one I've got, and I want to keep it,' I replied.

He looked blank for a short while, and then recovered.

'Ah, the English sense of humour. Allow me to take you to your table.'

Once we were comfortably seated he handed us menus, and Mamselle the wine list, and floated off to fawn on someone else. I browsed through a list of French dishes. Fortunately they had English translations, and sounded, to my surprise, pretty solid.

'Do you have to be nasty to people like poor Ernesto?' Fi asked mildly. 'He's only doing his job.'

Poor Ernesto?

'Sorry, darling. Just can't stand people like that. "Yes, Sir, no Sir, may I kiss your boots, Sir?"'

'I think you feel intimidated by them.'

Ha. As if.

'Red or white? Their house wine is normally pretty good.'

'I don't suppose they do pints, do they?'

'Stop stirring. Red or white?'

'White.'

She put the wine list down. 'Good. Anything in the menu take your fancy?'

'Am I allowed to have the roast beef, Yorkshire pud and roast potatoes, or is that too downmarket?'

'Don't be silly. That's what I'm having. My special treat every so often.'

Ernesto reappeared in a wave of napkin waving, making sure the spotless tablecloth hadn't suddenly developed a bad case of untidiness.

'Mamselle, M'sieur, you are ready to order?'

'A bottle of house white, and I'll have my usual, Ernesto,' Fi said, handing menus over.

'I'll have her usual as well,' I said. He had to think about that for a couple of seconds, before saying, 'Ah, good, excellent,' and flourishing away.

I have to admit, for all the pretentiousness, they do a really good

Sunday roast. I even got a slightly larger portion than Fi, which she claimed was sexist. I agreed, but didn't offer to share. So she nicked some of my spuds while I wasn't looking.

I offloaded most of my peas on to her plate while she wasn't looking. Can't stand the things.

She pointed out the wall hangings designed by some famous artist or other, and when I looked back I seemed to have more peas than ever.

You have to be in love to understand.

'You know that article that Carney wrote?' she said at one point, 'about hanging and flogging people?'

'Lying sod said that I said that about traffic offences. I never said that at all.'

'I know. If he did report what you said you would have got more supporters. We had quite a few letters after that radio interview agreeing with what you said.'

Fi and Mrs G and a couple of others handle the letters. I was banned from touching them after they read one of my replies.

Apparently most of the writers don't have a sense of humour.

'Weird,' I said. 'I was only saying those things to demonstrate how little power the mayor will have. You mean people actually took it seriously?'

'There are a lot of strange people out there.' She paused and looked at me. 'darling, I don't want to worry you, but one or two of them – well, they were threats. Not very nice threats.'

I considered the concept.

'Can't say I've ever heard of a nice threat,' I said.

'You know what I mean. I don't think it's serious, the person who wrote them can't spell very well. And he finished them with "Allah is Great". Only he spelt it g-r-a-t-e.'

'Poor chap. Sounds like he needs some help. I wouldn't worry, Fi, I spoke to Sergeant whats-his-name the other day, and I'm well down in the threats league. Can't say I was too pleased. I mean, it's a bit much when the Tory candidate gets more threats than you.'

'I think you should take more care. Jimmie has offered to organise some bodyguards. He says he knows some people who would be pretty good.'

'Jimmie? I suppose he would. Only trouble is people would wonder if the Scots were invading again. Forget about it Fi. Tell me if there were any offers of money from rich old women. Or any offers from rich young women, come to that.'

'Now do you think I would tell you that if there were?' she asked with a twinkle in her eye.

'I'm an honest man,' I said, adopting a tone of an honest man feeling aggrieved. 'I would only touch them for a small contribution to our worthy effort.'

'Well you can just keep your touch and worthy effort where I can see them.'

She was smiling. Made a difference. All my previous relationships have ended with – totally unfounded – accusations of, how shall I put it, playing away.

Disgraceful.

We finished with dessert – a small slice of sticky toffee pudding with clotted cream, after which you're glad it was only a small slice, you'd never get up from the table otherwise, delicious stuff – and drove back to Fi's flat for a siesta.

The countryside can wait.

I woke up to find her looking down on me again – why do women do that?

'Have you ever thought of the future?' she asked, doing that nail-tracing thing over my face again.

Not that I'm complaining, mind.

'How do you mean?' I asked. To me the present was as perfect as life gets. Why would you want to spoil things by worrying about the future?

'Nothing,' she said, 'just wondering.' She lay back down next to me, a sure sign that I had missed something.

Cuddle in the shoulder = good. Lying next to you = bad.

I propped myself up.

'Well, darling, I might well be the next mayor, you know. Surely that counts as something?'

She looked up at me. There was a look of concern in her eyes.

'Darling,' she said. Then nothing. Then she closed her eyes and sighed. 'Nothing, darling. Kiss me, please.'

Bloody women, eh.

Still, couldn't refuse a plea like that, could I?

Later on she gave me a lift back here, dropping me off just before the gates. We had the best kiss the world has ever known. So we had it again. Then she pushed me away, and I sat trying to work out what that meant.

'I've got a bad feeling about tomorrow,' she said.

Tomorrow's our final appearance in public before the people go to vote. It's going to be a good one. Music and as many rabbits as you can shake a stick at. Everything planned down to the last minute. Sweeties for the kiddies. Optimism for the grown-ups. We're going to make them love us.

We've even got a lovely large rainbow flag to wave around.

'Shush, my sweet,' I said, stroking her cheek next to her gorgeous red hair. 'My intuition says that it's going to be a marvellous day. Best ever. We're going to sock it to them. They'll tell their grandchildren about it. Okay?'

'Okay,' she agreed, smiling demurely, and cuddled up for a final kiss.

If you'd told me that I would ever have described Ms Dervish The Infallible as demure, I'd have suggested immediate and severe therapy. Now I found she could play Beethoven's Fifth on my heart strings.

Don't try this at home, boys and girls.

So here I sit finishing off this great instalment for today.

Tomorrow we give it a last blast, and the day after we have the elections. Despite everything Carney might write and Archie-baby might threaten I remain optimistic. Whatever happens now, it doesn't

really matter. I have this strange feeling of happiness.
They can do what the hell they like now.

Chapter 10: After Kerry

Bill Dughaille

Monday 7th October

Editor's Note: general interviews
Colin:

"He was in a really good mood for some reason. I think he was glad that it was almost over. He never was very good surrounded by people. But he was good at doing things as they came into his head. He suddenly decided to lead the band down the street. It was about eleven o'clock I think. The spectators were all clapping, maybe that got him going. He always was impulsive."

Mrs Gladstone:

"Silly idiot. Taking the band marching down the street like that. But I can't say much, I suppose, because I was right behind him. He had dragged Fiona off by the hand like some love-lorn swain, and the band followed and I was in-between them, so I didn't have much choice. It seemed like a good idea. We were all laughing, having fun. I didn't even hear the sound of the shot above the noise of the band. I didn't realise anything was wrong at first. Thought he was lying on the ground being silly."

The major:

"Well, naturally I recognised the sound of a rifle being fired. Saw it as well. Chap dressed up as the Easter Bunny. Chased after him. Caught the little sod as well. If I'd known then what he had actually done he wouldn't have lived to see a fair trial."

Fiona:

"I just remember Fred laughing. He hardly ever laughed. Smiled a lot, but hardly ever laughed. Funny thing, that.

"We were leading the band, or he was, pulling me along, but I didn't object. He said something to me. I couldn't hear him above the noise of the band, so he mouthed it again. "I love you" he said. I love you. That's what he said, I love you.

"And then then he was in my arms, and I didn't know why he had this red stuff running down his head and his eyes looked puzzled and I couldn't hold him up and I didn't know what was happening and where the blood was coming from and there was the noise of the band and the people on the pavements and suddenly I was screaming for him not to leave me and the band stopped playing and the people on the pavements fell silent and his eyes were closed."

Jimmie:

"Feck."

From the Local Echo, 15th October
Muslims Fear Reprisals

Local Muslim leaders fear a backlash after revelations following the shooting of one of the mayoral candidates last week. The man the police believe to be responsible and currently in custody is known as Mohamed Mohamed, a Muslim convert. Originally known as Johnnie Greengage – or "Johnny The Fruit" by some of his friends – he had converted to Islam during one of many stints in jail for small time crime. It is reported that he was well known to have a tendency to develop fanatical devotion to various "good" causes, such as environmentalism, save the whales, anti-capitalism, and latterly Islam.

Police believe that his failure as a criminal revealed an inability to think his actions through, or as source put it, 'he wasn't what could be called the sharpest tool in the box.' Despite converting to Islam he continued to pursue a life of crime, maintaining each time that he was arrested that the police were being anti-Muslim.

Having come out of jail for the third time in short succession, he announced to friends that he was going straight. What he actually meant is open to discussion, since he immediately began to run an extortion racket against one of the local supermarkets, threatening to put broken glass into bottles of baby-food on their shelves if they didn't pay a ransom in the millions. It is understood he conceived of the idea while watching trial footage of a gang who had been convicted of a similar offence.

Unfortunately for him, Mohamed, religiously following his principles of saving the environment by recycling, had typexed out his name and address on an envelope, and used that for the extortion demand. The police arrested him the following day.

It appears that it was about that time that he started to believe that the police and security services were anonymously monitoring all his movements.

Another short stretch in jail ensured; the judge admitted that in other circumstances Mohamed would have been locked away for years, but he had taken into consideration the chief constable's feelings, which were that Mohamed was more likely to be a danger to himself than the general public, a statement which turned out to be false, but which seemed humorously accurate at the time.

During this latest stretch inside Mohamed discovered that it wasn't a good time to be a Muslim. It appears that, in his mind he decided that the chief objection of his tormentors was that Islam rejected democracy. Since he knew that democracy was a good thing – in the same way he knew that recycling was good, not through some logical reasoning, but rather just because he knew – and Islam was a good thing, obviously Islam believed in democracy, a point he made strenuously and repeatedly to the others in jail with him. They do not appear to have agreed, but Mohamed left jail with the notion that defence of democracy was a jihad, in which he intended to participate as an unquestioning foot-soldier.

This, according to police sources, is why he targeted the mayoral candidate; Mohamed concluded that the candidate's approach was anti-democratic. He acquired a .22 rifle from an unknown source, and began stalking the candidate while disguised as a rabbit. Why he dressed this way is not clear, but may well have some religious significance. It did impede a quick getaway and he was captured and held down by passers-by until the police arrived.

Superintendent Bixley of the local CID has assured the Muslim community that they will receive whatever protection is needed. He emphasized that the crime was not a religious one, and anyone targeting Muslims would be charged under the relevant legislation.

Editor's Note (2):

At the start of May, 2002, H'Angus the Monkey, mascot of Hartlepool's football team, was elected as mayor. Otherwise known as Stuart Drummond, he was elected on the promise of "free bananas for schoolchildren".

He subsequently gave up his job as monkey mascot.

Ray Mallon, independent, was elected as mayor of Middlesborough.

Formerly a police superintendent, his nickname was "robocop".

On October 16th mayoral elections were held in Stoke, Hackney, Mansfield and Bedford.

Mike Wolfe, an independent, former manager of the Citizen's Advice Bureau and gay rights campaigner won in Stoke. Steven Batkin from the British National Party came third, ahead of the Conservatives.

Tony Egginton, independent, newsagent, won in Mansfield.

Jules Pipe, Labour council leader, won Hackney.

Frank Branston, independent, newspaper owner, won Bedford.

Turnout was low in all elections, ranging from 18.5% in Mansfield to 25.3% in Bedford.

In June the BBC reported that Nick Raynsford, Local Government Minister, had reversed the policy of forcing local councils to hold referendums on whether or not to have a mayor.

Editor's Note (3):

Interview with Ms Fiona Dervish on Saturday 20th October:

All the men I've gone out with have been total shits. Either they were married and promised to leave their wives – which of course they never did, though at the time they were pretty convincing – or single and dedicated to their careers. I was just a useful bauble to have at dinner or whenever they wanted to impress their bosses. Until they found a better bauble, that is; they treated me like a car which could be traded in at any time for a newer model.

Thinking about it, they had more respect for their cars.

Then I finally found someone I thought I could be happy with. He didn't have much of a future, but with the others they had their wives or careers and I was the one without a future. With Fred there was also the slight problem of being on different sides of the fence, as it were, but that wasn't going to stop me. You're lucky if you get one shot at happiness in this life.

And, believe me, it was hard work. I dropped so many hints he was knee deep in them. Did he notice? The hell he did. There were times I could have cheerfully have strangled him. I did everything but fall into his arms, and he just stood there with that silly grin on his face.

Never mind having to put up with all his depression and sulks every so often.

Why do men do that?

So I finally had to resort to that excuse for going to my flat. Even bought that little electric shock thing to get things going. It worked a treat, though I was more shocked afterwards to find I hadn't put the little battery in.

Maybe it's only a backup.

So after all that hard work I finally have him, and like all men, having just discovered what's been staring him in the face for months, he suddenly wants everything to be perfect at once. Like you think of putting up a shelf and the next thing they're planning on rebuilding the room.

I'm not complaining, but he does have this habit of ignoring the minor things in life, like earning a living.

And then, just when it seems like things couldn't be better, what does he do? Goes and gets himself shot, the bastard. Would he listen to me? No, of course not, why should he bother about other people who are worried about his safety? Why should he worry that there might be others left behind crying their eyes out?

Just as soon as that son of a bitch is well enough again I'm going to kill him.

Other novels by Bill Dughaille:

The FFSG series (aka the Wellbury Chronics)

Summers

The first in the FFSG series.

Detective Sergeant Frank Summers is a man on a mission: to keep his head down, stay out of trouble and enjoy the relaxed atmosphere of the easy-going, genteel town of Wellbury, his new posting. It's a town just made for him, where, he believes, even the criminals take bank holidays off. But, while perceptive in his professional life, he tends to miss the subtleties in his private life. In this case he fails to realise that his own tranquillity is being threatened by three women and a philanderer. The fact that the women in question are his boss, his constable and the local pathologist adds just the touch of danger to his life that he had hoped to avoid. The philanderer has been dead several decades. The women are very much alive. And ticking.

The Eighty-five-percenters

The second in the FFSG series.

Detective Sergeant Frank Summers is faced with an unexpected crisis as the staid citizens of the genteel town of Wellbury rapidly descend into disorganised anarchy after a sociology professor announces on radio that eighty-five percent of the population will die in a coming cull. The prediction appears to be coming true as apparently total strangers are felled one by one according to a list of the ten-most-disliked Wellburians, from nagging neighbours to estate agents ... and the police, at a poorly performing number ten. But Frank fails to realise that there is a graver danger closer to home. Three women have decided that he is their responsibility: his boss, his constable and the local pathologist have agreed to become best of enemies. Now they intend to re-arrange his fate the way it should be. And they aren't asking anyone's permission.

Fakes, Fraud and Deception

The third in the FFSG series.

Detective Sergeant Frank Summers is in the doghouse, despite having recently arrested an internationally sought con-artist. And since he is in the doghouse he has no intention of pointing out that there is something very strange about the attractive French police woman who has come to interview the arrested man, not to mention the two detectives claiming to be from Scotland Yard. Oh, no, he is going to stay well out of the way this time. Definitely.

Jokers

The fourth in the FFSG series.

The doctors have pronounced Detective Sergeant Frank Summers physically fit following recovery after his shooting, but his colleagues fear that his sense of humour was extracted along with the bullet. They are, as always, more than willing to interfere in his life in the pursuit of a good cause. If that wasn't enough, a bunch of criminals calling themselves the Joker Gang are laughing at him, the university students are creating mayhem during their rag week, and someone called The Shocker is trying to kill him. The only advantage is that it take his mind off of the ultimatum the three women in his life have given him, one that he has only until the Sunday to resolve. Or leave town.

Prophecies

The fifth in the FFSG series.

Detective Sergeant Summers is under a hex, otherwise known as his colleagues. First they don't want him to get married, then it is imperative it must happen. Then they decide that a prophecy has been made which threatens the wedding. They don't believe in prophecies, but aren't sure that prophecies understand that. So they'll have to Do Something About It. And if their bumbling efforts aren't enough to ensure he never makes it to the altar, he has to cope with visiting aliens and resident ghosts. He does have tiny Squishy to protect him, but what match can even this plucky little kitten be against a prospective mother-in-law?

Loonymoon

The Inspectors Summers have tied the knot and embarked on their honeymoon in a small family-run hotel in Normandy. She has very definite ideas of what she wants out of a honeymoon: to set a seal on their love, and to form a foundation for life-long devotion. He just wants to nick a French police officer's kepi. He had a Bobby's helmet nicked from him once by a French girl while he was on crowd duty one New Year's Eve in London, and now he intends to return the favour. Neither is about to achieve their aim unless they can solve the mystery of the woman in the bath and the missing heroin. Which means pitting their minds against the French Inspectors Simenon. That's Mr and Mrs Simenon, whose marriage has gone beyond the rocks and is now beating itself to death against humdrum reality. One or either or both or neither could be the guilty crumpet. More importantly, is their marriage a portent of what could become of the Loonymooners? Ultimately the decisive question could well be: which side do the peas go?

Others:

The Window

Little does Jim Allbright realise just how much paperwork his letter containing a simple enquiry to his local council is about to produce, nor the strange events he will experience as a result of the 'system'. But if the system cannot be beaten the interchange of letters can be used to have a little fun and get to know some of the people struggling behind it, especially the woman who signs herself as "Sandi (pp the Administrator)", and perhaps, one day even meet her.

The Weekend At Longwood

A whodunnit in the classic sense, set against the backdrop of

World War II and the trials, tribulations and romances of nine suspects.

A group of friends get together during the last weekend of August 1939 at the rural retreat named Longwood, just a few miles from Portsmouth. They are there to celebrate the last time they will see Georgina Riley, famed American novelist and socialite, for some time, as she is scheduled to leave for her native New York in order to marry her childhood sweetheart. During the afternoon they good-humouredly assign to each other the most suitable names of the nine muses, the daughters of Zeus and Mnemosyne:

Calliope: the muse of epic poetry and rhetoric

Clio: history

Erato: love poems and mimicry

Euterpe: lyric poetry

Melpomene: tragedy

Polymnia: hymns to the gods and heroes

Terpsichore: dance

Thalia: comedy

Urania: astronomy, astrology and prophecy

The following morning Georgina is discovered in her bedroom covered in blood, her throat slit, barely alive. Her American maid is dead. A tiara Georgina had been flaunting the day before has disappeared.

Detective Inspector Rudman arrives to investigate. But with Georgina in a coma and no solid evidence there is little he can do apart from haunt their lives. With Germany's invasion of Poland a week later they disperse across the land, some to the air-force, some to the army, others to reserved civilian jobs.

But Rudman does not give up. Wherever they are he can be found. Whatever other duties he is tasked to, he will find time to keep tabs on them. Whatever the defeats and victories of the Allied cause, he has only one aim: to find the person responsible for the murder done that weekend in Longwood.

The war ends; some of the Muses have survived, some not.

Some have prospered, some married, some matured, others have found despair. And then comes invitation to spend another weekend at Longwood. The message is that Rudman has found the evidence he has been looking for.

And so one of the surviving couples motor slowly down to Portsmouth, remembering the original weekend, the trials and the tribulations of the past years, and wonder: what will be revealed during the coming weekend at Longwood?

Firelight

A modern-day tale of an ordinary family gathering at Christmas; the good, the bad, the dysfunctional and the forgotten.

George Browne and his wife Winifred have retired to a large, run-down pile in the country. Rumour has it that it was once the abode of a mad aristocratic family with a penchant for Satanism, and that both they and their victims still haunt the corridors. Other rumours are that it was a lunatic asylum for much of the nineteenth and twentieth century, and bodies of the inhabitants are buried around the large gardens in unmarked graves.

The Brownes are an unremarkable retired couple who, depending on who you might ask, have bought it as an investment, or alternatively as somewhere with enough bedrooms to accommodate their children, grand-children, and the little baby great-grandchildren. Too often in the past excuses have been made at special times, the most common of which has been of the "I don't want to put you to any trouble" variety. That excuse can no longer hold water.

Now it is approaching Christmas. Winter has set in, but the house is snug with oil heaters and real fires. As the various relations arrive, or don't arrive, it becomes clearer why invitations might have been refused in the past. The men of the family believe in having their way. The women of the family are strong-willed in their own different ways, and have various means of getting what they want.

The guests of the family - friends, boyfriends, girlfriends, wives and husbands - discover that their partners have a totally different side to them as the explosive hatreds of long-nurtured fights and feuds simmer to the surface before quickly boiling over.

One evening Winifred Browne encourages them to each tell a story as they sit in the lounge with the large fire warming them, the television off, no access to broadband, computers or mobile connections. Reluctantly at first they begin. As each evening passes: with different members taking turns, they announce in stories the feelings and hopes they cannot voice in public.

Finally it's the turn of Winifred Browne. Her story will be the one that tells them who they are, where they come from, and maybe why they have turned out the way they have.

For further details on these visit:
www . dughaille . Info

www.ingramcontent.com/pod-product-compliance
Lightning Source LLC
Chambersburg PA
CBHW071633260626
47170CB00001B/78